Veronika Decides to Die

"A highly original, moving, and ultimately life-affirming book."
—*The Sunday Mirror* (London)

Warrior of the Light: A Manual

"[A] sublime tome of daily wisdom." —*The Jakarta Post* (Indonesia)

The Fifth Mountain

"More ambitious . . . than *The Alchemist.* . . . A thought-provoking personal tale." —*Time* (International Edition)

By the River Piedra I Sat Down and Wept

"A wondrous book, full of mystery and light." —Oscar Hijuelos

The Valkyries

"A book that delights, fascinates, frightens, and enlightens all at once. . . . A delightful read that leaves you pondering eternal truths long after you put it down." —*NAPRA Review*

The Pilgrimage

"The keys to self-mastery . . . wrapped in suspense and adventure." —*Body Mind Spirit*

The Alchemist

"A magical little volume." —*San Francisco Chronicle*

THE
WINNER STANDS
ALONE

Also by Paulo Coelho

The Alchemist

The Pilgrimage

The Valkyries

By the River Piedra I Sat Down and Wept

The Fifth Mountain

Veronika Decides to Die

Warrior of Light: A Manual

Eleven Minutes

The Zahir

The Devil and Miss Prym

The Witch of Portobello

Brida

THE
WINNER STANDS
ALONE

PAULO COELHO

Translated from the Portuguese by Margaret Jull Costa

HARPER ● PERENNIAL

NEW YORK ● LONDON ● TORONTO ● SYDNEY ● NEW DELHI ● AUCKLAND

HARPER ● PERENNIAL

A hardcover edition of this book was published in 2009 by HarperCollins Publishers.

P.S.™ is a trademark of HarperCollins Publishers.

HarperCollins books may be purchased for educational, business, or sales promotional use. For information please write: Special Markets Department, HarperCollins Publishers, 10 East 53rd Street, New York, NY 10022.

FIRST HARPER PERENNIAL EDITION PUBLISHED 2010.

Library of Congress Cataloging-in-Publication Data is available upon request.

ISBN 978-0-06-175052-6

10 11 12 13 14   OV/RRD   10 9 8 7 6 5 4 3 2 1

O Mary conceived without sin,
pray for us who have recourse to thee. Amen.

For N.D.P.,
who came down to Earth in order to show us
the path of the Good Fight

And he said unto his disciples, Therefore I say unto you,
Take no thought for your life, what ye shall eat; neither for
the body, what ye shall put on. The life is more than meat,
and the body is more than raiment.

Consider the ravens: for they neither sow nor reap;
which neither have storehouse nor barn; and God feedeth
them: how much more are ye better than the fowls? And
which of you with taking thought can add to his stature one
cubit? If ye then be not able to do that thing which is least,
why take ye thought for the rest?

Consider the lilies how they grow: they toil not,
they spin not; and yet I say unto you, that Solomon in all
his glory was not arrayed like one of these.

LUKE 12: 22—27

Whoever you are holding me now in hand,
Without one thing all will be useless,
I give you fair warning before you attempt me further,
I am not what you supposed, but far different.

Who is he that would become my follower?
Who would sign himself a candidate for my affections?
The way is suspicious, the result uncertain, perhaps destructive,

You would have to give up all else, I alone would expect
to be your sole and exclusive standard,
Your novitiate would even then be long and exhausting,
The whole past theory of your life and all conformity to the lives
around you would have to be abandon'd,
Therefore release me now before troubling yourself any further,
let go your hand from my shoulders,
Put me down and depart on your way.

WALT WHITMAN, *Leaves of Grass*

FOREWORD

One of the recurrent themes in my books is the importance of paying a price for your dreams. But to what extent can our dreams be manipulated? For the past few decades, we have lived in a culture that privileged fame, money, power—and most people were led to believe that these were the real values that they were to pursue.

What we don't know is that, behind the scenes, the real manipulators remain anonymous. They understand that the most effective power is the one that nobody can notice—until it is too late, and you are trapped. *The Winner Stands Alone* is about this trap.

In this book, three of the four main characters face this ordeal:

Igor, a Russian millionaire, who believes that he can kill if he has a good reason for it—such as avoiding human suffering, or bringing back the attention of the woman he loves.

Hamid, a fashion magnate, who starts with good intentions, until he gets caught up by the very system he was trying to use.

Gabriela, who—like most people today—is convinced that fame is an end in and of itself, the supreme reward in a world that praises celebrity as the highest achievement in life.

With these characters in mind, I wrote *The Winner Stands Alone*—not a thriller, but a crude portrait of where we are now.

PAULO COELHO

THE
WINNER STANDS
ALONE

3:17 A.M.

The Beretta Px4 compact pistol is slightly larger than a mobile phone, weighs around seven hundred grams, and can fire ten shots. It is small, light, invisible when carried in a pocket, and its small caliber has one enormous advantage: instead of passing through the victim's body, the bullet hits bones and smashes everything in its path.

Obviously, the chances of surviving a shot of that caliber are fairly high; there are thousands of cases in which no vital artery was severed and the victim had time to react and disarm his attacker. However, if the person firing the pistol is experienced enough, he can opt either for a quick death—by aiming at the point between the eyes or at the heart—or for a slower one—by placing the barrel at a certain angle close to the ribs and squeezing the trigger. The person shot takes a while to realize that he has been mortally wounded and tries to fight back, run away, or call for help. The great advantage of this is that the victim has time to see his killer's face, while his strength ebbs slowly away and he falls to the ground, with little external loss of blood, still not fully understanding why this is happening to him.

It is far from being the ideal weapon for experts. "Nice and light—in a lady's handbag. No stopping power though," someone in the British Secret Service tells James Bond in the first film in the series, meanwhile confiscating Bond's old pistol and handing him a new model. However, that advice applied only to professionals, and for what he now had in mind it was perfect.

He had bought the Beretta on the black market so that it would be impossible to trace. There are five bullets in the magazine, although he intends to use only one, the tip of which he has marked with an "X," using a nail file. That way, when it's fired and hits something solid, it will break into four pieces.

He will only use the Beretta as a last resort. There are other ways of extinguishing a world, of destroying a universe, and she will probably understand the message as soon as the first victim is found. She will know that he did it in the name of love, and that he feels no resentment, but will take her back and ask no questions about her life during these past two years.

He hopes that six months of careful planning will produce results, but he will only know for sure tomorrow morning. His plan is to allow the Furies, those ancient figures from Greek mythology, to descend on their black wings to that blue-and-white landscape full of diamonds, Botox, and high-speed cars of no use to anyone because they carry only two passengers. With the little artifacts he has brought with him, all those dreams of power, success, fame, and money could be punctured in an instant.

He could have gone up to his room because the scene he had been waiting to witness occurred at 11:11 P.M., although he would have been prepared to wait for even longer. The man and his beautiful companion arrived—both of them in full evening dress—for yet another of those gala events that take place each night after every important supper, and which attracted more people than any film première at the Festival.

Igor ignored the woman. He shielded his face behind a French newspaper (a Russian newspaper would have aroused suspicions) so that she wouldn't see him. An unnecessary precaution: like all women who feel themselves to be queen of the world, she never looked at anyone else. Such women are there in order to shine and always avoid looking at what other people are wearing because, even if their own clothes and accessories have cost them a fortune, the number of diamonds or a particularly exclusive outfit worn by someone else might make them feel depressed or bad-tempered or inferior.

Her elegant, silver-haired companion went over to the bar and ordered champagne, a necessary aperitif for a night that promised new contacts, good music, and a fine view of the beach and the yachts moored in the harbor.

He noticed how extremely polite the man was, thanking the waitress when she brought their drinks and giving her a large tip.

The three of them knew each other. Igor felt a great wave of happiness as the adrenaline began to mingle with his blood. The following day he would make her fully aware of his presence there and, at some point, they would meet.

God alone knew what would come of that meeting. Igor, an orthodox Catholic, had made a promise and sworn an oath in a church in Moscow before the relics of St. Mary Magdalene (which were in the Russian capital for a week, so that the faithful could worship them). He had queued for nearly five hours and, when he finally saw them, had felt sure that the whole thing was something dreamed up by the priests. He did not, however, want to run the risk of breaking his word, and so he had asked for her protection and help in achieving his goal without too much sacrifice. And he had promised, too, that when it was all over and he could at last return to his native land, he would commission a golden icon from a well-known artist who lived in a monastery in Novosibirsk.

AT THREE IN THE MORNING, the bar of the Hotel Martinez smells of cigarettes and sweat. By then, Jimmy (who always wears different colored shoes) has stopped playing the piano, and the waitress is exhausted, but the people who are still there refuse to leave. They want to stay in that lobby for at least another hour or even all night until *something* happens!

They're already four days into the Cannes Film Festival and still nothing has happened. Every guest at every table is interested in but one thing: meeting the people with Power. Pretty women are waiting for a producer to fall in love with them and give them a major role in their next movie. A few actors are talking among themselves, laughing and pretending that the whole business is a matter of complete indifference to them—but they always keep one eye on the door.

Someone is about to arrive. Someone must arrive. Young directors, full of ideas and with CVs listing the videos they made at university, and who have read everything ever written about photography and scriptwriting, are hoping for a stroke of luck; perhaps meeting someone just back from a party who is looking for an empty table where he'll order a coffee and light a cigarette, someone who's tired of going to the same old places all the time and feels ready for a new adventure.

How naïve!

If that did happen, the last thing such a person would want to hear about is some "really fresh angle" on a hackneyed subject; but despair can deceive the desperate. The people with power who do occasionally enter merely glance around, then go up to their rooms. They're not worried. They have nothing to fear. The Superclass does not forgive betrayals and they know their limitations—whatever the legend may say, they didn't get where they are by trampling on others. On the other hand, if there is some important new discovery to be made—be it in the world of cinema, music, or fashion—it will emerge only after much research and not in some hotel bar.

The Superclass are now making love to the girl who managed to gatecrash the party and who is game for anything. They're taking off their makeup, studying the lines on their faces, and thinking that it's time for more plastic surgery. They're looking at the online news to see if the announcement they made earlier that day has been picked up by the media. They're taking the inevitable sleeping pill and drinking the tea that promises easy weight loss. They're ticking the boxes on the menu for their room service breakfast and hanging it on the door handle along with the sign saying "Do not disturb." The Superclass are closing their eyes and thinking: "I hope I get to sleep quickly. I've got a meeting tomorrow at ten."

HOWEVER, EVERYONE KNOWS THAT THE bar in the Hotel Martinez is where the powerful people hang out, which means there's always a chance of meeting them.

It doesn't even occur to the hopefuls that the Powerful only talk to the Powerful, that they need to get together now and then for lunches and suppers, to lend allure to the big festivals, to feed the fantasy that the world of luxury and glamour is accessible to all those with the courage to pursue an idea, to avoid any nonlucrative wars and to promote aggression between countries or companies where they feel this might bring them more power and more money, to pretend that they're happy, even though they're now hostage to their own success, to continue struggling to increase their wealth and influence, even when both those things are already vast, because the vanity of the Superclass consists in competing with itself to see who is the top of the tops.

In an ideal world, the Powerful would talk to the actors, directors, designers, and writers who are now bleary-eyed with tiredness and thinking about going back to their rented rooms in distant towns, so that tomorrow they can begin again the marathon of making requests, fixing possible meetings, and being endlessly ready and available.

In the real world, the Powerful are, at this moment, locked in their rooms, checking their e-mails, complaining that these Festival parties are always the same, that their friend was wearing a bigger jewel than they were, and asking how come the yacht a competitor has just bought has a totally unique décor?

Igor has no one to talk to, nor does he want to talk. The winner stands alone.

Igor is the successful owner and president of a telephone company in Russia. A year ago, he reserved the best suite in the Martinez (which makes everyone pay up-front for at least twelve nights, regardless of how long they'll be staying); he arrived this afternoon in his private jet, was driven to the hotel, where he took a bath and then went downstairs in the hope of witnessing one particular scene.

At first, he was pestered by actresses, actors, and directors, until he came up with the perfect response for them all:

"Don't speak English, sorry. Polish."

Or:

"Don't speak French, sorry. Mexican."

When someone ventured a few words in Spanish, Igor tried another ploy. He started writing down numbers in a notebook so as to look neither like a journalist (because everyone wants to meet journalists) nor like a movie mogul. Beside him lay a Russian economics magazine (most people can't tell Russian from Polish or Spanish) with the photo of some boring executive on the cover.

The denizens of the bar, who pride themselves on their keen understanding of the human race, leave Igor in peace, thinking that he must be one of those millionaires who comes to Cannes in search of a new girlfriend. That, at least, is the rumor doing the rounds by the time the fifth person has sat down at his table and ordered a mineral water, alleging that there are no other free seats. Igor is duly relegated to the category of "perfume."

"Perfume" is the slang term used by actresses (or "starlets," as they're called at the Festival) because, as with perfumes, it's easy enough to change brands, but one of them might just turn out to be a real find. "Perfumes" are sought out during the last two days of the Festival, if the actresses in question haven't managed to pick up anything or anyone of interest in the movie industry. For the moment, then, this strange, apparently wealthy man can wait. Actresses know that it's always best to leave the Festival with a new boyfriend (whom they might, later on, be able to transform into a film producer) than to move on to the next event and go through the same old ritual—drinking, smiling (must keep smiling), and pretending that you're not looking at anyone, while your heart beats furiously, time ticks rapidly on, and there are still gala nights to which you haven't yet been invited, but to which the "perfumes" have.

They know what the "perfumes" going to say because they always say the same thing, but they pretend to believe them anyway.

(a) "I could change your life."

(b) "A lot of women would like to be in your shoes."

(c) "You're young now, but what will become of you in a few years' time? You need to think about making a longer-term investment."

(d) "I'm married, but my wife . . ." (This opening line can have various endings: ". . . is ill," ". . . has threatened to commit suicide if I leave her," etc.)

(e) "You're a princess and deserve to be treated like one. I didn't know it until now, but I've been waiting for you. I don't believe in coincidences and I really think we ought to give this relationship a chance."

It's always the same old spiel. The only variable is how many presents you get (preferably jewelry, which can be sold), how many invites to yacht parties, how many visiting cards you collect, how many times you have to listen to the same chat-up lines, and whether you can wangle a ticket to the Formula 1 races, where you'll get to mingle with the same class of people and where your "big chance" might be there waiting for you.

"Perfume" is also the word used by young actors to refer to elderly millionairesses, all plastic and Botox, but who are, at least, more intelligent than their male counterparts. They never waste any time: they, too, arrive in the final days of the Festival, knowing that money provides their only pulling power.

The male "perfumes" deceive themselves: they think that the long legs and youthful faces have genuinely fallen for them and can now be manipulated at will. The female "perfumes" put all their trust in the power of their diamonds.

IGOR KNOWS NOTHING OF ALL this. This is his first time at the Festival. And he has just realized that, much to his surprise, no one here seems very interested in films, except the people in that bar. He has leafed through a few magazines, opened the envelope in which his company has placed the invitations to the most prestigious parties, but not one of them is for a film première. Before traveling to France, he tried to find out which films were in the running, but had great difficulty in obtaining this information. Then a friend said:

"Forget about films. Cannes is just a fashion show."

FASHION. WHATEVER CAN PEOPLE BE thinking? Do they think fashion is something that changes according to the season of the year? Did they really come from all corners of the world to show off their dresses, their jewelry, and their collection of shoes? They don't understand. "Fashion" is merely a way of saying: "I belong to your world. I'm wearing the same uniform as your army, so don't shoot."

Ever since groups of men and women first started living together in caves, fashion has been the only language everyone can understand, even complete strangers. "We dress in the same way. I belong to your tribe. Let's gang up on the weaklings as a way of surviving."

But some people believe that "fashion" is everything. Every six months, they spend a fortune changing some tiny detail in order to keep up their membership in the very exclusive tribe of the rich. If they were to visit Silicon Valley, where the billionaires of the IT industry wear plastic watches and beat-up jeans, they would understand that the world has changed; everyone now seems to belong to the same social class; no one cares anymore about the size of a diamond or the make of a tie or a leather briefcase. In fact, ties and leather briefcases don't even exist in that part of the world; nearby, however, is Hollywood, a relatively more powerful machine—albeit in decline—which still manages to convince the innocent to believe in haute-couture dresses, emerald necklaces, and stretch limos. And since this is what still appears in all the magazines, who would dare destroy a billion-dollar industry involving advertisements, the sale of useless objects, the invention of entirely unnecessary new trends, and the creation of identical face creams all bearing different labels?

How ridiculous! Igor cannot conceal his loathing for those whose decisions affect the lives of millions of honest, hardworking men and women leading dignified lives and glad to have their health, a home, and the love of their family.

How perverse! Just when everything seems to be in order and as families gather round the table to have supper, the phantom of the Superclass appears, selling impossible dreams: luxury, beauty, power. And the family falls apart.

The father works overtime to be able to buy his son the latest sneakers because if his son doesn't have a pair, he'll be ostracized at school. The wife weeps in silence because her friends have designer clothes and she has no money. Their adolescent children, instead of learning the real values of faith and hope, dream only of becoming singers or movie stars. Girls in provincial towns lose any real sense of themselves and start to think of going to the big city, prepared to do anything, absolutely anything, to get a particular piece of jewelry. A world that should be directed toward justice begins instead to focus on material things, which, in six months' time, will be worthless and have to be replaced, and that is how the whole circus ensures that the despicable creatures gathered together in Cannes remain at the top of the heap.

Igor is untouched by this destructive power, for he has one of the most enviable jobs in the world. He continues to earn more money in a day than he could spend in a year, even if he were to indulge in all possible pleasures, legal and illegal. He has no difficulty in finding women, regardless of whether they know how much money he has— he's tested it out on more than one occasion and never failed yet. He has just turned forty, is in good physical shape, and, according to his annual checkup, has no health problems. He has no debts either. He doesn't have to wear a particular designer label, go to a particular restaurant, spend his holidays at a beach where "everyone" goes, or buy a watch just because some successful sportsman is promoting it. He can sign major contracts with a cheap ballpoint pen, wear comfortable, elegant jackets, handmade by a tailor who has a small shop next to his office, and which carry no label at all. He can do as he likes and doesn't have to prove to anyone that he's rich; he has an interesting job and loves what he does.

––––––

PERHAPS THAT'S THE PROBLEM: HE still loves what he does. He's sure that this is why the woman who came into the bar some hours earlier is not sitting at his table with him.

He tries to keep thinking, to pass the time. He asks Kristelle for another drink—he knows the waitress's name because an hour ago, when the bar was emptier (people were having supper), he asked for a glass of whisky, and she said that he looked sad and should eat something to cheer himself up. He thanked her for her concern, and was glad that someone should care about his state of mind.

He is perhaps the only one who knows the name of the waitress serving him, the others only want to know the names—and, if possible, the job titles—of the people sitting at the tables and in the armchairs.

He tries to keep thinking, but it's gone three o'clock in the morning, and the beautiful woman and her courteous companion—who, by the way, looks remarkably like him—have not reappeared. Maybe they went straight up to their room where they are now making love, or perhaps they're still drinking champagne on one of the yachts where the parties only begin when the other parties are all coming to an end. Perhaps they're lying in bed, reading magazines, ignoring each other.

Not that it matters. Igor is alone and tired and needs to sleep.

7:22 A.M.

He wakes up at 7:22 A.M., much earlier than his body would like, but he hasn't yet adapted to the time difference between Moscow and Paris. If he was at work, he would already have held two or three meetings with his subordinates and be preparing to have lunch with some new client.

He has another task to fulfill here: he must find someone he can sacrifice in the name of love. He needs a victim, so that Ewa will get his message that very morning.

He has a bath, goes downstairs to have a coffee in an almost deserted restaurant, then sets off along the Boulevard de la Croisette on which nearly all the major luxury hotels are located. There is no traffic because one lane is blocked off and only cars with official permission are being allowed through. The other lane is empty because even the people who live in the city are still only just getting ready to go to work.

He feels no resentment. He has passed the really difficult phase, when he couldn't sleep because he was so filled with pain and hatred. Now he can understand Ewa's feelings: after all, monogamy is a myth that has been rammed down people's throats for far too long. He has read a lot on the subject. The inability to be monogamous isn't just a matter of excess hormones or vanity, but, as all the research indicates, a genetic configuration found in almost all animals.

Paternity tests given to birds, monkeys, and foxes revealed that simply because these species had developed a social relationship very similar to marriage did not necessarily mean that they had been faithful to each other. In seventy percent of cases, their offspring turn out to have been fathered by males other than their partners. Igor remembered something written by David Barash, professor of psychology at the University of Washington in Seattle, in which he said that the only species in nature that doesn't commit adultery and in which there seems to be one hundred percent monogamy is a flatworm, *Diplozoon paradoxum*. The male and female worms meet as adolescents, and their bodies literally fuse together.

This is why he cannot accuse Ewa of anything; she was merely following her human instincts. However, she had been brought up to believe in those unnatural social conventions and must be feeling guilty, thinking that he doesn't love her anymore and will never forgive her.

He is, in fact, prepared to do anything, even to send messages that will mean he has destroyed someone's world, just so that she'll know that not only is he willing to welcome her back, he will gladly bury the past and ask no questions.

H E S E E S A Y O U N G W O M A N setting out her wares on the pavement—various bits of craftwork and jewelry of rather dubious taste.

Yes, she will be the sacrifice. She is the message he must send, a message that will be understood as soon as it reaches its destination. Before going over to her, he observes her tenderly; she doesn't know that in a little while, if all goes well, her soul will be wandering the clouds, free forever from an idiotic job that will never take her where her dreams would like her to go.

"How much?" he asks in perfect French.

"Which piece do you want, sir?"

"All of them."

The young woman—who must be twenty at most—smiles.

"This isn't the first time someone has asked to buy everything. The next step is usually: 'Would you like to go for a walk? You're far too pretty to be here selling these things. I'm . . .'"

"No, I'm not. I don't work in the movies, nor am I going to make you an actress and change your life. I'm not interested in the things you're selling either. I just need to talk, and we can do that right here."

The young woman averts her gaze.

"My parents make these things, and I'm proud of what I do. One day, someone will come along who'll recognize their value. Please, go away. I'm sure you can find someone else to listen to what you have to say."

Igor takes a bundle of notes out of his pocket and puts them gently down beside her.

"Forgive my rudeness. I only said I wasn't interested in buying anything to see if you would lower the price. Anyway, my name is Igor Malev. I flew in from Moscow yesterday, and I'm still a little jet-lagged."

"My name's Olivia," says the young woman, pretending to believe his lie.

Without asking her permission, he sits down on the bench beside her. She shifts up an inch or so.

"What do you want to talk about?"

"First, take the money."

Olivia hesitates, then, looking around, realizes that she has no reason to be afraid. Cars are now driving down the one available lane, young people are heading for the beach, and an elderly couple are coming toward them down the pavement. She puts the money in her pocket, not even bothering to count it; she has enough experience of life to know that it's more than enough.

"Thank you for accepting my offer," says the Russian. "You asked me what I want to talk about? Well, nothing very important."

"You must be here for a reason. You need a reason to visit Cannes at this time of year when the city is as unbearable for the people who live here as it is for the tourists."

Igor is looking at the sea. He lights a cigarette.

"Smoking's bad for your health," she says.

He ignores this remark.

"What, for you, is the meaning of life?" he asks.

"Love."

Olivia smiles. This really is an excellent way to start the day, talking about deeper things than the price of each piece of handiwork or the clothes people are wearing.

"And for you?"

"Yes, love too. But for me it was also important to earn enough money to show my parents that I was capable of succeeding. I did that, and now they're proud of me. I met the perfect woman, we married, and I would like to have had children, to honor and fear God. The children, alas, never came."

Olivia doesn't like to ask why. The man, in his forties, continues in his perfect French:

"We thought of adopting a child. Indeed, we spent two or three years thinking about it, but then life began to get too busy what with business trips and parties, meetings and deals."

"When you sat down here to talk, I thought you were just another eccentric millionaire in search of an adventure, but I'm enjoying talking about these things."

"Do you think about the future?"

"Yes, I do, and I think my dreams are much the same as yours. Obviously, I'd like to have children as well . . ."

She pauses. She doesn't want to hurt the feelings of this unexpected new companion.

". . . if, of course, I can. Sometimes, God has other plans."

He appears not to have heard her answer.

"Do only millionaires come to the Festival?"

"Millionaires and people who think they're millionaires or want to become millionaires. While the Festival is on, this part of the city is like a madhouse. Everyone behaves as if they were terribly important, apart from the people who really are important; they're much politer; they don't need to prove anything to anyone. They don't always buy what I have to sell, but at least they smile, make some pleasant remark, and treat me with respect. What are you doing here?"

"God made the world in six days, but what *is* the world? It's what you or I see. Whenever someone dies, a part of the universe dies too. Everything a person felt, experienced, and saw dies with them, like tears in the rain."

"'Like tears in the rain' . . . I saw a film once that used that phrase. I can't remember now what it was."

"I didn't come here to cry. I came to send messages to the woman I love, and in order to do that, I need to destroy a few universes or worlds."

Instead of feeling alarmed by this last statement, Olivia laughs. This handsome, well-dressed man, speaking fluent French, doesn't seem like a madman at all. She was fed up with always hearing the same things: you're very pretty, you could be doing better for yourself, how much is this, how much is that, it's awfully expensive, I'll go away and think about it and come back later (which they never do, of course), etc. At least this Russian has a sense of humor.

"Why do you need to destroy the world?"

"So that I can rebuild my own world."

Olivia would like to try and console him, but she's afraid of hearing the famous words: "I think you could give meaning to my life," at which point the conversation would come to an abrupt halt because she has other plans for her future. Besides, it would be absurd on her part to try and teach someone older and more successful how to overcome his difficulties.

One way out would be to learn more about his life. After all, he's paid her—and paid her well—for her time.

"How do you intend to do that?"

"Do you know anything about frogs?"

"Frogs?"

"Yes, various biological studies have shown that if a frog is placed in a container along with water from its own pond, it will remain there, utterly still, while the water is slowly heated up. The frog doesn't react to the gradual increase in temperature, to the changes in its environment, and when the water reaches the boiling point, the frog dies, fat and happy.

"On the other hand, if a frog is thrown into a container full of already boiling water, it will jump straight out again, scalded, but alive!"

Olivia doesn't quite see what this has to do with the destruction of the world. Igor goes on:

"I was like that boiled frog. I didn't notice the changes. I thought everything was fine, that the bad things would just go away, that it was just a matter of time. I was ready to die because I lost the most important thing in my life, but, instead of reacting, I sat there bobbing apathetically about in water that was getting hotter by the minute."

Olivia plucks up the courage to ask:

"What did you lose?"

"The truth is I didn't lose anything. Life sometimes separates people so that they can realize how much they mean to each other. For example, last night, I saw my wife with another man. I know she wants to come back to me, that she still loves me, but she's not brave enough to take the first step. Some boiled frogs still think it's obedience that counts, not ability: those who can, lead, and those with any sense, obey. So where's the truth in all this? It's better to emerge from a situation slightly scalded, but alive and ready to act. And I think you can help me in that task."

Olivia tries to imagine what is going through the mind of the man beside her. How could anyone leave such an interesting person, someone who can talk about things she has never even thought about? Then again, there's no logic to love. Despite her youth, she knows that. Her boyfriend, for example, can be quite brutal and sometimes hits her for no reason, and yet she can't bear to be apart from him even for a day.

WHAT EXACTLY WERE THEY TALKING about? About frogs and about how she could help him. She can't help him, of course, so she'd better change the subject.

"And how do you intend to set about destroying the world?"

Igor points to the one free lane on the Boulevard de la Croisette.

"Let's say that I don't want you to go to a party, but I daren't say so openly. If I wait for the rush hour to begin and stop my car in the middle of the road, within ten minutes, the whole of the Boulevard opposite the beach will have come to a standstill. Drivers will think: 'There must have been an accident' and will wait patiently. In fifteen minutes, the police will arrive with a truck to tow the car away."

"That kind of thing is always happening."

"Ah, yes, but I—very carefully and without anyone noticing—will have got out of my car and scattered nails and other sharp objects on the road in front of it. And I will have carefully painted all of these objects black, so that they blend in with the asphalt. As the tow truck approaches, its tires will be punctured. Now we have two problems, and the tailback of traffic will have reached the suburbs of this small city, the very suburbs where you perhaps live."

"You clearly have a very vivid imagination, but you would still only have managed to delay me by about an hour."

It was Igor's turn to smile.

"Oh, I could come up with all kinds of ways of making the situation worse. When people started gathering round to help, for example, I would throw something like a small smoke bomb under the truck. This would frighten everyone. I would get into my car, feigning despair, and start the engine. At the same time, though, I would empty a bit of lighter fluid on the floor of the car and it would ignite. I would then jump out of the car in time to observe the scene: the car gradually going up in flames, the flames reaching the fuel tank, the explosion that would affect the car behind as well, and so on in a chain reaction. And I could achieve all that with a car, a few nails, a smoke bomb that you can buy in a shop, and a small amount of lighter fluid . . ."

Igor takes from his pocket a small flask containing some kind of liquid.

". . . about this much. I should have done that when I realized Ewa was about to leave me, to make her postpone her decision and reflect a little and consider the consequences. When people start to reflect on decisions they're trying to make, they usually change their mind—it requires a lot of courage to take certain steps.

"But I was too proud. I thought it was just a temporary move and that she would soon realize her mistake. I'm sure she regrets leaving me and, as I said, wants to come back. But for that to happen I need to destroy a few worlds."

The expression on his face has changed, and Olivia is no longer amused by the story. She gets up.

"Well, I need to do some work."

"But I paid you to listen to me. I paid enough to cover your whole working day."

She puts her hand in her pocket to give him back the money, but at that moment, she sees the pistol pointing at her face.

"Sit down."

Her first impulse is to run. The elderly couple are still slowly approaching.

"Don't run away," he says, as if he could read her thoughts. "I haven't the slightest intention of firing the gun if you'll just sit down again and hear me out. If you don't try anything and do as I say, then I swear I won't shoot."

A series of options pass rapidly through Olivia's head, the first being to run, zigzagging her way across the street, but she realizes that her legs have gone weak.

"Sit down," the man says again. "I won't shoot if you do as you're told. I promise."

Yes, it would be madness on his part to fire that gun on a sunny morning, with cars driving past outside, people going to the beach, the traffic getting heavier by the minute, and more pedestrians walking along the pavement. Best to do as the man says, even if only because she's in no state to do anything else; she's almost fainting.

She obeys. Now she just has to convince him that she's not a threat, to listen to his deserted husband's lament, to promise him that she has seen nothing, and then, as soon as a policeman appears, doing his usual round, throw herself to the ground and scream for help.

"I know exactly what you're feeling," the man says, trying to calm her. "The symptoms of fear have been the same since the dawn of time. They were the same when men had to face wild beasts and they continue to be so right up to the present day: blood drains away from the face and the epidermis, protecting the body and avoiding blood loss, that's why people turn pale. The intestines relax and release everything, so that there will be no toxic matter left contaminating the organism. The body initially refuses to move, so as not to provoke the beast in question by making any sudden movement."

"This is all a dream," thinks Olivia. She remembers her parents, who should have been here with her this morning, but who had been up all night making jewelry because the day looked likely to be a busy one. A few hours ago, she had been making love with her boyfriend, whom she believed to be the man of her life, even though he sometimes hit her; they reached orgasm simultaneously, something that hadn't happened for a long time. After breakfast, she decided not to take her usual shower because she felt free and full of energy and pleased with life.

No, this can't be happening. She must try to appear calm.

"Let's talk. The reason you bought all my stuff was so that we could talk. Besides, I wasn't getting up in order to run away."

He presses the barrel of the gun gently against the girl's ribs. The elderly couple pass by, glance at them, and notice nothing odd. "There's that Portuguese girl," they think, "trying, as usual, to impress some man with her dark eyebrows and childlike smile." It's not the first time they've seen her with a strange man, and this one, to judge by his clothes, has plenty of money.

Olivia fixes them with her eyes, as if trying to tell them what's going on just by looking. The man beside her says brightly:

"Good morning."

The couple move off without uttering a word. They're not in the habit of talking to strangers or of exchanging greetings with street vendors.

"Yes, let's talk," says the Russian, breaking the silence. "I'm not really going to try and disrupt the traffic. I was just giving that as an example. My wife will realize I'm here when she starts to receive the messages. I'm not going to take the obvious route, which would be to go and meet her. I need her to come to me."

This was a possible way out.

"I can deliver the messages, if you like. Just tell me which hotel she's staying at."

The man laughs.

"You suffer from the youthful vice of thinking you're cleverer than everyone else. The moment you left here, you'd go straight to the police."

Her blood freezes. Are they going to sit on this bench all day? Is he going to shoot her after all, now that she knows his face?

"You said you weren't going to shoot."

"I promised I wouldn't if you behaved in a more adult fashion and with due respect for my intelligence."

He's right. The adult thing to do would be to talk a little about herself. She might arouse the compassion that is always there in the mind of a madman by explaining that she's in a similar situation, even though it isn't true.

A boy runs past, an iPod in his ears. He doesn't even turn to look at them.

"I live with a man who makes my life hell, and yet I can't leave him."

The look in Igor's eyes changes.

Olivia thinks she's found a way of escaping from the trap.

"Be intelligent. Don't just give up; think of the woman who's married to the man sitting next to you. Be honest."

"He's cut me off from my friends. He's always jealous even though he can get all the women he wants. He criticizes everything I do and says I have no ambition. He even takes the little money I earn as commission."

The man says nothing but stares at the sea. The pavement is filling up with people; what would happen if she just got to her feet and ran? Would he shoot her? Is it a real gun?

She senses that she has touched on a topic of possible interest to him. It would be best not to do anything foolish, she thinks, remembering the way he spoke and looked at her minutes before.

"And yet, you see, I can't bring myself to leave him. Even if I were to meet the kindest, richest, most generous man in the world, I wouldn't give my boyfriend up for anything. I'm not a masochist, I take no pleasure in these constant humiliations, I just happen to love him."

She feels the barrel of the gun pressing into her ribs again. She has said the wrong thing.

"I'm not like that scoundrel of a boyfriend of yours," he says, his voice full of loathing now. "I worked hard to build up what I have. I worked long and hard, and survived many a setback. I was always honest in my dealings, although there were, of course, times when I had to be hard and implacable. I was always a good Christian. I have influential friends, and I've always been grateful to them. In short, I did everything right.

"I never harmed anyone who got in my way. Whenever possible, I encouraged my wife to do what she wanted to do, and the result: here I am, alone. Yes, I killed people during the idiotic war I was sent to fight, but I never lost my sense of reality. I'm not one of those traumatized war veterans who goes into a restaurant and machine-guns people. I'm not a terrorist. Of course, I could say that life has treated me unfairly and taken from me the most important thing there is: love. But there are other women, and the pain of love always passes. I need to act, I'm tired of being a frog slowly boiling to death."

"If you know there are other women and you know that the pain of love will pass, why are you so upset?"

Yes, she's behaving like an adult now, surprised at the calm way in which she's trying to deal with the madman by her side.

He seems to waver.

"I don't really know. Perhaps because I've been abandoned once too often. Perhaps because I need to prove to myself just what I'm capable of. Perhaps because I lied, and there is only one woman for me. I have a plan."

"What plan?"

"I told you before. I'm going to keep destroying worlds until she realizes how important she is to me and that I'm prepared to run any risk in order to get her back."

The police!

They both notice the police car approaching.

"I'm sorry," says the man. "I intended to talk a little more. Life hasn't treated you very fairly either."

Olivia realizes this is the end. And since she now has nothing to lose, she again tries to get up. Then she feels the hand of that stranger on her right shoulder, as if he were fondly embracing her.

Samozashchita Bez Orujiya, or Sambo, as it is better known among Russians, is the art of killing swiftly with one's bare hands, without the victim realizing what is happening. It was developed over the centuries, when peoples or tribes had to confront invaders unarmed. It was widely used by the Soviet state apparatus to eliminate people without leaving any trace. They tried to introduce it as a martial art in the 1980 Moscow Olympics, but it was rejected as being too dangerous, despite all the efforts of the Communists of the day to include in the Games a sport which they alone practiced.

Perfect. That way, only a few people know the moves.

Igor's right thumb is pressing down on Olivia's jugular vein, and the blood stops flowing to her brain. Meanwhile, his other hand is pressing on a particular point near her armpit, causing the muscles to seize up. There are no contractions, it's merely a question of waiting two minutes.

Olivia appears to have gone to sleep in his arms. The police car drives by behind them, using the lane that is closed to other traffic. They don't even notice the embracing couple; they have other things to worry about this morning, like doing their best to keep the traffic moving—an impossible task if carried out to the letter. The latest call over the radio tells them that some drunken millionaire has just crashed his car a mile or so away.

Still supporting the girl, Igor bends down and uses his other hand to pick up the cloth spread out in front of the bench and on which all those tasteless objects were to be displayed. He adroitly folds up the cloth to form an improvised pillow.

When he sees that no one else is around, he tenderly lays her inert body on the bench. She looks as if she were asleep; and in her dreams she must be remembering some particularly lovely day or else having nightmares about her violent boyfriend.

Only the elderly couple had noticed them sitting together. And if the crime were discovered—which Igor doubted, since there were no visible marks—they would describe him to the police as fairer or darker or older or younger than he really was; there wasn't the slightest reason to be worried; people never pay much attention to what's going on around them.

Before leaving, he plants a kiss on the brow of the sleeping beauty and murmurs:

"As you see, I kept my promise. I didn't shoot."

———

HE TAKES A FEW STEPS and his head begins to ache terribly. This is perfectly normal: the blood is flooding the brain, an understandable reaction in someone who has just been under extreme tension.

Despite the headache, he feels happy. Yes, he has done what he set out to do.

He can do it. And he's happier still because he has freed the soul from that fragile body, freed a spirit incapable of defending herself against a bullying coward. If her relationship with her boyfriend had continued, the girl would have ended up depressed and anxious and devoid of all self-respect, and would have been even more under her boyfriend's thumb.

This had never been the case with Ewa. She had always been capable of making her own decisions. He had given her both moral and financial support when she decided to open her haute-couture boutique; and she had been free to travel as much as she wanted. He had been an exemplary man and husband. And yet, she had made a mistake: she had been unable to understand his love or his forgiveness. He hoped, however, that she would receive these messages; after all, he had told her on the day she left that he would destroy whole worlds to get her back.

He picks up the throwaway mobile phone he has just bought and on which he has entered the smallest possible amount of credit. He sends a text message.

11:OO A.M.

It all began, they say, with an unknown nineteen-year-old posing in a bikini for photographers who had nothing better to do during the 1953 Cannes Festival. She immediately shot to stardom, and her name became legendary: Brigitte Bardot. And now others think they can do the same. No one understands the importance of being an actress; beauty is the only thing that counts.

That's why women with long legs and dyed hair, the bottle blondes of this world, travel hundreds or even thousands of miles to be in Cannes, even if only to spend the whole day on the beach, hoping to be seen, photographed, discovered. They want to escape from the trap that awaits all women: becoming a housewife, who makes supper for her husband every evening, takes the children to school every day, and tries to dig up some dirt on her neighbors' monotonous lives so as to have something to gossip about with her friends. What these women want is fame, glory, and glamour, to be the envy of the other people who live in their town and of the boys and girls who always thought of them as ugly ducklings, unaware that they would one day grow up to be a swan or blossom into a flower coveted by everyone. They want a career in the world of dreams even if they have to borrow money to get silicone breast implants or to buy some newer, sexier outfits. Drama school? Forget it, good looks and the right contacts are all you need. The cinema can work miracles, always assuming, of course, you can ever break into that world. Anything to escape from the prison of the provincial city and the long, dreary, repetitive days. There are millions of people who don't mind that kind of life, and they should be left to live their lives as they see fit. However, if you come to the Festival you must leave fear at home and be prepared for anything: making spur-of-the-moment decisions, telling lies if necessary, pretending to be younger than you are, smiling at people you loathe, feigning an interest in people who bore you, saying, "I love you" without a thought for the consequences, or stabbing in the back the friend who once helped you out, but who has now become an undesirable rival. Don't let feelings of remorse or shame get in your way. The reward is worth any amount of sacrifice.

Fame. Glory. Glamour.

Gabriela finds these thoughts irritating. It's definitely not the best way to start a new day. Worse, she has a hangover.

At least there's one consolation. She hasn't woken up in a five-star hotel next to a man telling her to put her clothes on and leave because he has important business to deal with, like buying or selling films.

She gets up and looks around to see if any of her friends are still in the apartment. Needless to say they're not. They've long since left for the Boulevard de la Croisette, for the swimming pools, hotel bars, yachts, possible lunch dates, and chance meetings on the beach. There are five fold-out mattresses on the floor of the small shared apartment, hired for the duration at an exorbitant rent. The mattresses are surrounded by a tangle of clothes, discarded shoes, and hangers that no one has taken the trouble to put back in the wardrobe.

"The clothes take up more room here than the people," she thinks.

Not that any of them could even dream of wearing clothes designed by Elie Saab, Karl Lagerfeld, Versace, or Galliano, but what they have nevertheless takes up most of the apartment: bikinis, miniskirts, T-shirts, platform shoes, and a vast amount of makeup.

"One day I'll wear what I like, but right now, I just need to be given a chance," she thinks.

And why does she want that chance?

Quite simple. Because she knows she's the best, despite her experience at school—when she so disappointed her parents—and despite the challenges she's faced since in order to prove to herself that she can overcome difficulties, frustrations, and defeats. She was born to win and to shine, of that she has no doubt.

"And when I get what I always wanted, I know I'll have to ask myself: do they love and admire me because I'm me or because I'm famous?"

She knows people who have achieved stardom on the stage and, contrary to her expectations, they're not at peace with themselves; they're insecure, full of doubts, unhappy as soon as they come offstage. They want to be actors so as not to have to be themselves, and they live in fear of making the one false step that could end their career.

"I'm different, though. I've always been me."

Is that true? Or does everyone in her position think the same?

SHE GETS UP AND MAKES herself some coffee. The kitchen is a mess, and none of her friends has bothered to wash the dishes. She doesn't know why she's woken up in such a bad mood and with so many doubts. She knows her job, she's devoted herself to it heart and soul, and yet it's as if people refuse to recognize her talent. She knows what human beings are like, too, especially men—future allies in a battle she needs to win soon, because she's twenty-five already and nearly too old for the dream factory. She knows three things:

(a) that men are less treacherous than women;
(b) that they never notice what a woman is wearing because they're always mentally undressing her;
(c) that as long as you've got breasts, thighs, buttocks, and belly in good trim, you can conquer the world.

Because of those three things, and because she knows that all the other women she's competing with try to emphasize their attributes, she pays attention only to item (c) on her list. She exercises and tries to keep fit, avoids diets, and, illogical though it may seem, dresses very discreetly. This has worked well so far, and she can usually pass for younger than her age. She's hoping that it'll do the trick in Cannes too.

Breasts, buttocks, thighs. They can focus on those things now if they want to, but the day will come when they'll see what she can really do.

She drinks her coffee and begins to understand her bad mood. She's surrounded by some of the most beautiful women on the planet! She certainly doesn't consider herself ugly, but there's no way she can compete with them. She needs to decide what to do. She had thought long and hard before making this trip, money is tight, and she doesn't have much time in which to land a contract. She went to various places during the first two days, giving people a copy of her CV and her photos, but all she achieved was an invitation to last night's party at a cheap restaurant, with the music at full blast, and where she met no one from the Superclass. In order to lose her inhibitions, she drank more than she should and ended up not knowing where she was or what she was doing there. Everything seemed strange to her—Europe, the way people dress, the different languages, the phony jollity—when the truth was everyone was wishing they could have been invited to some more important event, instead of being in that utterly insignificant place, listening to the same old music, and having to hold shouted conversations about other people's lives and the injustices committed by the powerful on the powerless.

Gabriela is tired of talking about these so-called injustices. That's simply the way it is. They choose the people they want to choose and don't have to explain themselves to anyone, which is why she needs a plan. A lot of other young women with the same dream (but not, of course, with as much talent as she) will be doing the rounds with their CVs and their photos; the producers who come to the Festival must be inundated with portfolios, DVDs, business cards.

What would make her stand out?

She needs to think. She won't get another chance like this, largely because she's spent all her savings on this trip. And—horror of horrors—she's getting old. She's twenty-five. This is her last chance.

While she drinks her coffee, she looks through the small kitchen window at the dead-end street down below. All she can see is a tobacconist's and a little girl eating chocolate. Yes, this is her last chance. She hopes it will turn out quite differently from the first one.

She thinks back to when she was eleven years old and performing in her first school play at one of the most expensive schools in Chicago. Her subsequent desire to succeed was not born of the unanimous acclaim she received from the audience, composed of fathers, mothers, relatives, and teachers. Far from it. She was playing the Mad Hatter in *Alice in Wonderland*. She had got the part—one of the best roles in the play—after auditioning along with a lot of other girls and boys.

Her first line was: "Your hair wants cutting." Then Alice would reply: "You should learn not to make personal remarks, it's very rude."

When the long-awaited moment came, a moment she had rehearsed and rehearsed, she was so nervous that she got the line wrong and said instead: "Your hair wants washing." The girl playing Alice said her next line anyway, and the audience would never have noticed anything was wrong if Gabriela, who knew she had made a mistake, hadn't promptly lost the power of speech. Since the Mad Hatter was an essential character if the scene was to continue, and since children are not good at improvising on stage (although they improvise happily enough in real life), no one knew what to do. Then, after several long minutes, during which the actors simply looked at each other, the teacher started applauding, announced it was time for an interval, and ordered everyone offstage.

Gabriela not only left the stage, she left the school in tears. The following day, she found out that the scene with the Mad Hatter had been cut, and the actors would instead move straight on to the game of croquet with the Queen. The teacher said this didn't matter in the least because the story of *Alice in Wonderland* is a lot of nonsense anyway, but during playtime, the other girls and boys ganged up on Gabriela and started beating her.

This wasn't so very unusual—it was a fairly regular occurrence—and she had learned to defend herself as energetically as when she, in turn, attacked the weaker children. On this occasion, however, she took the beating without uttering a word and without shedding a tear. Her reaction was so surprising that the fight lasted almost no time at all; her schoolmates expected her to scream and shout, and, when she didn't, rapidly lost interest. For with each blow, Gabriela was thinking:

"I'll be a great actress one day and then you'll be sorry."

Who says that children aren't capable of deciding what they want to do in life?

Adults do.

And when we grow to be adults ourselves, we believe that we really are wise beings who are always right. Many children had doubtless been through a similar experience, playing the role of the Mad Hatter or Sleeping Beauty or Aladdin or Alice, and decided there and then to abandon the spotlights and the applause. Gabriela, though, had never before lost a battle; she was the prettiest and most intelligent student in school and always got the best marks in class; and she knew intuitively that if she didn't fight back at once, she would be lost.

It was one thing to get a beating from her schoolmates—because she could give as good as she got—but it was quite another to carry a failure like that around with her for the rest of her life. As we all know, a fluffed line in a school play, an inability to dance as well as everyone else, or rude comments passed about skinny legs or a big head—which all children have to put up with—can have two radically different consequences.

Some people opt for revenge and try to be really good at whatever it is the others thought they couldn't do. "One day, you'll envy me," they think.

Most people, however, accept their limitations, and then things tend to go from bad to worse. They grow up insecure and obedient (although they dream of a day when they'll be free and able to do whatever they want), they get married to prove that they're not as ugly as other kids said they were (although deep down they still believe they are), they have children so that no one can say they're infertile (even though they never wanted kids anyway), they dress well so that no one can say they dress badly (although they know people will say that anyway).

By the following week, the incident at the play had been forgotten by everyone at school, but Gabriela had decided that, one day, when she was a world-famous actress, accompanied by secretaries, bodyguards, photographers, and legions of fans, she would go back to that school. She would put on a performance of *Alice in Wonderland* for needy children, she would make the news, and her childhood friends would say:

"I was on the same stage as her once!"

Her mother wanted her to study chemical engineering, and as soon as she finished high school, her parents sent her to the Illinois Institute of Technology. During the day, she studied protein paths and the structure of benzene, but she spent her evenings with Ibsen, Coward, and Shakespeare while attending a drama course paid for with money sent to her by her parents to buy clothes and course books. She trained with the best professionals and had excellent teachers. She received good reviews and letters of recommendation, she performed (without her parents' knowledge) as a backup singer for a rock group and as a belly dancer in a play about Lawrence of Arabia. It was always a good idea to accept any role that came along. There was always the chance that someone important might be in the audience, someone who would invite her to her first real audition, and then all those testing times and all her struggles to gain a place in the spotlight would be over.

The years passed. Gabriela made TV commercials, toothpaste ads, did some modeling work, and was even tempted to respond to an invitation from a group that specialized in providing escorts for businessmen because she desperately needed money to put together a proper portfolio to send to all the major modeling and acting agencies in the United States. Fortunately, God—in whom she never lost faith— saved her. That same day, she was offered a job as an extra in a video of a Japanese singer, which was going to be filmed beneath the viaduct of the Chicago El. She was paid much more than she expected (apparently the producers had demanded a fortune in fees for the foreign cast), and with that extra money she managed to produce the vital book of photos (or "book," as it's known in every language in the world), which also cost much more than she had imagined.

She was always telling herself that she was just at the beginning of her career, even though the days and months were beginning to fly by. She might have been picked to play Ophelia in *Hamlet* while she was in the drama course, but life mostly offered her only ads for deodorants and beauty creams. Whenever she went to an agency to show them her book and the letters of recommendation from teachers, friends, and colleagues, she found the waiting room full of girls who looked very like her, all of them smiling, all of them hating each other, and all doing whatever they could to get something, anything, that would give them "visibility," as the professionals called it.

She would wait hours for her turn to come, and meanwhile read books on meditation and positive thinking. She would end up sitting opposite someone—male or female—who ignored the letters and went straight to the photos, not that they ever commented on those either. They would make a note of her name. Sometimes, she would be called in for an audition, about one in ten of which bore fruit. There she would be again, with all her talent (or so she thought), standing in front of a camera and a lot of ill-mannered people, who were always telling her: "Relax, smile, turn to the right, drop your chin a little, lick your lips." And the result: a photo of a new brand of coffee.

And what happened when she wasn't called? She felt rejected, but soon learned to live with that and come to see it as a necessary experience, a test of her perseverance and faith. She refused to accept the fact that the drama course, the letters of recommendation, the CV listing minor roles performed in minor theaters, were of no use at all . . .

Her mobile phone rang.

. . . none at all.

It continued to ring.

She was still traveling back in time as she gazed out at the tobacconist's and at the little girl eating chocolate, then she finally emerged from her reverie, realized what was happening, and answered the phone.

A voice at the other end was saying that she had an audition in two hours' time.

She had an audition!

In Cannes!

So it *had* been worth crossing the ocean, arriving in a city where all the hotels were full, meeting up at the airport with other young women in exactly the same position as she (a Pole, two Russians, and a Brazilian), and going round knocking on doors until they found that shared, exorbitantly priced apartment. After all those years of trying her luck in Chicago and traveling now and then to Los Angeles in search of more agents, more advertisements, more rejections, it turned out that her future lay in Europe!

In two hours' time?

She couldn't catch a bus because she didn't know the routes. She was staying high up on a steep hill and had only been down it twice so far—to distribute copies of her book and to go to that stupid party last night. On both occasions, when she reached the bottom of the hill, she had hitched a lift from complete strangers, usually single men in magnificent convertibles. Everyone knew Cannes to be a safe place, and all women know that good looks help when trying to get a ride, but she couldn't leave anything to chance this time, she would have to resolve the problem herself. Auditions follow a rigorous timetable, that was one of the first things you learn at any acting agency. She had noticed on her first day in Cannes that the traffic was almost permanently gridlocked, and so all she could do was get dressed and leave at once. She would be there in an hour and a half; she remembered the hotel where the producer was staying because it was on the "pilgrimage route" she had followed yesterday, in search of some opportunity, some opening.

Now the problem was what to wear.

She fell upon the suitcase she had brought with her, chose some Armani jeans made in China and bought on the black market in Chicago for a fifth of the real price. No one could say they were fake because they weren't: everyone knew that the Chinese manufacturers sent eighty percent of what they produced to the original stores, with the remaining twenty percent being sold off by employees on the side. It was, shall we say, excess stock, surplus to requirements.

She was wearing a white DKNY T-shirt, which had cost more than the jeans. Faithful to her principles, she knew that the more discreet the clothes, the better. No short skirts, no plunging necklines, because if other women had been invited to the audition, that is what they would be wearing.

She wasn't sure about her makeup. In the end, she opted for a very light foundation and an even lighter application of lip liner. She had already lost a precious fifteen minutes.

11:45 A.M.

People are never satisfied. If they have a little, they want more. If they have a lot, they want still more. Once they have more, they wish they could be happy with little, but are incapable of making the slightest effort in that direction.

Is it just that they don't understand how simple happiness is? What can she want, that girl in the jeans and white T-shirt who just came running past? What could be so urgent that it stopped her taking time to contemplate the lovely sunny day, the blue sea, the babies in their strollers, the palms fringing the beach?

"Don't run, child! You'll never escape the two most important presences in the life of any human being: God and death. God accompanies your every step and will be annoyed because he can see that you're not paying attention to the miracle of life. Or indeed death. You just ran past a corpse and didn't even notice."

Igor has walked past the scene of the crime several times now. At one point, he realized that his comings and goings might arouse suspicion and so decided to remain a prudent two hundred yards from the scene, leaning on the balustrade that looked out over the beach. He's wearing dark glasses, but there's nothing suspicious about that, not only because it's a sunny day, but because in a celebrity town like Cannes, dark glasses are synonymous with status.

He's surprised to see that it's almost midday, and yet no one has realized that there's a person lying dead on the main street of a city which, at this time of year, is the focus of the world's attention.

A couple are approaching the bench now, visibly irritated. They start shouting at the sleeping beauty; they're the girl's parents, angry because she isn't working. The man shakes her almost violently. Then the woman bends over, obscuring Igor's field of vision.

Igor knows what will happen next.

The mother screams. The father takes his mobile phone from his pocket and moves away, clearly agitated. The mother is shaking her daughter's unresponsive body. Passersby stop, and now he can remove his dark glasses and join them as one more curious onlooker.

The mother is crying, clinging to her daughter. A young man gently pushes her away and attempts mouth-to-mouth resuscitation, but soon gives up; Olivia's face already has a slight purple tinge to it.

"Someone call an ambulance!"

Several people dial the same number, all of them feeling useful, important, caring. He can already hear the sound of the siren in the distance. The mother's screams are growing louder. A young woman tries to put a comforting arm around her, but the mother pushes her away. Someone attempts to sit the body up, and someone else tells them to lay her down again because it's too late to do anything.

"It's probably a drug overdose," the person next to him says. "Young people today are a lost cause."

Those who hear the comment nod sagely. Igor remains impassive while he watches the paramedics unload their equipment from the ambulance, apply electric shocks to Olivia's heart, while a more experienced doctor stands by, not saying a word, because although he knows there's nothing to be done, he doesn't want his colleagues to be accused of negligence. They place Olivia's body on the stretcher and put it in the ambulance, the mother still clinging to her daughter. After a brief discussion, they allow the mother to get in too, and the ambulance speeds away.

No more than five minutes have passed between the couple discovering the body and the ambulance leaving. The father is still standing there, stunned, not knowing where to go or what to do. Forgetting whom he's speaking to, the same person who made the comment about a drug overdose goes over to the father and gives him his version of the facts:

"Don't worry, sir. This kind of thing happens every day around here."

The father does not respond. He's stilling holding his mobile phone and staring into space. He either doesn't understand the remark or has no idea what it is that happens every day, or else he's in a state of shock that has sent him immediately into some unknown dimension where pain does not exist.

The crowd disperses as quickly as it appeared. Only two people remain: the father still clutching his phone and the man who has now taken off his dark glasses and is holding them in his hand.

"Did you know the girl?" Igor asks.

There is no reply.

It's best to do as everyone else has done, keep walking along the Boulevard de la Croisette and see what else is happening on this sunny morning in Cannes. Like the girl's father, he doesn't know quite what he is feeling: he has destroyed a world he will never be able to rebuild, even if he had all the power in the world. Did Ewa deserve that? From the womb of that young woman, Olivia—the fact that he knows her name troubles him greatly because that means she's no longer just a face in the crowd—might have sprung a genius who would have gone on to discover a cure for cancer or drafted an agreement that would ensure that the world could finally live in peace. He has destroyed not just one person, but all the future generations that might have sprung from her. What has he done? Was love, however great and however intense, sufficient justification for that?

He had chosen the wrong person as his first victim. Her death will never make the news and Ewa won't understand the message.

Don't think about it, it's done now. You have prepared yourself to go much further than this, so carry on. The girl will understand that her death was not in vain, but was a sacrifice in the name of a greater love. Look around you, see what's happening in the city, behave like a normal citizen. You've already had your fair share of suffering in this life; now you deserve a little peace and comfort.

Enjoy the Festival. This is what you have been preparing yourself for.

EVEN IF HE'D HAD HIS swimming things with him, he would have found it difficult to get anywhere near the seashore. The big hotels had, it seems, acquired the rights to great swaths of beach which they had filled with their chairs, logos, waiters, and bodyguards, who, at every entry point, demanded the guest's room key or some other form of identification. Other areas were occupied by huge white tents, where some production company, brewery, or cosmetics firm was launching its latest product at a so-called lunch. People here were dressed normally, if by "normal" you mean a baseball cap, bright shirt, and light-colored trousers for men, and jewelry, loose top, Bermudas, and low-heeled shoes for women.

Dark glasses were de rigueur for both sexes, and there was little bare flesh on show because members of the Superclass were too old for that now, and any such display would be considered ridiculous or, rather, pathetic.

Igor noticed one other thing: the mobile phone. The most important item of clothing.

It was essential to be receiving a constant stream of messages or calls, to be prepared to interrupt any conversation in order to answer a call that was not in the least urgent, to stand keying in endless texts via an SMS. They had all forgotten that these initials mean Short Message Service and instead used the keypad as if it were a typewriter. It was slow, awkward, and could cause serious damage to the thumb, but what did it matter? At that very moment, not only in Cannes, but in the whole world, the ether was being filled with messages like "Good morning, my love, I woke up thinking about you and I'm so glad to have you in my life," "I'll be home in ten minutes, please have my lunch ready and check that my clothes were sent to the laundry," or "The party here is a real drag, but I haven't got anywhere else to go, where are you?" Things that take five minutes to be written down and only ten seconds to be spoken, but that's the way the world is. Igor knows all about this because he has earned hundreds of millions of dollars thanks to the fact that the phone is no longer simply a method of communicating with others, but a thread of hope, a way of believing that you're not alone, a way of showing others how important you are.

And it was leading the world into a state of utter madness. For a mere five euros a month, via an ingenious system created in London, a call center would send you a standard message every three minutes. When you know you're going to be talking to someone you want to impress, you just have to dial a particular number to activate the system. The phone rings, you pick it up, open the message, read it quickly, and say "Oh, that can wait" (of course it can: it was written to order). This way, the person you're talking to feels important, and things move along more quickly because he realizes he's in the presence of a very busy person. Three minutes later, the conversation is interrupted by another message, the pressure mounts, and the user of the service can decide whether it's worth turning off his phone for a quarter of an hour or lying and saying that he really must take this call, and so rid himself of a disagreeable companion.

There is only one situation in which all mobile phones must be turned off. Not at formal suppers, in the middle of a play, during the key moment in a film, or while an opera singer is attempting the most difficult of arias; we've all heard someone's mobile phone go off in such circumstances. No, the only time when people are genuinely concerned that their phone might prove dangerous is when they get on a plane and hear the usual lie: "All mobile phones must be switched off during the flight because they might interfere with the onboard systems." We all believe this and do as the flight attendants ask.

Igor knew when this myth had been created: for years now, airlines had been doing their best to convince passengers to use the phones attached to their seat. These cost ten dollars a minute and use the same transmission system as mobile phones. The strategy didn't work, but the myth lingered on; they had simply forgotten to remove the warning from the list of dos and don'ts that the flight attendant has to read out before takeoff. What no one knew was that on every flight, there were always at least two or three passengers who forgot to turn their phones off, and besides, laptops access the Internet using exactly the same system as mobiles. And no plane anywhere in the world has yet fallen out of the sky because of that.

Now they were trying to modify the warning without alarming the passengers too much and without dropping the price. You could use your mobile phone as long as it was one you could put into flight mode. Such phones cost four times as much. No one has ever explained what "flight mode" is, but if people choose to be taken in like this, that's their problem.

HE KEEPS WALKING. HE'S TROUBLED by the last look the girl had given him before she died, but prefers not to think about it.

MORE BODYGUARDS, MORE DARK GLASSES, more bikinis on the beach, more light-colored clothes and jewelry attending "lunches," more people hurrying along as if they had something very important to do that morning, more photographers on every corner attempting the impossible task of snapping something unusual, more magazines and free newspapers about what's happening at the Festival, more people handing out flyers to the poor mortals who haven't been invited to lunch in one of the white tents, flyers advertising restaurants on the top of the hill, far from everything, where little is heard of what goes on in Boulevard de la Croisette, up there where models rent apartments for the duration of the Festival, hoping they'll be summoned to an audition that will change their lives forever.

All so unsurprising. All so predictable. If he were to go into one of those tents now, no one would dare ask for his identification because it's still early and the promoters will be afraid that no one will come. In half an hour's time, though, depending on how things go, the security guards will be given express orders to let in only pretty, unaccompanied girls.

Why not try it out?

He follows his impulse; after all, he's on a mission. He goes down some steps, which lead not to the beach, but to a large white tent with plastic windows, air-conditioning, and white chairs and tables, largely empty. One of the security guards asks if he has an invitation, and he says that he does. He pretends to search his pockets. A receptionist dressed in red asks if she can help.

He offers her his business card, bearing the logo of his phone company and his name, Igor Malev, President. He's sure his name is on the list, he says, but he must have left his invitation at the hotel; he's been at a series of meetings and forgot to bring it with him. The receptionist welcomes him and invites him in; she has learned to judge men and women by the way they dress, and "President" means the same thing worldwide. Besides, he's the president of a Russian company! And everyone knows how rich Russians like to show off their wealth. There was no need to check the list.

Igor enters, heads straight for the bar—it's a very well-equipped tent; there's even a dance floor—and orders a pineapple juice because it suits the atmosphere and, more important, because the drink, decorated with a tiny blue Japanese umbrella, comes complete with a black straw.

He sits down at one of the many empty tables. Among the few people present is a man in his fifties, with hennaed mahogany brown hair, fake tan, and a body honed in one of those gyms that promise eternal youth. He's wearing a torn T-shirt and is sitting with two other men, who are both dressed in impeccable designer suits. The two men turn to face Igor, and he immediately turns his head slightly, but continues to study them from behind his dark glasses. The men in suits try to work out who this new arrival is, then lose interest.

Igor's interest, however, increases.

The man does not even have a mobile phone on the table, although his two assistants are constantly fielding calls.

Given that this badly dressed, arrogant fellow has been let into the tent; given that he has his mobile phone turned off; given that the waiter keeps coming up to him and asking if he wants anything; given that he doesn't even deign to respond, but merely waves him away, he is obviously someone very important.

Igor takes a fifty-euro note out of his pocket and gives it to the waiter who has just started laying the table.

"Who's the gentleman in the faded blue T-shirt?" he asks, glancing in the direction of the other table.

"Javits Wild. He's a very important man."

Excellent. After someone as insignificant as the girl at the beach, a figure like Javits Wild would be ideal—not famous, but important. One of the people who decides who should be in the spotlight and who feels no need to take much care over his own appearance because he knows exactly who he is. He's in charge of pulling the strings, and the puppets feel themselves to be the most privileged and envied people on the planet, until one day, for whatever reason, the puppeteer decides to cut the strings, and the puppets fall down, lifeless and powerless.

He's clearly a member of the Superclass, which means that he has false friends and many enemies.

"One other question. Would it be acceptable to destroy a universe in the name of a greater love?"

The waiter laughs.

"Are you God or just gay?"

"Neither, but thank you for your answer."

He realizes he should not have asked that question. Firstly, because he doesn't need anyone's support to justify what he's doing; he's convinced that since everyone will die one day, some must do so in the name of something greater. That's how it's been since the beginning of time, when men sacrificed themselves in order to feed their tribe, when virgins were handed over to the priests to placate the wrath of dragons and gods. The second reason is because he has now drawn attention to himself and indicated an interest in the man at the next table.

The waiter's sure to forget, but there's no need to take unnecessary risks. He tells himself that at a Festival such as this, it's only normal that people should want to know about other people, and even more normal that such information should be rewarded. He himself has done the same thing hundreds of times in restaurants all over the world, and

others had doubtless done the same with him. Waiters aren't just accustomed to being given money to supply a name or a better table or to
send a discreet message, they almost expect it.

No, the waiter wouldn't remember anything. Igor knows that his
next victim is there before him. If he succeeds, and if the waiter is questioned, he'll say that the only odd thing to happen that day was a man
asking him if he thought it was acceptable to destroy a universe in the
name of a greater love. He might not even remember that much. The
police will ask: "What did he look like?" and the waiter will reply: "I
didn't pay much attention, to be honest, but I know he said he wasn't
gay." The police—accustomed to the kind of French intellectual who
sits in bars and comes up with weird theories and complicated analyses
of, for example, the sociology of film festivals—would quietly let the
matter drop.

Something else was bothering Igor though.

The name or names.

He had killed before—with weapons and the blessing of his country. He didn't know how many people he had killed, but he had rarely
seen their faces and certainly never asked their names. Knowing someone's name meant knowing that the other person was a human being
and not "the enemy." Knowing someone's name transformed him into
a unique and special individual, with a past and a future, with ancestors
and possibly descendants, a person who has known triumphs and failures. People are their names; they're proud of them; they repeat them
thousands of times in their lifetime and identify with them. It's the first
word they learn after "Daddy" and "Mummy."

Olivia. Javits. Igor. Ewa.

Someone's spirit, however, has no name; it is pure truth and inhabits
a particular body for a certain period of time, and will, one day, leave
it, and God won't bother asking, "What's your name?" when the soul
arrives at the final judgment. God will ask only: "Did you love while
you were alive?" For that is the essence of life: the ability to love, not
the name we carry around on our passport, business card, and identity
card. The great mystics changed their names, and sometimes abandoned them altogether. When John the Baptist was asked who he was,

he said only: "I am the voice of one crying in the wilderness." When Jesus found the man on whom he would build his church, he ignored the fact that the man in question had spent his entire life answering to the name of Simon and called him Peter. When Moses asked God his name, back came the reply: "I am who I am."

Perhaps he should look for another victim, one named victim was enough: Olivia. At this precise moment, however, he feels that he cannot turn back, but he decides that he will not ask the name of the next world he destroys. He can't turn back because he wants to do justice to the poor, vulnerable girl on the bench by the beach—such a sweet, easy victim. This new challenge—this sweaty, pseudo-athletic, henna-haired man with the bored expression and who is clearly someone very powerful—is much more difficult. The two men in suits are not just assistants; he notices that every now and then, they look around the tent, watching everything that's going on nearby. If he is to be worthy of Ewa and fair to Olivia, he must be brave.

He leaves the straw in the pineapple juice. People are beginning to arrive. He has to wait for the place to fill up, but not too long. He hadn't planned to destroy a world in broad daylight, in the middle of the Boulevard in Cannes, and he doesn't know exactly how to carry out this next project. Something tells him, though, that he has chosen the perfect place.

His thoughts are no longer with the poor young woman at the beach; adrenaline is filling his blood, his heart is beating faster, he's excited and happy.

Javits Wild wouldn't be wasting his time here just to get a free meal at one of the thousands of parties to which he must be invited every year. He must be here for some specific reason or to meet a particular person. That reason or person would doubtless be Igor's best alibi.

12:26 P.M.

Javits watches the other guests arriving. The place is getting crowded, and he thinks what he always thinks:

"What am I doing here? I don't need this. In fact, I need very little from anyone—I have all I want. I'm a big name in the movie world, I can have any woman I desire, even though I dress badly. In fact, I make a point of being badly dressed. Long gone are the days when I had only one suit, and, on the rare occasions when I received an invitation from the Superclass (after much crawling, begging, and making promises), I would prepare myself for a lunch like this as if it were the most important occasion of my life. Now I know that the only thing that changes are the cities these lunches are held in; otherwise, it's all utterly boring and predictable.

"People will come up to me and tell me they adore my work. Others will call me a hero and thank me for giving movie mavericks a chance. Pretty, intelligent women, who are not taken in by appearances, will notice the people gathering round my table and ask the waiter who I am and immediately find some way of approaching me, certain that the only thing I'm interested in is sex. Every single one of them has some favor to ask of me. That's why they praise and flatter me and offer me what they think I need. But all I want is to be left alone.

"I've been to thousands of parties like this, and I'm not here in this tent for any particular reason, except that I can't sleep, even though

I flew to France in my private jet, a technological marvel capable of flying at an altitude of over thirty-six thousand feet from California all the way to Cannes without having to make a refueling stop. I changed the original configuration of the cabin. It can comfortably carry eighteen passengers, but I reduced the number of seats to six and kept the cabin separate for the four crew members. Someone's always sure to ask: 'May I come with you?' And now I have the perfect excuse: 'Sorry, there's no room.'"

Javits had equipped his new toy, which cost around forty million dollars, with two beds, a conference table, a shower, a Miranda sound system (Bang & Olufsen had an excellent design and a good PR campaign, but they were now a thing of the past), two coffee machines, a microwave oven for the crew and an electric oven for him (because he hates reheated food). Javits only drinks champagne, and whoever wishes to is more than welcome to share a bottle of Moët & Chandon 1961 with him. However, the "cellar" on the plane had every drink any guest might conceivably want. And then there were the two twenty-one-inch LCD screens ready to show the most recent films, even those that hadn't yet made it into the cinemas.

The jet was one of the most advanced in the world (although the French insisted that the Dassault Falcon was even better), but regardless of how much money he had, he couldn't change the clocks in Europe. It was now 3:43 A.M. in Los Angeles, and he was just beginning to feel really tired. He had been awake all night, going from one party to the next, answering the same two idiotic questions that began every conversation:

"How was your flight?"

To which Javits always responded with a question:

"Why?"

People didn't know quite what to say and so they smiled awkwardly and moved on to the next question on the list:

"Are you staying here long?"

And Javits would again ask: "Why?" Then he would pretend he had to answer his mobile phone, make his excuses, and move on with his two inseparable besuited friends in tow.

He met no one interesting. But then who would a man who has almost everything money can buy find interesting? He had tried to change his friends and meet people who had nothing to do with the world of cinema: philosophers, writers, jugglers, executives of food-manufacturing companies. At first, it all went swimmingly, until the inevitable question: "Would you like to read a script I've written?" Or the second most inevitable question: "I have a friend who has always wanted to be an actor/actress. Would you mind meeting him/her?"

Yes, he would. He had other things to do in life apart from work. He used to fly once a month to Alaska, go into the first bar, get drunk, eat pizza, wander about in the wild, and talk to the people who lived in the small towns up there. He worked out for two hours a day at his private gym, but the doctors had warned him he could still end up with heart problems. He didn't care that much about being physically fit, what he really wanted was to off-load a little of the constant tension that seemed to weigh on him every second of the day, to do some meditation and heal the wounds to his soul. When he was in the country, he always asked the people he chanced to meet what "normal life" was like, because he had forgotten. The answers varied, and he gradually came to realize that, even when he was surrounded by other people, he was absolutely alone in the world.

He decided to draw up a list of what constituted normal attitudes and behavior, based on what people did rather than on what they said.

Javits glances around. There's a man in dark glasses drinking a fruit juice. He seems oblivious to his surroundings and is staring out to sea as if he were somewhere far from there. He's smartly dressed and good-looking, with graying hair. He was one of the first to arrive and must know who Javits is, and yet he's made no effort to come and introduce himself. It was brave of him to sit there alone like that. Being alone in Cannes is anathema; it means that no one is interested in you, that you're unimportant or don't know anyone.

He envies that man, who probably doesn't fit the list of "normal" behavior he always keeps in his pocket. He seems so independent and free; if Javits weren't feeling so tired, he would really like to talk to him.

He turns to one of his "friends."

"What does being normal mean?"

"Is your conscience troubling you? Have you done something you shouldn't have?"

Javits has clearly asked the wrong question of the wrong man. His companion will perhaps assume that he's regretting what he's made of his life and that he wants to start anew, but that isn't it at all. And if he does have regrets, it's too late to begin again; he knows the rules of the game.

"I asked you what being normal means?"

One of the "friends" looks bewildered. The other keeps surveying the tent, watching people come and go.

"Living like someone who lacks all ambition," the first "friend" says at last.

Javits takes his list out of his pocket and puts it on the table.

"I always have this with me and I add to it all the time."

The "friend" says that he can't look at it now because he has to keep alert to what's going on around them. The other man, though, more relaxed and confident, reads the list out loud:

1. Normal is anything that makes us forget who we are and what we want; that way we can work in order to produce, reproduce, and earn money.
2. Setting out rules for waging war (the Geneva Convention).
3. Spending years studying at university only to find at the end of it all that you're unemployable.
4. Working from nine till five every day at something that gives you no pleasure at all just so that, after thirty years, you can retire.
5. Retiring and discovering that you no longer have enough energy to enjoy life and dying a few years later of sheer boredom.
6. Using Botox.
7. Believing that power is much more important than money and that money is much more important than happiness.

8. Making fun of anyone who seeks happiness rather than money and accusing them of "lacking ambition."

9. Comparing objects like cars, houses, clothes, and defining life according to those comparisons, instead of trying to discover the real reason for being alive.

10. Never talking to strangers. Saying nasty things about the neighbors.

11. Believing that your parents are always right.

12. Getting married, having children, and staying together long after all love has died, saying that it's for the good of the children (who are, apparently, deaf to the constant rows).

12a. Criticizing anyone who tries to be different.

14. Waking up each morning to a hysterical alarm clock on the bedside table.

15. Believing absolutely everything that appears in print.

16. Wearing a scrap of colored cloth around your neck, even though it serves no useful purpose, but which answers to the name of "tie."

17. Never asking a direct question, even though the other person can guess what it is you want to know.

18. Keeping a smile on your lips even when you're on the verge of tears. Feeling sorry for those who show their feelings.

19. Believing that art is either worth a fortune or worth nothing at all.

20. Despising anything that was easy to achieve because if no sacrifice was involved, it obviously isn't worth having.

21. Following fashion trends, however ridiculous or uncomfortable.

22. Believing that all famous people have tons of money saved up.

23. Investing a lot of time and money in external beauty and caring little about inner beauty.

24. Using every means possible to show that, although you're just an ordinary human being, you're far above other mortals.

25. Never looking anyone in the eye when you're traveling on

public transport, in case it's interpreted as a sign you're trying to get off with them.

26. Standing facing the door in an elevator and pretending you're the only person there, regardless of how crowded it is.

27. Never laughing too loudly in a restaurant however good the joke.

28. In the northern hemisphere, always dressing according to the season: bare arms in spring (however cold it is) and woolen jacket in autumn (however hot it is).

29. In the southern hemisphere, covering the Christmas tree with fake snow even though winter has nothing to do with the birth of Christ.

30. Assuming, as you grow older, that you're the guardian of the world's wisdom, even if you haven't necessarily lived enough to know what's right and wrong.

31. Going to a charity tea party and thinking that you've done your bit toward putting an end to social inequality in the world.

32. Eating three times a day even if you're not hungry.

33. Believing that other people are always better than you—better-looking, more capable, richer, more intelligent—and that it's very dangerous to step outside your own limits, so it's best to do nothing.

34. Using your car as a weapon and as impenetrable armor.

35. Swearing when in heavy traffic.

36. Believing that everything your child does wrong is entirely down to the company he or she keeps.

37. Marrying the first person who offers you a decent position in society. Love can wait.

38. Always saying, "I tried" when you didn't really try at all.

39. Postponing doing the really interesting things in life for later, when you won't have the energy.

40. Avoiding depression with large daily doses of television.

41. Believing that you can be sure of everything you've achieved.

42. Assuming that women don't like football and that men aren't interested in home decoration and cooking.

43. Blaming the government for all the bad things that happen.
44. Thinking that being a good, decent, respectable person will mean that others will see you as weak, vulnerable, and easy to manipulate.
45. Being equally convinced that aggression and rudeness are synonymous with having a "powerful personality."
46. Being afraid of having an endoscopy (if you're a man) and giving birth (if you're a woman).

The "friend" laughs.

"You should make a film on the subject," he says.

"Not again," Javits thinks. "They have no idea. They're with me all the time, but they still don't understand what I do. I don't make films."

All films start out in the mind of a so-called producer. He's read a book, say, or had a brilliant idea while driving along the freeways of Los Angeles (which is really a large suburb in search of a city). Unfortunately, he's alone, both in the car and in his desire to transform that brilliant idea into something that can be seen on the screen.

He finds out if the film rights to the book are still available. If the response is negative, he goes in search of another product—after all, more than sixty thousand books are published each year in the United States alone. If the response is positive, he phones the author and makes the lowest possible offer, which is usually accepted because it's not only actors and actresses who like to be associated with the dream machine. Every author feels more important when his or her words are transformed into images.

They arrange to have lunch. The producer says that the book is "a work of art and highly cinematographic" and that the writer is "a genius deserving of recognition." The writer explains that he spent five years working on the book and asks to be allowed to help in the writing of the script. "No, really, you shouldn't do that, it's an entirely different medium," comes the reply, "but I know you'll love the result." Then he adds: "The film will be totally true to the book," which, as both of them know, is a complete and utter lie.

The writer decides that he should agree to the conditions, promising himself that next time will be different. He accepts. The producer now says that they have to interest one of the big studios because they need financial backing for the project. He names a few stars he claims to have lined up for the lead roles—which is another complete and utter lie, but one that is always wheeled out and always works as a seduction technique. He buys what is known as an "option," that is, he pays around ten thousand dollars to retain the rights for three years. And then what happens? "Then we'll pay ten times that amount and you'll have a right to two percent of the net profits." That's the financial part of the conversation over with, because the writer is convinced he'll earn a fortune from his slice of the profits.

If he were to ask around, he'd soon find out that the Hollywood accountants somehow manage it so that no film *ever* makes a profit.

Lunch ends with the producer handing the writer a huge contract and asking if he could possibly sign it now, so that the studio will know that the product is definitely theirs. With his eyes fixed on that (nonexistent) percentage and on the possibility of seeing his name in lights (which won't happen either, at most there'll be a line in the credits, saying: "Based on the book by . . ."), the writer signs the contract without giving the matter much thought.

Vanity of vanities, all is vanity, and there is nothing new under the sun, as Solomon said more than three thousand years ago.

The producer starts knocking on the doors of various studios. He's known in the industry already, and so some of those doors open, but his proposal is not always accepted. In that case, he doesn't even bother to ring up the author and invite him to lunch again, he just writes him a letter saying that, despite his enthusiasm for the project, the movie industry isn't yet ready for that kind of story and he's returning the contract (which he, of course, did not sign).

If the proposal is accepted, the producer then goes to the lowest and least well-paid person in the hierarchy: the screenwriter, the person who will spend days, weeks, and months writing and rewriting the original idea or the screen adaptation. The scripts are sent to the producer (but never to the author), who, out of habit, automatically rejects the first draft, knowing that the screenwriter can always do better. More weeks and months of coffee and insomnia for the bright young talent (or old hack—there are no halfway houses) who rewrites each scene, which are then rejected or reshaped by the producer. (And the screenwriter thinks: "If he can write so damn well, why doesn't he write the whole thing?" Then he remembers his salary and goes quietly back to his computer.)

Finally, the script is almost ready. At this point, the producer draws up a list of demands: the removal of any political references that might upset a more conservative audience; more kissing, because women like that kind of thing; a story with a beginning, a middle, and an end, and a hero who moves everyone to tears with his self-sacrifice and devotion; and one character who loses a loved one at the start of the film and finds him or her again at the end. In fact, most film scripts can be summed up very briefly as: Man loves woman. Man loses woman. Man gets woman back. Ninety percent of all films are variations on that same theme.

Films that break this rule have to be very violent to make up for it, or have loads of crowd-pleasing special effects. And since this tried and tested formula is a surefire winner, why take any unnecessary risks?

ARMED WITH WHAT HE CONSIDERS to be a well-written story, whom does the producer seek out next? The studio who financed the project. The studio, however, has a long line of films to place in the ever-diminishing number of cinemas around the world. They ask him to wait a little or to find an independent distributor, first making sure that the producer signs another gigantic contract (which even takes into account exclusive rights "outside of Planet Earth"), taking full responsibility for all money spent.

"And that's where people like me come in!" The independent distributor can walk down the street without being recognized, although at media-fests like this everyone knows who he is. He's the person who didn't come up with the idea, didn't work on the script, and didn't invest a cent.

Javits is the intermediary—the distributor!

He receives the producer in a tiny office (the big plane, the house with the swimming pool, the invitations to parties all over the world are purely for his enjoyment—the producer doesn't even merit a mineral water). He takes the DVD home with him. He watches the first five minutes. If he likes it, he watches to the end, but this only happens with one out of every hundred new films he's given. Then he spends ten cents on a phone call and tells the producer to come back on a certain date and at a certain time.

"We'll sign," he says, as if he were doing the producer a big favor. "I'll distribute the film."

The producer tries to negotiate. He wants to know how many cinemas in how many countries and under what conditions. These, however, are pointless questions because he knows what the distributor will say: "That depends on the reactions we get at the prelaunch screenings." The product is shown to selected audiences from all social classes, people specially chosen by market research companies. The results are analyzed by professionals. If the results are positive, another ten cents gets spent on a phone call, and, the following day, Javits hands the producer three copies of yet another vast contract. The producer asks to be given time for his lawyer to read it. Javits says he has nothing against him doing that, but he needs to finalize that season's program now and can't guarantee that by the time the producer gets back to him he won't have selected another film.

The producer reads only the clause that tells him how much he's going to earn. He's pleased with what he sees and so he signs. He doesn't want to miss this opportunity.

Years have passed since he sat down with the writer to discuss making a film of his book and he's quite forgotten that he is now in exactly the same situation.

Vanity of vanities, all is vanity, and there is nothing new under the sun, as Solomon said more than three thousand years ago.

JAVITS WATCHES THE TENT FILLING up with guests and again asks himself what he's doing there. He controls more than five hundred cinemas in the United States and has an exclusive contract with another five thousand around the world, where exhibitors are obliged to buy everything he offers them, even if the films don't always work out. They know that one box-office success more than makes up for the other five that fail to pull in the crowds. They rely on Javits, the independent megadistributor, the hero who managed to break the monopoly of the big studios and become a legend in the film world.

No one has ever asked how he did this, but since he continues to give them one big success for every five failures (the average in the big studios is one blockbuster for every nine flops), it really doesn't matter.

Javits, however, knows how he became so successful, which is why he never goes anywhere without his two "friends," who are, at that moment, busily answering calls, arranging meetings and accepting invitations. They both have reasonably normal physiques, not like the burly bouncers on the door, but they're worth a whole army. They trained in Israel and have served in Uganda, Argentina, and Panama. One fields phone calls and the other is constantly looking around, memorizing each person, each movement, each gesture. They alternate these tasks because, like simultaneous translators and air controllers, they need to rest every fifteen minutes.

What is he doing at this "lunch"? He could have stayed at the hotel, trying to get some sleep. He's tired of being fawned over and praised, and of having to smile every minute and tell someone that it's really not worth their while giving him their card because he'll only lose it. When they insist, he asks them gently to speak to one of his secretaries (duly housed at another luxury hotel on the Boulevard de la Croisette, where they are not allowed to sleep, but must answer the phone that rings nonstop or reply to the e-mails flooding in from cinemas all over the world, along with the promises of increased penis size or multiple orgasms that manage to elude all the spam filters). Depending on how he nods his head, one of his two assistants will either give the person the secretary's address or phone number, or say that unfortunately they're fresh out of cards.

Yes, what is he doing at this "lunch"? He would be sleeping now in

Los Angeles, however late he might have got home from a party. Javits knows the answer, but he doesn't want to accept it: he's afraid of being alone. He envies the man who arrived earlier and sat drinking his fruit juice, staring off into the distance, apparently relaxed and unconcerned about trying to look busy or important. He decides to invite him to join him for a drink, but notices he's no longer there.

Just then, he feels something prick him in the back.

"Mosquitoes! That's what I hate about beach parties."

When he goes to scratch the bite, he finds a small needle. It must be some stupid prank. He looks behind him and, about two yards away, separated from him by various other guests, a black guy with dread-locks is laughing loudly, while a group of women gaze at him with mingled respect and desire.

He's too tired to react to this provocation. Best let the guy play the fool if that's the only way he can impress other people.

"Idiot."

His two companions react to the sudden change in posture of the man they are paid to protect at the rate of $435 a day. One of them raises his hand to his right shoulder, where he keeps an automatic pistol in a holster that is entirely invisible beneath his jacket. The other man gets discreetly to his feet (they are at a party, after all) and places himself between the black man and his boss.

"It was nothing," says Javits. "Just a prank."

He shows them the needle.

These two idiots are prepared for attacks with firearms and knives, for acts of physical aggression or attempts on their boss's life. They're always the first to enter his hotel room, ready to shoot if necessary. They can sense when someone's carrying a weapon (a common enough occurrence now in many cities of the world), and they don't take their eyes off that person until they're sure he's harmless. When Javits gets into an elevator, he stands sandwiched between them, their two bodies forming a kind of wall. He has never seen them take out their guns because, if they did so, they would use them. They usually resolve any problem with a look or a few quiet words.

Problems? He has never had any problems since he acquired his two "friends," as if their mere presence were enough to drive away evil spirits and evil intentions.

"That man, one of the first people to arrive, who sat down alone at that table over there," says one of them. "He was armed, wasn't he?"

The other man murmurs something like "Possibly," but the man had left the party some time ago. And he had been watched the whole time because they couldn't tell what exactly he was looking at from behind his dark glasses.

They relax. One of them starts answering the phone again, the other fixes his gaze on the Jamaican, who looks fearlessly back. There's something strange about that man, but one false move on his part and he'll be wearing false teeth from now on. It would all be done as discreetly as possible, on the beach, far from prying eyes, and by only one of them, while the other stood waiting, finger on the trigger. Sometimes, though, such provocative acts are a ruse to get the bodyguard away from the intended victim. They're used to such tricks.

"Fine . . ."

"No, it's not fine. Call an ambulance. I can't move my hand."

What luck!

The last thing she was expecting that morning was to meet the man who would—she was sure—change her life. But there he is, as sloppily dressed as ever, sitting with two friends, because powerful people don't need to show how powerful they are, they don't even need bodyguards.

Maureen has a theory that the people at Cannes can be divided into two categories:

(a) the tanned, who spend the whole day in the sun (they are already winners) and have the necessary badge to gain entry to certain restricted areas of the Festival. They arrive back at their hotels to find several invitations awaiting them, most of which will be thrown in the bin.

(b) the pale, who scurry from one gloomy office to the next, watching auditions, and either seeing some really good films that will be lost in the welter of other things on offer, or having to put up with some real horrors that might just win a place in the sun (among the tanned) because the makers know the right people.

Javits Wild, of course, sports an enviable tan.

THE FESTIVAL THAT TAKES OVER this small city in the south of France for twelve days, putting up prices, allowing only authorized cars to drive through the streets, and filling the airport with private jets and the beaches with models, isn't just a red carpet surrounded by photographers, a carpet along which the big stars walk on their way into the Palais des Congrès. Cannes isn't about fashion, it's about cinema!

What strikes you most is the luxury and the glamour, but the real heart of the Festival is the film industry's huge parallel market: buyers and sellers from all over the world who come together to do deals on films that have already been made or to talk investments and ideas. On an average day, four hundred movies are shown, most of them in apartments hired for the duration, with people perched uncomfortably on beds, complaining about the heat and demanding that their every whim be met, from bottles of mineral water up, and leaving the people showing the film with their nerves in tatters and frozen smiles on their faces, for it's essential to agree to everything, to grant every wish, because what matters is having the chance to show something that has probably been years in the making.

However, while these forty-eight hundred new productions are fighting tooth and nail for a chance to leave that hotel room and get shown in a proper cinema, the world of dreams is setting off in a different direction: the new technologies are gaining ground, people don't leave their houses so much anymore because they don't feel safe, or because they have too much work, or because of all those cable TV stations where you can usually choose from about five hundred films a day and pay almost nothing.

Worse still, the Internet has made anyone and everyone a filmmaker. Specialist portals show films of babies walking, men and women being decapitated in wars, or women who exhibit their bodies merely for the pleasure of knowing that the person watching them will be enjoying their own moment of solitary pleasure, films of people "freezing" in Grand Central Station, of traffic accidents, sports clips, and fashion shows, films made with hidden video cameras intent on embarrassing the poor innocents who walk past them.

Of course, people do still go out, but they prefer to spend their money on restaurant meals and designer clothes because they can get everything else on their high-definition TV screens or on their computers.

The days when everyone knew who had won the Palme d'Or are long gone. Now, if you ask who won last year, even people who were actually there at the Festival won't be able to remember. "Some Romanian, wasn't it?" says one. "I'm not sure, but I think it was a German film," says another. They'll sneak off to consult the catalogue and discover that it was an Italian, whose films, it turns out, are only shown at art cinemas.

After a period of intense competition with video rentals, cinemas started to prosper again, but now they seem to be entering another period of decline, having to compete with Internet rentals, with pirating and those DVDs of old films that are given away free with newspapers. This makes distribution an even more savage affair. If one of the big studios considers a new release to be a particularly large investment, they'll try to ensure that it's being shown in the maximum number of cinemas at the same time, leaving little space for any new film venturing onto the market.

And the few adventurous souls who decide to take the risk—despite all the arguments against—discover too late that it isn't enough to have a quality product. The cost of getting a film into cinemas in the large capitals of the world is prohibitive, what with full-page advertisements in newspapers and magazines, receptions, press officers, promotion junkets, ever more expensive teams of people, sophisticated filming equipment, and increasingly scarce labor. And the most difficult problem of all: finding someone who will distribute the film.

And yet every year it goes on, the trudging from place to place, the appointments, the Superclass who are interested in everything except what's being shown on the screen, the companies prepared to pay a tenth of what is reasonable just to give some filmmaker the "honor" of having his or her work shown on television, the requests that the film be reworked so as not to offend families, the demands for the film to be recut, the promises (not always kept) that if the script is changed completely to focus on one particular theme, a contract will be issued next year.

People listen and accept because they have no option. The Superclass rules the world; their arguments are subtle, their voices soft, their smiles discreet, but their decisions are final. They know. They accept or reject. They have the power. And power doesn't negotiate with anyone, only with itself. However, all is not lost. In the world of fiction and in the real world, there is always a hero.

AND MAUREEN IS STARING PROUDLY at one such hero now! The great meeting that is finally going to take place in two days' time after nearly three years of work, dreams, phone calls, trips to Los Angeles, presents, favors asked of friends in her Bank of Favors, and the influence of an ex-boyfriend of hers, who had studied with her at film school, then decided it was much safer to work for an important film magazine than risk losing both his head and his money.

"I'll talk to Javits," the ex-boyfriend had said. "But he doesn't need anyone, not even the journalists who can promote or destroy his products. He's above all that. We once tried getting together an article trying to find out how it is that he has all these cinema owners eating out of his hand, but no one he works with was prepared to say anything. I'll talk to him, but I can't put any pressure on him."

He did talk to him and got him to watch *The Secrets of the Cellar*. The following day, she received a phone call, saying that Javits would meet her in Cannes.

At the time, Maureen didn't even dare to say that she was just ten minutes by taxi from his office; instead they arranged to meet in this far-off French city. She bought a plane ticket to Paris, caught a train that took all day to reach Cannes, showed her voucher to the bad-tempered manager of a cheap hotel, installed herself in her single room where she had to climb over her luggage to reach the bathroom, and (again thanks to her ex-boyfriend) wangled invitations to a few second-rate events—a promotion for a new brand of vodka or the launch of a new line in T-shirts—but it was far too late to apply for the pass that would allow her into the Palais des Festivals et des Congrès.

She has overspent her budget, traveled for more than twenty hours, but she will at least get her ten minutes. And she's sure that she'll emerge with a contract and a future before her. Yes, the movie industry is in crisis, but so what? Movies (however few) are still making money, aren't they? Big cities are plastered with posters advertising new movies. And what are celebrity magazines full of? Gossip about movie stars! Maureen knows—or, rather, believes—that the death of cinema has been declared many times before, and yet still it survives. "Cinema was dead" when television arrived. "Cinema was dead" when video rentals arrived. "Cinema was dead" when the Internet began allowing access to pirate sites. But cinema is still alive and well in the streets of this small Mediterranean town, which, of course, owes its fame to the Festival.

Now it's simply a case of making the most of this manna from heaven. And of accepting everything, absolutely everything. Javits Wild is here. He has seen her film. The subject of the film is spot-on: sexual exploitation, voluntary or forced, was getting a lot of media attention after a series of cases that had hit the headlines worldwide. It is just the right moment for *The Secrets of the Cellar* to appear on the posters put up by the distribution chain he controlled.

Javits Wild, the rebel with a cause, the man who was revolutionizing the way films reached the wider public. Only the actor Robert Redford had tried something similar with his Sundance Film Festival for independent filmmakers, but nevertheless, after decades of effort, Redford still hadn't managed to break through the barrier into a world that mobilized hundreds of millions of dollars in the United States, Europe, and India. Javits, though, was a winner.

Javits Wild, the savior of filmmakers, the great legend, the ally of minority interests, the friend of artists, the new patron, who obviously used some very intelligent system (she had no idea what it was, but she knew it worked) to reach cinemas all around the world.

Javits Wild has arranged a ten-minute meeting with her in two days' time. This can mean only one thing, that he has accepted her project and that everything else is merely a matter of detail.

"I will accept everything, absolutely everything," she repeats.

Obviously, in those ten minutes, Maureen won't have a chance to say a word about what she has been through in the seven years (yes, a quarter of her life) that have gone into making her film. There will be no point in telling him that she went to film school, directed a few commercials, made two short films that were warmly received in various small-town cinemas or in alternative bars in New York. That in order to raise the million dollars needed for a professional production, she had mortgaged the house she inherited from her parents. That this was her one chance because she didn't have another house to mortgage.

She had watched as her fellow students, after much struggling, opted for the comfortable world of commercials—of which there were more and more—or some safe but obscure job in one of the many companies that made TV series. After the warm reception given to her short films, she began to dream of higher things and then there was no stopping her.

She was convinced she had a mission: to make the world a better place for future generations, by getting together with like-minded people, to show that art isn't just a way of entertaining or amusing a lost society; by exposing world leaders as the flawed people they are; by saving the children who were now dying of hunger somewhere in Africa; by speaking out about environmental problems; by putting an end to social injustice.

This was, of course, an ambitious project, but she was sure she would achieve it if only through sheer doggedness. To do this she needed to purify her soul, and so she turned to the four forces that had always guided her: love, death, power, and time. We must love because we are loved by God. We must be conscious of death if we are to have a proper understanding of life. We must struggle in order to grow, but without falling into the trap of the power we gain through that struggle, because we know that such power is worthless. Finally, we must accept that our eternal soul is, at this moment, caught in the web of time with all its opportunities and its limitations.

Caught in the web of time she might be, but she could still work on what gave her pleasure and filled her with enthusiasm. And through her films, she could make her contribution to a world that seemed to be disintegrating around her and could try to change reality and transform human beings.

WHEN HER FATHER DIED, AFTER complaining all his life that he had never had the chance to do what he had always dreamed of doing, she realized something very important: transformations always occur during moments of crisis.

She didn't want to end her life as he had. She wouldn't like to have to tell her daughter: "There was something I wanted to do and there was even a point when I could have done it, but I just didn't have the courage to take the risk." When she received her inheritance, she knew then that it had been given to her for one reason only: to allow her to fulfill her destiny.

She accepted the challenge. Unlike other adolescent girls who always dreamed of being famous actresses, her dream had been to tell stories that subsequent generations could see, smile at, and dream about. Her great example was *Citizen Kane*. That first film by a radio producer who wanted to make an exposé of a powerful American press magnate became a classic not just because of its story, but because it dealt in a creative and innovative manner with the ethical and technical problems of the day. All it took was one film to gain eternal fame.

"His first film."

It *was* possible to get it right the first time. Even though its director, Orson Welles, never made anything as good again. Even though he had disappeared from the scene (that does happen) and was now only studied in courses about cinema, someone was sure to "rediscover" his genius sooner or later. *Citizen Kane* wasn't his only legacy; he had proved to everyone that if your first step was good enough, you would never lack for invitations thereafter. And she would take up those invitations. She had promised herself that she would never forget the difficulties she had been through and that her life would contribute to dignifying human life.

And since there can only ever be one first film, she had poured all her physical efforts, her prayers, and her emotional energy into one project. Unlike her friends, who were always firing off scripts, proposals, and ideas, only to end up working on several things at once without any of them ever really coming to anything, Maureen dedicated herself body and soul to *The Secrets of the Cellar*, the story of five nuns who are visited by a sex maniac. Instead of trying to convert him to Christian salvation, they realize that the only way they can communicate with him is by accepting the norms of his aberrant world; they decide to surrender their bodies to him so that he can understand the glory of God through love.

Her plan was a simple one. Hollywood actresses, however famous they might be, usually disappear from the cast lists when they reach thirty-five. They still continue to appear in the pages of the celebrity magazines, are seen at charity auctions and big parties; they embrace humanitarian causes, and when they realize that they really are about to vanish from the spotlight entirely, they start to get married or have messy divorces and create public scandals—and all for a few months, weeks, or days of glory. In that period between unemployment and total obscurity, money is of no importance. They will take any role if it gives them a chance to appear on screen.

Maureen approached actresses who, less than a decade earlier, had been at the top of the tree, but who now sensed that the ground was beginning to slip away from under them and that they desperately needed to get back to the way things were. It was a good script; she sent it to their agents, who demanded an absurd salary and got a straightforward no as an answer. Her next step was to approach each actress individually. She told them that she had the money for the project, and they all ended up accepting on the understanding that no one would know that they were working for almost nothing.

In something like the film industry, there was no point in being humble. Sometimes, the ghost of Orson Welles would appear to her in dreams: "Try the impossible. Don't start low down because that's where you are now. Climb those rungs quickly before they take the ladder away. If you're afraid, say a prayer, but carry on." She had an excellent script, a first-class cast, and knew that she had to produce something that was acceptable to the big studios and distributors, but without sacrificing quality. It was possible and, indeed, obligatory for art and commerce to go hand-in-hand. As for the rest, well, the rest consisted of various things: the kind of critic who's into mental mastur-bation and who loves films no one else understands; the small alterna-tive circuits where the same half dozen people emerge from showings and spend the small hours in bars, smoking and discussing one particu-lar scene (whose meaning was, very possibly, quite different from the one intended when it was filmed); directors giving lectures to explain what should be obvious to the audience; trade union meetings call-ing for more state aid for domestic cinema; manifestos in intellectual magazines—the result of interminable meetings, at which the same old complaints were made about the government's lack of interest in supporting the arts; the occasional letter published in the serious press and usually read only by the interested parties or the families of the interested parties.

Who changes the world? The Superclass. Those who do. Those who alter the behavior, hearts, and minds of the largest possible number of people.

That's why she wanted Javits, an Oscar, and Cannes.

And since she couldn't get those things "democratically"—other people were very willing to offer advice, but never to shoulder any of the risks—she simply gambled everything. She took on whoever was available, spent months rewriting the script, persuaded excellent—but unknown—art directors, designers, and supporting actors to take part, promising them almost no money, only increased visibility in the future. They were all impressed by the names of the five main actresses ("The budget must be astronomical!"), and initially asked for large salaries, but ended up convinced that participating in such a project would look really good on their CVs. Maureen was so enthusiastic about the idea that her enthusiasm seemed to open all doors.

Now came the final step, the one that would make all the difference.

It isn't enough for a writer or musician to produce something of quality, they have to make sure their work doesn't end up gathering dust on a shelf or in a drawer.

Vis-i-bil-i-ty is what's required!

She sent a copy of the film to just one person: Javits Wild. She used all her contacts. She suffered rejection, but carried on anyway. She was ignored, but that didn't diminish her courage. She was mistreated, ridiculed, excluded, but still she believed it was possible because she had poured her lifeblood into what she had done. Then her ex-boyfriend entered the scene, and Javits Wild agreed to see her film and to meet her.

She keeps her eyes on Javits all through lunch, savoring in anticipation the moment they will spend together in two days' time. Suddenly, she notices him go stiff, his eyes fixed on nothing. One of the friends with him glances behind and to the side, slips one hand inside his jacket. The other man starts frantically keying in a number on his mobile phone.

Has something happened? Surely not. The people nearest him are still talking, drinking, enjoying another day of Festival, parties, sun, and nice bodies.

One of the men tries to help Javits up and make him walk, but he appears incapable of movement. It can't be anything serious. Too much drink perhaps. Tiredness. Stress. No, it can't be anything serious. She has come so far, she is so close and . . .

She can hear a siren in the distance. It must be the police, cutting their way through the permanently congested traffic in order to reach some important person.

One of the men puts Javits's arm around his shoulder and more or less carries him toward the door. The siren is getting closer. The other man, still with his hand inside his jacket, keeps looking in all directions. At one point, their eyes meet.

Javits is being taken up the ramp by one of his friends, and Maureen is wondering how someone so slight can possibly carry such a heavily built man and with so little apparent effort.

The sound of the siren stops right outside the tent. Javits has, by now, disappeared with one of the friends, but the second man is walking toward her, one hand still inside his jacket.

"What happened?" she asks, frightened, because years of directing actors have taught her that this man's face is that of a professional killer, a face that looks as if it were carved out of stone.

"You know what happened," the man says in an accent she can't identify.

"I saw that he began to feel ill, but what *did* happen?"

The man keeps his hand inside his jacket, and at that moment, it occurs to Maureen that this might be a chance to transform a minor incident into a great possibility.

"Can I help? Can I go with him?"

The hand in the jacket seems to relax a little, but the eyes watch every move she makes.

"I'll come with you. I know Javits Wild. I'm a friend of his."

After what seems like an eternity, but which can't have been more than a fraction of a second, the man turns and walks quickly away toward the Boulevard, without saying a word.

Maureen's brain is working fast. Why did he say that she knew what had happened? And why did he suddenly lose all interest in her?

The other guests haven't noticed a thing, apart from the sound of the siren, which they probably attribute to something going on out in the street. Sirens have nothing to do with joy, sun, drinks, contacts, beautiful women, handsome men, with the pale and the tanned. Sirens belong to another world, a world of heart attacks, diseases, and crime. Sirens are of no interest to the people here.

Maureen's head begins to spin. Something has happened to Javits, and this could be a gift from the gods. She runs to the door and sees an ambulance speeding away, sirens blaring, down the blocked-off lane of the Boulevard.

"That's my friend," she says to one of the bodyguards at the entrance. "Where have they taken him?"

The man gives her the name of a hospital. Without pausing to think, Maureen starts running to find a taxi. Ten minutes later, she realizes that there are no taxis in the city, only those summoned by hotel porters, lured by the prospect of generous tips. Since she has no money in her bag, she goes into a pizzeria, shows someone working there the map she has with her, and learns that she must run for at least half an hour to reach her objective.

She's been running all her life, so half an hour won't make much difference.

"Good morning."

"You mean 'Good afternoon,' don't you?" one of the other girls replies. "It's midday."

Everything is exactly as she'd imagined. The five other young women waiting all rather resemble her, at least physically. They, however, are heavily made up, wear short skirts and low-cut tops, and are busy with their mobile phones and their texts.

No one speaks because they know they're soul mates who have all been through the same difficulties and have uncomplainingly faced the same challenges and accepted each knockout blow. They're all trying hard to believe that dreams have no sell-by date, that life can change from one second to the next, that somewhere the right moment is waiting for them, and that this is just a test of their willpower.

They've all perhaps quarreled with their families, who are convinced their daughters will end up working as prostitutes.

They've all been on stage and experienced the agony and the ecstasy of seeing the audience and knowing that every eye is fixed on them; they've felt the electricity in the air and heard the applause at the end. They've imagined a hundred times over that there will come a night when a member of the Superclass will be in the audience and visit them in their dressing room after the performance with something more substantial to offer than an invitation to supper, a request for their phone number, or compliments on a job well done.

To begin with, they accepted a few of those invitations, but the only place they led to was the bed of some powerful, older man—usually married, as all the "interesting" men are—concerned only with notching up another conquest.

They all had a boyfriend their own age, but when anyone asked if they were married or single, they always answered: "Free and unattached." They thought they were in control of the situation. They've all been told—hundreds of times now—that they have real talent and just need the right opportunity, and that the person there before them is the one who can transform their lives. They've occasionally believed this too. They've fallen into the trap of being overconfident and thinking they were in charge, until the next day came and the phone number they'd been given put them through to the extension of a very grumpy secretary who had no intention of letting them speak to her boss.

They've threatened to sell their story to the tabloids, saying that they had been deceived, although none of them has ever actually done so because they're still at the stage of thinking: "I mustn't spoil my chances in the acting world."

One or two may even have shared Gabriela's *Alice in Wonderland* experience, and now want to prove to their families that they're far more capable than they thought. Their families, of course, have all by now seen their daughters in commercials, on posters and billboards scattered round the city, and, after a few initial arguments, are convinced that those same daughters are on the verge of entering a world of "bright lights and glamour."

All the girls there believed that their dream was possible, that one day their talent would be recognized, until the penny dropped: there is only one magic word—"contacts." They had all distributed their books as soon as they arrived in Cannes, and now keep a constant eye on their mobile phone, getting invited to whatever launches and events they can and trying their best to get into those they can't, always dreaming that someone will ask them to one of the evening parties or, dream of dreams, award them that greatest of prizes, an invitation to walk down the red carpet at the Palais des Congrès. That, however, was probably the most difficult dream to realize, so difficult that they didn't really allow themselves to think about it, in case the feelings of rejection and frustration destroyed their ability to wear the happy face they must wear at all times, even when they're not happy at all.

Contacts.

After many cases of mistaken identity, they did find the occasional useful contact, which is why they're here. One such contact had led to a New Zealand producer calling them. None had asked what it was about; they knew only that they had to be punctual because no one has any time to lose, certainly not people in the film industry. The only ones who do are the five young women in the waiting room, busy with their mobile phones and their magazines, compulsively sending texts to see if they've been invited to something later in the day, trying to talk to their friends, and always making a point of saying that they're not free to speak right now because they have an important meeting with a film producer.

GABRIELA IS THE FOURTH PERSON to be called. She had tried to interpret the look in the eyes of the first three candidates who emerged from the room without saying a word, but then, of course, they're all actresses, capable of hiding any emotion, be it joy or sadness. All three strode determinedly to the door and wished the others a confident "Good luck," as if to say: "No need to be nervous, girls, you've got nothing to lose. The part's mine."

ONE OF THE WALLS IN the apartment is covered with a black cloth. The floor there is cluttered with all kinds of electric cables and lights covered with a metal mesh, and there's a kind of umbrella with a white cloth spread before it, as well as sound equipment, screens, and a video camera. In the corners stand bottles of mineral water, metal briefcases, tripods, bits of paper, and a computer. Sitting on the floor, a bespec-tacled, thirty-something woman is leafing through Gabriela's book.

"Awful," she says, not looking up at her. "Awful."

Gabriela doesn't know quite what to do. Perhaps she should pretend she isn't listening and go over to the group of chain-smoking technicians chatting brightly in one corner or perhaps she should simply stay where she is.

"This one's awful," said the woman again.

"That's me."

She can't help herself. She has run through half of Cannes to get there, waited nearly two hours, imagined yet again that her life is about to change forever (although she's less and less prone to such fantasies now and won't allow herself to get as excited as she used to), and she certainly doesn't need more reasons to be depressed.

"I know," says the woman, her eyes fixed on the photos. "They must have cost you a fortune. People make a career out of making books, writing CVs, running acting courses, and generally making money out of the vanity of people like you."

"If you think I'm so awful, why did you call me?"

"Because we need someone awful."

Gabriela laughs. The woman finally raises her head and looks her up and down.

"I liked your clothes. I hate vulgar people."

Gabriela's dream is returning. Her heart beats faster.

The woman hands her a sheet of paper.

"Go over there to the mark."

Then she turns to the crew.

"Put those cigarettes out and close the window. I don't want the sound messed up."

The "mark" is a cross made with yellow tape on the floor. This means that the actor is automatically in the right position for the lighting and the camera.

"It's so hot in here, I'm sweating. Could I at least go to the bathroom and put a little foundation on, some makeup?"

"Of course you can, but when you get back, there won't be time to do the recording. We have to hand this stuff over by this afternoon."

All the other girls who went in must have asked the same question and been given the same answer. Best not to waste time. She takes a paper handkerchief out of her pocket and dabs at her face as she makes her way over to the mark.

An assistant positions himself by the camera, while Gabriela battles against time, trying to read through what is written on that half sheet of paper.

"Test number twenty-five, Gabriela Sherry, Thompson Agency."

"Twenty-five?!" thinks Gabriela.

"And action," says the woman with the glasses.

Silence falls.

———

"No, I can't believe what you're saying. No one can commit a murder for no reason."

"Start again. You're talking to your boyfriend."

"No, I can't believe what you're saying. No one can commit a murder like that for no reason."

"The words 'like that' aren't in the script. Do you really think that the scriptwriter, who worked on this for months, didn't consider putting those words in, but decided against it because they're useless, superficial, unnecessary?"

Gabriela takes a deep breath. She has nothing to lose but her patience. She's going to do her best now, then leave, go to the beach, or go back to bed for a while. She needs to rest in order to be in good shape for the evening round of cocktail parties.

A strange, delicious calm comes over her. Suddenly, she feels protected, loved, grateful to be alive. No one's forcing her to be there, enduring yet another humiliation. For the first time in years, she's aware of her power, a power she had never thought existed.

"No, I don't believe what you're saying. No one can commit a murder for no reason."

"Next line."

There was no need for her to say that. Gabriela was going to continue anyway.

"We'd better go and see a doctor. I think you need help."

"No," said the woman in glasses, who was playing the part of the boyfriend.

"OK, no doctor, then. How about a little walk, and you can tell me exactly what's going on. I love you, you know, and even if no one else in the world cares about you, I do."

There are no more lines. Another silence. A strange energy fills the room.

"Tell the other girl out there she can go," says the woman in the glasses to one of the other people present.

Does this mean what Gabriela thinks it means?

"Go to the marina at the end of Boulevard de la Croisette, opposite Allée des Palmiers. A boat will be waiting there at 1:55 prompt to take you to meet Mr. Gibson. We're going to send him the video now, but he always likes to meet the people he might be working with."

A smile appears on Gabriela's face.

"I said 'might,' I didn't say '*will* be working with.'"

The smile remains. Mr. Gibson!

Lying on a stainless steel table between Inspector Savoy and the pathologist is a beautiful young woman of about twenty, completely naked. And dead.

"Are you sure?"

The pathologist goes over to a stainless steel sink, removes his rubber gloves, throws them in the bin, and turns on the tap.

"Absolutely. There's no trace of drugs."

"What happened, then? Could a young woman like her have had a heart attack?"

The only noise in the room is that of running water. The pathologist thinks:

"They always come up with the obvious: drugs, a heart attack . . ."

He takes longer than necessary to wash his hands—a little suspense never goes amiss. He applies disinfectant to his arms and throws away the disposable material used in the autopsy. Then he turns round and asks the inspector to study the body.

"No, really, take a good look. Don't be embarrassed. Noticing details is part of your job, isn't it?"

Savoy carefully examines the body. At one point, he reaches out to lift one of the girl's arms, but the pathologist stops him.

"No need to touch."

Savoy runs his eyes over the girl's naked body. He knows quite a lot about her now—Olivia Martins, the daughter of Portuguese parents, currently going out with a young man of no fixed profession, who is heavily into Cannes nightlife and is, at that moment, being interrogated at a police station some way away. A judge issued a search warrant for his apartment and they found some small flasks of THC (tetrahydrocannabinol, the main hallucinogenic element in marijuana, and which can be taken dissolved in sesame oil, which leaves no smell and has a far stronger effect than when the substance is absorbed through smoke). They also found six envelopes, each containing a gram of cocaine, and some bloodstains on a sheet which is now on its way to a laboratory for tests. He's probably, at most, a minor dealer. He's already known to the police, having spent a couple of spells in prison, but never for physical violence.

Olivia was lovely, even in death. Her dark eyebrows, that childlike air, her breasts . . . "No," he thinks, "I mustn't go there. I'm a professional."

"I can't see anything," he says.

The pathologist smiles, and Savoy finds his smugness slightly irritating. The expert points to a small, purplish, almost imperceptible mark between the girl's left shoulder and her throat. Then he shows him another similar mark on the right-hand side of her torso, between two of her ribs.

"I could begin by giving you the technical details. Death was caused by obstruction of the jugular vein and the carotid artery while, simultaneously, similar pressure was being applied to a particular sheaf of nerves, but so precisely that it caused the complete paralysis of the upper part of the body . . ."

Savoy says nothing. The pathologist realizes that this is not the moment to show off his knowledge or to make jokes. He feels rather sorry for himself. He works with death on a daily basis and spends each day surrounded by corpses and grave-faced people. His children never tell anyone what their father does, and he has nothing to talk about at supper parties because people hate discussing what they perceive to be macabre topics. He sometimes wonders if he hasn't perhaps chosen the wrong profession.

". . . in short, she was strangled."

Savoy still says nothing. His brain is working very fast: how could someone possibly be strangled on Boulevard de la Croisette in broad daylight? Her parents had been interviewed, and they said that their daughter had left the house that morning with the usual merchandise—illegal merchandise, it must be said, because street vendors pay no taxes and are, therefore, banned from trading. "Although that's hardly relevant now," he thinks.

"The intriguing thing about this particular case," says the pathologist, "is that in a normal case of strangulation, there are marks on both shoulders, that is, in the classic scene in which the attacker grabs the victim round the throat and the victim struggles to get free. In this case, only one hand, or, rather, one finger stopped the blood reaching the brain, while another finger paralyzed the body, rendering her incapable of fighting back. This requires a very sophisticated technique and a detailed knowledge of the human body."

"Could she have been killed somewhere else and carried to the bench where we found her?"

"If so, there would be other marks on her body. That was the first thing I looked for, assuming she was killed by just one person. When I found no marks, I looked for any indication that she had been grabbed by the wrists or ankles, if, that is, we were dealing with more than one killer. But there was nothing to indicate this, indeed, without wishing to go into more technical detail, there are certain things that happen at the moment of death which leave traces in the body. Urine, for example, and . . ."

"What are you saying?"

"That she was killed where she was found and that, judging by the finger marks on her body, only one person was involved; that since no one saw her trying to run away, she clearly knew her killer, who was seated on her left side; and that her killer must be someone highly trained and with an extensive knowledge of the martial arts."

Savoy nods his thanks and walks quickly to the exit. On the way, he phones the police station where the boyfriend is being interrogated.

"Forget about drugs," he says. "We have a murder on our hands. Try and find out what the boyfriend knows about martial arts. I'm coming straight over."

"No," says the voice at the other end. "Go straight to the hospital. I think we have another problem."

A seagull was flying over a beach, when it saw a mouse. It flew down and asked the mouse:

"Where are your wings?"

Each animal speaks its own language, and so the mouse didn't understand the question, but stared at the two strange, large things attached to the other creature's body.

"It must have some illness," thought the mouse.

The seagull noticed the mouse staring at its wings and thought:

"Poor thing. It must have been attacked by monsters that left it deaf and took away its wings."

Feeling sorry for the mouse, the seagull picked it up in its beak and took it for a ride in the skies. "It's probably homesick," the seagull thought while they were flying. Then, very carefully, it deposited the mouse once more on the ground.

For some months afterward, the mouse was sunk in gloom; it had known the heights and seen a vast and beautiful world. However, in time, it grew accustomed to being just a mouse again and came to believe that the miracle that had occurred in its life was nothing but a dream.

This was a story from her childhood, but right now, she's up in the sky: she can see the turquoise sea, the luxurious yachts, the people small as ants below, the tents on the beach, the hills, the horizon to her left, beyond which lay Africa and all its problems.

The ground is approaching fast. "It's best to view humankind from on high," she thinks. "Only then can we see how very small we are."

Ewa seems bored, either that or nervous. Hamid never really knows what's going on in his wife's head, even though they've been together for more than two years now. Cannes, it's true, is a trial for everyone concerned, but he can't leave the Festival any earlier than planned. Besides, she should be used to all this because the life of her ex-husband hadn't been so very different, with suppers to attend, events to organize, and having constantly to change country, continent, and language.

"Was she always like this or is it that she doesn't love me as much as she did at first?"

A forbidden thought. Concentrate on other things, please.

The noise of the engine doesn't allow for conversation, unless you use the headphones with the microphone attached. Ewa hasn't even picked hers up from the hook beside her seat. Not that there's any point asking her to put them on so that he can tell her for the thousandth time that she's the most important woman in his life and that he'll do his best to make sure she enjoys the week at this, her first Cannes Festival. The sound system on board is set up so that every conversation can be overheard by the pilot, and Ewa hates public displays of affection.

There they are, in that glass bubble, just about to touch down. He can see the huge white car, a Maybach, the most expensive and most sophisticated car in the world. Even more exclusive than Rolls-Royce. Soon they'll be sitting inside, listening to some relaxing music, and drinking iced champagne or mineral water.

He consults his platinum watch, which is a certified copy of one of the first models produced in a small workshop in the town of Schaffhausen. Women can get away with spending a fortune on diamonds, but a watch is the only piece of jewelry allowed to a man of good taste, and only the true cognoscenti knew the significance of that watch, which was rarely advertised in the glossy magazines.

That could be a definition of true sophistication: knowing where to find the very best even if other people have never heard of it, and producing the very best too, regardless of what others might say.

It was already nearly two o'clock in the afternoon, and he needed to talk to his stockbroker in New York before trading opened on the stock exchange. When he arrived, he would make a call—just one—with his instructions for the day. Making money at the "casino," as he called the investment funds, was not his favorite sport; however, he had to pretend to be keeping an eye on what his managers and financial engineers were up to. He could rely on the protection, support, and vigilance of the sheikh, but nevertheless he had to demonstrate that he was up-to-date on what was happening.

He might, in the end, have to make two phone calls, but give no concrete instructions on what to buy or sell. His energy is focused on something else: that afternoon, at least two actresses—one famous and one unknown—will be walking down the red carpet wearing his dresses. Obviously, he has assistants who can take care of everything, but he likes to be personally involved, even if only to remind himself that every detail is important and that he hasn't lost touch with the basis on which he built his empire. Apart from that, he wants to spend the rest of his time in France trying to enjoy Ewa's company to the full, introducing her to interesting people, strolling on the beach, lunching together in some small restaurant in a nearby town, or walking along, hand-in-hand, through the vineyards he can see on the horizon.

He had always felt he was incapable of falling in love with anything other than his work, although the list of his conquests includes an enviable series of relationships with some even more enviable women. The moment Ewa appeared on the scene, though, he was a different man. They have been together for two years and his love is stronger and more intense than ever. In love. Him, Hamid Hussein, one of the most famous designers on the planet, the public face of a gigantic international conglomerate selling luxury and glamour. The man who had battled against everything and everyone, who had challenged all the West's preconceived ideas about people from the Middle East and their religion, the man who had used the ancestral knowledge of his tribe to survive, learn, and reach the top. Contrary to rumor, he was not from a rich oil family. His father had been a seller of cloth who, one day, had found favor with a sheikh simply because he refused to do as he was told.

Whenever Hamid had doubts about what decision to make, he liked to remember the example he had received in adolescence: Say no to powerful people, even when doing so means taking a great risk. It had almost always worked. And on the few occasions when it hadn't, the consequences were not as grave as he had imagined.

His father had not, alas, lived to see his son's success. When the sheikh started buying up all the available land in that part of the desert in order to build one of the most modern cities in the world, his father had had the courage to say to one of the sheikh's emissaries:

"I'm not selling. My family has been here for centuries. We buried our dead here. We learned to survive storms and invaders. We cannot sell the place that God charged us to take care of."

The emissaries increased their offer. When he still refused, they got angry and threatened to do whatever was necessary to remove him. The sheikh, too, began to grow impatient. He wanted to start his project straightaway because he had big plans. The price of oil had risen on the international market, and the money needed to be spent before the oil reserves ran out and any possibility of building an infrastructure to attract foreign investments vanished.

Still old Hussein refused to sell his property, whatever the price. Then the sheikh decided to go and speak to him directly.

"I can offer you anything you desire," he said.

"Then give my son a good education. He's sixteen now, and there are no prospects for him here."

"Only if you sell me your house."

There was a long silence, then his father, looking straight at the sheikh, said something the latter had never expected to hear.

"You, sir, have a duty to educate your subjects, and I cannot exchange my family's future for its past."

Hamid recalls the look of immense sadness in his father's eyes as he went on:

"But if you can at least give my son a chance in life, then I will accept your offer."

The sheikh left without saying another word. The following day, he asked Hamid's father to send his son to him so that they could talk.

After walking down blocked roads, past gigantic cranes, laborers tirelessly working, and whole quarters in the process of being demolished, Hamid finally reached the palace that had been built beside the old port.

The sheikh came straight to the point.

"You know that I want to buy your father's house. There is very little oil left in our country, and we must wean ourselves off oil and find other paths before the oil wells run dry. We will prove to the world that we can sell not only oil, but our services too. Meanwhile, in order to take those first steps, we need to make some major reforms, like building a good airport, for example. We need land so that foreigners can build on it. My dream is a just one and my intentions are good. One thing we're going to need are more experts in the field of finance. Now, you heard the conversation between myself and your father . . ."

Hamid tried to disguise his fear, for there were more than a dozen people listening to their conversation. However, his heart had an answer ready for each question he was asked.

". . . so tell me, what do you want to do?" asked the sheikh.

"I want to study haute couture."

The other people present looked at each other. They might not even have known what he meant.

"My father sells much of the cloth he buys to foreigners, who then turn his cloth into designer clothes and earn a hundred times more from it than he does. I'm sure we could do the same here. I'm convinced that fashion could be one way of breaking down the prejudices the rest of the world has about us. If they could be made to see that we don't dress like barbarians, they would find it easier to accept us."

This time, he heard murmurings in the court. Was he talking about clothes? That was something for Westerners, who were more concerned with how people looked on the outside than with what they were like inside.

"On the other hand, the price my father is paying is very high. I would prefer to keep our house. I will work with the cloth he has, and if Merciful God so desires it, I will realize my dream. I, like Your Majesty, know what I want."

The court listened in amazement to hear this boy not only challenging their region's great leader, but refusing to accept his own father's wishes. The sheikh, however, smiled.

"And where does one study haute couture?"

"In France or Italy, working with the great masters. There are universities where one can study, but there's no substitute for experience. It won't be easy, but if Merciful God so wishes, I will succeed."

The sheikh asked him to come back later that afternoon. Hamid strolled down to the port and visited the bazaar, where he marveled at the colors, the cloths, and the embroidery. He loved visiting the bazaar and it saddened him to think that it would soon be destroyed because a part of the past and part of tradition would be lost. Was it possible to stop progress? Would it be sensible to try and stop the development of a nation? He remembered the many nights he had sat up late drawing by candlelight, copying the clothes the Bedouin wore, afraid that tribal costumes would also one day be destroyed by the cranes and by foreign investment.

At the appointed hour, he returned to the palace. There were even more people with the sheikh now.

"I have made two decisions," said the sheikh. "First, I am going to pay your expenses for a year. We have enough boys interested in a career in the financial sector, but you are the first to express a wish to learn sewing. It seems utter madness, but then everyone tells me my dreams are mad too, and yet look where they've got me. I cannot go against my own example.

"On the other hand, none of my assistants has any contacts among the people you mentioned, and so I will be paying you a small monthly allowance to keep you from having to beg in the streets. You will return a winner; you will represent our country, and it's important that other nations should learn to respect our culture. Before leaving, you will have to learn the languages of the countries to which you are going. Which languages are they?"

"English, French, and Italian. I am most grateful to you for your generosity, but what about my father . . ."

The sheikh gestured to him to be silent.

"My second decision is as follows. Your father's house will remain where it is. In my dreams it will be surrounded by skyscrapers, no sun will enter its windows, and, in the end, he will have to move. However, the house will stay there forever. In the future, people will remember me and say: 'He was a great man because he changed his country. And he was just because he respected the rights of a seller of cloth.' "

THE HELICOPTER LANDS AT THE very end of the pier, and he leaves aside his memories. He gets out first and then proffers Ewa a helping hand. He touches her skin and looks proudly at this blonde woman, all dressed in white, her clothes glowing in the sunlight, her other hand holding on to the lovely, discreet beige hat she is wearing. They walk past the ranks of yachts moored on either side, toward the car that awaits them and the chauffeur standing with the door already open.

He holds his wife's hand and whispers in her ear:

"I hope you enjoyed the lunch. They're great collectors of art, and it was very generous of them to provide a helicopter for us."

"Yes, I loved it."

But what Ewa really means is: "No, I hated it. Worse, I'm feeling really frightened. I've just received a text on my mobile phone and I know who sent it, even though I can't identify the number."

They get into the vast car made for just two people, the rest being empty space. The air-conditioning is set at the ideal temperature, the music is exactly right for such a moment, and no outside noise penetrates their perfect isolation. He sits down on the comfortable leather seat, opens the mini-bar in front of them, and asks if Ewa would like some champagne. No, she says, mineral water will be fine.

"I saw your ex-husband yesterday in the hotel bar, before we left for supper."

"That's impossible. He has no business in Cannes."

She would like to have said: "You may be right. I've just received a text. We should board the next plane out of here."

"Oh, I'm quite sure it was him."

Hamid notices that his wife is not in the mood to talk. He has been brought up to respect the privacy of those he loves, and so he makes himself think of something else.

Having first asked Ewa's permission, he makes the obligatory phone call to his stockbroker in New York. He listens patiently for two or three sentences, then politely interrupts any further news on market trends. The whole call lasts no more than two minutes.

He makes another call to the director he has chosen for his first film. The director is on his way to the boat to meet with the Star, and yes, a young actress has been chosen and should be joining them shortly.

He turns to Ewa again, but she still seems disinclined to talk, her gaze absent, staring out of the limousine windows at nothing. Perhaps she's worried because she'll have so little time at the hotel. She'll have to change immediately and go straight to a rather insignificant fashion show by a Belgian designer, where Hamid wants to see for himself the young African model, Jasmine, whom his assistants tell him will be the ideal face for his next collection.

He wants to know how the girl will survive the pressures of an event in Cannes. If everything goes to plan, she'll be one of his star models at the Fashion Week in Paris set for October.

EWA KEEPS HER EYES FIXED on the window, not that she's interested in what's going on outside. She knows the gentle, creative, determined, well-dressed man by her side very well. She knows that he desires her as no man has ever desired a woman, apart, that is, from the man she left. She can trust him, even though he lives surrounded by some of the most beautiful women in the world. He's an honest, hardworking man who has met and overcome many challenges in order to be chauffeured around in that limo and to be able to offer her a glass of champagne or her favorite mineral water. He is powerful and capable of protecting her from any danger, except one, the worst of all. Her ex-husband.

She doesn't want to arouse suspicions now by picking up her phone again to reread the message; she knows the message by heart.

"I have destroyed a world for you, Katyusha."

She has no idea what these words mean, but no one else would call her by that name.

She has taught herself to love Hamid, although she detests the life he leads, the parties they go to, and his friends. She doesn't know yet if she has succeeded in making herself love him; there are moments when she feels almost suicidal with despair. All she knows is that he was her salvation at a time when she thought she was lost forever, incapable of escaping the trap of her marriage.

MANY YEARS BEFORE, SHE HAD fallen in love with an angel with a sad childhood, who had been called up into the Soviet army to fight in an absurd war in Afghanistan only to return to a country verging on collapse. Despite this, he had overcome all difficulties to succeed. He began to work very hard, getting loans from some very shady people, then lying awake at night, worrying about the risk he was taking and wondering how he could ever repay those loans. He put up uncomplainingly with the endemic corruption, accepting that he would have to bribe a government official each time he needed a new license for a product that would improve the quality of life of his own people. He was idealistic and affectionate. By day, his leadership went unquestioned because life had taught him how to lead, and military service had helped him understand exactly how hierarchies work. At night, he would cling to her and ask her to protect and advise him, to pray for everything to go well and for him to avoid the many traps that lay in his path each day.

Ewa would stroke his hair and assure him that everything was fine, that he was a good man, and that God always rewarded the just.

Gradually, the difficulties gave way to opportunities. The small business he had started—after almost begging people to sign contracts—began to grow because he was one of the few to have invested in something that no one believed could work in a country still plagued by near-obsolete communication networks. The government changed and corruption diminished. Money began to come in, slowly at first, then in vast quantities. However, they never forgot the difficult times they had been through and never wasted a penny. They made contributions to charities and to associations for ex-soldiers; they lived unostentatiously, dreaming of the day when they could put it all behind them and go and live in a house away from the world. When that happened, they would forget that they had once been obliged to have dealings with people who had no ethics and no dignity. They spent much of their time in airports, planes, and hotels; they worked eighteen hours a day, and for years never managed to take a month's holiday together.

They nurtured the same dream: the moment would come when that frenetic pace of life would be but a distant memory. The scars from that period would be like medals won in a war waged in the name of faith and dreams. After all, each human being—or so she believed then— had been born to love and to live with their beloved.

The whole process of finding work was suddenly turned on its head. Instead of them having to hunt down contracts, they began to appear spontaneously. Her husband was featured on the front cover of an important business magazine, and the local bigwigs started sending them invitations to parties and events. They began to be treated like royalty, and ever greater quantities of money flowed in.

They had to adapt to these changed circumstances: they bought a beautiful house in Moscow, a house with every possible comfort. For reasons she didn't and preferred not to know, her husband's old associates ended up in prison. (These were the same associates who had made those initial loans, of which, despite the exorbitant interest rates, Igor had paid back every penny.) From then on, Igor began to be accompanied everywhere by bodyguards, only two at first—fellow veterans and friends from the Afghan war—but they were later joined by others as the small company grew into a multinational giant with branches in several countries in seven different time zones, making ever more and ever more diverse investments.

Ewa spent her days in shopping malls or having tea with friends, who always talked about the same things. Igor, of course, wanted to go further . . . and further. After all, he had only got where he was by dint of ambition and hard work. Whenever she asked if they had not gone far beyond what they had planned and if it wasn't time to realize their dream of living only on the love they felt for each other, he always asked for a little more time. And he began to drink more heavily. One night, he came home after a long supper with friends during which much wine and vodka had been drunk, and she could contain her feelings no longer. She said she couldn't stand the empty existence she was leading; if she didn't do something soon, she would go mad. Wasn't she satisfied with what she had, asked Igor.

"Yes, *I'm* satisfied, but the problem is you're not, and never will be. You're insecure, afraid of losing everything you've achieved; you don't know how to quit once you're ahead. You'll end up destroying yourself. You're killing our marriage and my love."

This wasn't the first time she had spoken thus to her husband; they had always been very honest with each other, but she felt she was reaching a limit. She had had enough of the shopping and the tea parties and the ghastly television programs that she watched while waiting for him to come home from work.

"Don't say that, don't say I'm killing our love. I promise that soon we'll leave all this behind us, just be patient. Perhaps you should start some project of your own because your life at the moment really must be pretty hellish."

At least he recognized that.

"What would you like to do?" he asked.

Yes, she thought, perhaps that would be a way out.

"I'd like to work with fashion. That's always been my dream."

Her husband immediately granted her wish. The following week, he turned up with the keys to a shop in one of the best shopping malls in Moscow. Ewa was thrilled. Her life took on new meaning; the long days and nights spent waiting would be over for good. She borrowed money, and Igor invested enough in the business for her to have a good chance of success.

Suppers and parties—where she had always felt like an outsider— took on a new interest for her. In just two years, thanks to contacts made at such social events, she was running the most successful haute-couture shop in Moscow. Although she had a joint account with her husband, and he never questioned how much she spent, she made a point of paying back the money he had lent her. She started going off on business trips alone, looking for new designs and exclusive brands. She took on staff, got to grips with the accounts, and became—to her own surprise—an excellent businesswoman.

Igor had taught her everything. He was a great role model, an example to be followed. And just as everything was going so well and her life had taken on new meaning, the Angel of Light that had lit her path began to waver.

THEY WERE IN A RESTAURANT in Irkutsk, after spending a week-end in a fishing village on the shores of Lake Baikal. By that stage, the company owned two planes and a helicopter, so that they could travel as far as they liked and be back on Monday to start all over again. Neither of them complained about spending so little time together, but it was clear that the many years of struggle were beginning to take their toll. Still, they knew that their love was stronger than everything else, and, as long as they were together, they would be all right.

In the middle of a candlelit supper, a drunken beggar came into the restaurant, walked over to their table, sat down, and began to talk, interrupting their precious moment alone, far from the hustle and bustle of Moscow. A minute later, the owner offered to remove him, but Igor said he would take care of it. The beggar grew animated, picked up their bottle of vodka and drank from it; then he started asking questions ("Who are you? How come you've got so much money, when we all live in such poverty here?") and generally complaining about life and about the government. Igor put up with this for a few more minutes.

Then he got to his feet, took the man by the arm, and led him outside (the restaurant was in an unpaved street). His two bodyguards were waiting for him. Ewa saw through the window that her husband barely spoke to them, apart from issuing some order along the lines of "Keep an eye on my wife" and headed off toward a small side street. He came back a few minutes later, smiling.

"Well, he won't bother anyone again," he said.

Ewa noticed a different light in his eyes; they seemed filled by an immense joy, far greater than any joy he had shown during the weekend they had spent together.

"What did you do?"

Igor did not reply, but simply called for more vodka. They both drank steadily into the night—he happy and smiling and she choosing to understand only what she wanted to understand. He had always been so generous with those less fortunate than himself, so perhaps he had given the man money to help him out of his poverty.

When they went back to the hotel, he said:

"It's something I learned in my youth, when I was fighting in an unjust war for an ideal I didn't believe in. There's always a way of putting an end to poverty."

NO, IGOR CAN'T BE HERE in Cannes. Hamid must have made a mistake. The two men had only met once before, in the foyer of the building where they lived in London, when Igor had found out their address and gone there to beg Ewa to come back. Hamid had spoken to him, but hadn't allowed him to come in, threatening to call the police. For a whole week, she had refused to leave their apartment, claiming to have a headache, but knowing that the Angel of Light had turned into Absolute Evil.

She looks at her phone again and rereads the message.

Katyusha. Only one person would call her by that name. The person who lives in her past and will terrorize her present for the rest of her life, however protected she feels, however far away she lives, and even though she inhabits a world to which he has no access. The same person who, on their return from Irkutsk—as if he had sloughed off an enormous weight—had begun to speak more freely about the shadows that inhabited his soul.

"No one, absolutely no one, can threaten our privacy. We've spent long enough creating a fairer, more humane society. Anyone who fails to respect our moments of freedom should be removed in such a way that they'll never even consider coming back."

Ewa was afraid to ask what "in such a way" meant. She had thought she knew her husband, but from one moment to the next, it seemed that a submerged volcano had begun to roar, and the shock waves were getting stronger and stronger. She remembered certain late-night conversations with him when he was still a young man and how he had told her that, during the war in Afghanistan, he had sometimes been forced to kill in self-defense. She had never seen regret or remorse in his eyes.

"I survived, and that's what matters. My life could have ended one sunny afternoon, or at dawn in the snow-covered mountains, or one night when we were playing cards in our tent, confident that the situation was under control. And if I had died, nothing would have changed in the world. I would have been just another statistic for the army and another medal for my family.

"But Jesus helped me, and I was blessed with quick reactions. And because I survived the hardest tests a man can face, fate has given me the two most important things in life: success at work and the person I love."

It was one thing killing in order to save your own life, but quite another to "remove for good" some poor drunk who had interrupted their supper and who could easily have been shepherded away by the restaurant owner. She couldn't get the idea out of her head. She started going ever earlier to the shop and, when she came home, sitting at her computer until late into the night. There was a question she wanted to avoid. She managed to carry on like this for some months, following the usual routine: business trips, parties, suppers, meetings, charity auctions. She even wondered if she had misunderstood what her husband had said in Irkutsk and blamed herself for making such a snap judgment.

Time passed, and the question became less important, until the night they attended a gala supper–cum–charity auction at one of the most expensive restaurants in Milan. They were both there for different reasons: Igor in order to firm up the details of a contract with an Italian firm, and Ewa in order to attend the Fashion Week, where she intended to make a few purchases for her Moscow shop.

And what had happened in the middle of Siberia was repeated in one of the most sophisticated cities in the world. This time, a friend of theirs, rather the worse for wear, sat down at their table uninvited and started joking and making inappropriate remarks. Ewa saw Igor's hand grip the handle of his knife more tightly. As tactfully and politely as possible, she asked the friend to go away. By then, she had already drunk several glasses of Asti Spumante, as the Italians refer to what used to be called champagne because the use of the word "champagne" was banned under the so-called Protected Designation of Origin. Champagne simply means a white wine made using a particular bacteria which, when rigorously controlled, begins to generate gases inside the bottle as the wine ages over a period of at least fifteen months. The name refers to the region where it's produced. Spumante is exactly the same thing, but European law doesn't allow it to be known by the French name, since the vineyards are in Italy and not in the Champagne region of France.

They started talking about champagne and about the laws governing names, while she tried to drive from her head the question she had tried to suppress and which was now returning in full force. While they were talking, she kept drinking, until there came a moment when she could hold back no longer.

"What does it matter if someone gets a little drunk and comes over to talk to us?"

When he answered, Igor's voice had changed.

"Because we so rarely travel together. Besides, you know what I think about the world we live in: that we're being suffocated by lies, encouraged to put our faith in science rather than in spiritual values and to feed our souls with the things society tells us are important, when, in reality, we're slowly dying because we know what's going on around us, that we're being forced to do things we never planned to do, and yet even so, are incapable of giving it all up and devoting our days and nights to true happiness, to family, nature, love. And why is that? Because we feel obliged to finish what we started, so that we can achieve the financial stability we need in order to enjoy the rest of our lives devoting ourselves to each other because we're responsible people. I know you sometimes think I work too much, but it's not true. I'm building our future and soon we'll be free to dream and to live out our dreams."

Financial stability was hardly something they lacked. They had no debts and they could have got up from that table there and then with just their credit cards and simply left behind them the world Igor apparently hated and start all over again, and never have to worry about money. She had often spoken to him about this, and Igor always said the same thing: "It won't be much longer." Besides, this wasn't the moment to discuss their future as a couple.

"God thought of everything," he went on. "We are together because he decided we should be. You may not fully appreciate your importance in my life, but without you, I would never have got where I am today. He placed us side by side and lent me his power to defend you whenever necessary. He taught me that everything is part of a plan, and I must respect that plan down to the last detail. If hadn't done so, I would either be dead in Kabul or living in poverty in Moscow."

And it was then that the Spumante or champagne revealed what it was capable of, regardless of what it was called.

"What happened to that beggar in Siberia?" she asked.

Igor didn't at first know what she was talking about. Ewa reminded him of what had happened in the restaurant there.

"I'd like to know what you did."

"I saved him."

She gave a sigh of relief.

"I saved him from a filthy, hopeless life in those freezing winters, with his body being slowly destroyed by booze. I let his soul depart toward the light because the moment he came into that restaurant to destroy our happiness, I knew that his spirit was inhabited by the Evil One."

Ewa felt her heart begin to pound. She didn't need him to say outright: "I killed him." It was clear that he had.

"Without you I don't exist. Anything and anyone who tries to separate us or to destroy the little time we have together at this particular moment of our lives gets the treatment they deserve."

Meaning perhaps that they deserved to be killed? Could such a thing have happened before without her noticing? She drank and drank some more, and Igor began to relax again. Since he never opened his heart to anyone else, he loved their conversations.

"We speak the same language," he went on. "We see the world in the same way. We complete each other with a perfection that is granted only to those who put love above all else. As I said, without you I don't exist.

"Look at the Superclass around us. They think they're so important, so socially aware, because they're willing to pay a fortune for some useless item at a charity auction or to attend a supper organized to raise funds to help the homeless in Rwanda or to save the pandas in China. Pandas and the homeless are all one to them. They feel special, superior to the average person, because they're doing something useful. Have they ever fought in a war? No. They create wars, but they don't fight in them. If the war turns out well, they get all the credit. If not, others get the blame. They're in love with themselves."

"My love, I'd like to ask you something else . . ."

At that point, a presenter climbed onto the stage and thanked everyone for being there that night. The money raised would go toward buying medicine for refugee camps in Africa.

"What he doesn't say," Igor went on, as if he hadn't heard her, "is that only ten percent of the total amount raised will reach its destination. The rest will be used to pay for this event, for the cost of this supper, for the publicity and the organizers, in short, for the people who had the 'brilliant idea' in the first place, and all at an exorbitant price. They use poverty as a way to get even richer."

"So why are we here?"

"Because we need to be. It's part of my work. I have no intention of saving Rwanda or sending medicine to refugees, but at least I know that I don't. The other guests here tonight are using their money to wash their consciences and their souls clean of guilt. When the genocide was going on in Rwanda, I financed a small army of friends, who prevented more than two thousand deaths. Did you know that?"

"No, you never told me."

"I didn't need to. You know that I care about other people."

The auction began with a small Louis Vuitton travel bag. It sold for ten times its retail price. Igor watched the auction impassively, while she drank another glass of Spumante and wondered whether she should or shouldn't ask that question.

An artist danced to a soundtrack provided by Marilyn Monroe and simultaneously painted a picture. The bids for the finished work of art were sky-high—the price of a small apartment in Moscow.

Another glass of wine. Another item sold. For an equally absurd price.

She drank so much that night that she had to be carried back to the hotel. Before he put her into bed and before she fell asleep, she finally got up the courage to ask:

"And what if I were to leave you?"

"Drink less next time."

"Answer me."

"That could never happen. Our marriage is perfect."

Common sense returned, but she knew she had an excuse now and so pretended to be drunker than she was.

"Yes, but what if I did?"

"I'd make you come back, and I'm good at getting what I want, even if that means destroying whole worlds."

"And what if I met another man?"

He looked at her without rancor, almost benevolently.

"Even if you slept with every man on Earth, my love would still survive."

AND SINCE THEN, WHAT HAD seemed a blessing began to turn into a nightmare. She was married to a monster, an assassin. What was that story about financing an army of mercenaries to intervene in a tribal war? How many other men had he killed to keep them from troubling their marital peace? She could blame the war, the traumas he had suffered, the hard times he had been through, but many other men had endured the same experiences, without emerging from them convinced that they were the instrument of Divine Justice, carrying out some Grand Plan.

"I'm not jealous," Igor used to say whenever he or she set off on a business trip, "because you know how much I love you, and I know how much you love me. Nothing will ever happen to destabilize our marriage."

She was more convinced than ever that this was not love. It was something sick and morbid, which she would either have to accept and live the rest of her life a prisoner to fear, or else free herself as soon as possible, at the first opportunity.

Several opportunities arose, but the most insistent, the most persistent was the very last man with whom she would have imagined building a real relationship: the couturier who was dazzling the fashion world, growing ever more famous, and receiving a vast amount of money from his own country so that the world would understand that the nomadic tribes had solid moral values that were completely at odds with the reign of terror imposed by a religious minority. He was a man who, increasingly, had the world at his feet.

Whenever they met at fashion shows, he would drop whatever other commitments he had, cancel lunches and suppers, just so that they could spend some time together in peace, locked in a hotel room, often without even making love. They would watch television, eat, drink (although he never touched a drop of alcohol), go for walks in parks, visit bookshops, talk to strangers, speak very little of the past, never of the future, and a great deal about the present.

She resisted for as long as she could, and, although she was never in love with him, when he proposed that she leave everything and move to London, she accepted at once. It was the only possible way out of her private hell.

ANOTHER MESSAGE APPEARS ON HER phone. It can't be; they haven't been in touch for two years.

"I've just destroyed another world because of you, Katyusha."

"Who's it from?"

"I haven't the slightest idea. It doesn't show a number."

What she meant to say was that she was terrified.

"We're nearly there. Remember, we haven't got much time."

The limousine has to maneuver its way toward the entrance of the Hotel Martinez. On both sides, behind the metal barriers erected by the police, people of all ages spend the whole day hoping to get a close-up look at some celebrity. They take photos with their digital cameras, tell their friends whom they've seen, and send messages over the Internet to the virtual communities they belong to. They would feel the long wait was justified for that one moment of glory: catching a glimpse of an actress, an actor, or even a TV presenter!

Although it's only thanks to them that the celebrity industry keeps going, they are kept at a safe distance; strategically positioned bodyguards ask anyone going into the hotel for proof that they are staying there or meeting someone. Then you either have to get out the magnetic card that serves as your room key or else be turned away in full view of the public. If you're having a business meeting or have been invited for a drink at the bar, they give your name to the security people and, with everyone watching, wait to see if what you say is true or false. The bodyguard uses his radio to call reception, and you wait there for what seems like an eternity, and then, finally, after that very public humiliation, you're allowed in. Those who arrive in limousines, of course, are treated quite differently.

The two doors of the Maybach are opened, one by the chauffeur and the other by the hotel porter. The cameras turn on Ewa and start to shoot; even though no one knows who she is, if she's staying at the Martinez and has arrived in a fancy car, she must be important. Perhaps she's the mistress of the man she's with, and if she is and he's having an extramarital affair, there's always a chance they can send the photos to some scandal rag. Or perhaps the beautiful blonde is a famous foreign celebrity as yet unknown in France. Later, they'll find her name in the so-called people magazines and be glad that they were once only four or five yards from her.

Hamid looks at the small crowd pressed up against the metal barriers. He has never understood this phenomenon, having been brought up in a place where such things simply don't happen. Once he asked a friend why there was so much interest in celebrities.

"Don't assume they're all fans," said his friend. "Since time immemorial, men have believed that being close to something unattainable and mysterious can bring blessings. That's why people make pilgrimages to visit gurus and sacred places."

"But Cannes?!"

"It can be anywhere they might catch a distant glimpse of some elusive celebrity. For the adoring crowd, a wave from a celebrity is like being scattered with ambrosia dust or manna from heaven.

"It's the same everywhere. Take, for example, those massive pop concerts that seem more like religious meetings, or the way people are willing to wait outside some sell-out performance at a theater just to see the Superclass entering and leaving. Take the crowds who go to football stadiums to watch a bunch of men chasing after a ball. Celebrities are idols, icons if you like, after all, they do resemble the paintings you see in churches and can become cult images in the bedrooms of adolescents or housewives, and even in the offices of industrial magnates, who, despite their own enormous wealth, envy their celebrity.

"There's just one difference: in this case, the public is the supreme judge, and while they may applaud today, tomorrow they'll be equally happy to read some scandalous revelation about their idol in a gossip magazine. Then they can say: 'Poor thing. I'm so glad I'm not like him.' They may adore their idol today, but tomorrow they'll stone and crucify him without a twinge of conscience."

Unlike the other girls who arrived for work this morning and are now using their iPods and mobile phones to while away the five hours that separate having their makeup and hair done from the actual fashion show, Jasmine is reading a book, a poetry book:

> Two roads diverged in a yellow wood,
> And sorry I could not travel both
> And be one traveler, long I stood
> And looked down one as far as I could
> To where it bent in the undergrowth;
>
> Then took the other, as just as fair,
> And having perhaps the better claim,
> Because it was grassy and wanted wear;
> Though as for that the passing there
> Had worn them really about the same,
>
> And both that morning equally lay
> In leaves no step had trodden black.
> Oh, I kept the first for another day!
> Yet knowing how way leads on to way,
> I doubted if I should ever come back.

I shall be telling this with a sigh
Somewhere ages and ages hence:
Two roads diverged in a wood, and I—
I took the one less traveled by,
And that has made all the difference.

She had chosen the road less traveled, and though it cost her dearly, it has been worth it. Things arrive at the right moment. Love had appeared when she most needed it and was still there with her now. She did her work with, for, and out of love, or, rather, out of love for one particular person.

Jasmine's real name is Cristina. Her CV says she was discovered by Anna Dieter on a trip to Kenya, but there was little detail about this, leaving in the air the possibility of a childhood spent suffering and starving, caught up in the middle of a civil war. In fact, despite her black skin, she was born in the very traditional Belgian city of Antwerp, the daughter of parents fleeing the eternal conflicts between Hutus and Tutsis in Rwanda.

One weekend, when she was sixteen, she was helping out her mother on one of the latter's endless cleaning jobs, when a man came up to them and introduced himself, saying he was a photographer.

"Your daughter is extraordinarily beautiful," he said. "I'd like her to work with me as a model."

"You see this bag I'm carrying? It's full of cleaning materials. I work day and night so that she can go to a good school and, one day, get a university degree. She's only sixteen."

"That's the ideal age," said the photographer, handing his card to Cristina. "If you change your mind, let me know."

They carried on walking, but her mother noticed that her daughter kept the card.

"Don't be deceived. That isn't your world. They just want to get you into bed."

Cristina didn't need to be told this. Even though all the girls in her class envied her and the boys all wanted to take her to parties, she was keenly aware of her origins and her limitations.

She still didn't believe it when the same thing happened again. She had just gone into an ice-cream parlor when an older woman remarked on her beauty and said that she was a fashion photographer. Cristina thanked her, took her card, and promised to phone her, even though she had no intention of doing so and even though becoming a model was the dream of every girl her age.

Given that things never happen only twice, three months later, she was looking in the window of a shop selling extremely expensive clothes, when the owner of the shop came out to speak to her.

"What do you do for a living?"

"You should really be asking me what will I be doing. I'm going to study to be a vet."

"Well, you're on the wrong path. Wouldn't you like to work with us?"

"I haven't got time to sell clothes. Whenever I can, I help my mother."

"I'm not suggesting you sell anything. I'd like you to do a few photo shoots wearing our designs."

And if it hadn't been for an episode that occurred a few days later, these encounters would have been nothing but pleasant memories to look back on when she was married with children, loved by her family and fulfilled by her career.

She was with some friends at a nightclub, dancing and feeling glad to be alive, when a group of ten boys burst in, shouting. Nine of them were carrying clubs with razor blades embedded in them and were ordering everyone to get out. Panic spread, and people started running. Cristina didn't know what to do, although her instincts told her to remain where she was and look the other way.

Before she could do anything, however, she saw the tenth boy take a knife out of his pocket, go over to one of her friends, grab him from behind, and slit his throat. The gang left as quickly as they had appeared, while the other people present were either screaming, trying to run away, or sitting on the floor, crying. A few went over to the victim to see if they could help, knowing that it was too late. Others, like Cristina, simply stared at the scene in shock. She knew the murdered boy and the murderer too, and even knew the motive for the crime (a fight in a bar shortly before they had gone to the nightclub), but she seemed to be floating somewhere in the clouds, as if it had all been a dream from which she would soon wake up, drenched in sweat, relieved to know that all nightmares come to an end.

This, however, was no dream.

It took only a few minutes for her to return to earth, screaming for someone to do something, screaming for people to do nothing, screaming for no reason at all, and her screams seemed to make people even more nervous. Then the police arrived, carrying guns, and were followed by paramedics and then detectives, who lined all the young people up against the wall and started questioning them, demanding to see their documents, their mobile phones, their addresses. Who had killed the boy and why? Cristina could say nothing. The body, covered by a sheet, was taken away. A nurse forced her to take a pill and told her that she must on no account drive home, but take a taxi or use public transport.

Early the next morning, the phone rang. Her mother had decided to spend the day at home with her daughter, who seemed somehow detached from the world. The police insisted on speaking to Cristina directly, saying that she must be at the police station by midday and ask for a particular inspector. Her mother refused. The police threatened her, and so, in the end, Cristina and her mother had no choice.

THEY ARRIVED AT THE APPOINTED time. The inspector asked Cristina if she knew the murderer.

Her mother's words were still echoing in her mind: "Don't say anything. We're immigrants, they're Belgians. We're black, they're white. When they come out of prison, they'll track you down." So she said:

"I don't know who the boy was. I'd never seen him before."

She knew that by saying this, she risked losing her love of life.

"Of course you know who he was," retorted the policeman. "Look, don't worry, nothing's going to happen to you. We've arrested almost the whole group, and we just need witnesses for the trial."

"I don't know anything. I was nowhere near. I didn't see who did it."

The inspector shook his head in despair.

"You'll have to repeat that at the trial," he said, "knowing that you're committing perjury, that is, lying to the judge, a crime for which you could spend as long in prison as the murderers themselves."

Months later, she was called as a witness. The boys were all there with their lawyers and seemed almost to be enjoying the situation. One of the other girls who had been at the club that night identified the murderer in court.

Then it was Cristina's turn. The prosecutor asked her to identify the person who had slit her friend's throat.

"I don't know who did it," she said.

She was black and the daughter of immigrants. She had a student grant from the government. All she wanted was to recover her will to live, and to feel once again that she had a future. She had spent weeks staring at her bedroom ceiling, not wanting to study or to do anything. The world in which she had lived up until then did not belong to her anymore. At sixteen, she had learned in the hardest way possible that she was incapable of fighting for her own security. She needed to leave Antwerp, to travel the world, to recover her joy and her strength.

The boys were let off for lack of evidence; the prosecution had needed two witnesses to corroborate the charges and ensure that the guilty parties paid for their crime. After leaving court, Cristina phoned the numbers on the business cards given her by the two photographers and made appointments to see them. Then she went back to the dress shop where the owner had come out especially to speak to her and ask if she would model his clothes. The saleswomen, however, said that the owner had shops all over Europe and was a very busy man, and no, they couldn't give her his phone number.

Fortunately, photographers have better memories, and both immediately recognized her name and arranged to meet her.

Cristina went back home and told her mother what she had decided to do. She didn't ask her advice or try to convince her, she simply said that she wanted to leave Antwerp for good, and that her one chance was to get work as a model.

***

JASMINE LOOKS AROUND HER AGAIN. It's still three hours until the fashion show, and the other models are eating salad, drinking tea, and talking about where they'll be going next. They come from various countries, are about the same age as her—nineteen—and probably have just two things on their minds: getting a new contract that evening and finding a rich husband.

She knows their beauty routine. Before sleeping, they apply sundry creams to cleanse their pores and keep their skin moisturized, thus, from early on, making their organism dependent on artificial substances to maintain an ideal equilibrium. In the morning, they apply more cream and more moisturizer. They drink a cup of black coffee with no sugar, and eat some fruit and fiber, so that any other food they consume during the day will pass quickly through. Then they do a few stretching exercises before setting off in search of work. They're too young to start working out in a gym and, besides, their bodies might start taking on masculine contours. They get on the scales three or four times a day, in fact, most of them always have their own scales with them just in case, because sometimes they stay in boardinghouses rather than hotels. They get depressed each time the pointer on the scales tells them they've gained another ounce.

Most of the models are only seventeen or eighteen, and so their mothers go with them whenever possible. The girls never admit to being in love with anyone—although most of them are—because love makes the traveling seem longer and more unbearable and arouses in their boyfriends the strange sense that they're losing the woman (or girl) that they love. Yes, the girls think about money and earn an average of four hundred euros a day—an enviable salary for someone who is often still too young to have a license and drive a car. Their dreams go beyond being a model, however; they know that soon they'll be overtaken by new faces, new trends, and so urgently need to show that they can do more than just stride down a catwalk. They're always nagging their agencies to get them a screen test, so that they can demonstrate that they've got what it takes to become an actress—their great dream.

The agencies, of course, agree to do this, but advise them to wait a little; after all, their careers are only just beginning. The truth is that most model agencies don't have many contacts outside the fashion world; they earn a good percentage, compete with other agencies, and the market isn't that big. It's best to get what they can now, before time passes and the model crosses the dangerous age barrier of twenty, by which time her skin will have been spoiled by too many moisturizers, her body ruined by too much low-calorie food, and her mind already affected by the remedies she takes to inhibit appetite and which end up leaving eyes and head completely empty.

Contrary to what most people think, models pay their own expenses—flights, hotels, and those inevitable salads. They are summoned by a designer's assistant to do what is known as "casting," namely, selecting who will appear on the catwalk or in the photos. They are faced at these sessions by a lot of disgruntled people who use the little power they have to vent their own day-to-day frustrations and who never say a kind or encouraging word: "awful" or "dreadful" are the ones most commonly heard. The girls leave that test and move on to the next, clinging to their mobile phones for dear life, as if these were about to offer some divine revelation or at least put them in contact with the Higher World to which they dream of ascending and from where they'll be able to look down on all those other pretty faces and where they will be transformed into stars.

Their parents are proud that their daughters have got off to a good start and regret their initial opposition to such a career; after all, their daughters are earning money and helping the family. Their boyfriends get upset, but keep a lid on their feelings because it's good for one's ego to be seen going out with a professional model. The models' agents work with dozens of girls of similar age and with similar fantasies, and are ready with pat answers to the kind of questions the girls all ask: "Couldn't I take part in the Fashion Week in Paris?" "Do you think

I have what it takes to get into the movies?" The girls' friends envy them—either secretly or openly.

These young models go to any party they're invited to. They behave as if they were much more important than they are, knowing, deep down, that they would love someone to break through the artificial barrier of ice they create around themselves. They look at older men with a mixture of revulsion and attraction; they know that such men have the necessary money to help them make the big leap, but, at the same time, don't want to seem to be nothing but high-class whores. They're always seen with a glass of champagne in one hand, but that's just part of the image they want to project. They know that alcohol can affect their weight and so their preferred drink is a glass of still mineral water because although fizzy water doesn't affect the weight, it has immediate consequences on the shape of the stomach. They have ideals, dreams, dignity, but all these things will vanish one day, when they can no longer disguise the early onset of cellulite.

They make a secret pact with themselves never to think about the future. They spend much of what they earn on beauty products promising eternal youth. They adore shoes, but they're so expensive; nevertheless, they sometimes treat themselves and buy a pair of the very best. They get clothes from friends in the fashion world at half the usual price. They share a small apartment with their parents, a brother who's at university and a sister who's chosen to be a librarian or a scientist. Everyone assumes the girls must be earning a fortune and frequently ask them for loans, to which the girls agree because they want to appear important, rich, generous, and different from other mortals. When they go to the bank, though, their account is always in the red and they've overshot their credit card limit.

They acquire hundreds of business cards, meet well-dressed men who make proposals of work they know to be false, but they phone them now and then to keep in touch, conscious that they might need help one day, even though that help comes at a price. They all fall into the same traps. They all dream of easy success, only to realize that it doesn't exist. By seventeen, they have all suffered innumerable disappointments, betrayals, humiliations, and yet still they believe.

They sleep badly because of the various pills they take. They listen to stories about anorexia—the commonest illness in their world, a kind of mental disturbance caused by an obsession with weight and one's physical appearance, and which culminates in the body rejecting all nourishment. They say it won't ever happen to them, but never notice when the first symptoms appear.

They step out of childhood straight into a world of glitz and glamour, without passing through adolescence. When asked what their plans are for the future, they always have the answer on the tip of their tongue: "I'm going to study philosophy. I'm just working to pay for my studies."

They know this isn't true. Or rather, they know that something about these words doesn't ring true, but they can't quite put their finger on what it is. Do they really want a degree? Do they really need that money for their studies? They don't have time for college because there's always a casting session in the morning, a photo shoot in the afternoon, a cocktail party before dark, then another party they have to go to in order to be seen, admired, and desired.

To other people, they seem to lead a fairy-tale existence. And, for a while, they, too, believe that this is the real meaning of life; after all, they have almost everything they once envied in the girls who appeared in magazines and cosmetic ads. With a little discipline, they can even save a little money, until, after a careful, daily examination of their skin, they discover the first mark left by age. After that, they know it's only a matter of time before a designer or a photographer notices the same thing. Their days are numbered.

I took the one less traveled by,
And that has made all the difference.

Instead of going back to her book, Jasmine gets up, fills her glass with champagne (it's always there, but rarely drunk), picks up a hot dog, and goes over to the window. She stands there in silence, looking out at the sea. Her story is different.

1:46 P.M.

He wakes up bathed in sweat. When he looks at the clock on the bedside table, he realizes that he's only been asleep for forty minutes. He's exhausted, frightened, in a state of panic. He had always thought himself incapable of harming anyone, and yet this morning he has already killed two innocent people. It isn't the first time he's destroyed a world, but, before, he had always had good reasons for doing so.

He dreamed that the girl on the bench near the beach came to see him and instead of condemning him, blessed him. He lay in her lap, weeping and begging her to forgive him, but she seemed not to care about that, and simply stroked his hair and told him not to upset himself. Olivia, the image of generosity and forgiveness. He wonders now if his love for Ewa is worth what he is doing.

He prefers to believe that it is. The fact that Olivia is on his side, that he met with her on a higher plane closer to the Divine, and that everything has been so much easier than he imagined, all this indicates that there must be a reason behind what is happening.

———

IT HADN'T BEEN DIFFICULT TO evade the vigilant eyes of Javits's friends. He knew that such men, as well as being physically prepared to react rapidly and precisely, were trained to memorize each face, follow every movement, second-guess any danger. They probably knew he was armed, which is why they watched him for a while, but relaxed when they realized he didn't constitute a threat. They might even have thought he was in the same line of work and had gone to the tent to check out the place and see if it was safe for his own boss.

He had no boss. And he *was* a threat. The moment he went into the tent and decided who would be his next victim, there was no turning back, or only at the risk of losing all self-respect. He saw that the ramp leading into the tent was guarded, but that it was perfectly easy to slip out onto the beach. He left ten minutes after he had arrived, hoping that Javits's friends would notice that he had gone. He then walked round the tent and came back up the ramp reserved for guests at the Hotel Martinez (he had to show his key card) and into the area reserved for the "lunch." Walking on sand in one's shoes wasn't the pleasantest thing in the world, and Igor noticed that he was still feeling tired from the flight, from the fear that his plan might prove impossible to achieve, and from the tension he felt after destroying the universe and future generations of that poor young vendor of craftwork. Nevertheless, he had to go on.

BEFORE RETURNING TO THE TENT, he took from his pocket the drinking straw that he had made a point of keeping. He opened the small glass flask he had shown to Olivia. It did not, as he had told her, contain petrol, but something quite insignificant: a needle and a piece of cork. Using a thin metal blade, he made a hole in the cork the same diameter as the straw.

THEN HE REJOINED THE PARTY, which, by then, was full of guests strolling around, kissing and embracing, giving little yelps of recognition, clutching cocktails of every possible hue just to have something to do with their hands and to keep a check on their anxiety, as they waited for the buffet to open. They could eat then, in moderation, of course, because there were diets and plastic surgery to be considered and suppers at the end of the day, where they would have to eat even though they weren't hungry because that was what etiquette required.

Most of the guests were older people, which meant that this was an event for professionals. The age of the guests further favored his plan, since almost all of them would need glasses. Needless to say, no one was wearing them because "tired eyes" are a sign of age. There, every-one had to dress and behave like people in the prime of life, "young at heart" and "in excellent health," and to pretend that they were indiffer-ent to what was going on around them because they were preoccupied with other things, when the truth was that they couldn't actually see. Their contact lenses meant that they could just about identify a person a few yards away, and, besides, they would find out soon enough who it was they were talking to.

Only two of the guests noticed everything and everyone—Javits's "friends." This time, however, they were the ones being observed.

Igor placed the needle inside the straw, and pretended to put it back in his drink.

A group of pretty girls standing near Javits's table appeared to be listening, entranced, to the extraordinary tales told by a Jamaican man. In fact, each girl was plotting how to get rid of her rivals and carry the man off to bed because Jamaicans have such a reputation as studs.

Igor moved closer to Javits, took the straw from the glass, and blew through it, projecting the needle inside in the direction of his victim. He stayed only long enough to see Javits put his hand to his back. Then he left and went straight back to the hotel to try and get some sleep.

CURARE, ORIGINALLY USED BY SOUTH American Indians for hunting with darts, can also be found in European hospitals because, under controlled conditions, it can be used to paralyze certain muscles, thus facilitating the surgeon's work. A fatal dose—like that on the point of the needle he had shot into Javits's back—could kill a bird in just two minutes. Boar, on the other hand, take fifteen minutes to die, and large mammals—a man, for example—twenty.

As soon as it gets into the bloodstream, the nervous fibers of the body relax, then stop functioning altogether, causing gradual asphyxia. The strangest thing—or the worst, some might say—is that the victim remains conscious throughout, but cannot move in order to ask for help nor stop the slow process of paralysis overtaking his body.

If someone cuts his finger on a poisoned dart or arrow during a hunting expedition in the jungle, the Indians know exactly what to do. They use mouth-to-mouth resuscitation and an herbal antidote that they always carry with them because such accidents are commonplace. In cities, the paramedics can do nothing because they think they're dealing with a heart attack.

Igor did not look back as he walked to the hotel. He knew that just then one of the two "friends" would be frantically searching out the perpetrator, while the other would be ringing for an ambulance, which would arrive quickly enough, but the crew would have little idea what was going on. They would be wearing colorful uniforms and high-visibility jackets, and carrying a defibrillator—to apply a series of shocks to the heart—and a portable electrocardiogram. In the case of curare, the heart seems to be the last muscle affected and continues beating even after brain death has occurred.

The paramedics would notice nothing strange about his heartbeat, and so would put him on a drip, assuming he was suffering from some form of heat stroke or food poisoning, although they would still take all the usual measures, even applying an oxygen mask. By then, the twenty minutes would be up, and although the body might still be alive, it would now be in a vegetative state.

YES, HE HAD PLANNED EVERYTHING. He had used his private plane so that he could enter France with an unregistered gun and with the various poisons he had obtained via his connections with the Chechen mafia working in Moscow. Each step, each move had been carefully studied and rehearsed, as if he were planning a business meeting. He had made a list of victims in his head. Apart from the one he had met and talked to, the others were all to be of different classes, ages, and nationalities. He had spent months analyzing the lives of serial killers, using a computer program that was very popular with terrorists and which left no record of any searches you made. He had taken all the necessary steps to escape unnoticed once he had carried out his mission.

He is sweating. No, it's not remorse—perhaps Ewa really does deserve such a sacrifice—but the thought of the possible futility of the project. He needed the woman he most loved to know he was capable of doing anything for her, including destroying universes, but was it really worth it? Or is it sometimes necessary to accept fate and allow things to develop in their own way and simply wait for people to come to their senses in their own time?

He's tired. He can't think straight anymore and, who knows, perhaps martyrdom was better than murder, surrendering himself and thus making a greater sacrifice, offering up his own life for love. Jesus was the best example of that. When his enemies saw Jesus defeated and hung upon a cross, they thought it was all over. They felt proud of what they, the victors, had done, convinced that they had put paid to the problem once and for all.

Igor is confused. His intention was to destroy universes, not relinquish his freedom out of love. In his dream, the girl with the dark eyebrows had resembled Notre Dame de Piétat; the mother with her son in her arms, at once proud and long-suffering.

He goes into the bathroom, puts his head under the shower, and turns on the cold water. Perhaps it's lack of sleep, being in a strange place, in a different time zone, or the fact that he was actually doing the thing he had planned to do, but never thought he would. He remembers the promise he made before the relics of St. Mary Magdalene in Moscow. But is what he's doing right? He needs a sign.

Sacrifice. Yes, he should have thought of that, but perhaps he needed the experience of destroying those two worlds this morning to be able to see more clearly what is going on. The redemption of love through total surrender. His body will be handed over to the executioners who judge only one's gestures and who forget about the intentions and reasons that lie behind any act that society considers "insane." Jesus (who understands that love merits any amount of sacrifice) will receive his spirit, and Ewa will have his soul. She will know what he was capable of: surrender, self-immolation, and all for the sake of one person. He won't be condemned to death because the guillotine was abolished in France decades ago, but he might spend many years in prison. Ewa will repent of her sins. She'll come to see him, bring him food, they'll have time to talk, reflect, love, and even though their bodies do not touch, their souls will be closer than ever. Even if they have to wait years before they can live in the house he intends to build on the shores of Lake Baikal, that period of waiting will purify and bless them.

Yes, sacrifice. He turns off the shower, looks at his face in the mirror for a moment, and sees not himself, but the Lamb prepared to be slaughtered once again. He puts on the same clothes he was wearing this morning, goes out into the street, heads for the place where the little street vendor used to sit, and goes up to the first policeman he meets.

"I killed the girl who used to work here."

The policeman looks at him and sees a well-dressed man with disheveled hair and dark circles under his eyes.

"The one who used to sell craftwork?"

Igor nods.

The policeman doesn't take much notice of him. He greets a couple who are walking by, laden with shopping.

"You should get a maid!"

"If you'll pay her wages," retorts the woman, smiling. "You just can't get the staff these days!"

"Oh, come on, money can't be the reason. You have a different diamond on your finger every week."

Igor cannot understand what's going on. He has just confessed to a murder.

"Did you hear what I said?"

"Look, it's very hot. Go and lie down for a bit. Cannes has a lot to offer its visitors."

"But what about the girl?"

"Did you know her?"

"I'd never seen her before in my life. She was here this morning. I . . ."

". . . you saw the ambulance arrive and someone being taken away and concluded she'd been murdered. I don't know where you're from, sir, I don't know if you've got children yourself, but just watch out for drugs. People say they're not as bad as all that, but look what happened to that poor girl."

And the policeman moves away without waiting for a response.

Should Igor have insisted, given more details? Then would the policeman have taken him seriously? But, of course, it's impossible to kill someone in broad daylight and on the main street in Cannes. He had even been ready to own up to the other world he had destroyed at a party packed with people.

But the representative of law and order and good manners hadn't wanted to listen to him. What kind of world was he living in? Would he have to take the gun out of his pocket and start firing in all directions for them to believe him? Would he have to behave like a barbarian who kills for no reason before they would finally listen to him?

Igor watches the policeman cross the road and go into a snack bar. He decides to wait for a while, just in case he should change his mind, get further information from the police station and come back and ask him for more details of the crime.

However, he's pretty certain that won't happen. He remembers the policeman's remark to the woman about the diamond on her finger. Did he perhaps know where it came from? Of course not; if he did, he would have taken her straight to the police station and charged her with handling criminal property.

As far as the woman was concerned, the diamond had magically appeared in some high-class shop, having—as the shop assistants always said—first been cut by Dutch or Belgian jewelers. It would be classified according to cut, color, clarity, and carat weight. The price could vary from a few hundred euros to something most mere mortals would consider truly outrageous.

A diamond, or brilliant to give it its other name, is, as everyone knows, just a piece of coal that has been worked on by heat and time. Since it contains no organic matter, it is impossible to know how long it takes for its structure to change, although geologists estimate something between three hundred million and a billion years. Diamonds generally form ninety miles below the Earth's crust and gradually rise to the surface, where they can be mined.

Diamond is the hardest and most resistant of natural materials, and it takes a diamond to cut another diamond. The particles produced by this process are used in machines made for polishing and cutting. The real importance of diamonds lies in their use as jewels. A diamond is the supreme manifestation of human vanity.

A few decades ago, in a world that seemed about to return to more practical things and greater social equality, diamonds began to disappear from the market. Then the largest mining company in the world, with its headquarters in South Africa, decided to commission one of the best advertising agencies in the world. Superclass met with Superclass, research was carried out, and the result was a three-word phrase:

"Diamonds are forever."

Problem solved. Jewelers took up the slogan, and the industry began to flourish again. If diamonds are forever, what better way to express one's love, which, in theory at least, should also be eternal? What better way of distinguishing the Superclass from the other billions of inhabitants who make up the bottom half of the pyramid? The demand for the stones increased and prices started to rise. In a matter of a few years, that same South African company, which had, up until then, set the rules for the international market, found itself surrounded by corpses.

Igor knows what he's talking about. When he helped form an army to get involved in a tribal conflict in Africa, it had proved an extremely difficult task. Not that he regrets it because, although few people knew about the project, he managed to save many lives. He had mentioned it once in passing to Ewa over some now-forgotten supper, but had decided to say no more. When he performed a charitable act, he preferred his right hand not to know what his left hand was doing. Diamonds had helped him save many lives, although that fact will never appear in his biography.

The policeman who takes no notice when a criminal confesses to a crime, but praises the jewel on the finger of a woman carrying bags packed with toilet paper and cleaning materials, is simply not fit for the job. He doesn't know that this pointless industry creates about fifty billion dollars a year, employs a vast army of miners, transporters, private security companies, diamond factories, insurance companies, wholesalers, and luxury boutiques. He doesn't realize that it begins in the mud and has to cross whole rivers of blood before it reaches a shop window.

The mud is where the miner spends his life looking for the stone that will eventually bring him the fortune he so desires. He finds several and sells each stone for an average of twenty dollars, a stone that will end up costing the consumer ten thousand dollars. But he's happy enough because, where he lives, people earn less than fifty dollars a year, and five stones are enough for him to enjoy a short but happy life, working as he does in the worst possible conditions.

THE STONES ARE BOUGHT BY unidentified buyers and immediately passed on to irregular armies in Liberia, in the Congo, and in Angola. In those countries, a man, surrounded by guards armed to the teeth, is designated to go to an airstrip where planes can land illegally. A plane duly lands, a man in a suit gets out, usually accompanied by another man in shirtsleeves, carrying a small suitcase. There is a perfunctory exchange of greetings. The man with the bodyguards hands over a few small packages; perhaps for superstitious reasons, the packages are always made from old tights.

The man in shirtsleeves takes a special jeweler's eyeglass from his pocket, puts it to his left eye, and begins to check each piece, one by one. After about an hour and a half, he has a good idea of what he's dealing with; he then takes a small precision electronic weighing balance from his case and empties the contents of the packages onto the scale. He makes a few calculations on a sheet of paper. The material is placed in the suitcase along with the balance; the man in the suit signals to the armed guards, and five or six of them board the plane. They start to unload large crates, which they pile up beside the airstrip until the plane leaves again. The whole operation takes most of the day.

The large crates are opened. They contain precision rifles, anti-personnel mines, and bullets that explode on impact, releasing dozens of small, deadly metal balls. The arms are handed out to mercenaries and soldiers, and soon the country finds itself facing another ruthless coup d'état. Whole tribes are murdered, children's legs or arms are blown off by cluster bombs, women are raped. Meanwhile, a long way away—usually in Antwerp or in Amsterdam—earnest men are working with love and dedication, painstakingly cutting the stones, exhilarated by their own skill, hypnotized by the flashes of light that begin to emerge from each new facet of that piece of coal whose structure was transformed by time. Diamond cutting diamond.

On the one hand, women screaming in despair beneath a smoke-shrouded sky. On the other, beautiful old buildings seen through the windows of well-lit rooms.

In 2002, the United Nations adopted a resolution, the Kimberley Process, that tried to trace the origin of diamonds and forbade jewelers from buying any that came from war zones. For some time, the respectable European diamond cutters went back to buying stones from the South African monopoly. However, ways were found of making a diamond "official," and the resolution became a mere sham that allowed politicians to claim that they were doing something to put an end to "blood diamonds," as these became known.

Five years ago, Igor had swapped diamonds for arms and created a small group intended to put an end to a bloody conflict in the north of Liberia, and he had succeeded—only the murderers were killed. Peace returned to the small villages, and the diamonds were sold to jewelers in America, with no awkward questions asked.

When society doesn't act to stop crime, men have the right to do whatever they think correct.

SOMETHING SIMILAR HAD HAPPENED A few minutes ago on that beach. As soon as both murders were discovered, someone would turn to the public and say what they always said:

"We're doing our best to identify the murderer."

So be it. Once again, ever-generous destiny had shown the way ahead. Sacrifice wasn't enough. Besides, when he thought about it, Ewa would have found his absence unbearable, with no one to talk to during the long nights and endless days while she awaited his release. She would weep whenever she thought of him in his cold cell, staring at the blank prison walls. And when the time finally came for them to go and live in the house on the shores of Lake Baikal, they might be too old to experience all the adventures they had planned together.

The policeman comes out of the snack bar and joins him on the pavement.

"Are you still here, sir? Are you lost? Do you need help?"

"No, thank you."

"Like I said, go and have a rest. The sun can be very dangerous at this time of day."

He goes back to the hotel and takes a shower. He asks the receptionist to wake him at four, that way he should be rested enough to recover the necessary clarity of mind not to go doing any more such foolish things. He had very nearly ruined his whole plan.

He phones the concierge and reserves a table on the hotel terrace for when he wakes up; he'd like to drink some tea there undisturbed. Then he lies down, staring up at the ceiling and waiting for sleep to come.

What does it matter where diamonds are from, as long as they shine?

In this world, only love deserves absolutely everything. Nothing else makes sense.

As he has many times before in his life, Igor feels a sense of total freedom. The confusion in his head is slowly disappearing and lucidity is returning.

He had placed his fate in Jesus' hands, and Jesus had decided that he should continue with his mission.

He falls asleep without any feeling of guilt whatsoever.

1:55 P.M.

Gabriela decides to walk very slowly to the place where she is to pick up the boat. She needs to put her thoughts in order, she needs to calm down. She is at a point where not only her most secret dreams might become reality, but also her worst nightmares.

Her phone rings. It's a text message from her agent.

CONGRATULATIONS. ACCEPT WHATEVER THEY OFFER. XXX

She watches the crowds of people who seem to be wandering aimlessly up and down the Boulevard. She, on the other hand, has a goal! She isn't just another of the opportunists who come to Cannes and don't know quite where to start. She has a solid CV, some respectable professional baggage, she's never tried to get ahead in life merely by using her physical attributes, and she has real talent! That's why she's been chosen to meet this famous director, without any help from anyone, without having to dress in a provocative manner, without even having time to rehearse her role. He would, of course, take all these things into consideration.

She stops for a snack—she hasn't eaten anything all day—and as soon as she takes her first sip of coffee, her thoughts seem to come back down to earth.

Why had she been chosen?

What exactly would her role in the film be?

And what if, when Gibson saw the video of the audition, he decided she wasn't the person he was looking for?

"Calm down."

She has nothing to lose, she tells herself, but another voice insists:

"This is your one and only chance."

There's no such thing as a "one and only chance"; life always gives you another chance, but the voice says again:

"Maybe, but how long before another chance comes along? You know how old you are, don't you?"

Of course she does. She's twenty-five, in a world in which actresses, even the most committed, etc. etc.

She doesn't need to go over all that again. She pays for the sandwich and the coffee and makes her way over to the quay, this time trying to control her optimism, telling herself not to refer to other people as "opportunists," mentally reciting the rules of positive thinking that she can remember, anything to avoid dwelling on that all too imminent meeting.

"If you believe in victory, then victory will believe in you."

"Risk everything in the name of chance and keep well away from everything that offers you a world of comfort."

"Talent is a universal gift, but it takes a lot of courage to use it. Don't be afraid to be the best."

It isn't enough to focus on what great teachers have said, she needs help from the heavens. She starts to pray, as she always does when she's anxious. She feels the need to make a promise and decides that, if she does get the role, she will walk all the way from Cannes to the Vatican. If the film gets made. If it's a worldwide success.

No, it would be enough just to get a part in a film with Gibson because that would attract the attention of other directors and producers. Then she will make the promised pilgrimage.

She reaches the appointed place, looks at the sea and again at the message she received from her agent; if her agent already knows about it, that must mean the director is serious. But what did "accept whatever they offer" mean? That she should sleep with the director or with the starring actor?

She's never done that before, but she's prepared to do anything now. Besides, who hasn't dreamed of sleeping with a movie star?

She looks at the sea again. She could have gone back to the apartment and changed her clothes, but she's superstitious. If a pair of jeans and a white T-shirt were enough to get her this far, she should at least wait until the end of the day to change her clothes. She loosens her belt and sits in the lotus position and starts to do some yoga breathing. She breathes slowly, and body, heart, and thoughts all settle into place.

She sees the launch approaching. A man jumps out and says:

"Gabriela Sherry?"

She nods, and the man asks her to go with him. They get into the launch and set off across a sea crowded with yachts of all types and sizes. The man doesn't say another word, as if he were far away, perhaps dreaming about what might be going on in the cabins of those small boats or how good it would be to own one. Gabriela hesitates: her head is full of questions and doubts, and a sympathetic word can often make a stranger into an ally who might help with valuable tips on how to behave. But she doesn't know who he is. He might have influence with Gibson or be merely a no-account assistant who gets landed with jobs like picking up unknown actresses and taking them to his boss.

Best to say nothing.

Five minutes later, they draw up alongside a huge white boat. The name on the prow is *Santiago*. A sailor climbs down a ladder and helps her aboard. She passes through the spacious central reception room in which preparations are under way for what looks like a big party later that night. She walks toward the stern of the ship, where there is a small swimming pool, two tables shaded by parasols, and a few sun loungers. Enjoying the afternoon sun are Gibson and the Star!

"I wouldn't mind sleeping with either of them," she thinks, smiling to herself. She feels more confident, although her heart is beating faster than usual.

The Star looks her up and down and gives her a friendly, reassuring smile. Gibson gives her a firm handshake, gets up, takes one of the chairs from the nearest table, and tells her to sit down.

Then he phones someone and asks for the number of a hotel room. He repeats it out loud, looking at her.

It was just as she imagined—a hotel room.

He switches off his phone.

"When you leave here, go straight to this suite at the Hilton. That's where Hamid Hussein's clothes are on display. You've been invited to tonight's party in Cap d'Antibes."

It wasn't at all as she imagined. The part was hers. And she would be going to a party in Cap d'Antibes, *a party in Cap d'Antibes!*

He turns to the Star.

"What do you think?"

"I think we should hear what she has to say."

Gibson nods and makes a gesture meaning "Tell us a little about yourself." Gabriela starts with the drama course she took and the advertisements she's appeared in. She notices that the two men are no longer listening. They must have heard the same story thousands of times. And yet she can't stop, she's talking faster and faster, feeling that she has nothing more to say and that this chance of a lifetime depends on finding just the right word, which she is patently failing to do. She takes a deep breath and tries to appear at ease; she wants to seem witty and so she makes a joke, but she's incapable of departing from the script her agent taught her to follow in such interviews.

After two minutes, Gibson interrupts her.

"That's great, but we know all that from your CV. Why don't you talk about you?"

Some inner barrier suddenly crumbles. Instead of panicking, her voice grows calmer and steadier.

"I'm just one of millions of people in the world who have always dreamed of being on a yacht like this, looking at the sea, and talking about the possibility of working with at least one of you gentlemen. And you both know that. I doubt there's anything else I might say that will change anything very much. Am I single? Yes. But as is the case with all single women, there's a man back home who's madly in love with me and is waiting for me in Chicago right now, hoping that things here will all go horribly wrong."

Both men laugh, and she relaxes a little more.

"I want to get as far as I can, although I know I'm almost at the limit of what's possible, given that in the world of movies, my age is already against me. I know there are lots of people out there with as much or more talent than me, but I was chosen—why I don't know—and I've decided to run with it. This might be my last chance, and perhaps the fact that I'm saying this now will decrease my value, but I have no choice. All my life, I've imagined a moment like this: doing an audition, getting chosen, and being able to work with real professionals. It's finally happened. If it goes no further than this meeting and I return home empty-handed, at least I know I got here because of two qualities: integrity and perseverance.

"I'm my own best friend and my own worst enemy. Before coming here, I was thinking that I didn't deserve it, that I wouldn't be able to meet your expectations, and that you had probably chosen the wrong candidate. At the same time, my heart was telling me that I was being rewarded because I hadn't given up and had fought to the end."

She looks away and suddenly feels an intense desire to cry, but controls herself because that might be seen as emotional blackmail. The Star's mellow voice breaks the silence.

"There *are* honest people in the movie world, people who value professionalism, just as there are in any industry. That's why I've got where I am today, and the same with our director here. I've been through exactly what you're going through now. We know how you feel."

Her whole life passes before her eyes. All the years of seeking without finding, of knocking on doors that wouldn't open, of asking and never getting an answer and being met with blank indifference, as if she didn't exist. All the nos she had heard when no one even seemed to notice she was alive and at least deserved a response.

"I mustn't cry."

She thinks about all the people who have told her over the years that she's chasing an impossible dream and who, if this turned out right, would be sure to say: "I always knew you had talent!" Her lips start to tremble. It's as if all these thoughts were suddenly flowing out of her heart. She's glad to have had the guts to show that she's human and frail and that being chosen has made a huge difference to her soul. If Gibson were now to change his mind about her, she could take the launch back to shore with no regrets. At the moment of battle, she had shown real courage.

She depends on other people. It's taken her a long time to learn this lesson, but she's finally accepted that it's true. She knows people who are proud of their emotional independence, although the truth is they're as fragile as she is and weep in private and never ask for help. They believe in the unwritten rule that says, "The world is for the strong" and "Only the fittest survive." If that were true, human beings would never have survived because, as a species, we require care and protection for several years. Her father once told her that we only acquire some ability to survive alone by the age of nine, whereas a giraffe takes a mere five hours and a bee achieves independence in less than five minutes.

"What are you thinking?" asks the Star.

"That I don't need to pretend I'm strong, which is an enormous relief. I used to have a lot of problems with relationships because I thought I knew better than anyone else how to get where I wanted. All my boyfriends hated me for this, and I couldn't understand why. Once, though, when I was on tour with a play, I came down with the most terrible flu and couldn't leave my room, even though I was terrified that someone else would take my part. I couldn't eat, I was delirious with fever, and eventually they called a doctor, who ordered me home. I thought I had lost both my job and the respect of my colleagues. But that wasn't the case at all: they showered me with flowers and phone calls. They all wanted to know how I was. Suddenly, I realized that the people I believed to be my rivals, competing for the same place in the spotlight, were really concerned about me. One of the other actresses sent me a card on which she'd written the words of a doctor who went abroad to work in some far-off country. He wrote:

" 'We've all heard about an illness in Central Africa called sleeping sickness. What we should also know is that a similar disease exists that attacks the soul. It's very dangerous because the early stages often go unnoticed. At the first sign of indifference or lack of enthusiasm, take note! The only preventive against this disease is the realization that the soul suffers, suffers greatly, when we force it to live superficially. The soul loves all things beautiful and deep.' "

WORDS. THE STAR THINKS OF his favorite line from a poem, one that he learned when still at school, and which frightens him more and more as time passes: "You would have to give up all else, I alone would expect to be your sole and exclusive standard." Choosing is perhaps the most difficult thing any human being has to do. As the actress tells her story, he sees his own experiences being reflected back at him.

He remembers his first big chance, which he won thanks to his talent as a theater actor. He remembers how his life changed from one minute to the next, and the fame that overtook him so fast that he didn't really have time to adapt and ended up accepting invitations to places he shouldn't have gone to and rejecting meetings with people who would have helped him go much further in his career. Then there was the money he earned, which wasn't actually that much, but which gave him a sense that he could do anything; there were the expensive presents, the forays into an unfamiliar world, the private planes, the five-star restaurants, and the hotel suites that resembled the palatial rooms of kings and queens as imagined by a child. There were the first reviews, full of respect and praise and words that touched his heart and soul; there were the letters that flooded in from around the world and which he used to answer individually, even arranging to meet some of the women who sent him their photos, until he realized that he simply couldn't keep up that pace, and his agent terrified him by warning him that he could easily become the victim of some entrapment. Nevertheless, even now he still gets a special pleasure out of meeting the fans who have followed every step of his career, who create Web pages devoted to his work, distribute little magazines describing everything that's going on in his life—the positive things, that is—and defend him against any attacks in the press, when some performance of his doesn't receive the praise it deserves.

And with the passing years, what had once seemed a miracle or the luckiest of chances and which he had always promised himself he would never become enslaved by, has gradually become his sole reason to go on living. Then he looks ahead and feels a twinge of anxiety that it all might end one day. There were always younger actors prepared to accept less money in exchange for more work and more visibility. He's noticed that people talk only about the great film that propelled him to fame and which everyone knows about, even though he's made another ninety-nine films since that no one really remembers.

The financial conditions are no longer the same either because he made the initial mistake of thinking he would always have work and forced his agent to keep his fee very high. As a result, he got fewer and fewer offers, even though now he charges only half his normal fee to appear in a film. Feelings of despair are beginning to stir in a world which, up until then, had been made up entirely of the hope that he would get ever farther, ever higher, and ever more quickly. He cannot allow himself to lose his value just like that, and so now, whenever a script arrives, regardless of its quality, he has to say that he really loves the part they're offering him and that he is willing to do it even if they're unable to offer him his usual fee. The producers pretend to believe him, and his agent pretends that he's managed to pull the wool over their eyes, but he knows that his "product" needs to keep being seen at festivals like this one, always busy, always polite, always slightly distant, as movie legends should be.

His press officer has suggested that he should be photographed kissing a famous actress so that the resulting photo can appear on the cover of one of the scandal rags. They've already been in contact with the actress in question, who is also in need of a little extra publicity, so now it's simply a matter of choosing the right moment during tonight's gala supper. The clinch should appear spontaneous, although they'll have to be sure there's a photographer nearby, without, of course, seeming to be aware that they're being watched. Later on, when the photos are published, they'll hit the headlines again, denying any love interest and declaring that the photo was an invasion of privacy; lawyers will start legal proceedings against the magazines, and the press officers of both parties will do their best to keep the affair alive for as long as possible.

Despite his many years of work and despite being internationally famous, his situation is not so very different from that of this young actress.

You would have to give up all else, I alone would expect to be your sole and exclusive standard.

GIBSON INTERRUPTS THE THIRTY-SECOND SILENCE that has fallen upon this perfect scene: the yacht, the sun, the iced drinks, the cries of the seagulls, the cooling breeze.

"I assume you'd like to know about the role you'll be playing because the title of the film could change between now and its première. Well, you'll be playing opposite him."

And he indicates the Star.

"That is, you'll be playing one of the principal roles. Your next question, logically enough, must be: why me and not some big-name movie star?"

"Exactly."

"Money. For the script I've been asked to direct, and which will be the first film produced by Hamid Hussein, we have a very limited budget, half of which will go on promotion rather than on the final product. So we need a big name to pull in the crowds and a complete unknown, who'll be cheap, but will get lots of media attention. This isn't anything new. Ever since the movie industry became a force in the world, the studios have always done this in order to keep alive the idea that fame and money are synonymous. I remember, when I was a boy, seeing those great Hollywood mansions and thinking that all actors must earn a fortune.

"Well, it's a lie. There are maybe ten or perhaps twenty stars worldwide who can honestly say that they do earn a fortune, the rest live on appearances: in a house rented by the studio, wearing clothes and jewelry lent by couturiers and jewelers, driving cars on short-term loan from companies who want their name to be associated with the high life. The studio pays for all that glamour, and the actors earn very little. This isn't the case of our friend here, of course, but it will be with you."

THE STAR DOESN'T KNOW IF Gibson is being sincere and if he really does include him among the major stars, or if he's just being sarcastic. Not that it matters, just as long as they sign the contract, the producer doesn't change his mind at the last minute, the screenwriters manage to deliver the script on time, they keep strictly to the budget, and an excellent PR campaign is set in motion. He's seen hundreds of projects come to nothing; that's just a fact of life. However, his last film went almost unnoticed by the public, and he desperately needs a runaway success. And Gibson is in a position to produce just that.

"I accept," says the young woman.

"We'll discuss everything with your agent. You'll sign an exclusive contract with us. For the first film, you'll earn five thousand dollars a month for a year, and you'll have to attend parties and be promoted by our PR department, go wherever we send you and say what we want you to and not what you think. Is that clear?"

Gabriela nods. What could she say? A secretary in Europe could earn five thousand dollars a month, but it was either take it or leave it, and she doesn't want to appear even a tiny bit hesitant. She understands the rules of the game.

"So," Gibson says, "you'll be living like a millionairess and behaving like a big star, but always remember: none of that is true. If all goes well, we'll increase your salary to ten thousand dollars for the next film. Then we'll talk again because you'll probably be thinking: 'One day, I'll get my revenge.' Naturally, your agent has heard our terms and knows what to expect. Or perhaps you didn't realize that."

"It doesn't matter, and I have no intention of seeking revenge."

Gibson pretends not to have heard.

"I didn't call you here to talk about your test: it was great, the best I've seen in a long time. The casting director thought the same. I called you here to make sure you understand, from the start, just what you're getting into. After their first film, when they feel like the world is at their feet, a lot of actresses or actors want to change the rules. But they've signed contracts and know that's impossible. Then they fall into a kind of black depression, go into auto-destruct mode, that kind of thing. So our policy now is to set out plainly how it's going to be. If you're successful, you'll have to learn to live with two women: one of them will be adored by people around the world, while the other will be constantly aware that she has no power at all.

"So, before you go to the Hilton to collect your clothes for the night, think long and hard about the consequences. When you enter that hotel suite, you'll find four copies of a vast contract waiting for you. Before you sign it, the world is yours and you can do what you like with your life, but the moment you sign, you're no longer the mistress of anything. We will control everything from the way you cut your hair to where you eat, even if you're not hungry. Obviously you can use your new-won fame to earn money from advertising, which is why people accept these conditions."

The two men get up. Gibson asks the Star:

"Do you think you'll enjoy acting with her?"

"She'll be great. She showed real feeling in a situation where most people are simply trying to look competent."

"Oh, and, by the way, don't go thinking this yacht is mine," says Gibson, after calling someone to accompany her to the launch that will return her to shore.

She gets the message.

"Let's go up to the terrace and have a coffee," says Ewa.

"But the show starts in only an hour from now, and you know what the traffic's like."

"There's still time for a cup of coffee."

They go up the stairs, turn right, and walk to the end of the corridor. The security guard there knows them already and barely acknowledges them. They walk past glass cases full of jewelry studded with diamonds, rubies, and emeralds, and emerge into the sunlight on the first-floor terrace. The same very famous jewelry firm hires the area every year to receive friends, celebrities, and journalists. It's furnished in the very best of taste, and there's always a table groaning with a constantly replenished supply of delicacies. They sit down at a table shaded by a parasol. A waiter comes over, and they order a sparkling mineral water and an espresso. The waiter asks if they would like something from the buffet, but they decline, saying that they've already eaten. In less than two minutes, he's back with their order.

"Is everything all right?" he asks.

"Yes, thank you, excellent."

"No," thinks Ewa, "things couldn't be worse, although at least the coffee's good."

Hamid knows that something strange is going on with his wife, but prefers to leave that conversation for another time. He doesn't want to think about it. He doesn't want to risk hearing something along the lines of "I'm leaving you." He is disciplined enough to control his feelings.

At one of the other tables sits one of the most famous designers in the world, with his camera beside him. He's staring into space, as if hoping to make it clear that he doesn't want to be disturbed. No one approaches him, and whenever some ill-advised person attempts to do so, the hotel's PR lady, a pleasant woman in her fifties, asks them politely to leave him alone; he needs a respite from the constant barrage of models, journalists, clients, and impresarios.

Hamid remembers their first meeting, so many years ago now that it seems like an eternity. He had been in Paris for eleven months, made a few friends in the fashion world, knocked on various doors and, thanks to contacts furnished by the sheikh (who may have known no one in that particular world, but had influential friends in high places), had landed a job as a designer for one of the most respected names in haute couture. Instead of making sketches based on the materials he was given, he used to stay at the studio until late at night, working with the fabrics he had brought from his own country. During that period, he was twice summoned home. The first occasion was when he learned that his father had died and left him the small family business. Even before he'd had time to think about it, he was informed by one of the sheikh's emissaries that someone would be taking over the business and making the necessary investments to ensure that it prospered, but that ownership would remain in his name.

He asked why, since the sheikh had shown no knowledge of or interest in the subject.

"A French luggage manufacturer is setting up business here. The first thing they did was seek out local fabrics, which they've promised to use in some of their luxury goods. So not only do we already have one client, we can continue to honor our traditions and keep control of the raw material."

Hamid returned to Paris knowing that his father's soul was in Paradise and that his memory would remain in the land he had so loved. He continued working late into the night, making designs with Bedouin themes and experimenting with the fabrics he had brought back with him. If that French company—known for its innovative designs and good taste—was showing an interest in local products, then news of this would soon reach the capital of fashion and there was sure to be a big demand. It was only a matter of time, but news traveled fast.

One morning, he was called in to see the director. This was the first time he had entered that inner sanctum, the great couturier's office, and he was astonished to see how untidy it was. There were newspapers everywhere, papers piled high on the couturier's antique desk, a vast quantity of photos taken of him with various celebrities, framed magazine covers, fabric samples, and a vase full of white feathers of all sizes.

"You're very good at what you do. I had a look at the sketches you leave around for all to see. I'd be careful about doing that if I were you. You never know when someone might change jobs and steal any good ideas they picked up here."

Hamid didn't like to think he was being spied on, but he said nothing, and the great couturier went on:

"Why do I think you're good? Because you come from a country where people dress very differently, and you're beginning to understand how to adapt those fashions to the West. There's just one problem: we can't buy those fabrics here; also your designs have religious connotations, and fashion is, above all, about clothing the body, although it does inevitably reflect a great deal of what's going in the soul as well."

He went over to one of the piles of magazines, and as if he knew exactly what was there, he picked up a particular copy, possibly bought from the *bouquinistes*—the booksellers who have been selling their wares on the banks of the Seine since the days of Napoleon. It was an old *Paris Match* with a picture of Christian Dior on the cover.

"What makes this man a legend? I'll tell you: his ability to understand human beings. Of all the many fashion revolutions, one merits special mention. Immediately after the Second World War, when cloth was in such short supply in Europe that there was barely enough to make clothes at all, he started designing dresses that required an enormous amount of fabric. By doing so, he was not only showing off a beautiful woman beautifully dressed, he was selling the dream that we would once again return to a time of elegance, abundance, and plenty. He was attacked and insulted for doing this, but he knew he was going in the right direction, which is always the opposite direction to everyone else."

He put the magazine back exactly where he had taken it from and returned, holding another one.

"And here is Coco Chanel. She was abandoned by her parents, became a cabaret singer, and was just the kind of woman who could expect only the worst from life. But she seized the one chance she had—in her case, a series of rich lovers—and transformed herself into the most important female couturier of her day. What did she do? She liberated women from the slavery of corsets, those instruments of torture that imprisoned the torso and prevented all natural movement. She made only one mistake: she concealed her past, when that would, in fact, have helped her become an even greater legend—the woman who had survived despite all."

He put that magazine back in its place too. Then he went on:

"You might ask: why didn't they do that before? We'll never know. People must have tried—couturiers who have been completely forgotten by history because they failed to reflect in their collections the spirit of the times they were living in. Chanel needed more than creative talent and rich lovers to have the impact she had. Society had to be ready for the great feminist revolution that took place at the same time."

The couturier paused.

"Now it's the turn of the Middle East, precisely because all the tension and the fear that keep the world in limbo are coming from your country. I know this because I'm the director of this company. After all, everything starts with a meeting of the main suppliers of dyes."

HAMID GLANCES AGAIN AT THE designer sitting alone on the terrace, his camera resting on the armchair beside him. Perhaps he had noticed Hamid arrive and is now wondering just where Hamid got the money that had enabled him to become his biggest competitor.

The man now staring into space and feigning indifference had done everything possible to prevent Hamid from being admitted into the Fédération. He believed Hamid was being financed by oil money and felt that this constituted unfair competition. He didn't know that the director of the label Hamid was working for at the time had offered him a better job (not that "better" meant his name would appear anywhere; the company had contracted another designer to shine in the spotlight and on the catwalk), nor did he know that two months after this and eight months after the death of his father, Hamid had been summoned to a face-to-face meeting with the sheikh.

WHEN HAMID ARRIVED HOME, HE found it hard to recognize the city that had once been his. The skeletons of skyscrapers lined the city's one avenue; the traffic was unbearable; the old airport was in near chaos; but the sheikh's idea was beginning to take shape. The city would be a place of peace in the midst of war, an investment paradise in the midst of turbulent financial markets, the visible face of a nation that so many people took pleasure in criticizing, humiliating, and stereotyping. Other countries in the region had also now begun to believe in that city being built in the middle of the desert, and money was starting to flow in, first in a trickle and then like a rushing river.

The palace, however, was the same, although another much larger one was being built not far from there. Hamid arrived at the meeting in an excellent mood, saying that he had just received an excellent job offer and no longer needed the sheikh's financial help; indeed, he would pay back every penny invested in him.

"Hand in your resignation," said the sheikh.

Hamid didn't understand. He knew that the business his father had left him was doing well, but he had other dreams for his future. However, he couldn't defy this man who had done so much to help him— not a second time.

"At our first meeting, I was able to say no to Your Highness because I was defending my father's rights, which were always paramount. Now, though, I must bow to your will. If you think you have lost money by investing in my work, I will do whatever you ask. I will come home and look after my inheritance. If I have to give up my dream in order to honor the code of my tribe, I will do so."

He spoke these words without a tremor. He dared not show any weakness before a man who so respected other men's strength.

"I'm not asking you to come home. The fact that you were promoted is a sign that you're ready to set up your own company. That is what I want you to do."

"To set up my own company?" thought Hamid. "Did I hear him right?"

"More and more of the big fashion companies are setting up business here," the sheikh went on. "And they're no fools. Our women are beginning to change the way they think and dress. Fashion has had an even bigger impact on our region than foreign investment. I've spoken to men and women who know about these things. I'm just an old Bedouin who, when he saw his first car, thought it would have to be fed like a camel.

"I'd like foreigners to read our poets, listen to our music, to sing and dance to the songs that were passed down from generation to generation by our ancestors, but no one, it seems, is interested in that. There is only one way in which they can learn to respect our tradition, and that is via the world in which you work. If they can understand who we are by the way we dress, they will eventually understand everything else."

The following day, Hamid met a group of investors from various other countries. They placed at his disposal an enormous sum of money and gave him a deadline by which it had to be repaid. They asked him if he was ready and prepared to accept the challenge.

Hamid asked for time to think. He went to his father's grave and prayed all afternoon and evening. That night, he walked in the desert, felt the wind freezing his bones, then returned to the hotel where the foreign investors were staying. "Blessed be that which gives your children wings and roots," says an Arabic proverb.

He needed his roots. There is a place in the world where we are born, where we learn our mother tongue and discover how our ancestors overcame the problems they had to face. There always comes a point when we feel responsible for that place.

He needed wings too. They reveal to us the endless horizons of the imagination, they carry us to our dreams and to distant places. It is our wings that allow us to know the roots of our fellow men and to learn from them.

He asked for inspiration from God and began to pray. Two hours later, he remembered a conversation he had overheard between his father and a friend in his father's shop:

"This morning, my son asked me for money to buy a sheep. Should I help him, do you think?"

"Since it clearly isn't a matter of urgency, wait another week before giving him your answer."

"But I have the means to help him now. What difference will a week make?"

"A very great difference indeed. Experience has taught me that people only give value to a thing if they have, at some point, been uncertain as to whether or not they'll get it."

Hamid made the investors wait a week and then accepted the challenge. He needed people who would take care of the money and invest it as he wanted. He needed staff, preferably people who came from his own village. He needed another year in the job he was doing, so that he could learn what he still needed to know. That was all.

"EVERYTHING STARTS WITH A MEETING of the main suppliers of dyes."

Well, that isn't exactly true: everything begins when the companies involved in studying market trends (*cabinets de tendence* in French, "trend adapters" in English) take note of the different things—among them fashion—in which each layer of society is currently interested. This research is based on interviews with consumers, the close monitoring of samples, but, above all, on careful observation of a particular cohort of people—usually aged between twenty and thirty—who go to nightclubs, hang out on the streets, and read the blogs on the Internet. They never look at what's in the shop windows, even at name brands, because everything there has already reached the general public and is therefore condemned to die.

The trend adapters want to know what will be the *next* thing to capture the consumers' imagination? Young people don't have enough money to buy luxury goods and so have to invent new ways of dressing. Since they live glued to their computer screens, they share their interests with like-minded others, and these interests can often become a kind of virus that infects the whole community. Young people influence their parents' views of politics, literature, and music, and not, as ingenuous adults believe, the other way round. However, parents influence young people's "system of values." Adolescents may be rebellious by nature, but they always believe the family is right; they may dress strangely and enjoy listening to singers who howl and break guitars, but that's as far as it goes. They don't have the courage to go any further and provoke a real revolution in behavior.

"They did that in the past, but, fortunately, that particular wave has passed and returned to the sea."

All these studies of market trends show that society is now heading toward a more conservative style, far from the dangers posed by suffragettes (the women at the beginning of the twentieth century who fought for and achieved the right to vote) or by hairy, unhygienic hippies (a group of crazies who believed that peace and free love were real possibilities).

IN 1960, FOR EXAMPLE, THE world was caught up in the bloody wars of the post-colonial era, terrified by the threat of nuclear war, and although we were also living through a period of economic prosperity, we were all desperately in need of a little joy. Just as Christian Dior had understood that the hope of future abundance could be expressed through clothes using yards of material, the designers of the sixties went in search of a combination of colors that would lift people's morale and came to the conclusion that red and violet were simultaneously calming and stimulating.

Forty years later, the collective view had changed completely: the world was no longer under the threat of war, but of grave environmental problems. Designers were opting for colors drawn from the natural world: the sands of the desert, the jungles, the sea. Between these two periods, various other trends—psychedelic, futuristic, aristocratic, nostalgic—arose and vanished.

Before the great designer collections are fully defined, these studies of market trends are used to give a snapshot of the world's current state of mind. It seems now that—despite wars, famine in Africa, terrorism, the violation of human rights, and the arrogant attitude of certain developed countries—our main preoccupation is saving poor planet Earth from the many threats created by human society.

"Ecology. Save the planet. How ridiculous."

Hamid knows, however, that there's no point in fighting the collective unconscious. The colors, the accessories, the fabrics, the so-called charity events attended by the Superclass, the books being published, the music being played on the radio, the documentaries made by ex-politicians, the new films, the material used to make shoes, the new bio-fuels, the petitions handed in to members of parliament and congressmen, the bonds being sold by the largest of the world banks, everything appears to focus on one thing: saving the planet. Fortunes are made overnight; large multinationals are given space in the press because of some completely irrelevant action they are taking; unscrupulous NGOs place advertisements on the major TV channels and receive hundreds of millions of dollars in donations because everyone seems obsessed with the fate of the Earth.

Whenever he reads articles in newspapers or magazines written by politicians using global warming or the destruction of the environment as a platform for their electoral campaigns, he thinks:

"How can we be so arrogant? The planet is, was, and always will be stronger than us. *We* can't destroy *it*; if we overstep the mark, the planet will simply erase us from its surface and carry on existing. Why don't they start talking about not letting the planet destroy us?

"Because 'saving the planet' gives a sense of power, action, and nobility. Whereas 'not letting the planet destroy *us*' might lead to feelings of despair and impotence, and to a realization of just how very limited our capabilities are."

However, this is what the trends reveal, and fashion must adapt to the desires of the consumers. The dye works were already busy producing what were deemed to be the best colors for the next collection. The cloth manufacturers were on the hunt for natural fibers; the creators of accessories such as belts, bags, glasses, and wristwatches were doing their best to adapt, or at least pretend to adapt, by publishing leaflets printed on recycled paper explaining the lengths they had gone to in order to preserve the environment. All of this would be shown to the major designers at the largest of the fabric shows—closed to the public—and bearing the evocative name of "Première Vision."

After that, each designer would apply his or her creativity to the new collection and feel that haute couture was something inventive, original, and different. Not true. They were all merely slavishly following what the market trends dictated. The more important the brand, the less willing they were to take any risks, given that the jobs of hundreds of people around the world depended on the decisions of a small group of people, the Superclass of the haute-couture world, which was already weary of pretending that it had something different to sell every six months.

THE FIRST DESIGNS WERE MADE by "misunderstood geniuses" who dreamed of one day having their own label. They worked for approximately six to eight months, at first with pencil and paper, then with prototypes made out of cheap fabric, which could be photographed on models and analyzed by the directors. Out of every one hundred prototypes, about twenty would be chosen for the next show. Adjustments were made—new buttons, a different cut of sleeve, or some unusual stitching.

Then more photos would be taken, this time with the models sitting, lying down, or walking, and still further adjustments, because remarks such as "only suitable for the catwalk" could ruin a whole collection and place a particular label's reputation at risk. During this process, some of the "misunderstood geniuses" were summarily dismissed, with no right to compensation because they were only there as trainees. The more talented of those who remained would have to rethink their creations several times, aware that, however successful the design, only the name of the label would be mentioned.

They all vowed revenge one day. They told themselves that eventually they would open their own shop and get the recognition they deserved. Meanwhile, they smiled and continued working as if they were thrilled to have been chosen. As the final models were being selected, more people were dismissed and more people taken on (for the next collection), and finally, the genuine fabrics were used to make the clothes that would appear on the catwalk, as if this were the first time they were being shown to the public. This, of course, was part of the legend because, by then, retailers worldwide already had in their hands photos of the various designs taken from every conceivable angle, as well as details of the accessories, the texture of the fabric, the recommended retail price, and the addresses of suppliers. Depending on the brand's size and importance, the "new collection" was already being produced on a large scale in various countries around the world.

Then, finally, the big day arrived, or, rather, the three weeks that marked the beginning of a new era (which, as they all knew, would last only six months). It began in London, then went on to Milan, and ended in Paris. Journalists were invited from all over the world, photographers jockeyed for the best places, and everything was treated with the greatest secrecy; newspapers and magazines devoted pages and pages to the latest designs; women were dazzled, and men regarded with a certain scorn what they thought of as a mere "fashion item" and thought sourly about how they would have to spend a few thousand dollars on something of not the slightest importance to them, but which their wives considered to be an emblem of the Superclass.

A week later, something that had been described as "exclusive" was already available in shops around the world. No one asked how it had managed to travel so fast and be produced in such a short space of time. The legend, however, is more important than the reality.

The consumers didn't realize these new fashions were created by those who were merely following the existing fashions, that exclusivity was just a lie they chose to believe, that many of the collections praised by the specialist press belonged to the large manufacturers of luxury goods, who supported those same magazines and journals by placing full-page advertisements. There were, of course, exceptions, and, after a few years of struggle, Hamid Hussein was one of them, and therein lay his power.

HE NOTICES THAT EWA IS again checking her mobile phone, which she doesn't normally do. The fact is that she hates the thing, perhaps because it reminds her of a past relationship, a period of her life about which he still knows little or nothing because neither of them ever refers to it. He glances at his watch. They still have time to finish their coffee without rushing. He looks again at the other designer. If only it did all begin with a meeting of dye manufacturers and end on the catwalk, but that wasn't the case.

HE AND THE MAN NOW sitting alone and staring out at the horizon first met at Première Vision. Hamid was still working for the major fashion house that had taken him on as a designer, although the sheikh had, by then, already started organizing the small army of eleven people who would put into practice the idea of using fashion as a window onto their world, their religion, and their culture.

"Most of the time we stand here listening to explanations of how to present simple things in the most complicated way possible," Hamid had said.

They were walking past stands displaying the latest fabrics, the latest revolutionary techniques, the colors that would be used over the next two years, the ever more sophisticated accessories—platinum belt buckles, push-button credit card holders, watch straps the size of which could be minutely regulated with the help of a diamond-encrusted dial.

The couturier looked him up and down.

"The world always was and always will be complicated."

"I don't think so, and if I ever leave the company I'm working for now, it will be to open my own business, which will go against all these beliefs."

The couturier laughed.

"You know what the world of fashion is like. You've heard of the Fédération, haven't you, well, it takes foreigners a very, very long time to get accepted."

The Fédération Française de la Couture was one of the world's most exclusive clubs. It decided who could or couldn't take part in the Fashion Weeks in Paris, as well as setting the parameters to be followed by participants. First created in 1868, it had enormous power. It trademarked the expression "haute couture" so that no one outside the Fédération could use it without running the risk of being sued. It published the ten thousand copies of the Official Catalogue for the two great annual events, decided which journalists would receive the two thousand press passes, selected the major buyers, and selected the venue for each show according to the importance of the designer.

"Yes, I know what the world of fashion is like," said Hamid, bringing the conversation to a close. He sensed that the man he was talking to would, in the future, be a great designer, but he knew, too, that they would never be friends.

Six months later, everything was ready for his great adventure. He resigned from his job, opened his first shop in St-Germain-des-Près, and started to fight as best he could. He lost many battles, but realized one thing: he could not bow to the tyranny of the companies who dictated the fashion trends. He had to be original, and he succeeded because he brought with him the simplicity of the Bedouin, a knowledge of the desert, everything he had learned at the company where he had worked for over a year, as well as the advice of certain financial experts, together with textiles that were completely new and original.

Two years later, he had opened five or six large shops throughout France and had been accepted by the Fédération, not just because of his talent, but through the sheikh's contacts, whose emissaries controlled which French companies could open branches in their country.

More water flowed under the bridge, people changed their minds, presidents were elected or stepped down, the new technology grew in popularity, the Internet began to dominate world communications, public opinion became more influential in all spheres of human activity, luxury and glamour regained the position they had lost. His work grew and expanded. He wasn't just involved now in fashion, but in accessories, furniture, beauty products, watches, and exclusive fabrics.

Hamid was now the master of an empire, and all those who had invested in his dream were richly rewarded with the dividends paid to shareholders. He continued to supervise much of what his businesses produced, attended the most important photo shoots, still designed most of the clothes, and visited the desert three times a year to pray at his father's grave and give an account of his activities to the sheikh. Now he has taken up a new challenge; he is going to produce a film.

He glances at his watch again and tells Ewa it's time to go. She asks if it really is so very important.

"No, it's not, but I'd like to be there."

Ewa gets to her feet. Hamid takes one last look at the famous couturier, sitting alone and contemplating the Mediterranean, oblivious to everything.

The young all have the same dream: to save the world. Some quickly forget this dream, convinced that there are more important things to do, like having a family, earning money, traveling, and learning a foreign language. Others, though, decide that it really is possible to make a difference in society and to shape the world we will hand on to future generations.

They start by choosing their profession: politicians (whose initial impulse always stems from a desire to help their local community), social activists (who believe that the root of all crime lies in class differences), artists (who believe there's no hope at all and that we'll just have to start again from zero) . . . and policemen.

Savoy had been sure he could be a useful member of society. Having read a great deal of detective fiction, he imagined that once the baddies were all behind bars, the goodies would be able to enjoy their place in the sun forever. He went to police college where he studied assiduously, received excellent marks for his theory exams, prepared himself physically for dangerous situations, and trained as a sharpshooter, although he hoped never to have to kill anyone.

During his first year, he felt that he was learning about the nitty-gritty of the profession. His colleagues complained about low salaries, incompetent judges, other people's preconceived ideas about the job, and the almost complete absence of any real action in their particular area. As time passed, life as a policeman and the complaints continued more or less the same, apart from the addition of one thing: paper.

Endless reports on the where or how or why of a particular incident. A simple case of someone dumping some rubbish, for example, required the rubbish in question to be meticulously searched for evidence of the guilty party's identity (there are always clues, like envelopes or plane tickets), the area then had to be photographed, a map drawn, the perpetrator identified and sent a friendly warning, followed by a rather less friendly warning and, if the transgressor refused to take the matter seriously, by a visit to court, where statements were taken and sentences handed down, all of which, of course, required the services of competent lawyers. Two whole years might pass before the case was finally relegated to the files, with no real consequences for either side.

Murders, on the other hand, were extremely rare. Recent statistics showed that most of the crime in Cannes involved fights between rich kids in expensive nightclubs, break-ins at holiday apartments, traffic offenses, black marketeering, and domestic disputes. He should, of course, be pleased about this. In an ever more troubled world, the South of France was an oasis of peace, even during the Festival when Cannes was invaded by thousands of foreigners visiting the beach or buying and selling films. The previous year, he'd had to deal with four cases of suicide (these involved about fifteen pounds of paperwork) and two violent attacks that had ended in death. And now there had been likely two deaths in a matter of hours. What *was* going on?

THE BODYGUARDS HAD DISAPPEARED BEFORE they could even give a statement, and Savoy made a mental note to send a written reprimand—as soon as he had time—to the officers in charge of the case. After all, they had let slip the only two witnesses to what had happened, because the woman in the waiting room clearly knew nothing. It took him no time at all to establish that she had been standing some way away when the poison had been administered, and that all she wanted was to take advantage of the situation to get close to a famous film distributor. All he has to do now is to read more paper.

He's sitting in the hospital waiting room with two reports before him. The first, written by the doctor on duty, consists of two pages of boring technical details, analyzing the damage to the organism of the man now in the intensive care unit: poisoning by an unknown substance (currently being studied in the laboratory) and which was injected into the bloodstream through a needle that perforated the left lumbar region. The only agent on the list of poisons capable of provoking such a rapid and violent reaction is strychnine, but this normally sends the body into convulsions. According to the security men in the tent, and as was confirmed both by the paramedics and by the woman in the waiting room, there were no such symptoms. On the contrary, they had noticed an immediate paralysis of the muscles and a stiffening of the chest, and the victim had been able to be carried from the tent without attracting the attention of the other guests.

The second, much longer report was from the EPCTF (European Police Chiefs Task Force) and Europol, who had been following the victim's every move since he set foot on European soil. The agents were taking turns during the surveillance, and, at the time of the incident, the victim was being watched by a black agent originally from Guadeloupe, but who looked Jamaican.

"Even so, the person charged with watching him noticed nothing. Or, rather, at that precise moment, his view was partially blocked by a man walking past holding a glass of pineapple juice."

Although the victim had no police record and was known in the movie world as one of the few revolutionary film distributors around, his business was, in fact, just a front for something far more profitable. According to Europol, Javits Wild had been just another second-rate film producer; then, five years ago, he was recruited by a cartel specializing in the distribution of cocaine in the Americas to help them change dirty money into clean.

"It's starting to get interesting."

For the first time, Savoy feels pleased by what he's reading. He may have an important case on his hands, far removed from the routine of fly-tipping, domestic disputes, holiday apartments being burgled, and those two murders a year.

He knows how these things work. He knows what the report is talking about. Traffickers earn fortunes from selling their products, but because they can't show where that money came from, they can't open bank accounts; buy apartments, cars, or jewels; or transfer large sums of money from one country to another because the government is sure to ask: "How did this guy get to be so rich? Where did he earn all this money?"

To overcome this obstacle, they use a financial mechanism known as money laundering, that is, transforming money earned by criminal means into respectable financial assets which can then become part of the economic system and generate still more money. The expression is said to have originated with the Chicago gangster Al Capone, who bought a chain of laundries known as the Sanitary Cleaning Shops and then used those shops as a front for the money he was earning from the illegal sale of drinks during the Prohibition Era. So if anyone asked him how he came to be so rich, he could always say: "People are washing more clothes than ever. This line of business has turned out to be a really good investment."

"He did everything right," thought Savoy, "apart from forgetting to file a tax return."

Money laundering was used not only for drugs, but for many other things: politicians getting commission on the over-invoicing of construction work, terrorists needing to finance operations in various parts of the world, companies wanting to conceal profits and losses from shareholders, individuals who deem income tax to be an unacceptable invention. Once, all you had to do was open a numbered account in a tax haven, but then governments started drawing up a series of mutual collaboration treaties, and the money launderers had to adapt to these new times.

One thing was certain, however: the criminals were always several steps ahead of the authorities and the tax inspectors.

How does it work now? Well, in a far more elegant, sophisticated, and creative way. They just have to follow three clear stages: placement, layering, and integration. Take several oranges, make some juice, and serve it up—no one need ever suspect where the fruit came from.

Making the orange juice is relatively easy: you set up a series of accounts and start moving small amounts of money from one bank to another, often using computer-generated systems, with the aim of bringing it all together again at some future date. The routes taken are so circuitous that it's almost impossible to follow the traces left by the electronic impulses because, once the money has been deposited, it ceases to be paper and is transformed into digital codes composed of just two numbers: 0 and 1.

Savoy thinks about his own bank account; the little he has in there is entirely at the mercy of codes traveling up and down wires. What if the bank decided, from one moment to the next, to change the whole system? What if that new program didn't work? How could he prove he had the amount of money he said he had? How could he convert those numbers into something more concrete, like a house or food bought at the supermarket?

He can do nothing because he's in the hands of the system. However, he decides that as soon as he leaves the hospital, he'll visit an ATM and get a balance statement. He makes a note in his diary to do this every week; that way, if some calamity does occur in the world, he'll have proof on paper.

Paper. That word again. How did he get on to this subject in the first place? Ah, yes, money laundering.

He goes back to what he knows about laundering money. The final stage is the easiest of all; the money is put into a respectable account, for example, one belonging to a property development company or an investment fund. If the government asks: "Where did this money come from?" the answer's easy enough: "From small investors who believe in what we're selling." After that, it can be invested in more shares, more land, in planes and other luxury goods, in houses with swimming pools, in credit cards with no cash limit. The partners in these companies are the very same people who first financed the buying of drugs, guns, or some other illicit merchandise. The money, though, is clean; after all, any company can earn millions of dollars speculating on the stock market or on property.

This left only the first step to consider, the most difficult of all: "Who are these small investors?"

And that's where criminal creativity comes in. The "oranges" are people who hang around in casinos using money lent to them by a "friend," in countries where there's corruption aplenty and few restrictions on betting. There's always a chance someone will win a fortune. If they do, there are arrangements in place with the owners, who keep a percentage of the money that crosses their tables. And the gambler—someone on a low income—can justify the enormous sum deposited in his bank account by saying that it was all a matter of luck.

The following day, he'll transfer nearly all the money to the "friend" who lent it to him and hold back just a small percentage.

The preferred method used to be buying up restaurants, which could charge a fortune for their food and deposit the profits in an account without arousing suspicion. Even if an inspector came by and found the tables completely empty, they couldn't prove that no one had eaten there all day. Now, however, with the growth of the leisure industry, a more creative option has opened up. The ever imponderable, arbitrary, incomprehensible art market!

A middle-class couple, say, with little money will bring some extremely valuable piece to auction, alleging that they found it in the attic of their grandparents' old house. The piece is sold for a lot of money, then resold the following week to specialist galleries for ten or twenty times the original price. The "oranges" are happy, thank the gods for their generosity, deposit the money in their joint account, and resolve to invest it in some foreign country, always taking care to leave a small amount—their percentage—in that first account. The gods in this case are the real owners of the paintings who will buy it back from the galleries and put it on the market again, with different vendors this time.

There are, however, more expensive products still, like the theater and the production and distribution of films. That is where the invisible hands of the money launderers can really make a killing.

Savoy is now reading about the man currently in intensive care and trying to fill in a few blanks in his own imagination.

The man had been an actor who dreamed of becoming a major star.

He couldn't find any work—although he still took great care of his physical appearance, as if he really were a star—but he got to know the industry. In middle age, he managed to raise some money from investors and make a couple of films, both of which were resounding flops because they didn't get the right distribution. Nevertheless, his name appeared on the credits, and he became known in the specialist magazines as someone who had at least tried to make something different from the films being churned out by the big studios.

Just as he was beginning to despair, unsure what to do with his life, with no one willing to give him another chance, and weary of begging money from people who were only interested in investing in surefire hits, he was approached by a group of people, some of whom were very affable, while others were completely silent.

They made him an offer. He would start up as a film distributor, and his first purchase should be something guaranteed to reach a wider public. The major studios would offer vast sums of money for the film, but he needn't worry—any sum offered would be matched by his new friends. The film would be shown in lots of cinemas and earn a fortune. Javits would get what he most needed—a reputation. No one would be likely to delve into the life of a frustrated film producer. Two or three films later, the authorities might start to ask where all the money was coming from, but by then, the first step was safely concealed behind the five-year time limitation on all tax investigations.

So Javits began a glorious career. His first films as a distributor were highly profitable; exhibitors began to believe in his ability to select the best films on the market; directors and producers were soon queuing up to work with him. To keep up appearances, he always made sure to accept two or three low-budget projects every six months, the rest being films made with megabudgets, top-ranking stars, able technicians, and a lot of money to spend on promotion, money that came from groups based in tax havens. Box-office earnings were deposited in a normal investment fund, above suspicion, which had "shares" in the movie.

Fine. The dirty money was thus transformed into a marvelous work of art, which, naturally, didn't make as much money as was hoped, but was still capable of yielding millions of dollars that would immediately be invested by one of the partners in the enterprise.

At one point, however, a sharp-eyed tax inspector—or perhaps a whistle-blower at one of the studios—noticed one very simple fact: why was it that so many previously unknown producers were employing big stars and the most talented directors, spending a fortune on publicity, and using only one distributor for their films? The answer: the big studios are only interested in their own productions, whereas Javits is the hero, the man standing out against the monopoly of the giant corporations, a David to their Goliath, battling an unfair system.

A more conscientious tax inspector decided to proceed with his investigation, despite all these apparently reasonable explanations. He began in great secrecy and learned that all the companies who had invested in the biggest box-office successes were always limited companies based in the Bahamas, in Panama, or in Singapore. A mole in the tax office (there is *always* a mole) warned Javits's backers that they had better find another distributor to launder money from now on.

Javits was in despair. He had grown accustomed to the millionaire lifestyle and to being treated as if he were a demigod. He had traveled to Cannes, which provided an excellent front for sorting things out with his backers and personally handing over the codes of various numbered accounts. He had no idea that he was being followed, that a prison term would almost certainly ensue, pending decisions made by men in ties in ill-lit offices. They might let him continue for a while longer, in order to get more proof, or they might end the story right there.

His backers, however, never took unnecessary risks. Their man could be arrested at any moment, make a deal with the court, and give details of how the whole scam worked, as well as naming names and identifying people in photos taken without his knowledge.

There was only one way to solve the problem—they would have to kill him.

Things couldn't be clearer, and Savoy can see exactly how things developed. Now he just needs to do what he always does. Fill in more forms, draw up a report, hand it to Europol, and let their bureaucrats find the murderers because it's a case that could well lead to promotions and revive stagnant careers. The investigation has to produce a result, and none of his superiors would believe that a detective from a small town in France would be capable of making any major discoveries (because however glitzy and glamorous Cannes was during the Festival, for the other 350 days of the year it was just a small provincial town).

He suspects that the perpetrator may have been one of the bodyguards at the table, since the poison could only have been administered by someone standing very close. However, he won't mention that. He'll fill up more paper about the people working in the tent, find no further witnesses, then close the file—having first spent a few days exchanging faxes and e-mails with other more important departments.

He'll go back to his two murders a year, to the fights and the fines, having been so close to something that could have international repercussions. His adolescent dream of improving the world; contributing to creating a safer, fairer society; getting promoted; landing a job at the Ministry of Justice; giving his wife and children a more comfortable life; helping to change the public perception of the law; and showing that there *are* still some honest policemen, all came down to the same thing—more paperwork.

4:16 P.M.

The terrace outside the bar is packed, and Igor feels proud of his ability to plan things, because even though he's never been to Cannes before, he had foreseen precisely this situation and reserved a table. He orders tea and toast, lights a cigarette, and looks around him at the same scene you might see in any chic place anywhere in the world: women who are either anorexic or use too much Botox; ladies dripping with jewelry and eating ice cream; men with much younger female companions; bored couples; smiling young women sipping low-calorie drinks and pretending to be listening to what their friends are saying when they're really on the lookout for someone more interesting to hove into view.

There is one exception: three men and a woman are sitting at a table strewn with papers and beer cans, discussing something in low voices and constantly checking figures on a calculator. They appear to be the only ones who are really engaged in some project, but that isn't quite true; everyone there is working hard in a way, in search of one thing: vis-i-bil-i-ty, which, if all goes well, will turn into Fame, which, if all goes well again, will turn into Power, the magic word that transforms any human being into a demigod, a remote, inaccessible icon accustomed to having his every desire met and to getting jealous looks when he sweeps past in his limousine with the smoked-glass windows or in his expensive sports car, someone who no longer has mountains to climb or impossible conquests to make.

The people on the terrace have clearly leaped over certain barriers already; they are not outside with the photographers, behind the metal barriers, waiting for someone to come out of the main door and fill their universe with light. They have already made it into the hotel lobby, and now all they need is fame and power, and they really don't mind what form these take. Men know that age isn't a problem, all they need are the right contacts. The young women—who keep as keen an eye on the terrace as any trained bodyguard—know that they're reaching a dangerous age, when any chance of achieving something through their beauty alone will suddenly vanish. The older women there would like to be recognized and respected for their gifts and their intelligence, but the diamonds they're wearing make it unlikely that their talents will be discovered. The men sitting with their wives are waiting for someone to pass by and say hello and for everyone to turn and look and think: "He must be well-known, or even famous, who knows?"

The celebrity syndrome. It can destroy careers, marriages, and Christian values, and can blind both the wise and the ignorant. A few examples. Great scientists who, on being given an important prize, abandon the research that might have helped humanity and decide instead to live off lectures that feed both their ego and their bank balance. The Indian in the Amazon jungle who, on being taken up by a famous singer, decides that he's being exploited for his poverty. The campaigner for justice who works hard defending the rights of the less fortunate, decides to run for public office, wins the election, and subsequently considers himself above the law, until he's discovered one day in a motel room with a prostitute paid for by the taxpayer.

The celebrity syndrome. When people forget who they are and start to believe what other people say about them. The Superclass, everyone's dream, a world without shadows or darkness, where yes is the only possible answer to any request.

Igor is a powerful man. He has fought all his life to get where he is now. To that end, he has sat through boring suppers, endless lectures, and meetings with people he loathed, has bestowed smiles when he would rather have bestowed insults, and insults when he actually felt genuinely sorry for the poor creatures being singled out for punishment, as an example to others. He worked day and night and weekends too, deep in discussions with lawyers, administrators, officials, and press officers. He started with nothing just after the fall of the Communist regime and he reached the top. He has, moreover, managed to survive all the political and economic storms that swept his country during the first two decades of the new regime. And why? Because he fears God and knows that the road he has traveled in his life is a blessing that must be respected; if not, he will lose everything.

There were, of course, moments when something told him he was forgetting about the most important part of that blessing: Ewa; but for many years he persuaded himself that she would understand and accept that it was simply a temporary phase and that soon they would be able to spend as much time together as they wished. They made great plans—journeys, cruises, a remote house in the mountains with a blazing log fire, and the certain knowledge that they could stay there for as long as they wanted, with no need to worry about money, debts, or obligations. They would find a school for the many children they planned to have together; they would spend whole afternoons walking through the surrounding forests; they would have supper at small, cozy local restaurants.

They would have time to garden, read, go to the cinema, and do the simple things that everyone dreams of doing, the only things truly capable of filling anyone's life. When he got home, his arms full of papers which he would then spread out on the bed, he would ask her to be patient for a little while longer. When his phone rang on the very day they'd chosen to go out to supper together, and he had to interrupt their conversation and spend a long time talking to whoever had called, he would again ask her to be patient. He knew Ewa was doing everything she could to make things easy for him, although she did complain now and then, very sweetly, that they needed to make the most of life while they were still young; after all, they had money enough for the next five generations.

Igor would say: "Right, I'll stop today." And Ewa would smile and stroke his cheek, and then he would remember something important he'd forgotten to do and go over to the phone to ring someone or to the computer to send an e-mail.

A MAN IN HIS FORTIES gets up, looks around the terrace, and, brandishing a newspaper, shouts:

"'Violence and horror in Tokyo' says the headline. 'Seven people killed in a shop selling electronic toys.'"

Everyone looks at him.

"Violence! They don't know what they're talking about. This is where you get real violence!"

A shudder runs down Igor's spine.

"If some madman stabs to death a few innocent people, the whole world is shocked, but who cares about the intellectual violence being perpetrated in Cannes? Our festival is being killed in the name of a dictatorship. It's not a question of choosing the best film, but of committing crimes against humanity, forcing people to buy products they don't want, putting fashion above art, choosing to go to a lunch or a supper rather than watch a film. That's disgraceful. I'm here to—"

"Be quiet," someone says. "No one cares why you're here."

"I'm here to denounce the enslavement of man's desires, for we have stopped using our intelligence to make choices and instead allow ourselves to be manipulated by propaganda and lies! People get all steamed up about these stabbings in Tokyo, but they don't give a damn about the death by a thousand cuts suffered by a whole generation of filmmakers."

The man pauses, expecting a standing ovation, but there isn't even a thoughtful silence. Everyone resumes their conversations, indifferent to his words. He sits down again, trying to look dignified, but with his heart in shreds for making such a fool of himself.

"VIS-I-BIL-I-TY," THINKS IGOR. "THE PROBLEM is that no one took any notice."

It's his turn to look around. Ewa is staying at the same hotel, and a sixth sense born of many years of marriage tells him that she's sitting not very far away on that same terrace. She will have received his messages and is probably looking for him now, knowing that he, too, must be near.

He can't see her, but neither can he stop thinking about her——his obsession. He remembers one night being driven home in his imported limousine by the chauffeur who doubled as his bodyguard——they had fought together in Afghanistan, but fortune had smiled on them in very different ways——and remembers asking the driver to stop outside the Hotel Kempinski. He left his mobile phone and his papers in the car and went up to the terrace bar. Unlike this terrace in Cannes, the place was almost empty and getting ready to close. He gave a generous tip to the waiters and asked them to stay open for another hour, just for him.

And that was when he understood. It wasn't true that he would give up work next month or next year or even next decade. They would never have the house in the country and the children they dreamed of. He asked himself that night why this was impossible and he had only one answer.

On the road to power, there's no turning back. He would be an eternal slave to the road he'd chosen, and if he did ever realize his dream of abandoning everything, he would plunge immediately into a deep depression.

Why was he like that? Was it because of the nightmares he had about the trenches, remembering the frightened young man he'd been then, fulfilling a duty he hadn't chosen and being forced to kill? Was it because he couldn't forget his first victim, a peasant who had strayed into the line of fire when the Red Army was fighting the Afghan guerrillas? Was it because of the many people who hadn't believed in him and had humiliated him when he was looking for investors for his mobile phone business? Was it because in the beginning he'd had to associate with shadows, with the Russian mafia eager to launder the money they earned through prostitution?

He'd managed to repay those questionable loans without himself being corrupted and without owing any favors. He'd managed to negotiate with the shadows and still keep his own light burning. He knew that the war belonged to the distant past and that he would never again set foot on a battlefield. He'd found the love of his life. He was doing the kind of work he'd always wanted to do. He was rich, very rich, and, just in case the Communist regime were to return tomorrow, he kept most of his personal fortune abroad. He was on good terms with all the political parties. He'd met famous people from around the world. He'd set up a foundation to care for the orphans of those soldiers killed during the Soviet invasion of Afghanistan.

But it was only when he was sitting on that terrace café near Red Square, knowing that he had power and money enough to pay the waiters to work all night if necessary, that he finally understood.

He understood because he saw the same thing happening to his wife. Ewa was also constantly traveling, and even when she was in Moscow, she would arrive home late and go straight to her computer as soon as she walked in the door. He understood that, contrary to what most people think, total power means total slavery. When you get that far, you don't ever want to give it up. There's always a new mountain to climb. There's always a competitor to be convinced or crushed. Along with two thousand other people, he formed part of the most exclusive club in the world, which met only once a year in Davos in Switzerland, at the World Economic Forum. All the members were millionaires, and they all worked from dawn until late at night, always wanting to go further, never changing tack—acquisitions, stock markets, market trends, money, money, money. They worked not because they needed to, but because they judged themselves to be necessary; they felt that thousands of families depended on them and that they had a huge responsibility to their governments and their associates. They genuinely thought they were helping the world, which might be true, but they had to pay for this with their own lives.

THE FOLLOWING DAY, HE DID something he hated having to do: he went to a psychiatrist. Something must be wrong. He discovered then that he was suffering from an illness that was fairly common among those who had achieved something beyond the grasp of ordinary folk. He was a compulsive worker, a workaholic. According to the psychiatrist, workaholics run the risk of becoming depressed when not immersed in the challenges and problems of running a company.

"We don't yet know the origin of the disorder, but it's associated with insecurity, childhood fears, and a desire to block out reality. It's as serious an addiction as drugs. Unlike drugs, however, which diminish productivity, the workaholic makes a great contribution to the wealth of his country. So it's in no one's interests to seek a cure."

"And what are the consequences?"

"You should know, because that's presumably why you've come to see me. The gravest consequence is the damage it causes to family life. In Japan, one of the countries where the illness is most common and where the consequences are sometimes fatal, they've developed various ways of controlling the obsession."

Igor couldn't remember listening to anyone in the last two years with the respect and attention he was paying that bespectacled, mustachioed man before him.

"So there is a way out, then?"

"When a workaholic seeks help from a psychiatrist that means he's ready to be cured. Only about one in every thousand cases realizes that he needs help."

"Oh, I need help, and I have enough money . . ."

"That's what all workaholics say. Yes, I know you have enough money, you all do. I know who you are as well. I've seen photos of you at charity balls, at congresses, in private audience with our president, who, by the way, shows the same symptoms. Money isn't enough. What I want to know is this: do you really want to change?"

Igor thought of Ewa, of the house in the mountains, the family he'd like to have, the hundreds of millions of dollars he had in the bank. He thought of his position in society and of the power he possessed and how difficult it would be to give all that up.

"I'm not saying you should abandon what you're doing," said the psychiatrist, as if he'd read his thoughts. "I'm simply suggesting that you use work as a source of happiness and not as a compulsion."

"Yes, I can do that."

"And what would be your main motive for doing so? All workaholics think they're happy doing what they're doing, and none of their friends, who are in the same position, will see why they should seek help."

Igor lowered his eyes.

"Shall I tell you what your main motive is? As I said before, you're destroying your family."

"No, it's worse than that. My wife is starting to show the same symptoms. She's been distancing herself from me ever since a trip we made to Lake Baikal. And if there's anyone in the world I would be capable of killing again for . . ."

Igor realized he'd said too much, but the psychiatrist seemed entirely unmoved.

"If there's anyone in the world for whom I would do anything, absolutely anything, that person is my wife."

The psychiatrist summoned his assistant and asked her to make a series of appointments. He didn't consult his patient to see if he would be available on those dates; it was part of the treatment to make it quite clear that any other commitment, however important, could be postponed.

"May I ask a question?"

The psychiatrist nodded.

"Couldn't overwork also be considered rather noble? A proof of my deep respect for the opportunities God has given me in this life? A way of putting society to rights, even if sometimes I have to use methods that are a little . . ."

Silence.

"A little what?"

"Oh, nothing."

Igor left the consulting room feeling both confused and relieved. Perhaps the psychiatrist had failed to understand the essence of what he did. Life has its reasons. We are all of us linked, and often it's necessary to cut out the malignant tumors so that the rest of the body can remain healthy. People are locked up in their selfish little worlds; they make plans that don't include their fellow man; they believe the planet is simply land to be exploited; they follow their instincts and desires and care nothing for the collective well-being of society.

He wasn't destroying his family, he simply wanted to leave the world a better place for the children he dreamed of having, a world without drugs or wars or people trafficking, a world in which love would be the great force uniting all couples, peoples, nations, and religions. Ewa would understand this, even if their marriage was currently going through a crisis, a crisis doubtless sent by the Evil One.

The following day, he asked his secretary to cancel all subsequent appointments with the psychiatrist; he had more important things to do. He was drawing up a great plan to purify the world, a plan for which he would need help; indeed, he'd already contacted a group prepared to work with him.

Two months later, the wife he loved left him—because of the Evil that had possessed her, because he hadn't been able to understand her feelings.

THE SOUND OF A CHAIR being shifted returns him to the reality of Cannes. Before him sits a woman holding a glass of whisky in one hand and a cigarette in the other. She's well-dressed but visibly drunk.

"May I sit here? All the other tables are occupied."

"You already are sitting here."

"It's just not possible," says the woman, as if she'd known him for years. "It's simply not possible. The police made me leave the hospital. And the man for whose sake I traveled by train for almost a whole day, for whom I rented a hotel room at twice the normal price, is now hovering between life and death. Damn!"

Is she from the police? Or does what she's saying have nothing to do with what he thinks it does?

"Anyway, what are *you* doing here, if you don't mind my asking?

Aren't you hot? Wouldn't you be cooler without your jacket on, or are you trying to impress everyone with your elegance?"

As usual, people choose their own destiny, and this woman is doing just that.

"I always wear a jacket regardless of the temperature. Are you an actress?"

The woman gives an almost hysterical laugh.

"Yes, let's say I'm an actress, yes I am. I'm playing the part of someone who has had the same dream since she was an adolescent, has grown up with it, battled seven miserable years of her life to make it a reality, who's mortgaged her house, worked ceaselessly . . ."

"Oh, I know what that's like."

"No, you don't. It means thinking about just one thing day and night, going to places uninvited, shaking hands with people you despise, phoning once, twice, ten times until you get the attention of people who aren't worth half what you are, who don't have half your courage, but who've reached a certain position and are determined to take out on you all their domestic frustrations by making your life impossible . . ."

". . . it means only finding pleasure in pursuing your dream, having no other diversions, finding everything else deadly dull, and ending up destroying your family."

The woman looks at him, taken aback. She no longer seems drunk.

"Who *are* you? How do you know what I'm thinking?"

"I was thinking about exactly the same thing when you arrived. And I don't in the least mind you asking me what I'm doing here. I think I can help you."

"No one can help me. The only person who could is now in the intensive care unit. And from what I could glean before the police arrived, he probably won't survive. Oh God!"

She drinks the remaining whisky in her glass. Igor signals to the waiter, who ignores him and goes to serve another table.

"I've always preferred a cynical compliment to a bit of constructive criticism. Please, tell me I'm beautiful and that I've got what it takes."

Igor laughs.

"How do you know I can't help you?"

"Are you by any chance a film distributor? Do you have contacts and a chain of cinemas around the world?"

They were perhaps referring to the same person. If so and if this was a trap, it was too late to run away. He's obviously being watched, and as soon as he stands up, he'll be arrested. He feels his stomach contract, but why should he be afraid? Only a short time ago, he'd tried, without success, to hand himself over to the police. He'd chosen martyrdom, offered up his freedom as a sacrifice, but that gift had been rejected by God. Now, however, the heavens had obviously reconsidered their decision.

He must think how best to deal with what will ensue: the suspect is identified, a woman pretending to be drunk is sent on ahead to confirm the facts. Then, very discreetly, a man will walk over and ask him to come with him for a little chat. That man will be a policeman. Igor has what looks like a pen in his jacket pocket, but that will arouse no suspicions; the Beretta though will give him away. He sees his whole life flash before him.

Could he use the gun to defend himself? The policeman who is sure to appear as soon as he has been identified will have colleagues watching the scene, and Igor will be dead before he can make so much as a move. On the other hand, he didn't come here to kill innocent people in a barbarous, indiscriminate way; he has a mission, and his victims— or martyrs for love as he prefers to call them—are serving a greater purpose.

"No, I'm not a distributor," he says. "I have absolutely nothing to do with the world of cinema, fashion, or glamour. I work in telecommunications."

"Good," says the woman. "So you must have money. You must have had dreams in your life, so you know what I'm talking about."

He's beginning to lose the thread of the conversation. He signals to another waiter. This time the waiter comes over and Igor orders two cups of tea.

"Can't you see I'm drinking whisky?"

"Yes, but as I said, I think I can help you. To do that, however, you need to be sober and aware of what you're doing."

Maureen feels a change come over her. Ever since this stranger proved himself able to read her thoughts, she feels as if she were being restored to reality. Perhaps he really can help her. It's been years since anyone tried to seduce her with that most clichéd of chat-up lines in the film business: "I have some very influential friends." There's nothing more guaranteed to change a woman's state of mind than knowing that someone of the opposite sex desires her. She feels tempted to get up and go to the restroom and check her makeup in the mirror. That can wait. First, she needs to send out some clear signals that she's interested.

Yes, she needs company, she's open to whatever surprises fate may hold in store; when God closes a door, he opens a window. Why, of all the tables on that terrace, was this the only table occupied by just one person? There was a meaning in this, a hidden sign: the two of them were meant to meet.

She laughs at herself. In her current despairing state anything is a sign, a way out, a piece of good news.

"Firstly, tell me what you need," says the man.

"I need help. I have a movie with a top-line cast ready and waiting; it was going to be distributed by one of the few people in the industry who still has faith in the talent of people outside the studio system. I was going to meet him tomorrow. I was even at the same lunch as him today, when suddenly I noticed he was feeling unwell."

Igor starts to relax. Perhaps it's true, reality really is stranger than fiction.

"I left the lunch, found out which hospital he'd been taken to, and went there. On the way, I imagined what I was going to say, about how I was his friend and we were going to be working together. I've never even spoken to him, but I think anyone in a situation like that feels more comfortable knowing that someone, anyone, is near."

"In other words, turning someone else's tragedy to your own advantage," thinks Igor.

People are all the same.

"And what exactly is a top-line cast?" he asks.

"Will you excuse me? I need to go to the bathroom."

Igor politely stands up, puts on his dark glasses, and, as she walks away, tries to look as calm as possible. He drinks his tea, all the while scanning the terrace. At first sight, there appears to be no immediate threat, but it would still be wise to leave that terrace as soon as the woman comes back.

Maureen is impressed by her new friend's gentlemanly behavior. It's been years since she's seen anyone behave according to the rules of etiquette taught them by their mothers and fathers. As she leaves the terrace, she notices that some pretty young women at the next table, who have doubtless heard part of their conversation, are looking at him and smiling. She notices, too, that he's put on his dark glasses, possibly to be able to observe the young women without them knowing. Perhaps, by the time she gets back, they'll all be drinking tea together.

But then life is like that: don't complain and don't expect too much either.

She looks at her face in the mirror. Why would a man be interested in her? She really does need to get to grips with reality again, as he suggested. Her eyes look empty and tired; she's exhausted like everyone else taking part in the Festival, but she knows that she has to carry on fighting. Cannes isn't over yet, Javits might recover, or someone representing his company might turn up. She has tickets to see other people's films, an invitation to a party held by *Gala*—one of the most prestigious magazines in France—and she can use the time available to see how independent European producers and directors go about distributing their films. She needs to bounce back quickly.

As for the handsome stranger, she mustn't have any illusions in that regard. She returns to the table convinced that she'll find two of the young women sitting there, but he's still alone. Again he rises politely to his feet and draws back her chair so that she can sit down.

"Sorry, I haven't introduced myself. My name's Maureen."

"I'm Igor. Pleased to meet you. You were saying that you had the ideal cast."

She decides to get a dig in at the girls at the next table. She speaks slightly more loudly than usual.

"Here in Cannes, or indeed at any other festival, new actresses are discovered every year, and every year really great actresses lose out on getting a great role because the industry thinks they're too old, even if, in fact, they're still young and full of enthusiasm. Among the new discoveries" (and, she thinks: "I just hope the girls next to us are listening"), "some choose the path of pure glamour. They don't earn much on the movies they make—all directors know this and take full advantage—and so they invest in the one thing they shouldn't invest in."

"Namely . . ."

"Their own beauty. They become celebrities, start to charge for attending parties, they're asked to appear in advertisements, promoting various products. They end up meeting the most powerful men and the sexiest actors in the world. They earn a vast amount of money because they're young and pretty and their agents get them loads of contracts.

"In fact, they allow themselves to be entirely guided by their agents, who constantly feed their vanity. An actress of this type becomes the dream of housewives, of adolescent girls and would-be actresses who don't even have enough money to travel to the nearest town, but who consider her a friend, someone who's having the kind of experiences they would like to have. She continues making movies and earns a little more, although her press agent always puts it about that she's earning an enormous salary, which is a complete lie that not even the journalists believe, but which they publish anyway because they know the public prefers news to information."

"What's the difference?" asks Igor, who's feeling more relaxed now, while still keeping a close eye on what's going on around him.

"Let's say you were to buy a gold-plated computer in an auction in Dubai and decided to write a new book using that technological marvel. When a journalist finds out about the computer, he'll phone you up and ask: 'So how's your gold-plated computer?' That's news. The information—the nature of the new book you're writing—is of no importance whatsoever."

"Perhaps Ewa is receiving news rather than information," thinks Igor. The idea had never occurred to him before.

"Go on."

"Time passes, or, rather, seven or eight years pass. Suddenly, the film offers dry up. The revenue from parties and advertisements begins to dwindle. Her agent seems suddenly much busier than before and doesn't always call her back. The 'big star' rebels: how can they do this to her, the great sex symbol, the great icon of glamour? She blames her agent and decides to find another one; to her surprise, he doesn't appear to mind at all. On the contrary, he asks her to sign a statement saying how well they have always got on together; then he wishes her good luck, and that's the end of their relationship."

Maureen looks around the terrace to see if she can find an example of what she's describing: people who are still famous, but who have vanished from the scene and are desperately seeking some new opportunity. They still behave like divas, they still have the same distant air, but their hearts are full of bitterness, their skin full of Botox and covered with the invisible scars left by plastic surgery. She could see plenty of evidence of Botox and plastic surgery, but no celebrities from the previous decade. Perhaps they didn't even have enough money now to attend a festival like this, but were instead appearing as a special guest at dances in provincial towns or fronting the launch of some new brand of chocolate or beer, still behaving as if they were the person they once were, but knowing that they weren't.

"You mentioned two types of people."

"Yes. The second group of actresses have exactly the same problem, but there's one important difference." Again her voice grows louder because now the girls at the next table are clearly interested to hear what someone in the know has to say. "They know that beauty is a transient thing. They don't appear in ads or on magazine covers because they're busy honing their art. They keep studying and making contacts that will be useful in the future. They lend their name and appearance to certain products, not as models, but as partners. They earn less, of course, but it means a lifelong income.

"And then along comes someone like me, with a good script and enough money, plus I want them to be in my film. They accept and have enough talent to play the parts I give them and enough intelligence to know that even if the film doesn't turn out to be a huge success, at least they will still have a presence on the screen and be seen to be working as mature actresses, and who knows, that might spark the interest of another producer."

Igor is also aware that the girls are listening to their conversation.

"Perhaps we should go for a walk," he says quietly. "There's no privacy here. I know a place where we can be alone and watch the sun go down; it's beautiful."

That's precisely what she needs at this moment—an invitation to go for a walk! To see the sunset, even though it'll be quite some time before the sun goes down! He's not one of those vulgar types who says: "Let's go up to my room for a moment, I need to change my shoes" and "Nothing will happen, I promise," and who, once they're in his room, will say as he tries to make a grab for her: "I have contacts and I know just the people you need to talk to."

To be honest, she wouldn't mind being kissed by this seemingly charming man. She knows absolutely nothing about him, of course, but the elegance with which he's seducing her is something she won't forget in a long time.

They get up from the table, and he asks for the drinks to be put on his tab (so, she thinks, he's staying at the Martinez!). When they reach the Boulevard de la Croisette, he suggests they turn to the left.

"There are fewer people in that direction; besides, the view should be even better, with the sun setting behind the hills."

"Igor, who are you?"

"A good question," he says. "I'd like to know the answer to that one myself."

Another point in his favor. He doesn't immediately launch into some spiel about how rich and intelligent and talented he is. He simply wants to watch the sunset with her, that's all. They walk to the end of the beach in silence, passing all kinds of different people—older couples who seem to inhabit another world, quite oblivious to the Festival; young people on roller skates, wearing tight clothes and listening to iPods; street vendors with their merchandise set out on a mat, the ends of which have string looped through them so that at the first sign of a policeman, they can transform their "shop window" into a bag;

there's even an area that seems to have been cordoned off by the police for some reason—after all, it's only a bench. She notices that her companion keeps looking behind him, as if he were expecting someone, but he's probably just spotted an acquaintance.

They walk along a pier where the boats partially conceal the beach from view, and they finally find an isolated spot. They sit down on a comfortable bench with a backrest. They're completely alone. Well, why would anyone else come to a place where there's nothing to do? She's in an excellent mood.

"It's lovely here! Do you know why God decided to rest on the seventh day?"

Igor doesn't understand the question, but she proceeds to explain anyway:

"Because on the seventh day, before he'd finished work and left the world in a perfect state for human beings, a group of producers from Hollywood came over to him and said: 'Don't you worry about the rest! We'll take care of providing the Technicolor sunset, the special storm effects, the perfect lighting, and the right sound equipment so that whenever Man hears the waves, he'll think it's the real sea!'"

She laughs to herself. The man beside her is looking more serious now.

"You asked me who I am," he says.

"I've no idea who you are, but you obviously know the city well. And I have to say, it was real luck meeting you like that. In just one day, I've experienced, hope, despair, loneliness, and the pleasure of finding a new companion. That's a lot of emotions."

He takes something out of his pocket; it looks like a wooden tube less than six inches long.

"The world's a dangerous place," he says. "It doesn't matter where you are, you're always at risk of being approached by people who have no scruples about attacking, destroying, killing. And we never learn how to defend ourselves. We're all in the hands of those more powerful than us."

"You're right. I suppose that wooden tube is your way of fending them off."

He twists the upper part of the tube. As delicately as a painter putting the final touch to a masterpiece, he removes the lid. It isn't in fact a lid, but the head of what looks like a long nail. The sun glitters on the metal blade.

"You wouldn't get through airport security carrying that in your case," she says, and laughs.

"No, I wouldn't."

Maureen feels that she's with a man who is polite, handsome, doubtless wealthy, but who is also capable of protecting her from all dangers. She has no idea what the crime statistics are for Cannes, but it's as well to think of everything. That's what men are for: to think of everything.

"Of course, you need to know exactly how to use it. It may be made of steel, but because it's so thin it's also very fragile and too small to cause any real damage. If you don't use it with great precision, it won't work."

He places the blade level with Maureen's ear. Her initial reaction is one of fear, soon replaced by excitement.

"This would be one of the ideal places, for example. Any higher, and the cranial bones would block the blow, any lower, and the vein in the neck would be cut; the person might die, but would also be able to fight back. If he was armed, he could shoot me, especially at such close range."

The blade slides slowly down her body. It passes over her breast, and Maureen realizes that he's trying both to shock and to arouse her.

"I had no idea someone working in telecommunications could know so much about killing, but from what you say, killing someone with that blade is quite a complicated business."

This is her way of saying: "I'm interested in what you're telling me. I find you really fascinating. But please, just take my hand and let's go and watch the sunset together."

The blade slides over her breast, but does not stop there. Nevertheless, it's enough to make her feel aroused. It stops just under her arm.

"Here I'm on a level with your heart. It's protected by a natural barrier, the rib cage. In a fight, it would be impossible to injure someone with this blade. It would almost certainly hit a rib, and even if it did penetrate the body, the wound wouldn't bleed enough to weaken your enemy. He might not even feel the blow. But right here, it would be fatal."

What is she doing in this isolated spot with a complete stranger talking about such a macabre subject? Just then, she feels a kind of electric shock that leaves her paralyzed. His hand has driven the blade inside her body. She feels at first as if she were suffocating and tries to breathe, but then immediately loses consciousness.

Igor puts his arms around her, as he had with his first victim. This time, though, he positions her body so that she remains sitting. He then puts on some gloves and makes her head drop forward onto her chest.

If anyone ventures into that corner of the beach, all they will see is a woman sleeping, exhausted perhaps from chasing after producers and distributors at the Festival.

THE BOY LURKING BEHIND THE old warehouse—where he often hides so as to masturbate while he watches canoodling couples—is now furiously phoning the police. He saw everything. At first, he thought it was some kind of joke, but the man really did stick that blade into the woman! He'll have to wait for the police to arrive before leaving his hiding place. That madman could return at any moment and then he would be lost.

IGOR THROWS THE BLADE INTO the sea and walks back to the hotel. This time, his victim had chosen death. When she joined him, he'd been sitting alone on the terrace, wondering what to do next and thinking about the past. He never imagined she would agree to go for a walk to such an isolated spot with a complete stranger, but she did. She could have run away when he started showing her the different places where the blade would cause a mortal wound, but she didn't.

A police car passes, driving along the side of the road closed to the public. He decides to watch where it goes and, to his surprise, he sees it drive onto the pier where no one seems to go during the Festival period. It had been as empty that morning as it had this afternoon, even though it was the best place from which to see the sunset. A few seconds later, an ambulance passes with its deafening siren blaring and its lights flashing. It, too, heads for the pier.

He keeps walking, sure of one thing: someone must have witnessed the murder. But how would that someone describe him? A man with grayish hair, wearing jeans, a white shirt, and a black jacket. That possible witness would help the police make an Identi-Kit picture, a process that would not only take time, but lead them to the conclusion that there are tens or maybe thousands of men who look just like him.

Ever since he tried to give himself up to that policeman and was sent back to his hotel, he has felt sure that no one would be able to interrupt his mission. The doubts he feels now are of a different nature: is Ewa worth the sacrifices he's offering up to the universe? When he arrived in Cannes, he had felt sure she was; now, though, something else is filling his soul: the spirit of the little street vendor with her dark eyebrows and innocent smile.

"We are all part of the divine spark," she seems to be saying. "We all have a purpose in creation and that purpose is called Love. That love, however, shouldn't be concentrated in just one person, it should be scattered throughout the world, waiting to be discovered. Wake up to that love. What is gone cannot return. What is about to arrive needs to be recognized."

He struggles against the idea that perhaps we only discover that a plan is wrong when we take it to its ultimate consequences, or when all-merciful God leads us in another direction.

He looks at his watch: he still has another twelve hours in Cannes, time enough before he gets on the plane with the woman he loves and goes back to . . .

. . . goes back to what? To his work in Moscow after everything he has experienced, suffered, thought, planned? Or to find rebirth through his victims and choose absolute freedom and discover the person he didn't know he was, and from then on do all the things he had dreamed of doing when he was still with Ewa?

4:34 P.M.

Jasmine is sitting staring out at the sea while she smokes a cigarette and thinks of nothing. At such moments, she feels a deep connection with the infinite, as if it were not she who was there, but something more powerful, something capable of extraordinary things.

SHE REMEMBERS AN OLD STORY she once read.

Nasrudin appeared at court wearing a magnificent turban and asking for money for charity.

"You come here asking for money and yet you're wearing an extremely expensive turban on your head. How much did that extraordinary thing cost?" asked the sultan.

"It was a gift from someone very rich. And it's worth, I believe, five hundred gold coins," replied the wise Sufi.

The sultan's minister muttered: "That's impossible. No turban could possibly be worth that much."

Nasrudin insisted:

"I didn't come here only to beg, I also came to do business. I know that only a true sovereign would be capable of buying this turban for six hundred gold coins so that I could give the surplus to the poor."

The sultan was flattered and paid what Nasrudin asked. On the way out, Nasrudin said to the minister:

"*You may know the value of a turban, but I know how far a man's vanity will take him.*"

And that's what the world around her is like. She has nothing against her profession, she doesn't judge people by their desires, but she knows what's really important in life and wants to keep her feet on the ground, even though there are temptations at every turn.

Someone opens the door and says there's just half an hour before the show begins. The worst part of the day, the long period of tedium that precedes any fashion show, is coming to an end. The other girls put down their iPods and their phones; the makeup artists do any necessary retouching; the hairdressers comb back into place any stray locks.

Jasmine sits in front of the dressing room mirror and lets them get on with their work.

"Don't be nervous just because it's Cannes," says the makeup artist.

"I'm not nervous."

Why should she be? On the contrary, whenever she steps onto a catwalk, she feels a kind of ecstasy, a surge of adrenaline. The makeup artist seems in a mood to talk, and tells her about the many celebrity wrinkles she has smoothed, suggests a new face cream, says she's tired of her job, asks if Jasmine has a spare ticket to a party that night. Jasmine listens to all this with infinite patience. In her mind she's back in the streets of Antwerp on the day she decided to get in touch with the two photographers who had approached her earlier. She had met with a slight initial difficulty, but it had all worked out in the end.

As it would today and as it had then, when—along with her mother, who, eager for her daughter to recover from her depression as quickly as possible, had agreed to go with her—she rang the bell of the first photographer, the one who had stopped her in the street. The door opened to reveal a small room with a transparent table covered in photographic negatives, another table, on which sat a computer, and a kind of drawing board piled with papers. With the photographer was a woman of about forty, who looked at her long and hard, before smiling and introducing herself as the events coordinator. Then the four of them sat down.

"I'm sure your daughter has a great future as a model," said the woman.

"Oh, I'm just here to keep her company," said Jasmine's mother. "If you have anything to say, speak directly to her."

The woman, slightly taken aback, paused for a few seconds, then picked up a card and started noting down details and measurements, saying:

"Of course, Cristina isn't a good name for a model. It's too ordinary. The first thing we need to do is to change that."

"There's another reason why Cristina isn't a good name," Jasmine was thinking. Because it belonged to a girl who had ceased to exist when she witnessed a murder and denied what her eyes now refused to forget. When she decided to change everything, she began with the name she'd been called ever since she was a child. She needed to change everything, absolutely everything. She had her answer ready.

"My professional name is Jasmine Tiger—a combination of sweetness and danger."

The woman seemed to like the name.

"A career in modeling isn't an easy one, and you're lucky to have been picked out to take the first step. Obviously, there are a lot of things to sort out, but we're here to help you get to where you want to be. We take photos of you and send them to the appropriate agencies. You'll also need a composite."

She waited for Cristina to ask: "What's a composite?" But no question came. Again the woman was temporarily thrown.

"A composite, as I'm sure you know, is a sheet of paper with, on the one side, your best photo and your measurements, and, on the other, more photos in different poses, for example, in a bikini, dressed as a student, perhaps one of just your face, another that shows you wearing more makeup, so that they won't necessarily exclude you if they want someone older. Your bust . . ."

Another pause.

". . . your bust is perhaps a little large for a model."

She turned to the photographer.

"We need to disguise that. Make a note."

The photographer duly made a note. Cristina—who was rapidly becoming Jasmine Tiger—was thinking: "But when they meet me, they'll see I've got a bigger bust than they were expecting!"

The woman picked up a handsome leather briefcase and took out a list.

"We'll need to call a makeup artist and a hairdresser. You haven't any experience on a catwalk, have you?"

"None."

"Well, you don't stride down a catwalk as if you were walking down the street. If you did, you'd stumble because you'd be moving too fast or else trip over your high heels. You have to place one foot in front of the other, like a cat. You mustn't smile too much either. Even more important is posture."

She ticked off three things on the list.

"And you'll have to hire some clothes."

Another tick.

"And I think that's all for now."

She again put her hand inside the elegant briefcase and took out a calculator. She went down the list, tapped in a few numbers, then added them up. No one else in the room dared utter a word.

"That will be around two thousand euros, I think. We won't include the photos because Yasser"—she turned to the photographer—"is very expensive, but he's prepared to do the work for free, as long as you give him permission to use the material. We can have the makeup artist and the hairdresser here tomorrow morning and I'll get in touch with the people who run the course to see if there's a vacancy. I'm sure there will be, just as I'm sure that by investing in yourself, you're creating new possibilities for your future and will soon recover any initial expenses."

"Are you saying I have to pay?"

Again the "events coordinator" seemed taken aback. Usually, the girls who came to see her were so mad keen to realize the dream of a whole generation—being considered one of the sexiest women in the world—that they never asked indelicate questions like that.

"Listen, Cristina . . ."

"Jasmine. The moment I walked through that door, I became Jasmine."

The photographer's mobile phone rang. He took it out of his pocket and moved away to the far end of the room, which had, until then, been in darkness. When he drew one of the curtains, Jasmine saw a wall draped with a black cloth, tripods mounted with flashes, boxes with blinking lights, and several spotlights suspended from the ceiling.

"Listen, Jasmine, there are thousands and millions of people who would like to be in your position. You were chosen by one of Antwerp's finest photographers, you'll have the help of the best professionals, and I will personally manage your career. On the other hand, as with everything else in life, you have to believe that you're going to succeed and, for that to happen, you need to invest money. I know you're beautiful enough to enjoy great success as a model, but that isn't enough in this highly competitive world. You have to be the best, and that costs money, at least to begin with."

"But if you think I have all those qualities, why don't you invest *your* money in me?"

"I will later on. At the moment, we need to know just how committed you are. I want to be sure that you really do want to be a professional model or if you're just another young woman excited by the possibility of traveling, seeing the world, and finding a rich husband."

The woman's tone of voice had grown severe. The photographer returned from the studio end of the room.

"It's the makeup artist. She wants to know what time she should arrive tomorrow."

"If the money's essential, I can probably . . ." Jasmine's mother began to say, but Jasmine had got up and was walking over to the door, without shaking hands with either the woman or the photographer.

"Thank you very much, but I don't have that kind of money, and even if I did, I would spend it on something else."

"But it's your future!"

"Precisely. It's my future, not yours."

JASMINE BURST INTO TEARS AFTERWARD. First, she had gone to that expensive boutique where they'd not only been rude to her, but implied that she was lying when she said she'd met the owner. Then, just when she thought she was about to start a new life and had discovered the perfect new name for herself, she learned that it would cost her two thousand euros just to take the first step!

Mother and daughter made their way home in silence. Jasmine's mobile rang several times, but she just glanced at the number and put the phone back in her pocket.

"Why don't you answer it? We've got another appointment this afternoon, haven't we?"

"Because we don't have two thousand euros."

Her mother grasped Jasmine's shoulders. She knew what a fragile state her daughter was in and had to do something.

"Yes, we do. I've worked every day since your father died, and we do have two thousand euros. We have more than that if you need it. Cleaners earn good money here in Europe because no one here wants to clean up other people's messes. Besides, we're talking about your future. We can't go home now."

The phone rang again. Jasmine became Cristina again and did as her mother asked. The woman she had the appointment with that afternoon was ringing to apologize and explain that another commitment meant that she would be a couple of hours late for their meeting.

"That's all right," said Cristina. "But before you waste any more time, I'd like to know how much it's going to cost me."

"How much it's going to cost?"

"Yes. I've just had a meeting with another photographer and he and his colleague were going to charge me two thousand euros for the photos, the makeup . . ."

The woman at the other end laughed.

"No, it won't cost you anything. That's an old trick. We can talk about it when we meet."

HER STUDIO WAS SIMILAR TO the one they'd visited that morning, but the conversation they had was completely different. She asked Cristina why she looked so much sadder than when they'd first met; she clearly still remembered their initial encounter. Cristina told her what had happened with the other photographer, and the woman explained that it was common practice and one that the authorities were trying to clamp down on. At that very moment, in many places around the world, relatively pretty girls were being invited to reveal "the full potential of their beauty" and paying through the nose for the privilege. On the pretext of looking for new talent, agencies would rent rooms in luxury hotels, fill them with photographic equipment, promise the would-be models at least one fashion show a year or their money back, charge a fortune for any photos they took, call in failed professionals to act as makeup artists and hairdressers, suggest enrollment in particular modeling schools, and then, quite often, disappear without a trace. The studio Cristina had visited was, in fact, a genuine one, but she'd been quite right to reject their offer.

"They're appealing to people's vanity, and there's nothing necessarily wrong in that, as long as the person involved knows what they're getting into. It's not something that only happens in the world of fashion either, it goes on in other areas too: writers publishing their own books, painters sponsoring their own exhibitions, film directors who go into debt in order to buy their place in the sun with one of the big studios, girls your age who leave home and go to the big city to work as waitresses, hoping to be discovered one day by a producer who'll propel them to stardom."

No, they wouldn't take any photos now. She needed to get to know Cristina better; pressing the camera button was the last stage in a long process that began with uncovering your subject's soul. They arranged to meet the following day to talk more.

"You need to choose a name."

"It's Jasmine Tiger."

Yes, her love of life had returned.

THE PHOTOGRAPHER INVITED HER TO spend the weekend at her beach house near the Dutch border, and they spent eight hours a day experimenting with the camera.

She expected Jasmine to reveal on her face a whole range of emotions suggested by words such as "fire," "seduction," "water." Jasmine had to try and show both sides of her soul, good and bad. She had to look down, straight ahead, to the side, to stare off into space. She had to imagine seagulls and demons. She had to imagine she'd been attacked by a group of older men and left in the restroom in a bar, having been raped by one or more of them; she had to be sinner and saint, perverse and innocent.

Some photos were taken out in the open, and even though her body was freezing, she was able to react to each stimulus, to obey each suggestion. They also used a small studio set up in one of the rooms so that the photographer could play around with different types of music and lighting. Jasmine would do her own makeup, while the photographer did her hair.

"Am I any good?" Jasmine would ask. "Why are you spending so much time on me?"

But all the photographer would say was: "We'll talk about that later," and then spend the rest of the evening looking at the work they'd done that day, thinking and making notes, but never commenting on whether she was pleased or disappointed with the results.

Not until Monday morning did Jasmine (for Cristina was definitively dead by then) get an opinion. They were waiting at Brussels station for the connection to Antwerp when the photographer suddenly said:

"You're the best model I've ever worked with."

"You're joking."

The woman looked at her in surprise, then said:

"No, really, you are. I've been working in this field for twenty years now; I've taken photographs of countless people; I've worked with professional models and film actors, all of them highly experienced, but none of them had your ability to express emotion. And do you know what that's called? Talent. In certain professions, talent is quite easy to measure: managing directors who can turn around a business on the verge of bankruptcy and make it a going concern again; sportsmen who break records; artists whose work lives on for at least two generations; so how can I be so sure about you as a model? Because I'm a professional. You've managed to show your angels and your demons through the lens of a camera, and that's not easy. I'm not talking about young people who like to dress up as vampires and go to Goth parties; I'm not talking about girls who put on an innocent air to try to arouse the pedophile in men. I'm talking about real demons and real angels."

The station was full of people walking back and forth. Jasmine looked at the train timetable and suggested they go outside. She was dying for a cigarette, and smoking was forbidden within the station precinct. She was wondering whether she should say what was going on inside her just then.

"It may be that I do have talent, but if I do, there's only one reason I was able to show that talent. You know, during all the time we've spent together, you've never said anything about your private life and never asked about mine. Do you want me to help you with your luggage, by the way? Photography's basically a profession for men, isn't it? There's always so much equipment to lug around."

The woman laughed.

"There's nothing much to say, really, except that I adore my work. I'm thirty-eight, divorced, no kids, but with enough good contacts to be able to earn a comfortable living, but not to live in any great luxury.

There's something else I must add to what I said: if everything goes to plan you must never ever behave like someone who depends on her profession to survive, even if it's true. If you don't follow my advice, you'll be easily manipulated by the system. Obviously, I'll use your photos and earn money with them, but from now on, I'd suggest you get yourself a professional agent."

Jasmine lit another cigarette; it was now or never.

"Do you know why I was able to show my talent? Because of something I never imagined would happen in my life: I've fallen in love with a woman, a woman I would like to have by my side, guiding whatever steps I need to take, a woman who with her gentleness and her rigor managed to get inside my soul and release both the best and the worst that lie in those subterranean depths. She didn't do this by long instruction in meditation techniques or through psychoanalysis—which is what my mother thinks I need—she used . . ."

She paused. She felt afraid, but she had to go on. She had nothing now to lose.

"She used a camera."

Time stood still. The other people outside the station stopped moving, all noise ceased, the wind dropped, her cigarette smoke hung in the hair, the lights went out—there were just two pairs of eyes shining brighter than ever and fixed on each other.

"YOU'RE READY," SAYS THE MAKEUP artist.

Jasmine looks up and sees her partner pacing up and down in the improvised dressing room. She must be feeling nervous; after all, this is her first fashion show in Cannes, and if it goes well, she might get a fat contract with the Belgian government.

Jasmine feels like going over and reassuring her, telling her that everything will be fine, as it always has been before. She might get a response along the lines of: "You're only nineteen, what do you know about life?"

She would reply: "I know what your capabilities are, just as you know mine. I know about the relationship that changed our lives one day three years ago, outside a train station, when you gently touched my cheek. Do you remember how frightened we both were? But we survived that first feeling of fear. And thanks to that relationship, I'm here now; and you, as well as being an excellent photographer, are doing what you always dreamed of doing: designing and making clothes."

She knows it's best not to say anything. Telling a person to calm down only makes them even more nervous.

She goes over to the window and lights another cigarette. She's smoking too much, but then why shouldn't she? This is her first major fashion show in France.

4:43 P.M.

A young woman in a black suit and white blouse opens the door. She asks for her name, checks the list, and says she'll have to wait a little; the suite is currently occupied. Two men and another woman, possibly younger than her, are also waiting.

They all wait their turn in silence. "How long will this take? What exactly am I doing here?" Gabriela asks herself and hears two responses.

The first reminds her that she must keep going. Gabriela, the optimist, the one who has persevered in order to reach stardom and now needs to think about the première, the invitations, the flights by private jet, the posters put up in all the world's capitals, the photographers on permanent watch outside her house, interested in what she's wearing and where she buys her clothes, and in the identity of the blond hunk she was seen with in some fashionable nightclub. Then there will be the victorious return to the town where she was born, the astonished friends eyeing her enviously, and the charitable projects she intends to support.

The second response reminds her that Gabriela the optimist, the one who has persevered in order to reach stardom, is now walking along a knife edge from which it would be all too easy to slip and plunge into the abyss. Hamid Hussein doesn't even know of her existence; no one has ever seen her made up and ready for a party; the dress might not be her size, it might need adjusting, and then she might arrive late for her meeting at the Martinez. She's twenty-five years old, and, who knows, they might be interviewing some other candidate right now on that same yacht or they might have changed their minds; in fact, perhaps that was the idea: to talk to two or three possible candidates and see which of them stood out from the crowd. All three of them might be invited to the party, unaware of each other's existence.

Paranoia.

No, it isn't paranoia, she's just being realistic. Even the fact that Gibson and the Star only ever got involved in major projects was no guarantee of success. And if anything went wrong, it would all be her fault. The ghost of the Mad Hatter from *Alice in Wonderland* is still there. Perhaps she isn't as talented as she thinks, just very hardworking. She hasn't been as lucky as some others; nothing of great importance has so far happened in her life, despite fighting day and night, night and day. She hasn't stopped since arriving in Cannes: distributing her extremely expensive book to various casting companies and getting only one audition. If she really was that special, she would now be having to decide which of several roles to accept. She's getting above herself and will soon know the taste of defeat, all the more bitter because she has come so close and dipped her toes in the ocean of fame . . . only to fail.

"I'm attracting bad vibrations. I know they're out there. I must get a grip on myself."

She can't do any yoga exercises in front of that woman in the suit and the three other people waiting in silence. She needs to drive away those negative thoughts, but where exactly are they coming from? According to what she's read—and she had read a lot on the subject at a time when she felt she was failing to achieve as much as she could because of other people's envy—it was likely that another actress who had been rejected was, at that moment, focusing all her energies on getting the role back. Yes, she could feel it, it was true! The only escape is to make her mind leave that corridor and go off in search of her Higher Self, which is connected to all the forces of the universe.

She breathes deeply, smiles, and says to herself:

"I am spreading the energy of love all around me; it is more power-ful than the forces of darkness; the God in me greets the God who lives in all the inhabitants of the planet, even those who . . ."

She hears someone laugh. The door to the suite opens, and a group of smiling, happy young people of both sexes, accompanied by two female celebrities, are leaving and heading for the lift. The two men and the woman go into the room, collect the dozens of bags left beside the door, and join the group waiting for them by the lift. They must be assistants, chauffeurs, secretaries.

"It's your turn," says the woman in the suit.

"Meditation never fails," thinks Gabriela.

She smiles confidently at the receptionist, but the suite itself almost takes her breath away. It's like an Aladdin's cave, full of rail upon rail of clothes, and all kinds of pairs of glasses, handbags, jewelry, beauty products, watches, shoes, tights, and electronic devices. A blonde woman comes to meet her; she has a list in one hand and a mobile phone on a chain around her neck. She takes Gabriela's name and says:

"Follow me. We haven't much time, so let's get straight down to business."

They go into one of the other rooms, and Gabriela sees still more luxurious, glamorous treasures, things she has only ever seen in shop windows, but never had a chance to see close up, except when worn by someone else.

Yes, all this awaits her. She needs to be quick and decide exactly what she's going to wear.

"Can I start with the jewelry?"

"You don't get to choose anything. We know exactly what HH wants. And you'll have to return the dress to us tomorrow."

HH. Hamid Hussein knows what he wants her to wear!

They cross the room. The bed and the other furniture are clut-tered with more products: T-shirts, spices and seasonings, a picture of a well-known make of coffee machine, several of which are wrapped up as presents. They go down a corridor and through the doors into an even larger room. She had no idea hotel suites could be so big.

"This is the Temple."

An elegant long white poster bearing the designer's logo has been placed above the vast double bed. An androgynous creature—whether male or female, Gabriela cannot tell—is waiting for them in silence. The creature is extremely thin, with drab, straggly hair, shaven eyebrows, beringed fingers, and is wearing skin-tight trousers adorned with various chains.

"Get undressed."

Gabriela takes off her blouse and her jeans, still trying to guess the gender of the creature who has now gone over to one of the dress rails and selected a red dress.

"Take your bra off too. It makes bulges under the dress."

There's a large mirror in the room, but it's turned away from her and so she can't see how the dress looks.

"We need to be quick. Hamid said that as well as going to the party, she has to go up the steps."

Go up the steps!

The magic words.

The dress was all wrong. The woman and the androgyne are starting to get worried. The woman asks for two or three other dresses to be brought because Gabriela will be going up the steps with the Star, who is dressed and ready.

Going up the steps with the Star! She must be dreaming!

They decide on a long gold dress that clings to the body and has a neckline that plunges to the waist. At breast-height, a gold chain keeps the opening from getting any wider than the human imagination can bear.

The woman is very nervous. The androgyne goes out and returns with a seamstress, who makes the necessary alterations to the hem. If Gabriela could say anything at that moment, it would be to ask them to stop. Sewing the dress while she is actually wearing it means that her fate is also being sewn up and interrupted. But this is no time for superstitions, and many famous actresses must face the same situation every day without anything bad ever happening to them.

A third person arrives, carrying an enormous suitcase, goes over to one corner of the vast room, and starts dismantling the case, which is, in fact, a kind of portable makeup studio, including a mirror surrounded by lights. The androgyne is kneeling before her, like a repentant Mary Magdalene, trying shoe after shoe on her foot.

She's Cinderella and will shortly meet her Prince and go up the steps with him!

"Those are good," says the woman.

The androgyne starts putting the other shoes back in their boxes.

"OK, take it off. We'll put the final touches to the dress while you're having your hair and makeup done."

Gabriela feels relieved that they will no longer be sewing the dress while it is on her body. Her destiny opens up again.

Wearing only a pair of panties, she is led to the bathroom. A portable kit for washing and drying hair has already been installed there, and a shaven-headed man is waiting. He asks her to sit down and lean her head back into a kind of steel basin. He uses a hose attached to the tap to wash her hair, and, like everyone else, he's extremely agitated. He complains about the noise from outside; he needs quiet if he's to do a decent job, but no one pays any attention. Besides, he never has enough time; everything's always done in such a rush.

"No one understands the enormous responsibility resting on my shoulders," he says.

He's not talking to her, but to himself. He goes on:

"When you go up the steps, they're not looking at you, you know. They're looking at my work, at my makeup and at my hairstyling. You're just the canvas on which I paint or draw, the clay out of which I shape my sculptures. If I make a mistake, what will other people say? I could lose my job."

Gabriela feels offended, but she's obviously going to have to get used to this kind of thing. That's what the world of glamour is like. Later on, when she really is someone, she'll choose kind, polite people to work with her. For now, she focuses on her main virtue: patience.

The conversation is interrupted by the roar of the hair dryer, similar to that of a plane taking off. And he was the one complaining about the noise outside!

He rather roughly primps her hair into shape and asks her to move straight over to the portable makeup studio. His mood changes completely: he stands in silence, contemplating her face in the mirror, as if he were in a trance. He paces back and forth, using the dryer and the brush much as Michelangelo used hammer and chisel on his sculpture of David. And she tries to keep looking straight ahead and remember some lines written by a Portuguese poet:

The mirror reflects perfectly; it makes no mistakes because it doesn't think. To think is to make mistakes.

The androgyne and the woman return. In only twenty minutes the limousine will arrive to take her to the Martinez to pick up the Star. There's nowhere to park there, so they have to be right on time. The hairdresser mutters to himself, as if he were a misunderstood artist, but he knows he has to meet those deadlines. He starts working on her face as if he were Michelangelo painting the Sistine Chapel.

A limousine! The steps! The Star!

The mirror reflects perfectly; it makes no mistakes because it doesn't think.

She mustn't think either, because, if she does, she'll be infected by the prevailing anxiety and bad temper; those negative vibes will come back. She would love to know just what it is, this hotel suite packed with all these different things, but she must behave as if she were used to frequenting such places. Beneath the severe gaze of the woman and the distracted gaze of the androgyne, Michelangelo is putting the finishing touches to her makeup. Gabriela then stands up and is swiftly dressed and shod. Everything is in place, thank God.

From somewhere in the room, they grab a small leather Hamid Hussein bag. The androgyne opens it, removes some of the paper stuffing, studies the result with the same distracted air, and, when it appears to meet with his approval, hands it to her.

The woman gives her four copies of a huge contract, with small red markers along the edge, bearing the words: "Sign here."

"You can either sign without reading it or take it home, phone your lawyer, and say you need more time to think before deciding. You'll go up those steps regardless because it's too late to change anything now. However, if this contract isn't back here tomorrow morning, you just have to return the dress and that will be that."

She remembers her agent's words: accept everything. Gabriela takes the pen the woman is holding out to her, turns to the pages with the markers, and signs everything. She has nothing to lose. If there are any unfair clauses, she can probably go to the courts later on and say she was pressured into signing. First, though, she has to do what she has always dreamed of doing.

The woman takes the signed contract from her and vanishes without saying goodbye. Michelangelo is once again dismantling the makeup table, immersed in his own little world in which injustice rules, and in which his work is never recognized, where he never has enough time to do a proper job, and where, if anything goes wrong, the fault will be entirely his. The androgyne asks her to follow him to the door of the suite; he consults his watch—which, Gabriela notices, bears a death's head—and speaks to her for the first time since they have met.

"We've got another three minutes. You can't go down now and be seen by other people. And I have to go with you to the limousine."

The tension returns. She's no longer thinking about the limousine, about the Star, or going up those steps; she's afraid. She needs to talk.

"What's this suite for? Why are there all these things in it?"

"There's even a safari to Kenya," says the androgyne, pointing to one corner. She hadn't noticed the discreet advertising banner for an airline and a small pile of envelopes on the table. "It's free, like everything else in here, apart from the clothes and the accessories in the Temple."

Coffee machines, electronic gadgets, clothes, handbags, watches, jewelry, and a trip to Kenya.

All of it absolutely free?

"I know what you're thinking," says the androgyne in that voice which is neither male nor female, but the voice of some interplanetary being. "But it is all free, or, rather, given in fair exchange because noth-ing in this world is free. This is one of the many 'Gift Rooms' you get in Cannes during the Festival. The chosen few come in here and take whatever they want; they're people who will be seen around wearing a shirt designed by A or some glasses by B, they'll receive important guests in their home and, when the Festival's over, go into their kitchen and prepare some coffee with a brand-new coffee machine. They'll carry around their laptop in a bag made by C, recommend friends to use moisturizers by D, which are just about to be launched on the market, and they'll feel important doing that because it means they'll own something exclusive, which hasn't yet reached the specialist shops. They'll wear E's jewelry to the swimming pool and be photographed wearing a belt by F, neither of which are yet available to the public. When these products do come on the market, the Superclass will al-ready have done their advertising for them, not because they want to, but because they're the only ones who can. Then mere mortals will spend all their savings on buying the same products. What could be easier, sweetheart? The manufacturers invest in some free samples, and the chosen few are transformed into walking advertisements. But don't get too excited. You haven't reached those heights yet."

"But what has the safari to Kenya got to do with all that?"

"What better publicity than a middle-aged couple arriving back all excited from their 'jungle adventure' with loads of pictures in their camera, and recommending everyone else to go on the same exclusive holiday? All their friends will want to experience the same thing. As I say, nothing in this world is free. By the way, the three minutes are up, so we'd better go."

A white Maybach is waiting for them. The chauffeur, in gloves and cap, opens the door. The androgyne gives her final instructions:

"Forget about the film, that isn't why you're going up the steps. When you get to the top of the steps, greet the Festival director and the mayor, and then, as soon as you enter the Palais des Congrès, head for the restroom on the first floor. Go to the end of that corridor, turn left, and leave by a side door. Someone will be waiting for you there;

they know how you'll be dressed and will do some more work on your makeup and your hair, and then you can have a moment's rest on the terrace. I'll meet you there and take you to the gala supper."

"Won't the director and the producers be annoyed?"

The androgyne shrugs and goes back into the hotel with that strange swaying gait. The film is not of the slightest importance. What matters is *la montée des marches*, going up the red-carpeted steps to the Palais and along the ultimate corridor of fame, the place where all the celebrities in the worlds of cinema, the arts, and the high life are photographed, and their photos then distributed by news agencies to the four corners of the world to be published in magazines from west to east and from north to south.

"Is the air-conditioning all right for you, madame?"

She nods to the chauffeur.

"If you want anything to drink, there's a bottle of iced champagne in the cabinet to your left."

Gabriela opens the cabinet and gets out a glass; then, holding the bottle well away from her dress, she pops the cork and pours herself a glass of champagne which she downs in one and immediately refills. Outside, curious onlookers are trying to see who is inside the vast car with the smoked windows that is driving along the cordoned-off lane. Soon, she and the Star will be together, the beginning not just of a new career, but of an incredible, beautiful, intense love story.

She's a romantic and proud of it.

She remembers that she left her clothes and her handbag in the Gift Room. She doesn't have the key to the apartment she's renting. She has nowhere to go when the night is over. If she ever writes a book about her life, how could she possibly tell the story of that particular day: waking up with a hangover, unemployed and in a bad mood, in an apartment with clothes and mattresses scattered all over the floor, and six hours later being driven along in a limousine, ready to walk along the red carpet in front of a crowd of journalists, beside one of the most desirable men in the world.

Her hands are trembling. She considers drinking another glass of champagne, but decides not to risk turning up drunk on the steps of fame.

"Relax, Gabriela. Don't forget who you are. Don't get carried away by everything that's happening now. Be realistic."

She repeats these words over and over as they approach the Martinez. Whether she likes it or not, she can never go back to being the person she was before. There is no way out, except the one the androgyne told her about and which leads to a still higher mountain.

4:52 P.M.

Even the King of Kings, Jesus Christ, was tested as Igor is being tested now: being tempted by the Devil. And he needs to cling on tooth and nail to his faith if he's not to weaken in the mission with which he has been charged.

The Devil is asking him to stop, to forgive, to abandon his task. The Devil is a top-class professional and knows how to fill the weak with alarming feelings such as fear, anxiety, impotence, and despair.

When it comes to tempting the strong, he uses more sophisticated lures: good intentions. It's exactly what he did with Jesus when he found him wandering in the wilderness. Why, he asked, didn't he command that the stones be made bread, so that he could satisfy not only his own hunger, but that of all the other people begging him for food? Jesus, however, acted with the wisdom one would expect of the Son of God. He replied that man does not live on bread alone, but on every word from God's mouth.

Besides, what exactly were good intentions, virtue, and integrity? The people who built the Nazi concentration camps thought they were showing integrity by obeying government orders. The doctors who certified as insane any intellectuals opposed to the Soviet regime and had them banished to Siberia were convinced that Communism was a fair system. Soldiers who go to war may kill in the name of an ideal they don't properly understand, but they, too, are full of good intentions, virtue, and integrity.

No, that's not true. If sin achieves something good, it is a virtue, and if virtue is deployed to cause evil, it is a sin.

IN HIS CASE, THE EVIL One is trying to use forgiveness as a way to trouble his soul. He says: "You're not the only person to have been through this. Lots of people have been abandoned by the person they most loved, and yet managed to turn bitterness into happiness. Imagine the families of the people whom you have caused to depart this life; they'll be filled with rancor and hatred and a desire for revenge. Is that how you intend to improve the world? Is that what you want to give to the woman you love?"

Igor, however, is wiser than the temptations that seem to be possessing his soul. If he can hold out a little longer, that voice will grow tired and disappear. He thinks this largely because one of the people he sent to Paradise is becoming an ever more constant presence in his life. The girl with the dark eyebrows is telling him that everything is fine, and that there's a great difference between forgiving and forgetting. He has no hatred in his heart, and he's not doing this to have his revenge on the world.

The Devil may insist all he likes, but he must stand firm and remember why he's here.

HE GOES INTO THE FIRST pizzeria he sees, and orders a pizza margharita and a Coke. It's best to eat now because he won't be able to—he never can—eat properly over supper with a lot of other people round the table. Everyone feels obliged to keep up an animated but relaxed conversation, and someone always seems to interrupt him just as he's about to take a bite of the delicious food in front of him.

His usual way of avoiding this is to bombard his companions at table with questions, then leave them to come up with intelligent responses while he eats his meal in peace. Tonight, though, he will feel disinclined to be helpful and sociable. He will be unpleasant and distant. He can always claim not to speak their language.

He knows that in the next few hours, Temptation will prove stronger than ever, telling him to stop and give it all up. He doesn't want to stop, though; his objective is still to complete his mission, even if the reason for that mission is changing.

He has no idea if three violent deaths in one day would be considered normal in Cannes; if it is, the police won't suspect that anything unusual is happening. They'll continue their bureaucratic procedures and he'll be able to fly off as planned in the early hours of tomorrow. He doesn't know either if he has been identified: there was that couple who passed him and the girl this morning, there was one of the dead man's bodyguards, and the person who witnessed the other woman's murder.

Temptation is now changing its tactics: it wants to frighten him, just as it does with the weak. It would seem that the Devil has no idea what he has been through nor that he has emerged a much stronger man from the test fate has set him.

He picks up his mobile phone and sends another text.

He imagines Ewa's reaction when she receives it. Something tells him that she will feel a mixture of fear and pleasure. He is sure that she deeply regrets the step she took two years ago—leaving everything behind her, including her clothes and jewelry, and asking her lawyer to get in touch with him regarding divorce proceedings. The grounds: incompatibility. As if interesting people will ever necessarily think exactly the same way or have many things in common. It was clearly a lie: she had fallen in love with someone else.

Passion. Which of us can honestly say that, after more than five years of marriage, we haven't felt a desire to find another companion? Which of us can honestly say that we haven't been unfaithful at least once in our life, even if only in our imagination? And how many men and women have left home because of that, then discovered that passion doesn't last and gone back to their true partners? A little mature reflection and everything is forgotten. That's absolutely normal, part of human biology.

He has had to learn this very slowly. At first, he instructed his law-yers to proceed with the utmost rigor. If she wanted to leave him, then she would have to give up all claim to the fortune they had accumulated together over nearly twenty years, every penny of it. He got drunk for a whole week while he waited for her response. He didn't care about the money; he was doing it because he wanted her back, and that was the only way he knew of putting pressure on her.

Ewa, however, was a person of integrity. Her lawyers accepted his conditions.

It was only when the press got hold of the case that he found out about his ex-wife's new partner. One of the most successful couturiers in the world, someone who, like him, had built himself up from noth-ing; a man, like him, in his forties, and known, like him, for his lack of arrogance and his hard work.

He couldn't understand what had happened. Shortly before Ewa left for a fashion show in London, they had spent a rare romantic holiday alone in Madrid. They had traveled there in the company jet and were staying in a hotel with every possible comfort, but they had decided to rediscover the world together. They didn't book tables at expen-sive restaurants, they stood in long queues outside museums, they took taxis rather than chauffeured limousines, they walked for miles and got thoroughly lost. They ate a lot and drank even more, and would arrive back at the hotel exhausted and contented, and make love every night as they used to do.

For both of them it took a real effort to stop themselves from turn-ing on their laptops or their mobile phones, but they managed it. And they returned to Moscow with their hearts full of good memories and with smiles on their faces.

He plunged back into work, surprised to see that everything had continued to function perfectly well in his absence. She left for London the following week and never came back.

Igor employed one of the top private surveillance agencies—nor-mally used for industrial or political espionage—which meant having to look at hundreds of photos in which his wife appeared hand in hand with her new companion. Using information provided by her husband, the detectives managed to provide her with a made-to-measure "friend." Ewa met her "by chance" in a department store; she was from Russia and had, she said, been abandoned by her husband, couldn't get work in Britain because she didn't have the right papers, and had barely enough money to feed herself. Ewa was distrustful at first, but then resolved to help her. She spoke to her new lover, who decided to take a risk and get the friend a job in one of his offices, even though she was an illegal worker.

She was Ewa's only Russian-speaking "friend." She was alone. She had marital problems. According to the psychologist employed by the surveillance agency, she was ideally placed to obtain the desired information. He knew that Ewa hadn't yet adapted to her new life, and what could be more natural than to share her intimate thoughts with another woman in similar circumstances, not in order to find a solution, but simply to unburden her soul.

The "friend" recorded all their conversations, and the tapes ended up on Igor's desk, where they took precedence over papers requiring his signature, invitations demanding his presence, and gifts waiting to be sent to customers, suppliers, politicians, and fellow businessmen.

The tapes were far more useful and far more painful than any photos. He discovered that her relationship with the famous couturier had begun two years earlier, at the Fashion Week in Milan, where they had met for professional reasons. Ewa resisted at first; after all, he lived surrounded by some of the most beautiful women in the world, and she, at the time, was thirty-eight. Nevertheless, they ended up going to bed with each other in Paris, the following week.

When Igor heard this, he realized that he felt sexually aroused and couldn't understand why his body should react in that way. Why did the simple fact of imagining his wife opening her legs and being penetrated by another man provoke in him an erection rather than a sense of revulsion?

This was the only time he feared he might be losing his mind, and he decided to make a kind of public confession in an attempt to diminish his sense of guilt. In conversation with colleagues, he mentioned that "a friend of his" had experienced sexual pleasure when he found out that his wife was having an extramarital affair. Then came the surprise.

His colleagues, most of them executives and politicians from various social classes and nationalities, at first expressed horror at the thought. Then, after the tenth glass of vodka, they all admitted that this was one of the most exciting things that could happen in a marriage. One of them always asked his wife to tell him all the sordid details and the words she and her lover used. Another declared that swingers' clubs—places frequented by couples interested in group sex—were the ideal therapy for an ailing marriage. A slight exaggeration perhaps, but Igor was glad to learn that he wasn't the only man who found it arousing to know that his wife had slept with someone else. He was equally glad that he knew so little about human beings, especially the male of the species. His conversations usually focused on business matters and rarely entered personal territory.

HE'S THINKING NOW ABOUT WHAT was on those tapes. During their week in London (the fashion weeks are held consecutively to make life easier for the professionals involved), the couturier declared himself to be in love with her; hardly surprising, given that he had met one of the most unusual women in the world. Ewa, for her part, was still filled with doubts. Hussein was only the second man with whom she had made love in her life; they worked in the same industry, but she felt immensely inferior to him. She would have to give up her dream of working in fashion because it would be impossible to compete with her future husband, and she would go back to being a mere housewife.

Worse, she couldn't understand why someone so powerful should be interested in a middle-aged Russian woman.

Igor could have explained this had she given him a chance: her mere presence awoke the light in all those around her; she made everyone want to give of their best and to emerge from the ashes of the past filled with renewed hope. That is what had happened to him as a young man returning from a bloody and pointless war.

TEMPTATION RETURNS. THE DEVIL TELLS him that this isn't exactly true. He himself had overcome his traumas by plunging into work. Psychiatrists might consider working too hard to be a psychological disorder, but for him it had been a way of healing his wounds through forgiveness and forgetting. Ewa wasn't really so very important. He must stop focusing all his emotions on a nonexistent relationship.

"You're not the first," said the Devil. "You're being led into doing evil deeds in the erroneous belief that this will somehow create good deeds."

IGOR IS STARTING TO FEEL nervous. He's a good man, and whenever he's been obliged to behave harshly, it has been in the name of a greater cause: serving his country, saving the marginalized from unnecessary suffering, following the example of his one role model in life, Jesus Christ, and, like him, using a combination of turning the cheek and wielding the whip.

He makes the sign of the cross in the hope that Temptation will leave him. He forces himself to remember the tapes and what Ewa had said: that however unhappy she might be with her new partner, she would never return to the past because her ex-husband was "unbalanced."

How absurd. It appeared she was being brainwashed by her new environment. She must be keeping very bad company. He's sure she was lying when she told her Russian "friend" that she had only got married again because she was afraid of being alone.

In her youth, she had always felt rejected by others and never able to be herself. She always had to pretend to be interested in the same things as her friends, playing the same games, going to parties, and looking for some handsome man to be a faithful husband and give her security, a home, and children. "It was all a lie," she said on the tapes.

In fact, she always dreamed of adventure and the unknown. If she could have chosen a profession when she was still an adolescent, it would have been that of artist. When she was a child, she had loved making collages from photos cut out of Communist Party magazines; she hated the photos, but enjoyed coloring in the drab figures. Dolls' clothes were so hard to find that her mother had to make them for her, and Ewa loved those outfits and said to herself that, one day, she would make clothes too.

There was no such thing as fashion in the former Soviet Union. They only found out what was going on in the rest of the world when the Berlin Wall was torn down and foreign magazines started flooding into the country. As an adolescent, she was able to use these magazines to make brighter and more interesting collages. Then, one day, she decided to tell her family that her dream was to be a fashion designer.

As soon as she finished school, her parents sent her to law school. They were very happy with their new-won freedom, but felt that certain capitalist ideas were threatening to destroy the country, distracting people from real art, replacing Tolstoy and Pushkin with spy novels, and corrupting classical ballet with modern aberrations. Their only daughter must be kept away from the moral degradation that had arrived along with Coca-Cola and flashy cars.

At university, she met a good-looking, ambitious young man who thought exactly as she did, that they had to give up the idea that the old regime would return one day. It had gone for good, and it was time to start a new life.

She really liked this young man. They started going out together. She saw that he was intelligent and would go far in life, plus he seemed to understand her. He had, of course, fought in the Afghan war and been wounded in combat, but nothing very serious. He never complained about the past and never showed any signs of being unbalanced or traumatized.

One day, he brought her a bunch of roses and told her that he was leaving university to start his own business. He then proposed to her, and she accepted, even though she felt only admiration and friendship for him. Love, she believed, would grow over time as they became closer. Besides, the young man was the only one who really understood her and provided her with the intellectual stimulus she needed. If she let this chance slip, she might never find another person prepared to accept her as she was.

They got married with little fuss and without the support of their families. He obtained loans from people she considered dangerous, but she could do nothing to prevent the loans going ahead. Gradually, the company he had started began to grow. After almost four years together, she—shaking with fear—made her first demand: that he pay off the people who had lent him money in the past and who seemed suspiciously uninterested in recouping it. He followed her advice and often had reason to thank her for it later.

The years passed, there were the inevitable failures and sleepless nights, then things started to improve, and from then on, the ugly duckling began to follow the script of all those children's stories: it grew into a beautiful swan, admired by everyone.

Ewa complained about being trapped in her role as housewife. Instead of reacting like her friends' husbands, for whom a job was synonymous with a lack of femininity, he bought her a shop in one of the most sought-after areas of Moscow. She started selling clothes made by the world's great couturiers, but never tried to create her own designs. Her work had other compensations, though: she visited all the major fashion houses, met interesting people, and it was then that she first encountered Hamid. She still didn't know whether or not she loved him—possibly not—but she felt comfortable with him. When he had told her that he'd never met anyone like her and suggested they live together, she felt she had nothing to lose. She had no children, and her husband was so married to his work that he probably wouldn't even notice she was gone.

"I left it all behind," Ewa said on one of the tapes. "And I don't regret it one bit. I would have done the same even if Hamid—against my wishes—hadn't bought that beautiful estate in Spain and put it in my name. I would have made the same decision if Igor, my ex-husband, had offered me half his fortune. I would have taken the same decision because I know that I need to live without fear. If one of the most desirable men in the world wants to be by my side, then I'm obviously a better person than I thought."

On another tape, she commented that her husband clearly had severe psychological problems.

"My husband has lost his reason. Whether it stems from his war experiences or stress from overwork, I've no idea, but he thinks he knows what God intends. Before I left, I sought advice from a psychiatrist in order to try and understand him better, to see if it was possible to save our relationship. I didn't go into details so as not to compromise him and I won't do so with you now, but I think he would be capable of doing terrible things if he believed he was doing good.

"The psychiatrist explained to me that many generous, compassionate people can, from one moment to the next, change completely. Studies have been done of this phenomenon and they call that sudden change 'the Lucifer effect' after Lucifer, God's best-loved angel, who ended up trying to rival God himself."

"But why does that happen?" asked another female voice.

At that point, however, the tape ran out.

HE WOULD LIKE TO HAVE heard her answer because he knows he doesn't consider himself on a par with God and because he's sure that his beloved is making the whole thing up, afraid that if she did come back, she would be rejected. Yes, he had killed out of necessity, but what did that have to do with their marriage? He had killed when he was a soldier, with official permission. He had killed a couple of other people too, but only in their best interests because they had no means of living a decent life. In Cannes, he was merely carrying out a mission.

And he would only kill someone he loved if he saw that she was mad, had completely lost her way and begun to destroy her own life. He would never allow the decay of a mind to ruin a brilliant, generous past. He would only kill someone he loved in order to save her from a long, painful process of self-destruction.

IGOR LOOKS AT THE MASERATI that has just drawn up opposite him in a no-parking zone. It's an absurd, uncomfortable car which, despite its powerful engine—too low-powered for B roads and too high-powered for motorways—has to dawdle along at the same speed as other cars.

A man of about fifty—but trying to look thirty—opens the door and struggles out because the door is too low to the ground. He goes into the pizzeria and orders a quattro formaggi to go.

Maserati and pizza are something of a mismatch, but these things happen.

Temptation returns. It's not talking to him now about forgiveness and generosity, about forgetting the past and moving on, it's trying a different tack and placing real doubts in his mind. What if Ewa were deeply unhappy? What if, despite her love for him, she was too deep in the bottomless pit of a bad decision, as Adam was the moment he accepted the apple and condemned the whole human race?

He had planned everything, he tells himself for the hundredth time. He wanted them to get back together again and not to allow a little word like "goodbye" to erase their whole past life. He knows that all marriages have their crises, especially after eighteen years. However, he also knows that a good strategist has to be flexible. He sends another text message, just to make sure she gets it. He stands up and says a prayer, asking to have the cup of renunciation removed from him.

The soul of the little seller of craftwork is beside him. He knows now that he committed an injustice; it wouldn't have hurt him to wait until he had found a more equal opponent, like the pseudo-athlete with the hennaed hair, or until he could save someone from further suffering, as was the case with the woman on the beach.

The girl with the dark eyebrows seems to hover over him like a saint, telling him to have no regrets. He acted correctly, saving her from a future of suffering and pain. Her pure soul is gradually driving away Temptation, helping Igor to understand that the reason he's in Cannes isn't to revive a lost love; that's impossible. He's here to save Ewa from bitterness and decay. She may have treated him unfairly, but the many things she did to help him deserve a reward.

"I am a good man."

He goes over to the cashier, pays his bill, and asks for a small bottle of mineral water. When he leaves, he empties the contents of the bottle over his head.

He needs to be able to think clearly. He has dreamed of this day for so long and now he is confused.

Fashion may renew itself every six months, but one thing remains the same: bouncers always wear black.

Hamid had considered alternatives for his shows—dressing security guards in colorful uniforms, for example, or having them all dressed in white—but he knew that if he did anything like that, the critics would write more about "these pointless innovations" than about what really mattered: the new collection. Besides, black is the perfect color: conservative, mysterious, and engraved on the collective unconscious, thanks to all those old cowboy films. The goodies always wear white and the baddies wear black.

"Imagine if the White House was called the Black House. Everyone would think it was inhabited by the spirit of darkness."

Every color has a purpose, although people may think they're chosen at random. White signifies purity and integrity. Black intimidates. Red shocks and paralyzes. Yellow attracts attention. Green calms everything down and gives things the go-ahead. Blue soothes. Orange confuses.

Bouncers should wear black—so it was in the beginning and would be forever after.

AS USUAL, THERE ARE THREE different entrances. The first is for the press in general—a few journalists and a lot of photographers laden down with cameras. They seem perfectly polite, but have no qualms about elbowing a colleague out of the way to capture the best angle, an unusual shot, the perfect moment, or some glaring mistake. The second entrance is for the general public, and in that respect, the Fashion Week in Paris was no different from that show in a seaside resort in the South of France; the people who come in through the second entrance are always badly dressed and would almost certainly not be able to afford anything being shown that afternoon. However, there they are in their ripped jeans, bad-taste T-shirts, and, of course, their designer sneakers, convinced that they're looking really relaxed and at ease, which, of course, they aren't. Some do have what might well be expensive handbags and belts, but this seems somehow even more pathetic, like putting a painting by Velázquez in a plastic frame.

Finally, there is the VIP entrance. The security guards never have any idea who anyone is. They simply stand there, arms crossed, looking threatening, as if they were the real owners. A polite young woman, trained to remember famous faces, comes over to them with a list in her hand.

"Welcome, Mr. and Mrs. Hussein. Thank you so much for being here."

They go straight to the front. Everyone walks down the same corridor, but a barrier of metal pillars linked by a red velvet band marks out who are the most important people there. This is the Moment of Minor Glory, being singled out as special people, and even though this show isn't part of the official calendar—we mustn't forget that Cannes is, after all, a film festival—protocol must be rigorously observed. Because of that Moment of Minor Glory which occurs at all such similar events (suppers, lunches, cocktail parties), men and women spend hours in front of the mirror, convinced that artificial light is less harmful to the skin than the sun, against which they apply large amounts of sun factor. They are only two steps from the beach, but they prefer to use the sophisticated tanning machines in the beauty salons that are never more than a block away from the place where they're staying.

They could enjoy a lovely view if they were to go for a stroll along the Boulevard de la Croisette, but would they lose many calories? No. They are far better off using the treadmills in the hotel's mini-gym.

That way, they will be in good shape to attend the free lunches—for which they dress with studied casualness—where they feel important simply because they've been invited, or the gala suppers for which they have to pay a lot of money unless they have influential contacts, or the post-supper parties that go on into the small hours, or the last cup of coffee or glass of whisky in the hotel bar, all of which involve repeated visits to the toilets to retouch makeup, straighten ties, brush off any dandruff from jacket shoulders, and make sure one's lipstick is still perfect.

Finally, back in their luxurious hotel rooms, where they will find the bed made, the breakfast menu waiting, the weather forecast for the next day, a chocolate (which is immediately discarded as containing far too many calories), an envelope with their names exquisitely written (the envelope is never opened because all it contains is the standard-ized welcome letter from the hotel manager) beside a basket of fruit (devoured avidly because fruit is a rich source of fiber which is, in turn, good for the body and an excellent way of avoiding wind). They look in the mirror as they take off tie, makeup, dress, or dinner jacket, and say to themselves: "Nothing of much importance happened today. Per-haps tomorrow will be better."

EWA IS BEAUTIFULLY DRESSED IN an HH number that is at once discreet and elegant. They are ushered to two seats at the very front of the catwalk, next to the area reserved for the photographers, who are just coming in and setting up their equipment.

A journalist comes over and asks the usual question:

"Mr. Hussein, which would you say is the best film you've seen so far?"

"It's too early to give an opinion," he says, as usual. "I've seen a lot of very interesting things, but I prefer to wait until the end of the Festival before passing judgment."

In fact, he hasn't seen a single film. Later on, he'll talk to Gibson and ask him which he considers to be "the best film of the Festival."

The polite, smartly dressed blonde politely shoos the reporter away. She asks if they plan on going to the cocktail party being held by the Belgian government immediately after the show. She says that one of the ministers present would very much like to talk to him. Hamid considers the invitation, for he knows that the Belgians have put a lot of money into getting their couturiers a higher profile on the international scene, and thus recover some of the glory they once had as a colonial power in Africa.

"Yes, I might just drop in for a glass of champagne," he says.

"Aren't we meeting Gibson straight after this?" asks Ewa.

Hamid gets the message. He apologizes to the young woman. He had forgotten he had a prior commitment, but will be in touch with the minister later on.

A few photographers spot them and start taking photos. At the moment, they are the only people the press are interested in. Later, they're joined by a few models who were once all the rage and who pose and smile, sign autographs for some of the ill-dressed people in the audience, and do everything they can to be noticed, in the hope that their faces will once again appear in the press. The photographers turn their lenses on them, knowing that they're merely going through the motions to please their editors; none of the photos will be published. Fashion is about the present, and the models of three years ago—apart from those who keep themselves in the headlines either through carefully stage-managed scandals or because they really do stand out from the crowd—are only remembered by the people who wait behind the metal barriers outside hotels, or by ladies who can't keep up with the speed of change.

The older models who have just arrived are aware of this (and "older," of course, means anyone over twenty-five), but the reason they're in the audience isn't that they want to return to the catwalks, but because they're hoping to get a role in a film or a career as a presenter on some cable TV show.

WHO ELSE WILL BE ON the catwalk today, aside from the only reason Hamid is here, Jasmine?

Certainly not any of the four or five top models in the world, because they do only what they want to do, always charge a fortune, and would never dream of appearing at Cannes simply to lend prestige to someone else's show. Hamid reckons he will see two or three Class A models, like Jasmine, who will earn around fifteen hundred euros for that evening's work; you have to have a lot of charisma and, above all, a future in the industry; there will probably be another two or three Class B models, professionals who are brilliant on the catwalk, have the right kind of figure, but are not lucky enough to be taking part in any parallel events as special guests at the parties put on by the large conglomerates, and they will earn between six hundred and eight hundred euros. The rest will be made up of Class C models, girls who have recently entered the mad world of fashion shows and who earn between two hundred and three hundred euros simply "to gain experience."

Hamid knows what's going on in the heads of the girls in that third group: "I'm going to be a winner. I'm going to show everyone just what I can do. I'm going to be one of the most famous models in the world, even if that means having to sleep with a few older men."

Older men, however, are not as stupid as they think. The majority of these girls are underage, and in most countries in the world, anyone engaging in underage sex is likely to end up in jail. The legend differs greatly from the reality: no model gets to the top because of her sexual generosity; there's more to it than that.

Charisma. Luck. The right agent. Being in the right place at the right time. And the right time, according to the trend adapters, isn't what these girls new to the fashion world think it is. According to the latest research, everything indicates that the public is tired of seeing strange, anorexic creatures of indefinite age, but with provocative eyes. The casting agencies (who choose the models) are looking for something which is, apparently, extremely difficult to find: the girl next door, that is, someone who is absolutely ordinary and who transmits to everyone who sees her on posters or in fashion magazines the sense that she's just like them. And finding that extraordinary girl who appears to be so "ordinary" is an almost impossible task.

The days are long gone when mannequins were simply walking clothes hangers, although it has to be said that it is easier to dress someone thin—the clothes do hang better. The days are gone, too, of handsome men advertising expensive menswear. That worked well in the yuppie era, toward the end of the 1980s, but not anymore. There's no set standard for male beauty, and when men buy a product, they want to see someone they can associate with a work colleague or a drinking pal.

PEOPLE WHO HAVE ALREADY SEEN Jasmine on the catwalk had suggested her to Hamid as the perfect face for his new collection. They said things like: "She's got bags of charisma and yet other women can still identify with her." A Class C model is always chasing contacts and men who claim to be powerful enough to make her a star, but the best publicity you can get in the world of fashion—and possibly in all other worlds too—are recommendations from people in the know. Illogical though it may seem, as soon as someone is on the verge of being "discovered," everyone starts laying bets on their success or failure. Sometimes they win, sometimes they lose, but that's the way the market is.

THE ROOM IS BEGINNING TO fill up. The front-row seats are all reserved, and a group of elegantly dressed women and men in suits occupy some of those seats, while the rest remain empty. The general public are seated in the second, third, and fourth rows. The main focus of the photographers' attentions is now a famous model, who is married to a football player and has spent a lot of time in Brazil because, she says, she "just adores it." Everyone knows that "a trip to Brazil" is code for "plastic surgery," but no one says so openly. What happens is that, after a few days there, the visitor asks discreetly if a visit to a plastic surgeon might be fitted in between sightseeing trips to the beauties of

Salvador and dancing in the Rio carnival. There's a rapid exchange of business cards and the conversation ends there.

The nice blonde girl waits for the press photographers to finish their work (they, too, ask the model which, in her opinion, is the best film she's seen so far) and then leads her to the one free seat next to Hamid and Ewa. The photographers crowd round and take dozens of photos of the threesome—the great couturier, his wife, and the model-turned-housewife.

Some journalists ask Hamid what he thinks of the Belgian designer's work. Accustomed to this kind of question, he replies:

"That's what I came here to find out. I hear she's very talented."

The journalists insist, as if they hadn't heard his answer. They're nearly all Belgians; the French press aren't much interested. The nice blonde girl asks them to leave the guests in peace.

They move away. The ex-model sits down next to Hamid and tries to strike up a conversation, saying that she simply loves his work. He thanks her politely, and if she was expecting the response "Let's talk after the show," she's disappointed. Nevertheless, she proceeds to tell him everything that's happened in her life—the photos, the invitations, the trips abroad.

Hamid listens patiently, but as soon as he gets a chance (while the model is briefly talking to someone else), he turns to Ewa to ask her to save him from this dialogue of the deaf. His wife, however, is behaving even more strangely now and refuses to talk. His only alternative is to read the explanatory leaflet about the show.

The collection is a tribute to Ann Salens, who was considered the pioneer of Belgian fashion. She began designing in the sixties and opened a small boutique, but saw at once the enormous potential of the fashions created by the young hippies who were converging on Amsterdam from all over the world. She challenged—and triumphed over—the sober styles popular among the bourgeoisie at the time, and saw her clothes worn by various icons, including Queen Paola and that great muse of the French existentialist movement, the singer Juliette Gréco. She was one of the first to create the kind of fashion show that mixed clothes on the catwalk with lighting, music, and art. Nevertheless, she was little known outside her own country. She always had a terrible fear of cancer, and as Job says in the Bible, the thing that she greatly feared came upon her. She died of the dread illness and saw her business fail because of her own financial incompetence.

And, as with all things in a world that renews itself every six months, she had been completely forgotten. The designer who was about to show her own collection was displaying considerable courage in seeking inspiration in the past instead of trying to invent a future.

HAMID PUTS THE LEAFLET AWAY in his pocket. If Jasmine isn't all that he hopes, he'll go and talk to the designer afterward anyway and see if there's some project they can work on together. He's always open to new ideas, as long as his competitors are under his supervision.

He looks around him. The spotlights are well positioned, and, to his surprise, there are a good number of photographers present. Maybe the collection really is worth seeing, or perhaps the Belgian government has used its influence with the press, offering air tickets and accommodation. There's another possible explanation for so much interest, but Hamid hopes he's wrong. That reason is Jasmine. If he wants to proceed with his plans, he needs her to be someone completely unknown to the general public. Up until now, he's only heard comments from other people in the fashion business. If her face has already appeared in lots of magazines, then it will be a waste of time taking her on. Firstly, because it means someone has got there before him, and secondly, because it would make no sense to associate her with something fresh and new.

Hamid does a few calculations. This event must have been very expensive to put on, but, like the sheikh, the Belgian government is quite right: fashion for women, sport for men, celebrities for both sexes, those are the only things that interest everyone and the only things that can get a country's image recognized on the international scene. In the case of fashion, of course, there are often long negotiations with the Fédération to deal with first. However, he notices that one of the Fédération's directors is sitting alongside the Belgian politicians, so they are clearly losing no time.

More VIPs arrive, all of them shepherded in by the nice blonde girl. They seem slightly disoriented, as if they're not sure quite what they're doing here. They're overdressed, so this must be the first fashion show they've attended in France, having come straight from Brussels. They're certainly not part of the fauna currently invading the town to attend the Film Festival.

There is a five-minute delay. Unlike the Fashion Week in Paris, during which almost no show begins on time, there are a lot of other things happening in Cannes this week, and the press can't hang around for long. Then he realizes that he's wrong: most of the journalists present are talking to and interviewing the ministers; they're nearly all foreigners and from the same country. Only in a situation like this do politics and fashion meet.

The nice blonde girl goes over to the photographers and asks them to take their places; the show is about to begin. Hamid and Ewa have not exchanged a single word. She seems neither happy nor unhappy, and that bodes very ill indeed. If only she would complain or smile or say something! But she gives no clue as to what is going on inside her.

Best to concentrate on the screen at the far end of the catwalk from behind which the models will appear. At least fashion shows are something he can understand.

A few minutes ago, the models will have taken off all their underwear because bras and pants might leave visible marks underneath the clothes they'll be wearing. The models have already put on the first item they'll be showing and are waiting for the lights to dim, the music to start, and for someone—usually a woman—to tap them on the back to indicate the precise moment when they should head out toward the spotlights and the audience.

THE DIFFERENT CLASSES OF MODEL—A, B, and C—are all suffering from varying degrees of nerves, with the least experienced being the most excited. Some are saying a prayer, others are trying to peer through the curtain to see if anyone they know is there, or if their mother or father managed to get a good seat. There must be ten or twelve of them, each with their photo pinned up above the place where the clothes they'll be wearing are hung up in the order they'll be worn so that they can change in a matter of seconds and return to the catwalk looking completely relaxed, as if they'd been wearing the clothes all afternoon. The final touches have been given to makeup and hair. The models are repeating to themselves:

"I mustn't slip. I mustn't trip on the hem. I have been personally chosen by the designer from sixty other models. I'm in Cannes. There's probably someone important in the audience. I know that HH is here, and he might choose me for his brand. They say the place is full of photographers and journalists.

"I mustn't smile because that's against the rules. My feet must tread an invisible line. In these high heels I need to walk as if I were marching. It doesn't matter if that way of walking is artificial or uncomfortable—I must remember that.

"I must reach the mark, turn to one side, pause for two seconds, then come straight back at the same speed, knowing that as soon as I leave the catwalk, there'll be someone waiting to take off my clothes and put on the next set, and that I won't even have time to look in the mirror! I have to trust that everything will go well. I need to show off not only my body, not only the clothes, but the power of my gaze."

Hamid glances up at the ceiling: that is the mark, a spotlight brighter than the others. If the model overshoots that mark or stops beforehand, she won't photograph well, and then the magazine editors—or, rather, the Belgian magazine editors—will choose to show a photo of another model. The French press is currently camped outside the hotels or alongside the red carpet or at some evening cocktail party or else eating a sandwich before the main gala supper of the night.

The lights in the room go out, and the spotlights above the catwalk go on.

This is the big moment.

A powerful sound system fills the air with a soundtrack from the sixties and seventies. It transports Hamid to a world he never knew, but which he has heard people talk about. He feels a certain nostalgia for what he has never known and a twinge of anger—why didn't he get the chance to experience the great dream of all those young people traveling the world?

The first model comes on, and sound fuses with vision—the brightly colored clothes, full of life and energy, are telling a story that happened a long time ago, but one that the world still likes to hear. Beside him, he hears the click and whirr of dozens of shutters. The cameras are recording everything. The first model performs perfectly—she walks as far as the mark, turns to the right, pauses for two seconds, then walks back. She will have approximately fifteen seconds to reach the wings, when she will drop her pose and run to the hanger where the next dress is waiting; she quickly gets undressed, gets dressed even more quickly, takes her place in the queue, and is ready for her next appearance. The designer will be watching everything via closed circuit television, biting her lips and hoping that no one slips up, that the audience understands what she's trying to say, that she gets a round of applause at the end, and that the emissary from the Fédération is duly impressed.

The show continues. From where he is sitting, both Hamid and the TV cameras can see how elegantly the models walk, how firmly they tread. The people sitting on the side—who, like the majority of VIPs present, are not used to fashion shows—wonder why the girls "march" instead of walking normally, like the models they're used to seeing on fashion programs. Is this the designer trying to seem original?

No, thinks Hamid. It's because of the high heels. Only by marching like that can they be sure they won't stumble. What the cameras show—because they're filming head-on—isn't really a true representation of what's happening.

The collection is better than he expected, a trip back in time with a few creative, contemporary touches, nothing over-the-top, because the secret of good fashion, as with good cooking, lies in knowing how much of which ingredient to use. The flowers and beads are a reminder of those crazy years, but they're used in such a way that they seem absolutely modern. Six models have now appeared on the catwalk, and he notices that one of them has a pinprick on her knee that makeup cannot disguise. Minutes before, she must have injected herself there with a shot of heroin to calm her nerves and suppress her appetite.

Suddenly, Jasmine appears. She's wearing a long-sleeved white blouse, all hand-embroidered, and a white below-the-knee skirt. She walks confidently, but, unlike the others, her seriousness isn't put on, it's natural, absolutely natural. Hamid glances at the others in the audience; everyone in the room is mesmerized by Jasmine, so much so that no one even glances at the model leaving or entering after she has finished her turn and is walking back to the dressing room.

"Perfect!"

On her next two appearances on the catwalk, he studies every detail of her body, and sees that she radiates something more than just physical beauty. How could one define that? The marriage between Heaven and Hell? Love and Loathing going hand in hand?

As with any fashion show, the whole thing lasts no more than fifteen minutes, even though it has taken months of planning and preparation. At the end, the designer comes onto the catwalk to acknowledge the applause; the lights go up, the music stops, and only then does he realize how much he's been enjoying the soundtrack. The nice blonde girl comes over to them and says that someone from the Belgian government would very much like to speak to him. He takes out his leather wallet and offers her his card, explaining that he's staying at the Hotel Martinez and would be delighted to arrange to meet the following day.

"But I *would* like to talk to the designer and the black model. Do you happen to know which supper they'll be going to tonight? I'll wait here for a reply."

He hopes the nice blonde girl doesn't take too long. The journalists are gathering to ask him the usual questions, or, rather, the same question repeated by different journalists:

"What did you think of the show?"

"Very interesting," he says, which is the answer he always gives.

"And what does that mean?"

With the delicacy of a practiced professional, Hamid moves on to the next journalist. Always be polite to the press, but never give a direct answer and say only what seems appropriate at the time.

The nice blonde girl returns. No, they won't be going to the gala supper that night. Despite the presence of all those ministers, Film Festival politics are dictated by a different sort of power.

Hamid says that he'll have the necessary invitations sent to them, and his offer is accepted at once. The designer doubtless expected this response, knowing the value of the product she has in her hands.

Jasmine.

Yes, she's the one. He would only rarely use her in a show because she's more powerful than the clothes she's wearing, but as "the public face of Hamid Hussein" there could be no one better.

EWA TURNS ON HER MOBILE phone as they leave. Seconds later, an envelope flies across a blue sky, lands at the bottom of the screen, and opens, and all that to say: "You have a message."

"What a ridiculous bit of animation," thinks Ewa.

Again the name of the caller has been blocked. She's unsure whether to open the text, but her curiosity is stronger than her fear.

"It seems some admirer has found your phone number," jokes Hamid. "You don't usually get that many texts."

"Maybe you're right."

What she would really like to say is: "Don't you understand? After two years together, can you not see that I'm terrified, or do you just think I've got PMS?"

She pretends casually to read the message:

"I've destroyed another world because of you. And I'm beginning to wonder if it's really worth it because you don't appear to understand my message. Your heart is dead."

"Who's it from?"

"I haven't the slightest idea. It doesn't give the number. Still, it's always nice to have a secret admirer."

5:15 P.M.

Three murders. All the statistics have been overturned in only a matter of hours and are showing an increase of fifty percent.

He goes to his car and tunes in to a special frequency on his radio.

"I believe there's a serial killer at work in the town."

A voice murmurs something at the other end. The sound of static cuts out some of the words, but Savoy understands what is being said.

"No, I can't be sure, but neither do I have any doubts about it."

More comments, more static.

"I'm not mad, sir, and I'm not contradicting myself. For example, I can't be sure that my salary will be deposited in my account at the end of the month, but I don't actually doubt that it will. Do you see what I mean?"

More static and angry words.

"No, sir, I'm not asking for an increase in salary, I'm just saying that certainties and doubts can coexist, especially in a profession like ours. Yes, all right, let's leave that to one side and move on to what really matters. The man in hospital has just died, so it's quite possible that on the news tonight three murders will be reported. All we know, so far, is that each of the three murders was committed using a different but very sophisticated technique, which is why no one will suspect that they're connected, but suddenly Cannes is being seen as a dangerous town. And if this carries on, people are bound to start speculating about whether there is, in fact, only one murderer. What do you want me to do?"

More angry comments from the commissioner.

"Yes, they're here. The boy who witnessed the murder is telling them everything he knows. The place is swarming with photographers and journalists at the moment. I assumed they'd all be lined up and waiting by the red carpet, but it seems I was wrong. The problem with the Festival is that there are too many reporters and nothing to report."

More indignant remarks. He takes a notebook from his pocket and writes down an address.

"Fine. I'll go straight to Monte Carlo and talk to him."

The static stops. The person at the other end has hung up.

Savoy walks to the end of the pier, places the siren on the roof of his car, puts it on at maximum volume, and races off like a madman, hoping to lure the reporters away to some nonexistent crime. They, however, wise to this trick, stay where they are and continue interviewing the boy.

Savoy is beginning to feel excited. He can finally leave all that paperwork to be completed by an underling and devote himself to what he's always dreamed of doing: solving murders that defy all logic. He hopes he's right and that there really is a serial killer in town terrorizing the population. Given the speed with which news spreads these days, he'll soon be in the spotlight explaining that "nothing has yet been proved," but in such a way that no one quite believes him, thus ensuring that the spotlight will stay on him until the criminal is found. For all its glamour, Cannes is really just a small provincial town, where everyone knows everything that's going on, so it shouldn't be that hard to find the murderer.

Fame and celebrity.

Is he just thinking about himself rather than about the well-being of Cannes' citizens? Then again, what's wrong with seeking a little glory, when every year for years now, he's been forced to put up with twelve days of people trying to look far more important than they really are? It's infectious. After all, who doesn't want to gain public recognition for their work, whether they're policemen or film directors?

"Stop thinking about future glory. That will come of its own accord if you do your job well. Besides, fame is a very capricious thing. What if you're deemed incapable of carrying out this mission? Your humiliation will be public too. Concentrate."

After nearly twenty years in the police force in all kinds of jobs, getting promoted on merit, reading endless reports and documents, he's reached the conclusion that when it comes to finding criminals, intuition always plays just as important a part as logic. The danger now, as he drives to Monte Carlo, isn't the murderer—who must be feeling utterly exhausted from the sheer amount of adrenaline pumping through his veins, not to mention apprehensive, because someone saw him in the act—no, the great danger now is the press. Journalists also mix logic with intuition. If they manage to establish a link, however tenuous, between the three murders, the police will lose control of the situation and the Festival could descend into chaos, with people afraid to walk the streets, foreign visitors leaving earlier than expected, tradesmen accusing the police of inefficiency, and headlines in newspapers around the world. After all, a real-life serial killer is always far more interesting than any screen version.

In the years that follow, the Film Festival won't be the same: the myth of fear will take root, and the world of luxury and glamour will choose another more appropriate place to show its wares, and gradually, after more than sixty years, the Festival will become a minor event, far from the bright lights and the magazines.

He has a great responsibility, well, two great responsibilities: the first is to find out who is committing these murders and to stop him before another corpse turns up on his patch; the second is to keep the media under control.

He needs to think logically. How many of those journalists, most of whom come from far-flung places, are likely to know the murder statistics for Cannes? How many of them will take the trouble to phone the National Guard and ask?

The logical response? None of them. Their minds are focused on what has just happened. They're excited because a major film distributor suffered a heart attack during one of the Festival lunches. They don't yet know that he was poisoned—the pathologist's report is on the backseat of his car. They don't yet know—and possibly never will—that he was also involved in a huge money-laundering scam.

The illogical response is that there's always someone who thinks more laterally. It's therefore now a matter of urgency to call a press conference and give a full account, but only of the film director's murder on the beach; that way, the other incidents will be momentarily forgotten.

An important figure in the world of filmmaking has been killed, so who's going to be interested in the death of an insignificant young woman? They'll all reach the same conclusion as he did at the start of the investigation—that she died of a drug overdose. Problem solved.

To go back to the murdered film director; perhaps she isn't as important a figure as he thinks; if she was, the police commissioner would be calling him now on his mobile phone. The facts are as follows: a smartly dressed man of about forty, with slightly graying hair, had been seen talking to her as they watched the sunset, the two of them observed by a young man hiding nearby. After sticking a blade into her with all the precision of a surgeon, he had walked slowly away, and was now mingling with hundreds and thousands of other people, many of whom quite possibly fitted his description.

He turns off the siren for a moment and phones his deputy, who had remained at the scene of the crime and who is probably currently being interrogated by journalists rather than himself doing the interrogating. Savoy asks him to tell the journalists, whose hasty conclusions so often get them into trouble, that he is "almost certain" it was a crime of passion.

"Don't say we're certain, just say that the circumstances may indicate this, given that they were sitting close to each other like a courting couple. It clearly wasn't a robbery or a revenge killing, but possibly a dramatic settling of personal scores.

"Be careful not to lie; your words are being recorded and may be used in evidence against you."

"But why do I need to say that?"

"Because that is what the circumstances indicate. And the sooner we give them something to chew on, the better."

"They're asking about the weapon used."

"Tell them that everything indicates it was a knife, as the witness said."

"But he's not sure."

"If even the witness doesn't know what he saw, what else can you say apart from 'everything indicates that, etc. etc.'? Frighten the lad; tell him his words are being recorded by the journalists and could be used against him later on."

He hangs up before his subordinate starts asking awkward questions.

"Everything indicates" that it was a crime of passion, even though the victim had only just arrived in Cannes from the United States, even though she was staying at a hotel alone, even though, from what they have been able to glean, she had only attended one rather trivial meeting in the morning, at the Marché du Film next to the Palais des Congrès. The journalists, however, would not have access to that information.

And there is something even more important that no one else on his team knows, indeed, that no one else in the world knows but him.

The victim had been at the hospital. He and she had talked a little and then he'd sent her away—to her death.

He turns on the siren again, so that the deafening noise can drive away any feeling of guilt. After all, he wasn't the one who stuck the knife in her.

He could, of course, think: "She was obviously there in the waiting room because she had some connection with the drug mafia and was just checking that the murder had been a success." That was "logical," and if he told his superior about that chance encounter, an investigation along those lines would immediately be launched. It might even be true; she had been killed using a very sophisticated method, as had the Hollywood film distributor. They were both Americans. They had both been killed with sharp implements. It all seemed to indicate that the same group was behind the killings, and that there really was a connection between them.

Perhaps he's wrong, and there is no serial killer on the loose. The young woman found dead on the bench, apparently asphyxiated by an experienced killer, might have met up the previous night with someone from the group who had come to see the film distributor. Perhaps she was also peddling drugs along with the craftwork she used to sell.

Imagine the scene: a group of foreigners arrive to settle accounts. In one of Cannes' many bars, the local dealer introduces one of them to the pretty girl with the dark eyebrows, who, he says, works with them. They end up going to bed together, but the foreigner, feeling strangely relaxed on European soil, drinks more than he should; the drink loosens his tongue and he *says* more than he should too. The next morning, he realizes his mistake and asks the professional hit man—every gang has one—to sort things out.

It all fits so perfectly that it must be true.

It all fits so perfectly that it makes no sense at all. It just wasn't credible that a cocaine cartel would have decided to hold such a meeting in a town which, during the Film Festival, is heaving with extra police brought in from all over the country, with private bodyguards, with security guards hired for the various parties, and with detectives charged with keeping a round-the-clock watch on the priceless jewels being worn in the streets and elsewhere.

Although if that *were* true, it would be equally good for his career. A settling of accounts between mafia men would attract as much publicity as a serial killer.

HE CAN RELAX; WHATEVER THE truth of the matter, he will finally acquire the reputation he has always felt he deserved.

He turns off the siren. It has taken him half an hour to drive along the motorway and across an invisible barrier into another country, and he's only minutes from his destination. His mind, however, is mulling over what are, in theory, forbidden thoughts.

Three murders in one day. His prayers are with the families of the victims, as the politicians always say. And he knows that the state pays him to maintain order and not to jump up and down with glee when it's disrupted in such a violent manner. Right now, the commissioner will be pacing his office, conscious that he now has two problems to solve: finding the killer (or killers, because he may not be convinced by Savoy's theory) and keeping the press at bay. Everyone is very worried; other police stations in the region have been alerted and an Identi-Kit picture of the murderer sent via the Internet to police cars in the area. A politician may even have had his well-deserved rest interrupted because the chief of police believed the matter to be so very delicate that he felt it necessary to pass responsibility on to someone higher up the chain of command.

The politician is unlikely to take the bait, telling the chief of police to ensure that the town returns to normal as soon as possible because "millions or hundreds of millions of euros depend on it." He doesn't want to get involved; he has more important issues to resolve, like which wine to serve that night to a visiting foreign delegation.

"Am I on the right path?" Savoy asks himself.

The forbidden thoughts return. He feels happy. This is the high point of a career spent filling in forms and dealing with trivia. It had never occurred to him that such a situation would produce in him this state of euphoria—he can, at last, be a real detective, the man with a theory that goes against all logic, and who will end up being given a medal because he was the first to see what no one else could. He won't confess this to anyone, not even to his wife, who would be horrified and assume that he must have temporarily lost his reason under the strain of working on such a dangerous case.

"I'm happy. I'm excited," he thinks.

His prayers might well be with the families of the dead, but his heart, after many years of inertia, is returning to the world of the living.

SAVOY HAD IMAGINED A VAST library full of dusty books, piles of magazines, a desk strewn with papers, but the office is, in fact, painted entirely in immaculate white and furnished with a few tasteful lamps, a comfortable armchair, and a glass table on which sits a large computer screen and nothing else, just a wireless keyboard and a small notepad with an expensive Montegrappa pen lying on it.

"Wipe that smile off your face and at least try to look a little concerned," says the man with the white beard, who is dressed, despite the heat, in tweed jacket, tie, and tailored trousers, an outfit not at all in keeping with the décor or with the subject under discussion.

"What do you mean, sir?"

"I know how you're feeling. This is the biggest case of your career, in a town where normally nothing happens. I went through the same inner turmoil when I lived and worked in Penycae, Swansea. And it was thanks to a very similar case that I got transferred to Scotland Yard."

"*My* dream is to work in Paris," thinks Savoy, but he says nothing. The man invites him to take a seat.

"I hope you, too, get a chance to realize your professional dream. Anyway, nice to meet you. I'm Stanley Morris."

Savoy decides to change the subject.

"The commissioner is afraid that the press will start speculating about there being a serial killer on the loose."

"They can speculate all they like, it's a free country. It's the kind of thing that sells newspapers and brings a little excitement into the dull lives of pensioners who will watch all the media for any new tidbit on the subject with a mixture of fear and certainty that it will never happen to them."

"I hope you've received a detailed description of the victims. Does the evidence so far suggest to you a serial killer, or are we dealing here with some sort of revenge killing on the part of drug cartels?"

"Yes, I got the descriptions. By the way, they wanted to send them to me by fax, for heaven's sake. How old-fashioned! I asked them to send the information by e-mail, and do you know what they said? 'We don't usually do that.' Imagine! One of the best-equipped police forces in the world still relying entirely on a fax machine!"

Savoy shifts rather impatiently in his chair. He isn't here to discuss the pros and cons of modern technology.

"Let's get down to business," says Dr. Morris, who had been quite a celebrity at Scotland Yard, but had decided to retire to the South of France and was possibly as glad as Savoy to have a break from routine—in Morris's case one that now revolved around reading, concerts, charity teas, and suppers.

"Since this is the first time I've met such a case, could you perhaps tell me whether or not you agree with my theory that there is only one killer, just so that I know where I stand."

Dr. Morris explains that in theory, yes, he's right: three murders with certain common characteristics would normally be enough to indicate a serial killer. And such murders were usually confined to one geographical area (in this case, the town of Cannes), and . . .

"Whereas, a mass murderer . . ."

Dr. Morris interrupts him and asks him not to misuse terminology. Mass murderers are terrorists or immature adolescents who go into a school or a snack bar and shoot everyone in sight, and who are then either shot dead by the police or commit suicide. They have a preference for guns and bombs that will cause the maximum amount of damage in a short space of time, usually two to three minutes at most. Such people don't care about the consequences of their actions because they know exactly how it will end.

"In the collective unconscious, the concept of the mass murderer is easier to take on board because he's clearly 'mentally unbalanced' and therefore easily distinguishable from 'us.' The serial murderer, on the other hand, touches on something far more complicated—the destructive instinct we all carry within us."

He pauses.

"Have you read *Dr. Jekyll and Mr. Hyde* by Robert Louis Stevenson?"

Savoy explains that he has so much work that he has little time for reading. Morris's gaze grows icy.

"And do you think I don't have work to do?"

"No, no, I didn't mean that. Listen, Dr. Morris, I'm here on an urgent mission. I'm not interested in discussing technology or literature. I just want to know what conclusions you drew from the reports."

"I'm sorry, but I'm afraid we can't, in this instance, avoid literature. *The Strange Case of Dr. Jekyll and Mr. Hyde* is the story of an apparently normal individual, Dr. Jekyll, who, in seeking to explore his own violent impulses, discovers a way of transforming himself periodically into a creature entirely without morality, Mr. Hyde. We all have those impulses, Inspector. A serial killer doesn't just threaten our physical safety, he threatens our sanity too. Because whether we like it or not, we all carry around in us a great destructive power and have all, at some point, wondered what it would be like to give free rein to that most repressed of feelings—the desire to take someone else's life.

"There are many reasons for this: wanting to put the world to rights, to get revenge for something that happened in our childhood, to vent one's suppressed hatred of society, but, whether consciously or unconsciously, everyone has felt that desire at one time or another, even if only in childhood."

Another meaningful silence.

"I imagine that, regardless of your chosen profession, you must yourself have experienced this feeling. Tormenting a cat perhaps or torturing some perfectly harmless insect."

It's Savoy's turn now to give Morris an icy stare and say nothing. Morris, however, interprets his silence as consent and continues talking in the same easy, superior tone:

"Don't expect to find some visibly unbalanced person with wild hair and a hate-filled leer on his face. If you ever do have time to read—although I know you're a busy man—I would recommend a book by Hannah Arendt, *Eichmann in Jerusalem*. There she analyzes the trial of one of the worst serial killers in history. Obviously, Eichmann needed help to carry out the gigantic task he was given: the purification of the human race. Just a moment."

He goes over to his computer. He knows that the man with him wants results, but that simply isn't possible. He needs to educate him and prepare him for the difficult days ahead.

"Here it is. Arendt made a detailed analysis of the trial of Adolf Eichmann, who was responsible for the extermination of six million Jews in Nazi Germany. She says that the half a dozen psychiatrists charged with examining him had all concluded that he was normal. His psychological profile and his attitude toward wife, children, mother, and father were all within the social parameters one expects in a responsible man. Arendt goes on: 'The trouble with Eichmann was precisely that so many were like him, and that the many were neither perverted nor sadistic, that they were, and still are, terribly and terrifyingly normal. From the viewpoint of our legal institutions and of our moral standards of judgment, this normality was much more terrifying than all the atrocities put together. . .' "

Now he could get down to business.

"I notice from the autopsies that there was no sign of sexual abuse . . ."

"Dr. Morris, I have a problem to solve and I need to do so quickly. I want to know whether or not we're dealing with a serial killer. No one could possibly rape a man in the middle of a lunch party or a girl on a public bench in broad daylight."

He might as well have said nothing. Morris ignores him completely and continues.

". . . which is a common feature in many serial killers. Some have what you might call 'humane' motives. Nurses who kill terminally ill patients, people who murder beggars in the street, social workers who feel so sorry for certain pensioners or disabled people that they reach the conclusion they'd be better off in the next life—there was one such case in California just recently. There are also people bent on putting society to rights, and in those cases, the victims tend to be prostitutes."

"Dr. Morris, I didn't come here . . ."

This time Morris raises his voice slightly.

"And I didn't invite you. I'm doing you a favor. If you want to leave, please do so, but if you're going to stay, please stop interrupting my argument every two minutes. In order to catch someone, we have to understand the way he thinks."

"So you do believe we're dealing with a serial killer?"

"I haven't finished yet."

Savoy controls himself. After all, why was he in such a hurry?

Wouldn't it be more fun to let the press tie itself in knots and then present them with the solution?

"Please go on."

Morris moves the monitor so that Savoy can see more clearly. On the large screen is an engraving, possibly from the nineteenth century.

"This is the most famous of all serial killers: Jack the Ripper. He was active in London in the second half of 1888, and was responsible for killing five or possibly seven women in public and semi-public places. He would rip open their bellies and disembowel them. He was never found. He became a legend, and even today, there are still people trying to uncover his real identity."

The image on the screen changes to reveal what looks like something from an astrological chart.

"This is the signature of the Zodiac Killer. He's known to have killed five couples in California over a period of ten months, mostly courting couples who had parked their cars in isolated spots. He used to send letters to the police bearing this symbol, which is rather like a Celtic cross. No one has yet managed to identify him.

"Researchers believe that both Jack the Ripper and the Zodiac Killer were people who were trying to restore moral order and decency to their particular areas. They had, if you like, a mission to fulfill. And contrary to what the press would have us believe with the terrifying nicknames they invent, like the Boston Strangler and the Child Killer of Toulouse, these were ordinary folk who would get together with their neighbors at weekends and who worked hard to earn a living. None of them ever benefited financially from their criminal acts."

The conversation is beginning to interest Savoy.

"So it could be anyone who came to Cannes to attend the Film Festival . . ."

"Yes, having first made a conscious decision to create an atmosphere of terror for some completely absurd reason, for example 'to overthrow the dictatorship of fashion' or 'to put a stop to the making of films that provoke violence.' The press will come up with some blood-curdling soubriquet for him and start chasing various leads. Crimes that have nothing to do with the killer will start being attributed to him. Panic will ensue and only come to an end if by chance—and I repeat, by chance—the killer is caught. These killers are often only active for a short period of time and then disappear completely, having left their mark on history. They may perhaps write a diary that will be discovered after their death, but that's all."

Savoy has stopped looking at his watch. His phone rings, but he decides not to answer. The subject is far more complicated than he thought.

"So you agree with me?"

"Yes," says the expert from Scotland Yard, the man who had become a legend by solving five cases that everyone else had given up on.

"Why do you think we're dealing with a serial killer?" Savoy asks.

Morris sees what looks like an e-mail flash up on his computer and he smiles. The inspector has finally started to show a little respect for what he has to say.

"Because of the complete absence of motive. Most of these criminals have what we call a 'signature': they choose one type of victim, homosexuals, say, or prostitutes, beggars, courting couples. Others are known as 'asymmetrical killers': they kill because they can't control their impulse to kill. When they reach a point where that impulse is satisfied, they stop killing until the urge to kill again becomes unbearable. I think that is the kind of killer we have here.

"There are several points to consider in this case. The criminal is highly sophisticated. He has chosen a different weapon each time—his bare hands, poison, and a stiletto knife. He's not motivated by the usual things: sex, alcohol, or some evident mental disorder. He knows the human anatomy, and that, so far, has been his only 'signature.' He must have planned the crimes in advance because the poison he used isn't easy to obtain, and so we could classify him as a killer with a mission, but one who still doesn't quite know what that mission is. From what I know of the young girl's murder, and this is the only clue we have so far, he used a type of Russian martial art called Sambo.

"I could go further and say that it's part of his signature to get close to his chosen victim and befriend him or her for a while, but that theory doesn't fit with the murder committed in the middle of a lunch party on a beach in Cannes. The victim apparently had two bodyguards with him and they would have been sure to react if the killer had gone anywhere near their boss, plus the victim was under surveillance by Europol."

Russian. Savoy considers using his phone to ask for an urgent search of all the hotels in Cannes. A man, about forty, well-dressed, slightly graying hair—and Russian.

"The fact that he used a Russian martial art technique doesn't mean he himself is Russian," says Morris, reading Savoy's mind like the good ex-policeman he is. "Just as we cannot assume he's a South American Indian because he used curare."

"So what do we do?"

"We just have to wait for him to commit his next murder."

Cinderella!

If people believed more in fairy tales instead of just listening to their husbands and parents—who think everything is impossible—they would be experiencing what she's experiencing now, being driven along in one of the innumerable limousines that are slowly but surely heading for the steps and the red carpet—the biggest catwalk in the world.

The Star is by her side, smiling and wearing the obligatory beautifully cut suit. He asks if she's nervous. Of course not: tension, nerves, anxiety, and fear don't exist in dreams. Everything is perfect; it's just like in a movie—the heroine suffers, struggles, and finally achieves everything she has always wanted.

"If Hamid Hussein decides to go ahead with the project and the film is the success he hopes it will be, then prepare yourself for more such moments."

If Hamid Hussein decides to go ahead with the project? Isn't it all signed and sealed?

"But I signed a contract when I went to collect my outfit in the Gift Room."

"Look, forget what I said. I don't want to spoil your special moment."

"No, please, go on."

The Star was expecting the silly girl to say exactly that, and he takes enormous pleasure in doing as she asks.

"I've been involved in loads of projects that begin and never come to anything. It's all part of the game, but, like I say, don't worry about that now."

"But the contract . . ."

"Contracts are there for lawyers to argue over while they earn their money. Please, forget what I said. Enjoy the moment."

The "moment" is approaching. Because of the slow traffic, people can see who is inside the cars, despite the smoked-glass windows separating mere mortals from the chosen. The Star waves; hands bang on the window asking him to open it just for a moment, to give them an autograph, to have a photo taken.

The Star keeps waving, as if he didn't understand what they wanted and a smile from him was enough to flood the world with light.

There's a real air of hysteria out there. Women with their little portable stools on which they must have been sitting and knitting since the morning; men with beer bellies, bored to death, but obliged to accompany their middle-aged spouses, who are dressed to the nines as if they were the ones about to go up the steps and onto the red carpet; children who have no idea what's going on, but can sense that it's something important. Crammed behind the steel barriers that separate them from the line of limousines, stand people of all ages and colors, every one of them wanting to believe that they're only two yards away from the great legends, when, in fact, they're separated by thousands of miles; for it isn't just the steel barrier and the car window keeping them apart, it's chance, opportunity, and talent.

Talent? Yes, she wants to believe that talent counts too, but knows that really it's all the result of a game of dice played by the gods, who choose certain people and place others on the far side of an impassable abyss from where they can only applaud, worship, and, when the tide turns against their gods, condemn.

The Star pretends to be talking to her, but he's not actually saying anything, just looking at her and moving his lips, like the great actor he is. He doesn't do this out of desire or pleasure. Gabriela realizes that he simply doesn't want to appear unfriendly to his fans outside, but, at the same time, can't be bothered now to wave and smile and blow kisses.

"You must think me an arrogant, cynical person with a heart of stone," he says at last. "If you ever get where you want to get, then you'll understand what I'm feeling: that there's no way out. Success is both an addiction and an enslavement, and at the end of the day, when you're lying in bed with some new man or woman, you'll ask yourself: was it really worth it? Why did I ever want this?"

He pauses.

"Go on."

"I don't know why I'm telling you this."

"Because you want to protect me. Because you're a good man. Please, go on."

Gabriela may be ingenuous about many things, but she's still a woman and knows how to get almost anything she wants out of a man. In this case, the button to press is vanity.

"I don't know why I always wanted this." The Star has fallen into the trap and is now revealing his more vulnerable side, while, outside, the fans continue to wave. "Often, when I go back to the hotel after an exhausting day's work, I stand under the shower for ages, just listening to the sound of water falling on my body. Two opposing forces are battling it out inside me: one telling me I should be thanking God and the other telling me I should abandon it all while there's still time.

"At that moment, I feel like the most ungrateful person in the world. I have my fans, but I can't be bothered with them. I'm invited to parties that are the envy of the world, and all I want is to leave at once and go back to my room and sit quietly reading a good book. Well-meaning men and women give me prizes, organize events, and do everything to make me happy, and I feel nothing but exhaustion and embarrassment because I don't believe I deserve all this, I don't feel worthy of my success. Do you understand?"

For a fraction of a second, Gabriela feels sorry for the man beside her. She imagines the number of parties he must have to attend in a year, and how there must always be someone asking him for a photo or an autograph, someone telling him some tedious story to which he pretends to be listening, someone trying to sell him some new project or embarrassing him with the classic question: "Don't you remember me?," someone getting out his mobile phone and asking him to say a few words to his son, wife, or sister. And he must always be the consummate professional, happy, attentive, good-humored, and polite.

"Do you understand?"

"Yes, I do, but I wouldn't mind having those problems one day, although I know I've a long way to go before I do."

Only another four limousines and they'll be there. The chauffeur tells them to get ready. The Star folds down a small mirror from the roof of the car and adjusts his tie; Gabriela does the same and smooths her hair. She can see a bit of the red carpet now, although the steps are still out of sight. The hysteria has vanished as if by magic, and the crowd is now composed of people wearing identity tags round their necks, talking to each other and taking no notice at all of who is in the cars because they're tired of seeing the same scene repeated over and over.

Two more cars. Some steps appear to her left. Men in dinner jacket and tie are opening the doors, and the aggressive metal barriers have been replaced by velvet cords looped along bronze and wooden pillars.

"Damn!" cries the Star, making Gabriela jump.

"Damn! Look who's over there, just getting out of her car!"

Gabriela sees a female Superstar, also wearing a Hamid Hussein dress, who has just stepped onto the red carpet. The Superstar turns her back on the Palais des Congrès, and when Gabriela follows her gaze, she sees the most extraordinary sight. A human wall, almost nine feet high, filled with endlessly flashing lights.

"Good!" says the Star, relieved. "She's looking in the wrong direction."

He's no longer polite and charming and has forgotten all his existential angst. "They're not the accredited photographers. They're not important."

"Why did you say 'Damn'?"

The Star cannot conceal his irritation. There is one car to go before it's their turn.

"Can't you see? What planet are you from, child? When we step onto the red carpet, all the accredited photographers, who are positioned halfway along, will have their cameras aimed at her!"

He turns to the chauffeur and says:

"Slow down!"

The chauffeur points to a man in plainclothes, also wearing an identity tag, and who is signaling to them to keep moving and not hold up the traffic.

The Star sighs deeply; this really isn't his lucky day. Why did he say all those things to this mere beginner at his side? It's true that he's tired of the life he leads, and yet he can't imagine anything else.

"Don't rush," he says. "We'll try and stay down here for as long as possible. Let's leave a good space between her and us."

"Her" was the Superstar.

The couple in the car ahead of them don't appear to attract as much attention, although they must be important because no one gets as far as those steps without having scaled many mountains in life.

Her companion appears to relax a little, and now it's Gabriela's turn to feel tense, not knowing quite how to behave. Her hands are sweating. She grabs the handbag stuffed with paper, breathes deeply, and says a prayer.

"Walk slowly," says the Star, "and don't stand too close to me."

Their limousine draws up alongside the steps. Both doors are opened from outside.

Suddenly, an immense roar seems to fill the universe, shouts coming from all sides—she hadn't realized until then that she was in a soundproof car and could hear nothing. The Star gets out, smiling, as if his tantrum of two minutes ago had never happened and as if he were still the center of the universe, despite his apparently true confessions to her in the car. He is a man in conflict with himself, his world, and his past, and who cannot now turn back.

"What am I thinking about?" Gabriela tells herself. "I should be concentrating on the moment, on going up the steps!"

They both wave to the "unimportant" photographers and spend some time there. People hold out scraps of paper to him, and he signs autographs and thanks his fans. Gabriela isn't sure whether she should remain by his side or continue up toward the red carpet and the entrance to the Palais des Congrès; fortunately, she's saved by someone holding out pen and paper and asking for her autograph.

How she wishes this ceremony were being broadcast live to the whole world and that her mother could see her arriving in that dazzling dress, accompanied by a really famous actor (about whom she's beginning to have her doubts, but, no, she must drive away such negative thoughts), and see her giving the most important autograph of her twenty-five years of life! She can't understand the woman's name, so she smiles and writes something like "with love."

The Star comes over to her.

"Come on. The way ahead is clear now."

The woman to whom she has just addressed an affectionate message reads what she's written and says angrily:

"I don't want your autograph! I just need your name so that I can identify you in the photo."

Gabriela pretends not to hear; nothing in the world can destroy this magic moment.

They start going up the steps, with policemen forming a kind of security cordon, even though the public are a long way off now. On either side, on the building's façade, gigantic plasma screens reveal to the poor mortals outside what is going on in that open-air sanctuary. Hysterical screams and clapping can be heard in the distance. When they reach a broader step, as if they had reached the first floor, she notices another crowd of photographers, except this time, they are properly dressed and are shouting out the Star's name, asking him to turn this way, no, this way, just one more shot, please, a little closer, look up, look down! Other people pass them and continue up the steps, but the photographers aren't interested in them. The Star has lost none of his glamour; he looks as if he doesn't care and jokes around to show how relaxed and at ease he is with all this.

Gabriela notices that the photographers are interested in her too, although, of course, they don't shout out her name (they've no idea who she is), imagining that she must be his new girlfriend. They ask them to stand together so that they can get a photo of the two of them. The Star obliges for a few seconds, but keeps a prudent distance and avoids any physical contact.

Yes, they've successfully managed to avoid the Superstar, who will, by now, have reached the door of the Palais des Congrès to be greeted by the president of the Film Festival and the mayor of Cannes.

The Star gestures to her to continue up the stairs, and she obeys.

She looks ahead and sees another gigantic screen strategically placed so that people can see themselves. A loudspeaker announces:

"And now we have . . ."

And the voice gives the name of the Star and of his most famous film. Later, someone tells her that everyone inside the room is watching the same scene being shown on the plasma screen outside.

They go up the remaining steps, reach the door, greet the president of the Festival and the mayor, and go inside. The whole thing has lasted less than three minutes.

Now the Star is surrounded by people who want to talk to him and flatter him and take photos (yes, even the chosen take photos of themselves with famous people). It's suffocatingly hot inside, and Gabriela starts to worry that her makeup will run . . .

Her makeup!

She had completely forgotten. She's supposed to go through a door on the left where someone will be waiting for her outside. She walks mechanically down some steps and past a couple of security guards. One of them asks if she's going outside for a smoke and intends coming back in for the film. She says no and carries on.

She crosses another series of metal barriers and no one asks her anything because she's leaving, not trying to get in. She can see the backs of the crowd who are still waving and shouting at the limousines that continue to arrive. A man comes toward her, asks her name, and tells her to follow him.

"Can you just wait a minute?"

The man seems surprised, but nods his assent. Gabriela has her eyes fixed on an old carousel, which has possibly been there since the beginning of the last century and which continues to turn, while the children riding it rise up and down.

"Can we go now?" asks the man politely.

"Just one more minute."

"We'll be late."

Gabriela can no longer hold back the tears, the tension, the fear, and the terror of the three minutes she has just lived through. She sobs convulsively, not caring about her makeup now, which someone will fix for her anyway. The man offers her his arm to lean on, so that she won't stumble in her high heels, and they start walking across the square toward the Boulevard de la Croisette. The noise of the crowd grows ever more distant, and her sobs grow ever louder. She's crying out all the tears of the day, the week, and the years she had spent dreaming of that moment, and which was over before she could even take in what had happened.

"I'm sorry," she says to the man accompanying her.

He strokes her hair. His smile reveals affection, understanding, and pity.

He has finally understood that you cannot search out happiness at any price. Life has given him all it could, and he's beginning to see just how generous life has always been to him. Now and for the rest of his days, he will devote himself to disinterring the treasures hidden in his suffering and enjoying each second of happiness as if it were his last.

He has overcome Temptation. He is protected by the spirit of the girl who understands his mission perfectly, and who is now beginning to open his eyes to the real reason for his trip to Cannes.

For a few moments in that pizzeria, while he was remembering what he'd heard on those tapes, Temptation had accused him of being mentally unbalanced and of believing that anything was permitted in the name of love. His most difficult moment was, thank God, behind him now.

He is a normal person; his work requires discipline, routine, negotiating skills, and planning. Many of his friends say that he's become more of a loner; what they don't know is that he's always been a loner. Going to parties, weddings, and christenings, and pretending to enjoy playing golf on Sundays was merely part of his professional strategy. He's always loathed the social whirl, with all those people concealing behind their smiles the real sadness in their souls. It didn't take him long to see that the Superclass are as dependent on their success as an addict is on his drugs, and nowhere near as happy as those who want nothing more than a house, a garden, a child playing, a plate of food on the table, and a fire in winter. Are the latter aware of their limitations, and do they know that life is short and wonder what point there is in going on?

The Superclass tries to promote its values. Ordinary people complain of divine injustice, they envy power, and it pains them to see others having fun. They don't understand that no one is having fun, that everyone is worried and insecure, and that what the jewels, cars, and fat wallets conceal is a huge inferiority complex.

Igor is a man of simple tastes; indeed, Ewa always complained about the way he dressed. But what's the point of buying a ridiculously expensive shirt when no one is going to see the label anyway? What's the point of frequenting fashionable restaurants if nothing of interest is said there? Ewa used to say that he didn't talk very much at the parties and other work-related events. He tried to change his behavior and be more sociable, but none of it really interested him. He would look at the people around him talking on and on, comparing share prices, boasting about their marvelous new yacht, launching into long disquisitions on Expressionist painting (but really just repeating what a tour guide had told them on a visit to a Paris museum), and stating boldly that one writer is infinitely better than another (basing themselves entirely on the reviews they've read because, naturally, they never have time to read fiction).

They are so very cultivated, so very rich, and so utterly charming. And at the end of each day, they all ask themselves: "Is it time I stopped?" And they all reply: "If I did, there would be no meaning to my life."

As if they actually knew what the meaning of life was.

TEMPTATION HAS LOST THE BATTLE. It wanted to make him believe that he was mad: it's one thing to plan the sacrifice of certain people, quite another to have the capacity and the courage to carry it out. Temptation said that we all dream of committing crimes, but that only the unbalanced make that macabre idea a reality.

Igor is well-balanced and successful. If he wanted, he could hire a professional killer, the best in the world, to carry out his task and send the requisite messages to Ewa. Or he could hire the best public relations agency in the world, and by the end of the year, he'd be the talk not only of economics journals, but of magazines interested only in success and glamour. At that point, his ex-wife would weigh up the consequences of her mistaken decision, and he would know just the right moment to send her flowers and ask her to come back, all was forgiven. He has contacts at all levels of society, from businessmen who've reached the top through perseverance and hard work, to criminals who've never had a chance to show their more positive side.

He isn't in Cannes because he takes a morbid pleasure in seeing the look in a person's eyes as he or she confronts the inevitable. He's decided to place himself in the line of fire, in the dangerous position in which he finds himself now, because he's sure that every step he takes during this seemingly endless day will prove vital if the new Igor who exists within him is to be born again out of the ashes of his tragedy.

He's always been able to make difficult decisions and to see things through, although no one, not even Ewa, has ever known what went on in the dark corridors of his soul. For many years he endured in silence the threats made by various individuals and groups, and he reacted discreetly when he felt strong enough to rid himself of the people threatening him. He had learned to exercise enormous self-control so as not to be left traumatized by bad experiences. He never took his fears home with him, feeling that Ewa deserved a quiet life and to be kept in ignorance of the terrors that beset any businessman. He chose to save her from that, and yet he received nothing in return, not even understanding.

The girl's spirit soothes him with that thought, then adds something that hadn't occurred to him until then: he wasn't there to win back the person who had left him, but to see, at last, that she wasn't worth all those years of pain, all those months of planning, all his enormous capacity for forgiveness, generosity, and patience.

He has sent one, two, three messages now, and there's been no reaction from Ewa. It would be easy enough for her to find out where he's staying, although, admittedly, phoning the five or six top hotels wouldn't help because when he checked in, he gave a different name and profession. Then again, she who seeks, finds.

He's read the statistics. Cannes has only seventy thousand inhabitants, and that number usually triples during the Film Festival, but festivalgoers all haunt the same places. Where would she be staying? Given that he had seen the two of them the previous night, she was probably staying in the same hotel and visiting the same bar. Even so, Ewa isn't prowling the Boulevard de la Croisette looking for him. She isn't phoning mutual friends, trying to find out where he is. At least one of those friends has all the necessary information, for Igor had assumed that the woman he thought was the love of his life would contact that friend as soon as she realized Igor was in Cannes. The friend has instructions to tell her how she can find him, but so far, there has been no news.

HE TAKES OFF HIS CLOTHES and gets into the shower. Ewa isn't worth all this fuss. He's almost certain that he'll see her tonight, but this is growing less and less important with each passing moment. Perhaps his mission is about something much more important than simply regaining the love of the woman who betrayed him and who speaks ill of him to other people. The spirit of the girl with the dark eyebrows reminds him of the story told by an old Afghan in a break during a battle.

After many centuries of turmoil and bad government, the population of a city high up on one of the desert mountains of Herat province was in despair. They could not simply abolish the monarchy, and yet neither could they stand many more generations of arrogant, egotistical kings. They summoned the Loya Jirga, as the council of wise men is known locally.

The Loya Jirga decided that they should elect a king every four years, and that this king should have absolute power. He could increase taxes, demand total obedience, choose a different woman to take to his bed each night, and eat and drink his fill. He could wear the finest clothes, ride the finest horses. In short, any order he gave, however absurd, would be obeyed, and no one would question whether it was logical or just.

However, at the end of that period of four years, he would be obliged to give up the throne and leave the city, taking with him only his family and the clothes on his back. Everyone knew that this would mean certain death within three or four days because there was nothing to eat or drink in that vast desert, which was freezing in winter and like a furnace in summer.

The wise men of the Loya Jirga assumed that no one would risk standing for the position of king, and that they would then be able to return to the old system of democratic elections. Their decision was made public, and the post of king fell vacant. Initially, several people applied. An old man with cancer took up the challenge and died during the period of his rule with a smile on his face. A madman succeeded him, but left four months later (he had misunderstood the terms) and vanished into the desert. Then rumors started going around that the throne had a curse on it, and no one dared apply for the position. The city was left without a governor, confusion reigned, and the inhabitants realized that they must forget the monarchist tradition altogether and prepare to change their ways. The Loya Jirga felt pleased that its members had taken such a wise decision. They hadn't forced the people to make a choice, they had simply got rid of those who wanted power at any price. Then a young man, married and with three children, came forward.

"I accept the post," he said.

The wise men tried to explain the risks. They reminded him that he had a family and explained that their decision had merely been a way of discouraging adventurers and despots. However, the young man stood firm, and since it was impossible to go back on their decision, the Loya Jirga had no option but to wait another four years before they could put in place the planned return to elections.

The young man and his family proved to be excellent governors. They ruled fairly, redistributed wealth, lowered the price of food, organized popular festivals to celebrate the change of season, and encouraged craftwork and music. Every night, though, a great caravan of horses would leave the city, drawing heavy carts covered with jute cloth so that no one could see what was inside them. These carts never came back.

At first, the wise men of the Loya Jirga thought that the king must be removing treasure from the city, but consoled themselves with the fact that the young man rarely ventured beyond the city walls; if he had and had tried to climb the nearest mountain, he would have realized that the horses would die before they got very far. This was, after all, one of the most inhospitable places on the planet. They determined that, as soon as his reign was over, they would go to the place where the horses had died of exhaustion and the riders of thirst, and they would recover all that treasure.

They stopped worrying and waited patiently.

At the end of the four years, the young man left the throne and the city. The population was in an uproar; after all, it had been a long time since they had enjoyed such a wise and just governor!

However, the Loya Jirga's decision had to be respected. The young man went to his wife and children and asked them to leave with him.

"I will," said his wife, "but at least let our children stay. They will then survive to tell your story."

"Trust me," he said.

The tribal laws were very strict, and the wife had no alternative but to obey her husband. They mounted their horses and rode to the city gate, where they said goodbye to the friends they had made while governing the city. The Loya Jirga were pleased. They might have made many allies, but fate is fate. No one else would risk accepting the post of governor, and the democratic tradition would be restored at last. As soon as they could, they would recover the treasure abandoned in the desert, less than three days from there.

The family rode into the valley of death in silence. The wife didn't dare say a word, the children didn't understand what was going on, and the young man was immersed in thought. They climbed one hill, traveled for a whole day across a vast plain, and slept on the top of the next hill.

The woman woke at dawn, wanting to make the most of the final few days of her life to look her last on the mountains she had loved so much. She went up to the very top of the hill and gazed down on what should have been an empty plain, and she was startled by what she saw.

During those four years, the caravans leaving the city each night had not been carrying off jewels or gold coins. They had been carrying bricks, seeds, wood, roof tiles, spices, animals, and traditional tools that could be used to drill into the earth and find water.

Before her lay a far more modern, far more beautiful city than the old one, and all in working order.

"This is your kingdom," said the young man, who had just woken up and joined her. "Ever since I heard the decree, I knew it would be pointless to try and change in four years everything that centuries of corruption and bad governance had destroyed. I was certain of one thing, though, that it was possible to start again."

Igor, too, is starting again as he stands in the shower with the water cascading over his face. He has finally understood why the first person he spoke to in Cannes is by his side now, sending him off along a different path, helping him make the necessary adjustments, and explaining that her sacrifice was neither a chance event nor unnecessary. On the other hand, she has also made it plain to him that Ewa has always been naturally perverse and only interested in climbing the social ladder, even if doing so meant abandoning her family.

"When you go back to Moscow, try and do plenty of sport. That will help free you from your tensions," says the girl.

He can just make out her face in the clouds of steam in the shower. He has never felt as close to anyone as he does now to Olivia, the girl with the dark eyebrows.

"Carry on, even if you're not so sure now of what you're doing. God moves in mysterious ways, and sometimes the path only reveals itself once you start walking it."

"Thank you, Olivia," he thinks. Perhaps he is here in order to show the world the aberrations of modern life, of which Cannes is the supreme manifestation.

He's not sure, but whatever the case, he's here for a reason, and the last two years of tension, planning, fear, and uncertainty are finally justified.

HE CAN IMAGINE WHAT THE next Festival will be like: people being issued with swipe cards even to get into the lunch parties on the beach, sharpshooters on every rooftop, hundreds of plainclothes policemen mingling with the crowds, metal detectors at the door of every hotel, where those children-of-the-Superclass will have to wait while the police search their bags; women will have to take off their high heels and men be called back because the coins in their pockets have set off the alarm; gray-haired gentlemen will have to hold out their arms and be frisked like common criminals; the women will be led to a kind of canvas tent at the entrance—which clashes horribly with the former elegance of the place—where they'll have to wait patiently in line to be searched, until a policewoman discovers what triggered the alarm: the underwiring in a bra.

The city will begin to show its true face. Luxury and glamour will be replaced by tension, insults, wasted time, and the cool, indifferent gaze of the police. People will feel more and more isolated, this time by the system itself, rather than by the eternal arrogance of the chosen few. Army units will be sent to that simple seaside town with the sole objective of protecting people who are trying to have fun, and the prohibitive cost of this will, of course, fall on the taxpayers' shoulders.

There will be demonstrations by honest workers protesting at what they deem to be an absurdity. The government will issue a statement saying that they're considering the possibility of shifting the cost to the organizers of the Festival. The sponsors—who could easily afford the expense—lose interest when one of their number is humiliated by some insignificant little officer, who tells him to shut up and respect the security regulations.

Cannes will begin to die. Two years on, they'll see that everything they did to maintain law and order really has paid off, with zero levels of crime during the Festival period. The terrorists have failed in their attempt to sow further panic.

They'll try to turn the clock back, but they won't be able to. Cannes will continue to die. This new Babylon will be destroyed, this modern-day Sodom will be erased from the map.

HE STEPS OUT OF THE shower having made a decision. When he goes back to Russia, he will order his employees to find out the girl's family name. He will make anonymous donations through neutral banks. He will order some gifted author to write the story of her life and pay for it to be translated into different languages.

"The story of a young woman who sold craftwork, was beaten by her boyfriend, exploited by her parents, until the day she surrendered her soul to a stranger and thus changed one small corner of the planet."

He opens the wardrobe, takes out an immaculate white shirt, his carefully pressed dinner jacket, and his handmade patent-leather shoes. He has no trouble tying his bow tie because he does this at least once a week.

He turns on the TV in time for the local news bulletin. The parade of stars along the red carpet takes up much of the program, but there is also a brief report about a woman found murdered on the beach.

The police have cordoned off the area. The boy who witnessed the murder (Igor studies his face, but feels no desire for revenge) says that he saw the couple sit down to talk, then the man got out a small stiletto knife and appeared to run it lightly over the woman's body. The woman seemed quite happy, which is why he didn't call the police earlier because he thought it was some kind of joke.

"What did the man look like?"

White, about forty, wearing such-and-such clothes, and apparently very polite.

There's no need to worry. Igor opens his leather briefcase and takes out two envelopes. One contains an invitation to the party that is due to start in an hour (although everyone knows that the start will be delayed by ninety minutes), where he knows he will meet Ewa. If she won't come to him, too bad; he will go to her. It has taken less than twenty-four hours for him to see the kind of woman he married and that the sufferings of the last two years have been in vain.

The other envelope is silver and hermetically sealed. On it are the two words "For you" written in an exquisite hand that could be either male or female.

There are CCTV cameras in the corridors, as there are in most hotels nowadays. In some part of the basement is a dark room lined with TV screens before which a group of people sit, watching. They are on the lookout for anything unusual, like the man who kept going up and down stairs and who explained to the officer sent to investigate that he was simply enjoying a little free exercise. Since the man was a guest at the hotel, the officer apologized and left.

They take no interest in guests who go into another guest's room and don't leave until the next day, usually after breakfast has been served. That's normal and none of their business.

The screens are connected to special digital recording systems, and the resulting disks are stored for six months in a safe to which only the manager has the key. No hotel in the world wants to lose a customer because some rich, jealous husband manages to bribe one of the people watching one particular part of the corridor and then gives (or sells) the material to a tabloid newspaper, having first presented proof of adultery to the courts and thus ensured that his wife will get none of his fortune.

That would be a tragic blow to the prestige of a hotel that prides itself on discretion and confidentiality. The occupation rate would immediately plummet; after all, people choose a five-star hotel because they know that the people who work there are trained to see only what they're supposed to see. For example, if someone asks for room service, when the waiter arrives, he keeps his eyes fixed on the trolley, holds out the bill to be signed by the person who opens the door, but never— *ever*—looks over at the bed.

Prostitutes—male and female—dress discreetly, although the men in the screen-lined room know exactly who they are, thanks to a data system provided by the police. This is none of their business either, but in these cases, they always keep one eye on the door of the room they went into until they come out again. In some hotels, the switchboard operator is told to make a fake phone call just to check that the guest is all right. The guest picks up the phone, a female voice asks for some nonexistent person, hears an angry "You've got the wrong room" and the sound of the phone being slammed down. Mission accomplished; there's no need to worry.

Drunks who try their key in the lock of the wrong room and, when the door fails to open, start angrily pounding on it, are often surprised to see a solicitous hotel employee appear out of nowhere—he just happened to be passing, he says—and who suggests accompanying the drunken guest to the right room (usually on a different floor and with an entirely different number).

Igor knows that his every move is being recorded in the hotel basement: the day, hour, minute, and second that he comes into the lobby, gets out of the lift, walks to the door of his suite, and puts the swipe card into the lock. Once inside, he can breathe easy; no one has access to what is happening in the room itself, that would be a step too far in violating someone's privacy.

HE CLOSES HIS ROOM DOOR behind him.

He had made a point of studying the CCTV cameras as soon as he arrived the night before. Just as all cars have a blind spot when overtaking, regardless of how many rearview mirrors they may have, the cameras show every part of the corridor, except the rooms located in each of the four corners. Obviously, if one of the men in the basement sees someone pass by a particular place but fail to appear on the next screen, he'll suspect something untoward has happened—the person might have fainted—and immediately send someone up to check. If he gets there and finds no one, the person has obviously been invited into one of the rooms, and the rest is a private matter between guests.

Igor, however, doesn't intend to stop in the corridor. He walks nonchalantly to the point where the corridor curves away toward the elevators and slips the silver envelope under the door of the corner room or suite.

It all takes less than a fraction of a second, and if someone downstairs was observing his movements, they would have noticed nothing. Much later, when they check the disks to try and identify the person responsible for what happened, they will have great difficulty determining the exact moment of death. It may be that the guest wasn't there and only opened the envelope when he or she returned from one of that night's events. It may be that he or she opened the envelope at once, but that the contents took a while to act.

During that time, various people will have passed by the same place and every one of them will be considered suspicious; and if some shabbily dressed person or someone from the less orthodox worlds of massage, prostitution, or drugs had the misfortune to follow the same trajectory, they'll immediately be arrested and questioned. During a film festival, the chances of such an individual appearing on the scene are very high indeed.

He knows, too, that there's a danger he hadn't reckoned with: the person who witnessed the murder of the woman on the beach. After jumping through the usual bureaucratic hoops, the witness will be asked to view the recordings. Igor, however, had checked in using a false passport, and the photo shows a man with glasses and a beard (the hotel reception didn't even take the trouble to check, although if they'd asked, he would simply have said that he'd shaved off both beard and mustache and now wore contact lenses).

Assuming that they were much quicker off the mark than most policemen and had reached the conclusion that just one person was behind this attempt to derail the normal running of the Festival, they would be awaiting his return and he would be asked to give a statement. Igor, however, knows that this is the last time he'll walk down the corridors of the Hotel Martinez.

They'll go into his room and find an empty suitcase, bearing no fingerprints. They'll go into the bathroom and think to themselves: "What's a millionaire doing washing his own clothes in the sink! Can't he afford the laundry?"

A policeman will reach out to pick up what he considers evidence bearing DNA traces, fingerprints, and strands of hair, and drop it with a yelp, having burned his fingers in the sulfuric acid that is now dissolving everything Igor has left behind. He needs only his false passport, his credit cards, and some cash, and he has all of this in the pockets of his dinner jacket, along with the Beretta, that weapon so despised by the cognoscenti.

He has always found traveling easy; he hates luggage. Even though he had a complicated mission to carry out in Cannes, he chose things that would be easy and light to transport. He can't understand people who take enormous suitcases with them, even when they're only spending a couple of days away.

He doesn't know who will open the envelope, nor does he care; the choice will fall to the Angel of Death, not to him. A lot of things could happen in the meantime, or indeed nothing.

The guest might phone reception and say that the envelope has been delivered to the wrong person and ask that someone come and collect it. Or they might throw it in the trash, thinking it's just another of those charming letters from the management, asking if everything is going well; the guest has other things to read and a party to get ready for. If the guest is a man expecting his wife to arrive at any moment, he'll put it in his pocket, convinced that the woman he was flirting with that afternoon is writing to say yes. Or it might be a married couple, and since neither of them knows to whom the "you" on the envelope refers, they'll agree that this is no time for mutual suspicion and throw the envelope out of the window.

If, despite all these possibilities, the Angel of Death does decide to brush the recipient's face with his wings, then he or she will tear open the envelope and see the contents. Those contents had involved a great deal of work and required him to call on the help of the "friends and collaborators" who had given him their financial backing when he was first setting up his company, the same ones who had been most put out when he repaid that loan early. It had been a real godsend to them being able to invest money of suspect origin in a business that was perfectly legal and above-board, and they only wanted the money back when it suited them.

Nevertheless, after a period during which the two parties barely spoke, they had become friendly again, and whenever they asked him for a favor—getting a university place for their daughter or tickets for concerts that their "clients" wanted to attend—Igor always did all he could to help them. After all, regardless of their motives, they were the only people who had believed in his dreams. Ewa—whenever he thought of her now, Igor felt intensely irritated—used to say that they had played on her husband's innocence to launder money earned from arms trafficking, as if that made any difference. It wasn't as if he'd been involved in the actual buying or selling of arms, and besides, in any business deal, both parties need to make a profit.

And everyone has their ups and downs. Some of his former backers had spent time in prison, but he had never abandoned them, even though he no longer needed their help. A man's dignity isn't measured by the people he has around him when he's at the peak of his success, but by his ability not to forget those who helped him when his need was greatest. Whether those hands were drenched in blood or sweat was irrelevant: if you were clinging on to the edge of a precipice, you wouldn't care who it was hauling you up to safety.

A sense of gratitude is important; no one gets very far if he forgets those who were with him in his hour of need. Not that you have to be constantly thinking about who helped or was helped. God has his eyes fixed on his sons and daughters and rewards only those who behave in accordance with the blessings that were bestowed on them.

And so when he wanted to buy some curare, he knew where to go, although he had to pay an absurd price for a substance that is relatively commonplace in the jungles of South America.

HE REACHES THE HOTEL LOBBY. The party is more than half an hour away by car, and it would be very hard to find a taxi if he just stood out in the street. He long ago learned that the first thing you do when you arrive at a hotel is give a large tip to the concierge without asking anything in exchange; all successful businessmen do this, and they never have any trouble getting reservations at the best restaurants, or tickets for shows, or information about certain areas of the city that don't appear in the guidebooks, and which prefer not to shock the middle classes.

With a smile, he asks for and gets a taxi right there and then, while another guest beside him is complaining about the problems he's having finding transport. Gratitude, necessity, and the right contacts. You can get anything you want with those three things, even a silver envelope with the seductive words "For you" written in fine calligraphy. He had held off using it until the very end because if Ewa had failed to understand the other messages, this—the most sophisticated of all—would leave no room for doubt.

His old friends had come up trumps. They had offered to let him have it for nothing, but he had preferred to pay. He had enough money and didn't like to be in anyone's debt.

He hadn't asked too many questions about how it was made; he only knew that it was a very complicated process and that the person who created the hermetically sealed envelope had to wear gloves and a gas mask. The high price he had paid for the envelope was quite justified since it had to be handled very carefully indeed, even though the product itself wasn't that hard to get hold of: it's commonly used in steel tempering and in the production of paper, clothes, and plastic. It has a rather frightening name, hydrogen cyanide, but smells of almonds and looks perfectly harmless.

He stops thinking about who sealed the envelope and begins to imagine the person who will open it—holding it quite close to the face, as is normal. On the white card inside is a printed message in French:

"Katyusha, *je t'aime*."

"Katyusha? Who's that?" the person will ask, noticing that the card is covered in a kind of dust. Once in contact with the air, the dust will become a gas, and a strong smell of almonds will fill the room.

The person will be surprised and think: "Whoever sent it might have chosen a nicer smell." It must be an advertisement for perfume. He or she will remove the card and turn it this way and that, and the gas given off by the dust will start to spread ever more quickly.

"It must be some kind of joke."

That will be their last conscious thought. Leaving the card on the table at the door, they'll go into the bathroom to take a shower or to finish applying makeup or to adjust their tie.

They'll notice then that their heart is racing. They won't immediately connect this with the perfume filling the room; after all, they have no enemies, only competitors and adversaries. Before they even reach the bathroom, they will notice that they can no longer stand and they'll sit down on the edge of the bed. The next symptoms will be an unbearable headache and difficulty in breathing, followed by a desire to vomit. However, there will be no time for that; they will rapidly lose consciousness, still without making any connection between their physical state and the contents of the envelope.

In a matter of minutes—he had asked for the product to be as concentrated a possible—the lungs will stop working, the body will go into convulsions, the heart will stop pumping blood, and death will follow.

Painless. Merciful. Humane.

Igor gets into the taxi and gives the address: Hotel du Cap, Eden Roc, Cap d'Antibes.

Tonight's gala supper.

The androgyne—wearing a black shirt, white bow tie, and a kind of Indian tunic over the same tight trousers that draw attention to his scrawny legs—tells her that they could be arriving at either a very good moment or a very bad one.

"The traffic's better than I expected. We'll be one of the first to enter Eden Roc."

Gabriela, who, by now, has had her hair and makeup retouched yet again—this time by a makeup artist who seemed totally bored by her work—doesn't understand what this means.

"Given all the traffic holdups, isn't it best to be early? How could that be bad?"

The androgyne gives a deep sigh before replying, as if he were having to explain the obvious to someone who doesn't even know the most elementary rules of the world of glamour.

"It could be good because you'll be alone in the corridor . . ."

The androgyne looks at her, sees the blank expression on her face, utters another deep sigh, then says:

"No one walks straight into this kind of party through a door. You always have to go down a corridor first. On one side are the photographers and on the other is a wall bearing the logo of the party's sponsor. Haven't you ever seen photos in celebrity magazines? Haven't you ever noticed that the celebrities are always standing in front of a logo as they smile for the cameras?"

Celebrity. The arrogant androgyne has let slip the wrong word. He has unwittingly admitted that Gabriela is also a celebrity. Gabriela savors this victory in silence, although she's grown-up enough to know that she still has a very long way to go.

"And what's so bad about arriving on time?"

Another sigh.

"The photographers themselves might not have arrived yet, but let's hope I'm mistaken, that way I can hand out a few of these flyers."

"About me?"

"You surely don't imagine that everyone knows who you are, do you? Sorry to disappoint you, sweetheart. No, I'll have to go on ahead of you and give this wretched bit of paper to each photographer and tell them that the big star of Gibson's next film is about to arrive and that they should have their cameras ready. I'll signal to them as soon as you appear in the corridor.

"I won't be nice to them though. I mean, they're used to being treated as what they are, creatures on the lowest rung of power. I'll say I'm doing them a big favor, and they won't want to risk missing a chance and getting fired because there's no shortage of people in the world with a camera and an Internet connection, and who are mad keen to post something on the Web that everyone else has missed. I reckon that, in future, given the way circulation figures are going, newspapers will rely entirely on the services of anonymous photographers as a way of keeping down their costs."

He wants to show off his knowledge of the media, but the young woman beside him isn't interested. She picks up one of the bits of paper and starts reading.

"Who's Lisa Winner?"

"That's you. We've changed your name. Or rather, the name had been chosen even before you were selected. From now on, that's what you're called. Gabriela is too Italian, whereas Lisa could be any nationality. Market research shows that the general public find surnames with between four and six letters easiest to remember: Taylor. Burton. Davis. Woods. Hilton. Shall I go on?"

"No, thanks. I can see you know your market, but now I need to find out who I am—according to my new biography."

She makes no attempt to hide the irony in her voice. She was growing in confidence and beginning to behave like a real star. She starts reading: a major discovery chosen from among more than a thousand applicants to work on the first production by famous couturier and entrepreneur Hamid Hussein, etc. etc.

"The flyers were printed over a month ago," says the androgyne, tipping the scales back in his favor. "It was written by the group's marketing team, and they're always spot-on. Listen: 'She worked as a model and studied drama.' That's you, isn't it?"

"So I was chosen more for my biography than for the quality of my audition."

"No, it means that everyone there had the same biography."

"Look, shall we just stop making jibes at each other and try to be a little more human and friendly?"

"Here? In Cannes? Forget it. There's no such thing as friends, only self-interest. There are no human beings, just crazy machines who mow down everything in their path in order to get where they want or else end up plowing into a lamppost."

Despite this response, Gabriela feels she was right and that her companion's animosity is beginning to melt.

"Look at this," he goes on. " 'For years, she refused to work in the cinema, feeling that the theater was the best way to express her talent.' That gives you a lot of bonus points; it shows you're a person with integrity, who only accepted the role in the film because you really loved it, even though you'd been invited to do plays by Shakespeare, Beckett, or Genet, or whoever."

He's obviously very well-read, this androgyne. Everyone's heard of Shakespeare, but fewer people know about Beckett and Genet.

Gabriela—or Lisa—agrees. The car arrives, and there, once more, are the inevitable security guards in black suits, white shirts, and black ties, all clutching tiny radios as if they were real policemen (or perhaps that's the collective dream of all security guards). One of them waves the driver on because it's too early.

The androgyne—having weighed up the risks and decided that early is, in fact, best—jumps out of the limousine and goes over to one of the guards, a man twice his size. Gabriela tries to distract herself and think of other things.

"What sort of car is this?" she asks the chauffeur.

"A Maybach 57S," he replies. He has a German accent. "A real work of art, the perfect machine, the ultimate in luxury. It was built . . ."

But she's no longer listening. She can see the androgyne talking to the huge security guard. The man appears to ignore him and makes a gesture indicating that he should get into the car and stop holding up the traffic. The androgyne—a mere mosquito to the security guard's elephant—turns on his heel and walks back to the car.

He opens the door and tells Gabriela to get out; they're going in anyway.

Gabriela fears the worst, that there'll be an almighty row. She walks with the mosquito past the elephant, who says: "Hey, you can't go in there!," but they both keep straight on. Other voices shout: "Have a little respect for the rules! We haven't opened the door yet!" She doesn't have the courage to look back and imagines that the herd must be hot on their heels ready to trample them at any moment.

But nothing happens, even though the androgyne isn't walking any faster, perhaps out of respect for her long dress. They're passing through an immaculate garden now; the horizon is tinged with pink and blue; the sun is sinking.

The androgyne is enjoying this new victory.

"They're all very macho until you face up to them, but you just have to raise your voice, look them straight in the eye, and keep walking, and they won't come after you. I have the invitations and that's all I need. They may be big those guys, but they're not stupid, and they know that only someone important would speak to them as I did."

He concludes with surprising humility:

"I've got used to pretending to be important."

They reach the hotel, which is totally removed from the hustle and bustle of Cannes and suitable only for those guests who don't need to keep going back and forth along the Boulevard. The androgyne asks Gabriela/Lisa to go to the bar and order two glasses of champagne; this will indicate that she's not alone. No talking to strangers. Nothing vulgar, please. He'll go and see how the land lies and distribute the flyers.

"I'm only doing this for form's sake really. No one will publish your photo, but this is what I'm paid to do. I'll be back in a minute."

"But didn't you just say that the photographers . . ."

He has reverted to his former arrogant self. Before Gabriela can hit back, though, he has vanished.

THERE ARE NO EMPTY TABLES; the place is packed with men in dinner jackets and women in long dresses. They're all talking in low voices, those who *are* talking, for most have their eyes fixed on the sea that can be seen through the large windows. Even though this is their first time in such a place, a palpable, unmistakable feeling hovers over all these celebrated heads: a profound sense of tedium.

They have all attended hundreds, possibly thousands of parties like this. Once, they would have felt the excitement of the unknown, of possibly meeting a new love, of making important professional contacts; but now that they have reached the top of their careers, there are no more challenges; all that's left to do is to compare one yacht with another, one jewel with your neighbor's jewel, the people who are sitting at the tables nearest the window with those who are farther off—a sure sign of the former's superiority. Yes, this is the end of the line: tedium and endless comparisons. After decades of struggling to get where they are, there seems to be nothing left, not even the pleasure of having watched one more sunset in one more beautiful place.

What are they thinking, those rich, silent women, so distant from their husbands?

They're thinking about age.

They need to go back to see their plastic surgeon and redo what time is relentlessly undoing. Gabriela knows that one day this will happen to her as well, and suddenly—perhaps because of all the emotions of a day that is ending so very differently from the way it began—she can feel those negative thoughts returning.

Again there's that feeling of terror mingled with joy. Again the feeling that, despite the long struggle, she doesn't deserve what's happening to her; she's just a girl who's worked hard at her job, but who's still ill-prepared for life. She doesn't know the rules; she's going further than good sense dictates; this world doesn't belong to her and she'll never be a part of it. She feels helpless and can't remember now why she came to Europe; after all, it's not so dreadful being an actress in small-town America, doing exactly what she likes and not what other people make her do. She wants to be happy, and she's not entirely sure she's on the right path.

"Stop it! Stop thinking like that!"

She can't do any yoga exercises here, so she tries to concentrate on the sea and on the blue and pink sky. She has been given a golden opportunity; she needs to overcome her feelings of revulsion and to talk more to the androgyne in the few free moments they have before the "corridor." She mustn't make any mistakes; she has been lucky and she must make the most of it. She opens her handbag to take out her lipstick and touch up her lips, but all she sees inside is a lot of crumpled paper. She had been back to the Gift Room with the bored makeup artist, and had again forgotten to collect her things, but even if she had remembered, where would she have put them?

That handbag is an excellent metaphor for her current experience: lovely outside and completely empty inside.

She must control herself.

"The sun has just sunk below the horizon and will be reborn tomorrow with the same force. I need to be reborn now. The fact that I've dreamed of this moment so many times ought to have prepared me, made me more confident. I believe in miracles and I'm being blessed by God, who listened to my prayers. I must remember what the director used to say to me before each rehearsal: 'Even if you're doing the same thing over and over, you need to discover something new, fantastic, and unbelievable that went unnoticed the time before.'"

ENTER A HANDSOME MAN OF about forty, with graying hair and dressed in an impeccable dinner jacket handmade by some master tailor. He looks as if he were about to come over to her, but immediately notices the second glass of champagne and heads off to the other end of the bar. She would have liked to talk to him; the androgyne is taking such a long time. But she remembers his stern words:

"Nothing vulgar."

And it would indeed be reprehensible, inappropriate, embarrassing to see a young woman, all alone in the bar of a five-star hotel, go over to an older customer. What would people think?

She drinks her champagne and orders another glass. If the androgyne has disappeared for good, she has no way of paying the bill, but who cares? Her doubts and insecurities are disappearing as she drinks, and now she's afraid that she might not be able to get into the party and fulfill her commitments.

No, she's no longer the small-town girl who has struggled to get on in life, and she will never be that person again. The road rises before her; another glass of champagne, and the fear of the unknown becomes a dread that she might never have the chance to discover what it really means to be here. What terrifies her now is the sense that everything could change from one moment to the next; how can she make sure that the miracle of today continues tomorrow? What guarantee does she have that all the promises made earlier will ever be met? She has often before stood outside some magnificent door, some fantastic opportunity, and dreamed for days and weeks about the possibility that her life might change forever, only to find, in the end, that the phone didn't ring, or that her CV was mislaid, or that the director would call and offer his apologies, and tell her that they'd found someone more suitable for the part, "which isn't to say you don't have real talent, so don't be discouraged." Life has many ways of testing a person's will, either by having nothing happen at all or by having everything happen all at once.

The man who arrived alone has his eyes fixed on her and on the second glass of champagne. She so wishes he would come over to her! She hasn't had a chance to talk to anyone about what's been happening. She'd thought several times of phoning her family, but her phone was in her real bag and probably full of messages from her roommates, wanting to know where she is, if she has any spare invitations, if she'd like to go with them to some second-rate event where such-and-such a celebrity is going to make an appearance.

She can't share anything with anyone. She has taken a big step in her life, she's alone in a hotel bar, terrified that the dream might end, and at the same time knowing that she can never go back to being the person she was. She has nearly reached the top of the mountain: she must either hang on tight or be blown over by the wind.

The forty-something man with the graying hair, drinking an orange juice, is still there. At one point, their eyes meet, and he smiles. She pretends not to have seen him.

Why is she so afraid? Because with each new step she's taking, she doesn't know quite how to behave. No one helps her; all they do is give orders and expect them to be rigorously obeyed. She feels like a child locked in a dark room, trying to find her way to the door because some very powerful person is calling her and demanding to be obeyed.

Her thoughts are interrupted by the androgyne, who has just come back.

"Let's wait awhile longer. People are only just starting to arrive."

The handsome man gets up, pays his bill, and heads for the exit. He seems disappointed. Perhaps he was waiting for the right moment to come over, tell her his name, and . . .

". . . talk a little."

"What?"

She had let her guard drop. Two glasses of champagne and her tongue was looser than it should be.

"Nothing."

"No, you said you needed to talk a little."

She's the little girl in the dark room with no one to guide her. Humility. She must do what she promised herself she would do a few minutes earlier.

"Yes, I was just going to ask what you're doing here in Cannes, how you ended up in this world of which I understand almost nothing. It's not at all as I imagined it would be; believe it or not, when you went off to talk to the photographers, I felt really alone and frightened, but I know I can count on you for help, and I wondered whether or not you enjoy your work."

Some angel—who clearly likes champagne—is putting the right words in her mouth.

The androgyne looks at her in surprise. Is she trying to make friends with him? Why is she asking questions no one normally dares to ask, when she's only known him a few hours?

No one trusts him because he's not like anyone else—he's unique. Contrary to what most people think, he isn't homosexual, he has simply lost all interest in other human beings. He bleaches his hair, wears the clothes he's always dreamed of wearing, weighs exactly what he wants to weigh, and though he knows he makes a strange impression on people, he's not obliged to be nice to anyone as long as he does his job.

And now here's this woman asking him what he thinks, how he feels. He picks up the glass of champagne that has been waiting for him and drinks it down in one.

She must imagine that he works for Hamid Hussein and has some influence, and wants his cooperation and help so as to know what her next step should be. He knows all the steps, but he was only taken on for the duration of the Festival and to perform certain tasks, and he'll only do what he's been asked to do. When these days of luxury and glamour are over, he'll go back to his apartment in a Paris suburb, where he gets abuse from the neighbors simply because he doesn't fit the conventional model established by whatever madman once declared: "All human beings are equal." It's not true. All human beings are different and should take their right to be different to its ultimate consequences.

He'll watch TV, shop at the supermarket next door, buy magazines, and sometimes go to the cinema; and because he's considered to be a responsible person, he'll get the occasional call from agents who need experienced assistants in the world of fashion, people who know how to dress models and choose accessories, to help those new to the fashion world avoid making social blunders, and to explain what they should and absolutely shouldn't do.

Oh, he has his dreams. He's unique, he tells himself. He's happy because he expects nothing more from life, and although he looks much younger, he's actually forty years old. He did try to get a career as a designer, but couldn't get a decent job and fell out with the people who could have helped him. He no longer has any great expectations, even though he's cultured and has good taste and a will of iron. He no longer believes that someone will look at him, see the way he dresses, and say: "Great, we'd like to talk to you." He's had a few invitations to work as a model, but that was a long time ago, and he doesn't regret having turned them down because being a model wasn't part of his life plan.

He makes his own clothes from offcuts discarded by haute-couture studios. In Cannes, he's staying with two other people up on the hill, probably not very far from where the young woman is lodging. She, however, is getting her big chance, and however unfair he may feel life to be, he mustn't allow himself to be overwhelmed by frustration and envy. He'll do his very best because if he doesn't, he won't be invited back as "production assistant."

Of course he's happy; anyone who desires nothing is happy. He looks at his watch; it might be a good moment for them to go in.

"Come on. We'll talk another time."

He pays for the drinks and asks for a receipt, so that he can claim back every penny once the glitz and glamour are over and done with. Some other people are getting up and doing the same thing; he and Gabriela/Lisa need to hurry if she isn't to get lost in the crowd that is now beginning to arrive. They walk across the hotel lobby toward the "corridor"; he hands her two invitations, which he has kept safe in his pocket. After all, important people don't have to bother with such details, they always have an assistant to do that.

He is the assistant and she is the important person, and she's already beginning to show signs that "greatness" is going to her head. She'll find out soon enough just what this world is capable of: draining every ounce of her energy, filling her mind with dreams, manipulating her vanity, then discarding her just when she thinks she's ready for anything. That's what happened with him and it happens with everyone.

THEY GO DOWN THE STAIRS. They stop in the small hall just before the "corridor." There's no hurry; this is different from the red carpet. If anyone calls her name, she must turn and smile. If that happens, then the chances are that all the other photographers will start taking photos too, because if one of them knows her name, she must be important. She shouldn't spend more than two minutes posing because this is just the entrance to a party, even though it seems like something from another world. If she wants to be a star, then she must start behaving like one.

"Why am I going in alone?"

"Apparently there's been some hitch. He should be here—after all, he's a professional—but he's obviously been held up."

"He" is the Star. The androgyne could have told her what he thought had really happened: "He didn't leave his room when he should have done, which means he's probably met some girl who's got the hots for him." This, however, would hurt the feelings of the novice by his side, who's probably nursing entirely baseless dreams of some lovely love story.

He doesn't need to be cruel, just as he doesn't need to be her friend; he simply has to do his job and then leave. Besides, if the silly girl can't control her emotions, the photos taken of her in the corridor might turn out badly.

He stands in front of her in the queue and asks her to follow him, but to leave a yard or two between them. As soon as they enter the corridor, he'll go over to the photographers and see if he can get any of them interested.

GABRIELA WAITS FOR A FEW seconds, puts on her best smile, holds her handbag as she has been taught, straightens her back, and starts to walk confidently ahead, ready to face the flashbulbs. The corridor opens out into a brightly lit area, with a white wall plastered with the sponsor's logo. On the other side is a small gallery where various lenses are pointing in her direction.

She keeps walking, this time trying to be aware of each step; she doesn't want to repeat the frustrating experience of earlier that day, when her walk along the red carpet was over before she knew it. She must live the present moment as if a film of her life were being shown in slow motion. At some point, the cameras will start to whir.

"Jasmine!" someone shouts out.

Jasmine? But her name is Gabriela!

She stops for a fraction of a second, a smile frozen on her face. No, her name isn't Gabriela anymore. What is it? Jasmine?

Suddenly, she hears the sound of camera buttons being pressed, lenses opening and closing, except that all the lenses are pointing at the person behind her.

"Move!" says one photographer. "Your moment of glory is over. Get out of the way!"

She can't believe it. She keeps smiling, but starts to walk more rapidly now in the direction of the dark tunnel that seems to follow on from that corridor of light.

"Jasmine! Over here! Here!"

The photographers seem to be in the grip of a collective hysteria.

She reaches the end of the corridor without having heard anyone call out her name, a name she herself has forgotten anyway. The androgyne is waiting for her.

"Don't worry," he says, for the first time showing a little humanity. "The same thing will happen to others. Or worse. You'll see people who used to get their name shouted out, but who'll walk along the corridor tonight, a smile on their face, waiting for someone to take their photo, only to find that no one bothers."

She has to stay cool and in control. It wasn't the end of the world; no demons will appear just yet.

"Oh, I'm not worried. After all, I only started today. Who's Jasmine, though?"

"She started today too. It was announced this evening that she's just signed a huge contract with Hamid Hussein, but not to appear in his films, so don't worry."

She's not worried. She just wishes the Earth would open up and swallow her.

Smile.

Pretend you don't know why so many people are interested in your name.

Walk as if you were walking on a red carpet, not a catwalk.

Careful, other people are arriving, your quota of time for photos is over, it's best to keep moving.

However, the photographers insist on calling out her name, and she feels embarrassed because the next person—a couple, in fact—have to wait until the photographers are satisfied, which, of course, they never are, always looking for the perfect angle, the unique shot (as if such a thing were possible), the shot of her looking straight into the camera.

Now wave, still smiling, and walk on.

AS SHE REACHES THE END of the corridor, she's immediately surrounded by a crowd of journalists. They want to know everything about the huge contract she's just signed with one of the best-known couturiers in the world. She'd like to say: "It's not true," but instead she says:

"We're still studying the details."

They insist. A television reporter approaches, microphone in hand, and asks if she's happy about the news. She says she thought that afternoon's fashion show had gone off really well and that the designer—and she makes a point of saying her name—will be holding her next show during the Paris Fashion Week.

The journalist doesn't appear to know anything about that afternoon's show, and the questions keep coming, except now they're being filmed.

Don't drop your guard, only give the answers you want to give and not the one they're trying to get out of you. Pretend you don't know the details and just say again how well the show went, about it being a long-overdue tribute to Ann Salens, the forgotten genius who had the misfortune not to be born in France. A young man, who's a bit of a joker, asks how she's enjoying the party; she responds with equal irony: "Well, if you give me a chance to go in, I'll tell you." A former model, now working as a presenter on cable TV, asks how she feels about becoming the exclusive face of the next HH collection. A better-informed colleague wants to know if it's true that her salary will be more than six digits.

"They should have put 'seven-digit salary' on the press release, don't you think?" he says. "More than six digits sounds a touch absurd, don't you think? Or even better, they could have said that it's over a million euros, instead of making us count the digits, don't you think? In fact, instead of 'six-*digit* salary,' they could have said 'six-*figure*,' don't you think?"

She doesn't *think* anything.

"We're still looking into it," she says again. "Now let me get a little air, will you? I'll answer what questions I can later on."

This, of course, is a complete lie. Later on, she'll get a taxi straight back to the hotel.

Someone asks her why she isn't wearing a Hamid Hussein dress.

"I've always worked for . . ." and again she gives the designer's name. Some of the reporters there note it down, while others simply ignore it. What they want is a piece of publishable news, not the truth behind the facts.

She's saved by the pace at which things happen at parties like this. In the corridor, the photographers are already shouting out someone else's name. In an orchestrated movement, as if under the baton of an invisible conductor, the journalists surrounding her all turn and see that a bigger, more important celebrity has just arrived. Jasmine takes advantage of this hiatus and heads for the lovely walled garden that has been transformed into a salon where people are drinking, smoking, and walking up and down.

Soon she, too, will be able to drink, smoke, look up at the sky, thump the parapet, turn round, and leave.

However, a young woman and a very strange-looking creature—like an android out of a science-fiction movie—are staring at her, blocking her path. They clearly don't know what they're doing there either, so she might as well strike up conversation with them. She introduces herself. The strange creature takes his mobile phone out of his pocket, grimaces, and says he'll be back shortly.

The young woman is still staring at her with a look on her face that says, "You ruined my evening."

Jasmine is sorry she ever accepted tonight's invitation. It was delivered by two men, just as she and her partner were getting ready to go to a small reception put on by the BCA (the Belgian Clothing Association, the body that promotes and regulates fashion in her country). But it's not all bad news. If the photos are published, her dress will be seen, and someone might feel interested enough to find out the designer's name.

The men who delivered the invitation seemed very polite. They said that a limousine was waiting outside and that they were sure a model of her experience would need only fifteen minutes to get ready.

One of them opened a briefcase, took out a laptop and a portable printer, and announced that they were there to close the contract. It was simply a matter of fine-tuning the details. They would fill in the conditions, and her agent—they knew that the woman with her was also her agent—would sign.

They promised her partner every help with her next collection. And yes, of course she could keep her name on the label and even use their PR service. More than that, HH would like to buy the brand and thus inject the necessary money into it to ensure that she got good coverage in the Italian, French, and British press.

There were two conditions. First, the matter had to be decided right there and then, so that they could send a note to the press before the newspapers were put to bed for the night.

Second, she would have to transfer her contract with Jasmine Tiger to Hamid Hussein, for whom Jasmine would then work exclusively. There was, after all, no shortage of models, and the Belgian designer would soon find someone to replace her. Besides, as Jasmine's agent, she would earn a lot of money.

"I agree to the transfer of contract," her partner said, "but we'll have to talk about the rest."

How could she agree so quickly, the woman who was responsible for everything that had happened in her life, and who now seemed perfectly happy to lose her? She was being stabbed in the back by the person she loved most in the world.

One of the men took out his BlackBerry.

"We'll send a press release now, in fact, we've written it already: 'I'm thrilled to have this opportunity . . .'"

"Just a minute. *I'm* not thrilled at all. I don't even know what you're talking about."

Her partner, however, started editing the text, changing "thrilled" to "happy" and "opportunity" to "invitation." She studied each word and phrase. She demanded that they mention some absurdly high salary. The men disagreed, saying that this might inflate the market. No deal then, came the reply. The two men left the room to make a phone call and returned almost at once. They would put something vague about a six-digit salary, without mentioning an exact sum. They all shook hands; the two men complimented both the collection and the model, put laptop and printer back in the bag, and asked the designer to record a formal agreement on one of their mobile phones as proof that their negotiations regarding Jasmine had been successful. They left as quickly as they came, both talking on their mobile phones and, at the same time, urging Jasmine to take no longer than fifteen minutes to get ready; her presence at tonight's party was part of the contract.

"You'd better get ready, then," said her companion.

"You don't have the power to decide what I do with my life. You know I don't agree, but I wasn't even asked my opinion. I'm not interested in working for anyone else."

The woman went over to the dresses scattered round the room and chose the most beautiful one—a white dress embroidered with butterflies. She spent a moment considering which shoes and handbag Jasmine should wear; there was no time to lose.

"They didn't say anything about you wearing a dress by HH tonight, which means we have a chance to show off something from my collection."

Jasmine couldn't believe what she was hearing.

"Is that why you did it?"

"Yes, it is."

They were standing facing each and neither of them looked away.

"You're lying."

"Yes, I'm lying."

And they fell into each other's arms.

"Ever since that weekend on the beach, when we took those first photographs, I knew this day would come. It took a while, but you're nineteen now and old enough to accept a challenge. Other people have approached me before, but I've always said no, and I never knew whether it was just that I didn't want to lose you or because you weren't quite ready. Today, though, when I saw Hamid Hussein in the audience, I knew he wasn't there simply to pay tribute to Ann Salens and that he must have something else in mind, and that could only be you. Sure enough, I got a message saying he wanted to talk to us. I didn't know quite what to do, but I gave him the name of our hotel. It was no surprise when those two men arrived with the contract."

"But why did you accept?"

"If you love someone, you must be prepared to set them free. He can offer you far more than I can, and you have my blessing. I want you to have everything you deserve. We'll still be together because you have my heart, my body, and my soul. And I'll keep my independence, although I know how important sponsors can be in this world. If Hamid Hussein had come to me with a proposal to buy my label, I would have had no problem in selling it and going to work for him.

However, the deal wasn't about me, it was about you. And if I accepted the part of the proposal involving me, that would mean being untrue to myself."

She kissed Jasmine.

"Well, I can't accept either," declared Jasmine. "I was just a frightened child when I met you, terrified because I'd perjured myself in court, wretched because I'd been responsible for letting criminals go free, and so depressed that I was seriously considering suicide. You're responsible for everything that's happened in my life."

Her partner asked her to sit down in front of the mirror and, before doing anything else, she tenderly stroked her hair.

"When I met you, I'd lost all my zest for life as well. My husband had left me for someone younger, better-looking, and richer, and I was forced to become a photographer to make a living, spending my weekends at home reading, surfing the Internet, or watching old films on TV. My great dream of becoming a designer seemed to be moving ever farther off. I couldn't get the necessary financial backing, and I'd had enough of knocking on doors that never opened or talking to people who didn't listen to what I was saying.

"That's when you appeared. And that weekend, I have to confess, I was only thinking about myself. I knew I had a rare jewel in my hands, and could make a fortune if I could get you to sign an exclusive contract with me. I seem to remember that I even suggested I should become your agent. I didn't do that out of a desire to protect you from the world. My thoughts at the time were as selfish as Hamid Hussein's. I would know how to exploit my treasure. I would get rich on those photos."

She gave a few final touches to Jasmine's hair.

"And you, even though you were only sixteen then, showed me how love can change a person. It was through you that I discovered who I am. In order to show off your talent to the world, I started designing clothes for you to wear, clothes that had been in my head all the time, waiting to be transformed into fabrics, embroidery, accessories. We lived together and, even though I was more than twice your age, we learned together as well. Thanks to all these things, people started noticing what I was doing and decided to invest in it, and, for the first time, I began to realize my dreams. We traveled here to Cannes together, and no contract is going to part us."

She went to the bathroom to fetch the makeup case. Her tone grew more businesslike.

"You need to look really stunning tonight. Models rarely rise to stardom out of nowhere, so there'll be a lot of media interest. Just say you don't know the details yet; that's enough, but they'll keep asking and trying to get you to say things like: 'I've always dreamed of working with Hamid Hussein' or 'This is a very important step in my career,' etc."

She went with Jasmine down to the hotel lobby, where the waiting chauffeur opened the car door.

"Remember: you don't know the details of the contract yet; your agent is taking care of all that. Enjoy the party."

AT THE PARTY, OR RATHER, supper—although she can see neither tables nor food, only waiters walking about, proffering every possible kind of drink, including mineral water—people form into small groups, and anyone arriving alone looks somewhat lost. The event is taking place in a vast garden furnished with armchairs and sofas; there are also several pillars about three feet high on which half-clothed models with perfect bodies are dancing to the sound of music that emerges out of strategically positioned loudspeakers.

Celebrities continue to arrive. The guests seem happy; they smile and greet each other as if they'd known each other for years, although Jasmine knows this isn't so. They probably meet now and again on occasions like this and always forget each other's names, but they need to show how very influential, famous, admired, and well-connected they are.

The young woman, who initially looked so angry, reveals that she, too, is feeling completely lost. She asks for a cigarette and introduces herself. Within a matter of minutes, they know each other's life story. Jasmine leads her over to the balustrade overlooking the Mediterranean, and while the party fills up with strangers and acquaintances, they stand there gazing out to sea. They discover that they're now working for the same man, although on different projects. Neither of them has ever met him, and for both of them, everything has happened during this one day.

Men occasionally try to engage them in conversation, but Gabriela and Jasmine ignore them. Gabriela is the person Jasmine needed to meet, someone with whom to share her sense of having been abandoned, despite her partner's loving words. If she had to choose between her career and the love of her life, she would choose love over career every time, and she didn't care if such behavior seemed adolescent. Now it turns out that the love of her life wants her to put her career first and seems to have accepted HH's proposal simply so that she can feel proud of everything she's done for her, of the care with which she's guided her steps and corrected her mistakes, and the enthusiasm she's put into every word spoken and decision taken, however difficult.

Gabriela had needed to meet Jasmine too, to ask her advice, to feel less alone, and to see that good things happen to other people too. She confesses that she's worried that her companion has just left her there, when he's supposed to be introducing her to various people she needs to meet.

"He thinks he can hide his feelings, but I know something's wrong."

Jasmine tells her not to worry, to relax, drink some champagne and enjoy the music and the view. Unforeseen things are always happening, and there's a whole army of people ready to deal with them, so that no one ever finds out what really goes on behind the scenes of all that wealth and glamour. The Star is sure to be here soon.

"But, please, don't leave me on my own, will you? I'm not staying long."

Gabriela promises that she won't leave her alone. She's her only friend in this new world.

Yes, her only friend, but Jasmine's so young that Gabriela suddenly feels too old to be starting out on a new track. The Star had shown himself to be utterly superficial during the limousine drive to the red carpet; all his charm had vanished. And however much she likes the young girl by her side, she needs to find some new male companion for the night. She notices that the man who came into the bar earlier on is standing, like them, by the balustrade, looking out to sea, his back to the party, oblivious to everything else going on at this gala supper. He's charismatic, handsome, elegant, mysterious. When the opportunity arises, she'll suggest to her new friend that they go over to him and start a conversation, it really doesn't matter what about.

After all—and despite all—this has been her lucky day, and it might include finding a new love.

8:21 P.M.

The pathologist, the commissioner, Savoy, and a fourth person—who has not been introduced, but who arrived with the commissioner—are sitting round a table.

Their task is not to discuss the latest murder, but to draw up a joint statement to be presented to the journalists gathering outside. This time a really big Star has died, a well-known director is in intensive care, and the news agencies from around the world have obviously sent a stark message to their journalists: either come up with something we can print or you're fired.

"Legal medicine is one of the most ancient of the sciences, involved as it is with identifying poisons and producing antidotes. Nevertheless, in the past, royalty and the nobility always preferred to employ 'an official taster,' just to avoid any nasty surprises the doctors failed to foresee."

Savoy had met this "sage" earlier today. This time, he allows the commissioner to step in and put a stop to the pathologist's erudite lecture.

"That's enough showing off, Doctor. There's a criminal on the loose in Cannes."

The pathologist remains impassive.

"As a pathologist, I don't have the authority to determine the circumstances of a murder. I can't give opinions on the matter; I can only describe the cause of death, the weapon used, the identity of the victim, and the approximate time when the crime was committed."

"Do you see any link between the two deaths? Is there something that connects the murder of the film distributor and the actor?"

"Of course. They both worked in the movies."

He chuckles, but no one else moves a muscle. They clearly have no sense of humor.

"The only connection is that, in both cases, toxic substances were used, both of which affect the organism with extraordinary speed. What is really intriguing about the second murder, though, is the way in which the hydrogen cyanide was wrapped. The envelope had inside it a fine plastic membrane vacuum-sealed, but easily torn when the envelope was opened."

"Could it have been made here?" asks the fourth man, who has a strong foreign accent.

"Possibly, but I doubt it, because its actual manufacture is very complex, and the person who made it knew that it would be used to murder someone."

"So the murderer didn't make it?"

"I doubt it. A specialist group would almost certainly have been commissioned to produce it. In the case of the curare, the criminal himself could have dipped the needle in the poison, but hydrogen cyanide requires special techniques."

Savoy's thoughts immediately go to Marseilles, Corsica, Sicily, certain Eastern European countries, and terrorist groups in the Middle East. He leaves the room for a moment and phones Europol. He explains the gravity of the situation and asks them for a complete rundown on laboratories equipped to produce chemical weapons of that type.

He's put through to someone who tells him that they've just had a call from an American intelligence agency asking exactly the same thing. What's going on?

"Nothing. But please get back to me as soon as you have any information—in the next ten minutes at the latest."

"That's impossible," says the voice on the other end. "We'll give you the answer as soon as we have it, not before or afterward. We'll have to put in a request . . ."

Savoy hangs up and rejoins the group.

More paper.

This appears to be an obsession common to everyone working in the field of public security. No one wants to risk taking a step without first having a guarantee that their superiors approve of what they're doing. Men who once had a brilliant career ahead of them and began working with creativity and enthusiasm now cower fearfully in a corner, knowing the enormous problems they face: they need to act swiftly, but, at the same time, the hierarchy of command must be respected; the media are always quick to accuse the police of brutality, while the taxpayers complain that crimes are never solved. For all these reasons, it's always best to pass responsibility on to someone higher up.

His telephone call was really just a bit of play-acting. He knows who the killer is, and he alone will catch him; he doesn't want anyone else snatching from him the glory of having solved the biggest murder case in the history of Cannes. He must keep calm, but he's nevertheless impatient for this meeting to end.

When he goes back into the room, the commissioner informs him that Stanley Morris, formerly of Scotland Yard, has just phoned from Monte Carlo, telling them not to worry because he very much doubts that the criminal will use the same weapon again.

"We could be facing a new terror threat," says the foreigner.

"Yes, possibly," replies the commissioner, "but unlike you, the last thing we want to do is sow fear among the population. What we need to do is draw up a press statement to prevent journalists from leaping to their own conclusions and broadcasting them on tonight's TV news. This is an isolated terrorist incident, and may involve a serial killer."

"But . . ."

"There are no 'buts.'" The commissioner's voice is firm and authoritative. "We contacted your embassy because the dead man comes from your country. You are here at our invitation. In the case of the two other Americans murdered, you showed no interest at all in sending a representative, even though in one case poison was also used. So, if you're trying to insinuate that we're facing some kind of collective threat in which biological weapons are being used, you can leave now. We're not going to turn a criminal matter into something political. We want to have another Festival next year with all the usual glitz and glamour, so we're taking Mr. Morris's advice and will draw up a statement along those lines."

The foreigner says nothing.

The commissioner summons an assistant and asks him to tell the waiting journalists that they will have their conclusions in ten minutes. The pathologist tells him that it's always possible to track down the origin of hydrogen cyanide because it leaves a kind of "signature," but tracking it down will take not ten minutes, but a week.

"There were traces of alcohol in the body. The skin was red, and death was almost instantaneous. There's no doubt about which poison was used. If it had been an acid, we would have found burns around the nose and mouth, and in the case of belladonna, the pupils would have been dilated, and . . ."

"Please, Doctor, we know that you studied at university and are therefore equipped to tell us the cause of death, and we have no doubts about your competence in the field. Let us conclude that it was hydrogen cyanide."

The doctor nods and bites his lip, controlling his irritation.

"And what about the other man, who's currently in hospital. The film director . . ."

"We're treating him with pure oxygen, six hundred milligrams of Kelocyanor via intravenous drip every fifteen minutes, and if that doesn't work, we can add sodium thiosulfate diluted in twenty-five percent . . ."

The silence in the room is palpable.

". . . Sorry. The answer is, yes, he'll survive."

The commissioner makes some notes on a sheet of yellow paper. He knows that he's run out of time. He thanks everyone, and asks the foreigner not to come out with them, so as to avoid any further needless speculation. He goes to the bathroom, adjusts his tie, and asks Savoy to adjust his as well.

"Morris says that the murderer won't use poison next time. From what I've gleaned, the killer is following a pattern, although it may be an unconscious one. Do you know what it is?"

Savoy had thought about this as he was driving back from Monte Carlo. Yes, there was a pattern, which possibly not even the great Scotland Yard inspector had noticed. It was this:

The victim on the bench: the murderer was close.

The victim at the lunch: the murderer was far away.

The victim on the beach: the murderer was close.

The victim at the hotel: the murderer was far away.

Therefore, the next crime will be committed with the murderer at his victim's side, or, rather, that will be his plan, unless he's arrested in the next half hour. He learned all this from his colleagues at the police station, who gave him the information as if it were of no importance. And Savoy, in turn, had initially dismissed it as irrelevant too, but, of course, it wasn't; it was the missing link, the vital clue, the one piece needed to complete the puzzle.

His heart is pounding. He's dreamed of this all his life and cannot wait for this interminable meeting to end.

"Are you listening?"

"Yes, sir."

"Look, the people out there aren't expecting some official, technical statement, with precise answers to their questions. The fact is they'll do all they can to make us say what they want to hear, but we mustn't fall into that trap. They came here not to listen to us, but to look at us, and for their viewers and readers to be able to see us too."

He regards Savoy with a superior air, as if he were the most knowledgeable person on the planet. It would seem that Morris and the pathologist are not the only ones who like to show off their knowledge, well, everyone has their own way of saying: "I know my job."

"Think visual, by which I mean, remember that your face and body say more than words. Look straight ahead, keep your head up, and your shoulders down and slightly back. Raised shoulders mean tension and are a sure indication that we have no idea what is going on."

"Yes, sir."

THEY WALK OUT TO THE entrance of the Institute of Legal Medicine. Lights come on, microphones are thrust forward, people start to push. After a few minutes, this apparent disorder becomes more orderly. The commissioner takes the piece of paper out of his pocket.

"The actor was killed with hydrogen cyanide, a deadly poison that can be administered in various ways, although in this case it was used in the form of a gas. The film director survived the attack. His involvement was clearly accidental. He merely happened to enter the room while there were still remnants of the gas in the air. The CCTV footage shows a man walking down the corridor, going into one of the rooms, and, five minutes later, coming out again and falling to the floor."

He omits to say that the room in question is not actually visible to the camera. Omission is no lie.

"The security personnel took swift action and sent for a doctor, who immediately noticed the smell of almonds, which was, by then, too dilute to cause any harm. The police were called, and they arrived at the scene less than five minutes later and cordoned off the area. An ambulance came, and the doctors used oxygen to save the director's life."

Savoy is beginning to feel really impressed by the commissioner's easy manner. He wonders if all commissioners have to do a course in public relations.

"The poison was delivered in an envelope, but we have not as yet been able to establish whether the writing on the envelope was that of a man or a woman. Inside was a piece of paper."

He fails to mention that the technology used to seal the envelope was highly sophisticated. There was a chance in a million that one of the journalists present would know this, although, later on, that kind of question would become inevitable. He also fails to mention that another man in the film industry had been poisoned that same afternoon. Apparently, everyone thinks he died of a heart attack, although no one has actually told them this. Sometimes it's handy if the press—out of laziness or inattention—draw their own conclusions without bothering the police.

"What was on the paper?" is the first question.

The commissioner explains that he cannot reveal this now because doing so might hamper the investigation. Savoy is beginning to see the direction in which he's leading this interview and is filled with admiration; he really deserves his post as commissioner.

"Could it have been a crime of passion?" asks someone else.

"Anything is possible at the moment. Now, if you'll excuse me, ladies and gentlemen, we must get back to work."

He gets into his car, turns on the siren, and speeds away. Savoy walks to his own vehicle, feeling very proud of his boss. How amazing! He can imagine the headlines already: "Star thought to have been victim of crime of passion."

That was sure to capture people's interest. The power of celebrity was so great that the other murders would go unnoticed. Who cares about a poor young girl, who died possibly under the influence of drugs and was found on a bench near the beach? What did it matter if some henna-haired film distributor had a heart attack over lunch? What was there to say about a murder—another crime of passion— involving two complete nonentities who were never in the spotlight, on a beach away from all the hurly-burly of the Festival? It was the kind of thing that appeared every night on the television news, but the media would only continue speculating about it if a Major Celebrity was involved! And an envelope! And a piece of paper inside on which something was written!

He turns on the siren and drives in the opposite direction from the police station. In order not to raise suspicions, he uses the car radio. He finds the commissioner's frequency.

"Congratulations!"

The commissioner is also rather pleased with himself. They've gained a few hours, possibly days, but they both know that they're dealing with a serial killer of the male sex, well-dressed, with graying hair and about forty years old, and armed with sophisticated weapons. A man who is also experienced in the art of killing, and while he may be satisfied with the crimes he's already committed, he could easily strike again, at any moment.

"Have officers sent to all the Festival parties," orders the commissioner. "They should look out for any men on their own who correspond to that description. Tell them to keep any suspects under surveillance. Call for reinforcements. I want plainclothes policemen, discreetly dressed and in keeping with their surroundings—either jeans or evening dress. And I repeat, I want them at all the parties, even if we have to mobilize the traffic police as well."

Savoy immediately does as he is told. He has just received a message on his mobile phone. Europol needs more time to track down the laboratories, at least three days.

"Let me have that in writing, will you? I don't want to be held responsible if something else goes wrong here."

He chuckles quietly. He asks them to send a copy to the foreign agent as well, since he himself is no longer interested in the matter. He drives as fast as he can to the Hotel Martinez, leaves his car at the entrance, blocking other people's vehicles. When the porter complains, he shows him his policeman's ID, throws him the keys so that he can park the car somewhere else, and runs into the hotel.

He goes up to a private room on the first floor, where a police officer is waiting, along with the duty manager and a waiter.

"How much longer are we going to have to stay here?" asks the duty manager. Savoy ignores her and turns to the waiter.

"Are you sure that the murdered woman, whose picture appeared on the news, is the same woman who was sitting on the terrace this afternoon?"

"Yes, sir, pretty much. She looks younger in the photo with her hair dyed, but I'm used to remembering guests' faces, just in case one of them tries to leave without paying."

"And are you sure she was with the male guest who reserved the table earlier?"

"Absolutely. A good-looking man of about forty, with graying hair."

Savoy's heart almost leaps out of his mouth. He turns to the manager and the policeman.

"Let's go straight up to his room."

"Do you have a search warrant?" asks the manager.

Savoy's nerves snap:

"*No I haven't!* And I'm not filling in any more forms! Do you know what's wrong with this country, madame? We're all too obedient! In fact, that isn't a problem peculiar to us, it applies to the whole world! Wouldn't you obey if they wanted to send your son off to war? Wouldn't your son obey? Of course! Well, since you are an obedient citizen, either take me to that room or I'll have you arrested for aiding and abetting!"

The woman seems genuinely frightened. With the other policeman, they make their way over to the lift, which is coming down, stopping at every floor, unaware that a human life may depend on the speed with which those waiting for it can act.

They decide to take the stairs instead. The manager complains because she's wearing high heels, but Savoy simply tells her to take off her shoes and go up the stairs barefoot. They race up the marble stairs, gripping the bronze banister so as not to fall and passing various elegant waiting areas on the way. The people there wonder who this barefoot woman is, and what a uniformed policeman is doing in the hotel, running up the stairs like that. Has something bad happened? If so, why don't they take the elevator? Standards at the Festival are definitely dropping, they say to themselves; hotels aren't as selective about their guests as they once were; and the police treat the place as if they were raiding a brothel. As soon as they can, they will complain to the manager, who, unbeknownst to them, is the same barefoot woman they've just seen bounding up the stairs.

Savoy and the duty manager finally reach the door of the suite where the murderer is staying. A member of the "security squad" has already sent someone up to find out what's going on. He recognizes the manager and asks if he can help.

Savoy asks him to speak more quietly, but yes, he can help. Is he armed? The guard says that he is.

"Then you'd better stay here."

They are talking in whispers. The manager is instructed to knock on the door, while the three men—Savoy, the policeman, and the security guard—stand to one side, backs to the wall. Savoy takes his gun out of his holster. The other policeman does the same. The manager knocks several times, but gets no answer.

"He must have gone out."

Savoy asks her to use the master key. She explains that she doesn't have it with her, and even if she did, she would only open that door with the authorization of the managing director.

Savoy responds politely this time:

"No matter. I'll go downstairs and wait in the surveillance room with the security staff. He'll be back sooner or later, and I'd like to be the first to question him."

"We have a photocopy of his passport and his credit card number downstairs. Why are you so interested in him?"

"Oh, no matter."

9:02 P.M.

Half an hour's drive from Cannes, in another country where they speak the same language, use the same currency, and have no border controls, but where they have a completely different political system from France—it's ruled by a prince, as in the olden days—a man is sitting in front of a computer. Fifteen minutes ago, he received an e-mail informing him that a famous actor had been murdered.

Morris studies the photo of the victim. He hasn't been to the cinema for ages and so has no idea who he is. However, he must be someone important because there are reports of his death on one of the news portals.

Morris may be retired, but things like this used to be the equivalent of a chess game to him, a game in which he rarely allowed his opponent to win. It wasn't his career that was at risk now, it was his self-esteem.

There are certain rules he always liked to follow when he worked for Scotland Yard, one of which was to come up with as many flawed hypotheses as he could. This freed up your mind because you weren't necessarily expecting to get it right. At the tedious meetings with work evaluation committees, he used to enjoy provoking the people present: "Everything you know comes from experience accumulated over long years of work. However, those old solutions are only of use when applied to old problems. If you want to be creative, try to forget that you have all that experience."

The older members of such committees would pretend they were taking notes, the younger ones would stare at him in horror, and the meeting would continue as if he had said nothing. But he knew that the message had been received loud and clear, and soon afterward, his superiors—without giving him any of the credit, of course—would start demanding more new ideas.

He prints out the files sent by the police in Cannes. He normally tries to avoid using paper because he doesn't want to be accused of being a serial killer of forests, but sometimes it's necessary.

He starts studying the modus operandi, that is, the way the crimes were committed. Time of day (morning, afternoon, and night), weapons (hands, poison, stiletto knife), type of victim (men and women of different ages), closeness to victim (two involved direct physical contact, two involved no contact at all), the reaction of victims to their aggressor (none in all cases).

When he feels that he's faced by a dead end, the best thing is to let his thoughts wander for a while, while his unconscious mind goes to work. He opens a new screen on the computer, showing the New York Stock Exchange. Since he has no money invested in shares, it couldn't be more boring, but that's how it works: his years of experience analyze all the information he has received so far, and his intuition comes up with new, creative responses. Twenty minutes later, he goes back to the files, and his head is once again empty.

The process has worked. The murders do have things in common.

The murderer is an educated man. He must have spent days and weeks in a library, studying the best way to carry out his mission. He knows how to handle poisons and obviously hadn't touched the hydrogen cyanide himself. He knows enough about anatomy to be able to stick a knife in at exactly the right place without meeting a bone, and to kill someone with his bare hands. He knows about curare and its lethal power. He may have read about serial killings, and would be aware that some kind of "signature" always leads the police to the attacker, and so he had committed his murders in a completely random manner, with no fixed modus operandi at all.

But that's impossible. The unconscious mind of the murderer is bound to leave some signature, which Morris has not yet managed to decipher.

There's something more important still: he obviously has money, enough to follow a course in Sambo, in order to be absolutely sure which points on the body he needs to press in order to paralyze his victim. He also has contacts: he didn't buy those poisons from the corner pharmacist, not even from the local criminal underworld. They are highly sophisticated biological weapons, which require great care in their handling and application. He must have got other people to acquire them for him.

Finally, he works very quickly, which leads Morris to conclude that the murderer won't be staying long. Perhaps a week, possibly a few days more.

Where does all this take him?

The reason he can't reach a conclusion now is because he's got used to the rules of the game. He has lost the innocence he always demanded of his subordinates. That's what the world does to people; gradually, over the years, we become mediocre beings, concerned not to be seen as weird or overenthusiastic. Old age is considered a stigma, not a sign of wisdom. People assume that no one over fifty can keep up with the speed of change nowadays.

True, he can't run as fast as he could and needs reading glasses, but his mind is as sharp as ever, or so at least he wants to believe.

What about this crime though? If he's as intelligent as he thinks, why can't he solve something that seems so easy?

He can't get any further at the moment. He'll have to wait until the next victim appears.

A couple pass by. They smile and congratulate him on his luck at having two such lovely ladies by his side!

Igor thanks them, for he's genuinely in need of distraction. Soon the long-awaited meeting will take place, and although he's accustomed to all kinds of pressure, he reminds himself of the patrols he had to go on near Kabul and how before any very dangerous mission, he and his colleagues would drink and talk about women and sport, chatting away as if they weren't in Afghanistan, but were back in their hometowns, sitting round a table with family and friends. It was a way of quelling their nerves and recovering their true identities, and thus feeling better prepared for the challenges they would face the next day.

Like any good soldier, he knows that battles have more do with aims and objectives than with the actual fighting. Like any good strategist—he did, after all, build up his company from nothing to become one of the most respected in Russia—he knows that one's objective should always remain the same, even if the motive behind it may change over time. That is what has happened today: he arrived in Cannes for one reason, but only when he began to act did he understand the true motives behind what he was doing. He has been blind all these years, but now he can see the light; the revelation has finally come.

And precisely because of this, he needs to keep going. The decisions he made required courage, a degree of detachment, and, at times, even a little madness, not the kind of madness that destroys, but the sort that carries a person beyond his own limits. He's always been the same and has won precisely because he knew how to use that controlled madness whenever he had to make a decision. His friends would move with astonishing speed from saying, "It's too risky" to "I always knew you were doing the right thing." He was capable of surprising people, of coming up with fresh ideas, and, above all, of taking any necessary risks.

Here in Cannes, though—perhaps because he's in an unfamiliar place and still befuddled by lack of sleep—he has taken quite unnecessary risks, risks that might have forced him to abort his plan earlier than expected. Had that happened, he would never have reached his present clear-eyed position, one that cast an entirely different light on the woman he thought of as his beloved and whom he believed merited both sacrifice and martyrdom. He remembers the moment when he went up to the policeman to confess. That was when the change began. It was then that the spirit of the girl with the dark eyebrows began to protect him and to explain that he was doing the right things but for the wrong reasons. Accumulating love brings luck, accumulating hatred brings disaster. Anyone who stands outside the Door of Problems and fails to recognize it may well end up leaving it open and allowing tragedies to enter.

He had accepted the young girl's love. He had been an instrument of God, sent to rescue her from a dark future; now she was helping him to carry on.

He is aware, too, that, regardless of the many precautions he may have taken, he could not possibly have thought of everything, and his mission might yet be interrupted before he reaches the end. There is no reason, however, for regret or fear; he has done what he could, behaved impeccably, and, if God does not wish him to complete his task, then he must accept his decisions.

Relax, he tells himself. Talk to the young women by your side. Let your muscles rest a little before the final strike, that way, they'll be more prepared. Gabriela—the young woman who was alone at the bar when he arrived—seems very excited, and whenever the waiter comes by with more drinks, she hands him her glass, even if it's still half full, and picks up a fresh one.

"I love it when it's really icy!" she says.

Her happiness infects him a little too. Apparently, she's just signed a contract to appear in a film, although she knows neither the title of the film nor what role she'll be playing, but she will, in her words, be "the leading lady." The director is known for his ability to choose good actors and good scripts, and the leading actor, whom Igor knows and admires, certainly merits respect. When she mentions the name of the producer, he merely nods knowledgably, as if to say, "Yes, of course, I know who he is," aware that she'll interpret the nod as meaning: "I've no idea who he is, but I don't want to appear ignorant." She babbles on about rooms full of gifts, the red carpet, her meeting on the yacht, the rigorous selection process she went through, future projects . . .

"At this very moment, there are thousands of young women in Cannes and millions around the world who would like to be here to-night, talking to you and being able to tell these stories. My prayers have been answered and all my efforts rewarded."

The other young woman seems more discreet, but sadder too, per-haps because of her age and lack of experience. Igor had been there when she walked down the corridor and had heard the photographers calling out her name and clamoring to ask her questions afterward. Apparently, though, the other people at the party had no idea who she was; she had been so in demand at the start, and then, just as suddenly, had been dropped.

It was probably the talkative young woman who had decided to come over to him and ask him what he was doing there. At first, he'd felt rather constrained, but he knew that if they hadn't approached him, other solitary people would have done so, to avoid the impression that they were lost and alone and with no friends at the party. That's why he welcomed their conversation or, rather, their company, even though his mind was elsewhere. He told them his name was Gunther and explained that he was a German industrialist specializing in heavy machinery (a subject guaranteed to interest no one) and had been invited there by friends. He would be leaving tomorrow (which he hoped would be true, but God moves in mysterious ways).

When the actress learned that he didn't work in the film industry and wouldn't be staying long at the Festival, she almost moved away; however, the other girl stopped her, saying that it's always good to meet new people. And so there they are: he waiting for the friend who showed no signs of arriving, the actress waiting for her vanished assistant, and the quiet girl waiting for absolutely nothing, just a little peace.

SUDDENLY, THE ACTRESS NOTICES SOME fluff on his dinner jacket, and before he can stop her, she reaches out to brush it away. She says:

"Oh, do you smoke cigars?"

That's a relief, she thinks the object in his inside jacket pocket is a cigar.

"Yes, but only after supper."

"If you like, I could invite you both to a party on a yacht tonight. But first I need to find my assistant."

The other girl suggests that maybe she's being a little precipitate. She has only been signed up for one film and has a long way to go before she can surround herself with friends (or with an "entourage," that word universally used to describe the parasites who hover around celebrities). She should respect the rules and go to the party alone.

The actress thanks her for this advice. Then a waiter passes, and she again places her half-full glass of champagne on the tray and takes another one.

"I think you should stop drinking so much so quickly," says Igor/ Gunther, delicately taking the glass from her and pouring the contents over the balustrade. She makes a despairing gesture, then accepts that he's right, realizing that he has her best interests at heart.

"I'm just so excited," she says. "I need to calm down a little. Do you think I could smoke one of your cigars?"

"I'm afraid I only have one. Besides, it's been scientifically proven that nicotine is a stimulant, not a tranquilizer."

A cigar. Well, they are similar in shape, but that's all the two objects have in common. In his inside jacket pocket he has a suppressor, or as it's more commonly known, a silencer. It's about four inches long and, once attached to the barrel of the Beretta he has in his trouser pocket, it can work miracles, by changing BANG! into *puf*.

This is because when a gun is fired a few simple laws of physics come into effect. The speed of the bullet is slightly diminished as it's forced past a series of rubber baffles; meanwhile, the gases produced by the firing of the gun fill the hollow chamber around the cylinder, cool rapidly, and suppress the noise of the gunpowder exploding. A silencer is useless for long-range shooting because it affects the trajectory of the bullet, but it's ideal for firing at point-blank range.

IGOR IS BEGINNING TO GROW impatient. Could Ewa and her husband have canceled their invitation? Or could it be—and for a fraction of a second his head swims—that he had slipped the envelope under the door to the suite in which they were staying?

No, that's not possible; that would be such a stroke of bad luck. He thinks of the families of those who have died. If his sole objective was still to win back the woman who left him for a man who did not deserve her, all his work would have been in vain.

His composure begins to crack. Could that be why Ewa hasn't attempted to contact him, despite all the messages he's sent her? He has twice rung their mutual friend, only to be told there was no news.

His doubt is beginning to become a certainty. Yes, the couple were both dead. That would explain the sudden departure of the actress's "assistant" and why no one was bothering with the nineteen-year-old model who was supposed to appear at the great couturier's side.

Was God punishing him for having loved a woman he did not deserve and had loved too much? His ex-wife had used his hands to strangle a young woman who had her whole life ahead of her, who might have gone on to discover a cure for cancer or a way of making humanity realize that it was destroying the planet. Ewa may have known nothing about the murder, but she it was who had made him use those poisons. He had been sure that he would only have to destroy one world and that the message would reach its intended recipient. He had taken that whole small arsenal with him knowing it was all just a game, certain that on the first night, she would go to the bar for a glass of champagne before joining the party, sense his presence there, and realize that she had been forgiven for all the evil and destruction she had unleashed around her. He knows that, according to scientific research, people who have spent a lot of time together can sense their partner's presence in a place, even if they don't know exactly where they are.

That didn't happen. Ewa's indifference last night—or perhaps her guilt at what she had done to him—had prevented her from noticing the man trying to hide behind a pillar, but who had left on the table various Russian economics journals, which should have been a large enough clue for anyone who was constantly looking for what she had lost. When you're in love you imagine that you'll see the love of your life everywhere—in the street, at a party, or in the theater—but Ewa had perhaps exchanged love for a life of glamour.

He's beginning to feel calmer now. Ewa was the most powerful poison on earth, and if she had been killed by hydrogen cyanide, that was nothing. She deserved far worse.

The two young women continue talking; Igor moves away from them; he cannot allow himself to be overwhelmed by the fear that he might have destroyed his own work. He needs solitude, calm, the ability to react swiftly to this sudden change in direction.

He goes over to another group of people, who are animatedly discussing various methods of giving up smoking. This was one of the favorite topics in that particular world: showing your friends that you had the necessary willpower to defeat the foe. To take his mind off other things, he lights a cigarette, knowing full well that this is a provocative act.

"It's very bad for your health, you know," says a skeletally thin woman dripping with diamonds and holding an orange juice in one hand.

"Just being alive is bad for the health," he replies. "It always ends in death sooner or later."

The men laugh. The women eye this newcomer with interest. However, just at that moment, in the corridor—about twenty yards away from where he's standing—the photographers start shouting:

"Hamid! Hamid!"

Even from a distance, and with his view blocked by the people strolling about in the garden, he can see the couturier and his companion, the same woman who, in other parts of the world, had walked into rooms with him, the same woman who used to hold his arm in that same affectionate, delicate, elegant way.

Even before he has time to utter a sigh of relief, something else attracts his attention and makes him look away: a man has just entered from the other side of the garden without being stopped by any of the security guards. The man glances this way and that, as if searching for someone, but that someone is clearly not a friend lost in the throng.

Without saying goodbye to the group he's with, Igor goes back to the two young women, who are still standing by the balustrade, talking. He takes the actress's hand in his and makes a silent prayer to the girl with the dark eyebrows. He asks forgiveness for having doubted, but we human beings are still so impure, incapable of understanding the blessings so generously bestowed on us.

"You're moving a bit fast, aren't you?" says the actress, making no attempt to move away.

"Yes, I am, but given what you've been telling me, everything in your life is moving fast today."

She laughs. The sad girl laughs too. The policeman passes by without noticing him. He's been told to look out for men in their forties with slightly graying hair, but for men on their own.

9:20 P.M.

Doctors look at test results which are completely at odds with what they believe the actual illness to be, and must then decide whether to trust science or their heart. They learn, with time and experience, to give more weight to their instincts and they find that the outcomes for their patients improve.

Successful businessmen pore over graphs and diagrams, then go completely against the market trend and grow still richer.

Artists write books or films about which everyone says: "That won't work. No one's interested in things like that," and end up becoming icons of popular culture.

Religious leaders preach fear and guilt rather than love, which should, in theory, be the most important thing in the world, and their congregations swell.

Only one group consistently fail to go against the current trend: politicians. They want to please everyone and stick rigidly to the rules of political correctness. They end up having to resign, apologize, or contradict themselves.

MORRIS KEEPS OPENING ONE WINDOW after another on his computer. This has nothing to do with technology, but with intuition. He's tried distracting himself with the Dow Jones Index, but wasn't pleased with the results. It would be best to focus a little on some of the characters he's lived with for much of his life.

He looks again at the video in which Gary Ridgway, the Green River Killer, is describing in a calm voice how he killed forty-eight women, most of them prostitutes. Ridgway is doing this not because he wants absolution for his sins or to relieve his conscience; the public prosecutor has offered to commute his death sentence to life imprisonment if he confesses, for despite having acted with impunity for a long time, Ridgway had left insufficient evidence to convict him. Or perhaps he had just grown weary of the macabre task he had set himself.

Ridgway had a steady job spraying trucks and could only remember his victims by relating them to whether he had been working that day. For twenty years, sometimes with more than fifty detectives on his trail, he managed to commit murder after murder without ever leaving any kind of signature or clue. One of the detectives on the tape comments that Ridgway wasn't very bright, wasn't too good at his job or very educated, but was a perfect killer.

In short, he was born to be a killer, even though he had always lived in the same place. His case, at one point, was even filed away as insoluble.

Morris has watched this same video hundreds of times. It has, in the past, given him the necessary inspiration to solve other cases, but not today. He closes down that window and opens another, which shows a letter written by the father of Jeffrey Dahmer, the Milwaukee Cannibal, who was responsible for killing and dismembering seventeen men between 1978 and 1991:

> *Initially, of course, I couldn't believe that it was really Jeff who had done the things the police had accused him of. How could anyone believe that his son could do such things? I had been in the actual places where they said he had done them. I had been in rooms and basements which at other moments, according to the police, had been nothing less than a slaughterhouse. I had looked in my son's refrigerator and seen only a scattering of milk cartons and soda cans. I had leaned casually on the black table they claimed my son had used both*

as a dissecting table and a bizarre satanic altar. How was it possible that all of this had been hidden from me—not only the horrible physical evidence of my son's crimes, but the dark nature of the man who had committed them, this child I had held in my arms a thousand times, and whose face, when I glimpsed it in the newspapers, looked like mine? If the police had told me that my son was dead, I would have thought differently about him. If they'd told me that a strange man had lured him to a seedy apartment, and a few minutes later, drugged, strangled, then sexually assaulted and mutilated his dead body—in other words, if they'd told me the same horrible things that they had to tell so many other fathers and mothers in July of 1991—then I would have done what they have done. I would have mourned my son and demanded that the man who'd killed him be profoundly punished. If not executed, then separated forever from the rest of us. After that, I would have tried to think of my son warmly. I would, I hope, have visited his grave from time to time, spoken of him with loss and affection, continued, as much as possible, to be the custodian of his memory. But I wasn't told what these other mothers and fathers were told, that their sons were dead at the hands of a murderer. Instead, I was told that my son was the one who had murdered their sons.

A satanic altar. Charles Manson and his "family." In 1969, three people burst into a house occupied by a film star and killed everyone there, including a young man who happened to be driving away from the house. Two more murders followed on the next day: a married couple, both of whom were businesspeople. Manson claimed to be capable of killing the whole of humanity.

For the thousandth time, Morris looks at the photo of the man behind those crimes, smiling at the camera, surrounded by hippie friends, including a famous pop musician of the day. They all seem perfectly harmless, talking about peace and love.

HE CLOSES DOWN ALL THE windows. Manson is the closest thing to what is happening now, involving as it does the cinema and well-known victims. A kind of political manifesto against luxury, consumerism, and celebrity. Manson, however, was only the brains behind the killings; he didn't actually murder anyone himself; he left that to his acolytes.

No, that's not it. And despite the e-mails he has sent, explaining that he can't provide answers in such a short space of time, Morris is beginning to experience what all detectives always feel about serial killers: it's becoming a personal matter.

On the one hand, there's a man, doubtless with some other profession, who, given the weapons he uses, has clearly planned the murders in advance, but who is on entirely unfamiliar territory, where he has no knowledge of the competence or otherwise of the local police force. He is, therefore, a vulnerable man. On the other hand, there's the accumulated experience of all kinds of security organizations accustomed to dealing with society's aberrants, but apparently incapable of stopping the bloody trail left by this rank amateur.

He should never have responded to the commissioner's call. He had decided to live in the South of France because the climate was better, the people more amusing, the sea close at hand, and because he hoped that he still had many years ahead of him in which to be able to enjoy life's pleasures.

He had left his job in London with a reputation for being the best. And now this one failure would be sure to reach the ears of his colleagues, and he would lose that reputation earned through hard work and great dedication. They'll say: "He was the first person to insist that modern computers be installed in our department, but despite all the technology at his disposal, he's simply too old to keep up with challenges of a new age."

He presses the off button. The software logo comes up and then the screen goes blank. Inside the machine, the electronic impulses disappear from the fixed memory and leave no feeling of guilt, remorse, or impotence.

His body has no off buttons. The circuits in his brain keep working, always arriving at the same conclusions, trying to justify the unjustifiable, bruising his self-esteem, telling him that his colleagues are right:

perhaps his instincts and his capacity for analysis *have* been affected by age.

He goes into the kitchen, turns on the espresso machine, which has been giving him problems lately. As with any modern domestic appliance, it's usually cheaper to throw the old one out and buy a new one. Fortunately, the machine decides to work this time, and he sips the resulting cup of coffee unhurriedly. A large part of his day involves pressing buttons: computer, printer, phone, lights, stove, coffeemaker, fax machine.

Now, though, he needs to press the right button in his brain. There's no point in rereading the documents sent through by the police. He needs to think laterally and make a list, however repetitive.

(a) The murderer is fairly well educated and sophisticated, at least as regards the weapons he uses. And he knows how to use them.

(b) He's not from the area; if he was, he would have chosen a better time to come, when there were fewer police around.

(c) He doesn't leave any clear signature, so he obviously has no desire to be identified. This may seem self-evident, but such "signatures" are often a desperate way of the Doctor trying to put a stop to the evils committed by the Monster, as if Dr. Jekyll were saying: "Please arrest me. I'm a danger to society, and I can't control myself."

(d) The fact that he was able to approach at least two of his victims, look them in the eye, and find out a little about them, means that he's used to killing without remorse. Therefore, he must, at some time, have fought in a war.

(e) He must have money, a lot of money, not just because Cannes is a very expensive place to stay during the Festival, but because of the high cost of producing the envelope containing the hydrogen cyanide. He must have paid around $5,000 in all—$40 for the poison and $4,460 for the packaging.

(f) He's not part of the drug mafia or involved in arms trafficking or that kind of thing; if he was, Europol would be on to him.

Contrary to what most such criminals believe, the only reason
they haven't been caught is because it isn't yet the right time
for them to be put behind bars. Their groups are regularly in-
filtrated by agents who are paid a fortune for their work.

(g) He doesn't want to be caught, and so he's very careful. On
the other hand, he can't control his unconscious mind and is,
unwittingly, following a set pattern.

(h) He appears to be completely normal and unlikely to arouse
suspicion; he may even be kind and friendly, capable of gaining the confidence of the people he lures to their death. He
spends some time with his victims, two of whom were women,
who tend to be more trusting than men.

(i) He doesn't choose his victims. They could be men or women of
any age or social class.

Morris pauses for a moment. There's something that doesn't fit with
the rest.

He rereads the list two or three times. On the fourth reading, he
spots the flaw.

(c) He doesn't leave any clear signature, so he obviously has no
desire to be identified.

This murderer isn't trying to cleanse the world as Manson was, or,
like Ridgway, to purify his hometown; he's not trying, like Dahmer, to
satisfy the appetite of the gods. Most criminals don't want to be caught,
but they do want to be identified, some in order to hit the headlines and
gain fame and glory, like Zodiac or Jack the Ripper. Others perhaps
think their grandchildren will be proud of what they did when, years
later, they discover a dusty diary in the attic. Others have a mission
to fulfill: for example, driving away prostitutes by making them too
afraid to walk the streets. Psychoanalysts have concluded that when
serial killers suddenly stop murdering from one moment to the next,
it's because they feel that the message they've been trying to send has
finally been received.

Of course, that's it! Why hadn't he thought of it before?

For one simple reason: because it would have sent the police hunt off in two different directions, in search of the murderer *and* the person to whom he was sending the messages. And this Cannes murderer is killing people very fast. Morris is almost sure that he will stop soon, once the message has been received. In two or three days at most. And as with other serial killers whose victims appear to have nothing in common, the message must be intended for one person, just one.

He goes back to the computer, turns it on, and sends a reassuring e-mail to the commissioner.

"Don't worry, the murders will stop soon, before the Festival is over."

Just for the hell of it, he copies the e-mail to a friend in Scotland Yard, as a way of letting him know that the French authorities respect him as a professional, have asked for his help and received it; that he's still capable of reaching conclusions which will, later on, prove correct; that he's not as old as they would like to think.

His reputation is at stake, but he's sure his conclusion is the right one.

10:19 P.M.

Hamid turns off his mobile phone. He isn't the slightest bit interested in what's going on in the rest of the world, and in the last half hour, his phone has been inundated with grim messages.

It's a sign that he should ditch the whole absurd idea of producing a film. He had clearly allowed himself to be carried away by vanity instead of listening to the advice of the sheikh and of his own wife. He's starting to lose touch with himself; the world of luxury and glamour is beginning to poison him, something he had always believed would never happen.

Tomorrow, when things have calmed down, he'll call a press conference for the world media present in Cannes and tell them that, despite having already invested a large amount of money in the project, he's decided to pull out because it was "a dream shared by all those involved, one of whom is no longer with us." A journalist is bound to ask if he has other projects in mind, and he'll reply that it's still too early to discuss such things and that "we need to respect the memory of the departed."

Like anyone with even a minimum of decency, he deeply regrets the fact that the actor who was going to appear in his first film should have died of poisoning and that his chosen director is still in hospital—although not now in danger of losing his life—but both these events carry a clear message: keep away from cinema. It isn't his world and he's bound to lose money and gain nothing in return.

Leave cinema to the filmmakers, music to the musicians, and literature to the writers. Ever since he first embarked on this adventure two months before, he has met with nothing but problems: wrestling with gigantic egos, rejecting outlandish budgets, editing a script that seemed to get worse with every new version, and putting up with condescending producers who treated him as if he knew absolutely nothing about films.

His intentions had been impeccable: to make a film about the culture of his home country, about the beauty of the desert and the Bedouins' ancient wisdom and code of honor. He felt he owed this to his tribe, although the sheikh had warned him not to stray from his original path.

"People get lost in the desert because they're taken in by mirages. You're doing an excellent job as a couturier; focus all your energies on that."

Hamid, however, wanted to go further, to show that he could still surprise people, go higher, take risks. He had committed the sin of pride, but that wouldn't happen again.

THE JOURNALISTS BOMBARD HIM WITH questions—news, it seems, is traveling even faster than usual. He says he doesn't yet know any details, but that he'll make a full statement tomorrow. He repeats the same answer over and over, until one of his own security guards comes to his aid and asks the press to leave the couple alone.

He summons an assistant and asks him to find Jasmine in the crowd of people in the garden and bring her to him. They need to have a few photos taken together, a new press release confirming the deal, and a good PR person to keep the issue alive until October and the Fashion Week in Paris. Later on, he'll try to persuade the Belgian designer to join him; he genuinely liked her work and is sure she would bring money and prestige to his group; however, he knows that, at the moment, she'll be thinking that he was only trying to buy her because he wanted her principal model. Approaching her now would not only up the price, it would seem inelegant. To everything its proper time; it would be best to wait for the right moment.

Ewa appears troubled by the journalists' questions. She says:

"I think we should leave."

"Absolutely not. I'm not hard-hearted, as you know, but I can't get upset over something that only confirms what you always told me, that I shouldn't get involved in cinema. Now, though, we're at a party, and we're going to stay here until the end."

His voice sounds sterner than he intended, but Ewa doesn't appear to notice, as if she were as indifferent to his love as to his hate. In a more equitable tone of voice, he adds:

"This party's just perfect, don't you think? Our host must be spending a fortune to be here in Cannes, what with the travel and accommodation expenses of the celebrities who've all been specially selected to be present at this lavish gala supper. But you can be sure that all the free publicity will send his profits soaring: full-page spreads in magazines and newspapers, TV airtime and hours of coverage on the cable channels that have nothing else to show. Women will associate his jewels with glamour; men will wear his watches as proof that they're powerful and wealthy; and young people will flick through the fashion pages and think: 'One day, I want to be there too, wearing exactly that.'"

"Please, let's leave now. I just have a really bad feeling about this party."

This was the last straw. He's put up with his wife's bad mood all day without complaint. She keeps turning on her mobile phone to see if there's another text message, and now he's beginning to think that there really is something strange going on. Another man perhaps? Her ex-husband, who he saw in the hotel bar, and who is perhaps doing everything he can to arrange a meeting? If that's the case, though, why doesn't she just tell him what she's feeling instead of withdrawing into herself?

"Don't talk to me about bad feelings. I'm trying to explain to you why people put on parties like this. If you ever decide to go into fashion as you always dreamed of doing or of once again owning a shop selling haute-couture clothes, you could learn something. By the way, when I told you that I'd seen your ex-husband in the bar last night, you told me that was impossible. Is he the reason you keep checking your mobile phone?"

"Why on earth would he be here?" she says, when what she feels like saying is: "I know who ruined your film project. And I know that he's capable of far worse. We're in danger here; please, let's leave."

"You didn't answer my question."

"The answer is yes. That's why I keep checking my mobile phone because I know him, and I know he's here somewhere, and I'm afraid."

Hamid laughs.

"But I'm here too."

Ewa picks up a glass of champagne and drinks it down in one. He says nothing, feeling that she's simply being provocative.

He looks around him, trying to forget the recent news that flashed up on his phone, and still hoping for a chance to have a few photos taken with Jasmine before they're all called into the room where supper will be served. The death of the actor couldn't have come at a worse moment. Now no one is asking about the big contract he's signed with an unknown model, and yet, half an hour earlier, it was all the press were interested in. Not anymore.

Despite his many years of working in this glamorous world, he still has a lot to learn: the contract he signed has been quickly forgotten, but the host of this party has managed to keep the media interest alive. None of the photographers and journalists present has left the party to go to the police station or the hospital to find out exactly what has happened. They are, admittedly, fashion journalists, but their editors wouldn't have dared order them to leave, for the simple reason that murders don't appear on the same pages as social events.

Makers of expensive jewelry don't get themselves mixed up in cinematographic adventures. Big promoters know that regardless of how much blood is being spilled in the world right now, people will always prefer photos depicting an ideal and inaccessible life of luxury.

Murders can take place next door or out in the street, but parties like this only occur at the very top of society. What could be of more interest to mere mortals than this perfect party, which would have been advertised months before in press releases, confirming that the jeweler would be holding his usual event in Cannes, and that all the invitations had already gone out. Not quite true; at the time, half of the guests would have received a kind of memorandum, politely asking them to keep the date free.

They would, of course, respond at once and reserve the date and buy their plane tickets and book their hotel room for twelve days, even if they're only staying for forty-eight hours. They need to prove to everyone that they're still members of the Superclass, membership of which is invaluable in making business deals, opening doors, and feeding egos.

The lavish invitation card would arrive two months later. The women would start worrying about which dress to wear for the occasion, and the men would contact a few acquaintances to ask if they could meet in the bar to discuss business before supper. This was the male way of saying: "I've been invited to the party. Have you?" Even if the acquaintance claimed he was too busy and wasn't sure he'd be able to travel to Cannes on that date, the message had been sent loud and clear: that "full diary" was just an excuse for not yet having been invited.

Minutes later, that "very busy man" would start mobilizing friends, advisors, and associates to wangle him an invitation. This meant that the host could then choose the second half of his guest list, basing himself on three things: power, money, contacts.

The perfect party.

A professional team of caterers would be signed up. On the day itself, the order will go out to serve as much alcohol as possible, preferably plenty of France's legendary and unbeatable champagne. Guests from other countries don't realize that they're being served a drink produced in the country itself and which is, therefore, much cheaper than they might think. The women feel—as even does Ewa at that moment—that the golden liquid in the glass is the best possible complement to dress, shoes, and bag. The men are all holding a glass as well, but they drink much less; they've come to make peace with a competitor, to cement relationships with a supplier, or to meet a potential distributor of their products. Hundreds of business cards are exchanged on such nights, most of them among professionals. A few, of course, are given to pretty women, who know they're not worth the paper they're printed on; no one has come here hoping to find the love of their life, but to make deals, to shine, and, possibly, to enjoy themselves a little. Enjoying yourself is optional and not of great importance.

The people here tonight come from three points of an imaginary triangle. At one point are those who have it all and spend their days playing golf or having lunch or hanging out at some exclusive club, and who, when they go into a shop, can buy anything they want without first asking the price. Having reached the top, they have realized something that had never even occurred to them before: they cannot bear to be alone. They can't stand the company of their husband or wife and they need to be on the go all the time, in the belief that they can still make a difference to humanity, although they've discovered, since they retired, that their day-to-day life is as dull as that of any other middle-class person: eat breakfast, read the newspapers, eat lunch, take a nap, eat supper, watch TV. They accept most of the supper invitations they receive. They go to social and sporting events at the weekend. They spend their holidays in fashionable places (even though they no longer work, they still believe in something called "holidays").

At the second point on the triangle are those who haven't yet achieved anything and who are doing their best to row in very choppy waters, to break the resistance of the have-it-alls, to look happy even if one of their parents happens to be in hospital, and they are having to sell off things they don't even own.

Finally, at the apex, is the Superclass.

This is the ideal mixture for a party. Those who have reached the top and yet carry on life as normal may well have enough money stashed away for several generations, but their influence has waned and they have realized, too late, that power is actually more important than wealth. Those who haven't yet reached the top put all their energy and enthusiasm into making the party go with a swing, thinking that they're making a really good impression, only to discover, in the weeks that follow, that no one phones them despite all the business cards they handed out. Finally, there are those who wobble about on the apex, knowing that it's very windy up there and that the slightest gust could blow them off into the abyss below.

PEOPLE KEEP COMING OVER TO talk to him, although no one mentions the murder, either because they don't know about it, since they live in a world where such things don't happen, or out of politeness, which he very much doubts. He looks around him and sees the thing he hates most in the fashion world: middle-aged women who dress as if they were still twenty. Haven't they noticed that it's time they changed their style? He speaks to one person, smiles at another, thanks someone else for a kind remark, introduces Ewa to the few who still don't know her. He has, however, only one thought in his mind: to find Jasmine within the next five minutes and pose for the photographers.

An industrialist and his wife are telling him in detail about the last time they met, a meeting of which Hamid has no recollection, although he nods wisely. They talk about trips they've made, people they've met, and projects they're involved in. No one touches on genuinely interesting topics like "Are you happy?" or "After all we've been through, what does victory actually feel like?" They are part of the Superclass and therefore obliged to behave as if they were contented and fulfilled, even if they're actually asking themselves: "What shall I do with my future, now that I have everything I ever dreamed of?"

A squalid creature in tight trousers and an Indian top approaches, looking like something out of a comic strip.

"Mr. Hussein, I'm terribly sorry . . ."

"Who are you?"

"I work for you, sir."

How absurd.

"Look, I'm busy right now, and I know everything I need to know about tonight's sad events, so there's no need for you to worry."

The creature, however, stays where he is. Hamid begins to feel embarrassed by his presence, mainly because friends nearby will have heard those dreadful words: "I work for you, sir." Whatever will they think?

"Mr. Hussein, I'm just about to bring over the actress who's going to be appearing in your film. I had to leave her for a moment because I got a phone message, but . . ."

"Later. At the moment, I'm waiting to meet Jasmine Tiger."

The strange creature leaves. The actress who's going to be appearing in his film! Poor girl: signed up and dismissed all in one day.

Ewa is holding a champagne glass in one hand and her mobile phone and an extinguished cigarette in the other. The industrialist takes a gold lighter out of his pocket and offers to light her cigarette.

"No, thank you, it's all right, I can do it myself," she says. "I'm deliberately keeping both hands occupied in an attempt to smoke less."

She would like to say: "I'm holding my mobile so as to protect this idiot, who refuses to believe me and who has never shown the slightest interest in my life or what I've been through. If I get another message, I'll make a scene and he'll be forced to leave and take me with him, whether he wants to or not. Even if he tells me off afterward, at least I can console myself with the thought that I saved his life. I know who the killer is. I can feel the presence of Absolute Evil very near."

A receptionist starts asking the guests to go into the main dining area. Hamid Hussein is prepared to accept his fate without complaint. The photo can wait until tomorrow when he goes up the steps with her. Just then, one of his assistants appears.

"Jasmine Tiger isn't here. She must have left."

"Never mind. Perhaps they forgot to tell her that we were supposed to meet."

He looks very calm, like someone accustomed to dealing with such situations. Inside, though, his blood is boiling. She's left the party? Who does she think she is?

IT'S SO EASY TO DIE. The human body may well be one of the most efficient mechanisms in creation, but all it takes is a small metal projectile to enter and cut through it at a certain speed, and that's that.

Death, according to the dictionary, is the end of a life (although life also needs to be properly defined), the permanent paralysis of the body's vital functions, like brain activity, breathing, blood flow to and from the heart. Only two things resist this permanent paralysis—the hair and the nails, which continue to grow for a few days or weeks.

The definition changes when it comes to religions: for some, death means moving to a higher state, while others believe that it is merely a temporary condition and that the soul inhabiting the body will return later on, either to pay for its sins or to enjoy in the next life the blessings denied it during the previous incarnation.

The young woman is standing very still by his side. Either the champagne has taken full effect or its effects have passed, and she now realizes that she knows no one, that this could be both her first and last invitation to such a party, and that dreams sometimes turn into nightmares. When he moved away for a moment with the other sadder girl, he noticed a few men approach the actress, but it seems she felt uncomfortable with all of them. When she saw him reappear, she asked him to stay with her for the rest of the party. She also asked if he had transport because she has no money and it doesn't look as if her companion will be coming back.

"Yes, of course, I'll be glad to take you home."

This wasn't in his plans, but having spotted the policeman observing the guests, he knows it's best to look as if he's with someone, that he's just another of the important, anonymous people there, proud to have a pretty, much younger woman with him, one who so perfectly fits the norm in that particular place.

"Don't you think we should go in?"

"Yes, but I know how these things work. It's best to wait until everyone else is seated. Several of the tables will have places reserved at them for certain people, and we don't want to find ourselves in the embarrassing position of sitting down where we shouldn't."

He notices that, for a moment, the girl looks slightly disappointed that he doesn't have one of those reserved places.

The waiters are collecting the empty glasses scattered around the garden. The models have stepped down from their ridiculous pedestals where their gyrations have persuaded the male guests at the party that life can still be interesting and reminded the female guests that they really must get some more liposuction, Botox, silicone, or plastic surgery.

"Please, let's go in. I need to eat. I'll get sick if I don't."

She takes his arm and they walk toward the room on the upper floor. It would seem that his last message to Ewa has been received and discarded, but then he knows now what to expect from a woman as corrupt as his ex-wife. The angel with the dark eyebrows continues by his side; she was the one who had made him turn round at the right moment and notice the plainclothes policeman, when, in theory, he should have been concentrating on the arrival of the famous couturier.

"All right, we'll go in."

They walk up the steps and into the dining room. As they do so, he asks her politely to let go of his arm, in case any friends there should misinterpret the situation.

"Are you married, then?"

"No, divorced."

YES, EWA IS THINKING, SHE had been right, her intuition was correct, the problems they have encountered so far this evening are as nothing compared with what she has just seen. Since Igor can have no professional reason for being at a film festival, his presence there can have only one possible motive.

"Igor!" Hamid says.

The man, accompanied by a much younger woman, looks straight at him. Ewa's heart starts pounding. She says to Hamid:

"What are you doing?"

Hamid has already got up from the table. He has no idea what he's doing. He's walking toward Absolute Limitless Evil, capable of anything. Hamid assumes that Igor is just another adult and that he can confront him with either physical force or logical argument. What he doesn't know is that Absolute Evil has the heart of a child and takes no responsibility for its actions and is convinced that it's right. And when it doesn't get what it wants, it's not afraid to use all possible means to satisfy its desires. Now she understands how it was that the Angel changed so quickly into a Devil: because he has always nursed vengeance and rancor in his heart, even though he claimed to have grown up and overcome all his traumas; because he's unbeatable when it comes to succeeding in life, thus confirming his belief in his own omnipotence; because he doesn't know how to give up, having survived the worst possible torments through which he walked without so much as a backward glance, all the while repeating to himself: "One day, I'll be back, and then you'll see what I'm capable of."

"Apparently, he's found someone more interesting to talk to than us," says a former Miss Europe, who is also sitting at the top table, along with another two celebrities and the host of the party.

Ewa tries to conceal her unease, but she doesn't know what to do. The host seems almost amused and is waiting for some explanation.

"I'm sorry. He's an old friend of mine."

Hamid goes over to Igor, who looks suddenly uncertain. The girl with him says loudly:

"Hello, Mr. Hussein. I'm your new actress!"

People at the other tables turn round to see what's happening. The host smiles. It's always good to have something unusual happen at a party; it will give his guests plenty to talk about. Hamid is now standing in front of the man; the host realizes that all is not well and says to Ewa:

"I think you'd better retrieve Hamid, or, if you like, we can get another chair for your friend. His companion will, I'm afraid, have to sit elsewhere."

The guests have turned their attention back to their food and their conversations about yachts, private planes, and the stock market. Only the host keeps a watchful eye on what's going on.

"Go and talk to them," he says.

Ewa, however, isn't there. Her thoughts are thousands of miles away in a restaurant in Irkutsk, near Lake Baikal. The scene was different then, with Igor leading another man outside. Making an enormous effort, she gets to her feet and joins the two men.

"Go back to the table," says Hamid quietly. "We're going outside to talk."

That is the most stupid thing he could possibly do. She grabs his arm and, smiling, pretends to be happy to be meeting someone she hasn't seen in a long time. With great aplomb, she says:

"But supper's only just beginning!"

She doesn't add "my love"; she doesn't want to open the doors of hell.

"She's right. We'd be better off talking here."

Did Igor say that? Perhaps she's been imagining things and it isn't at all as she thought? Has the child finally grown into a responsible adult? Has the Devil been forgiven for his arrogance and returned to the Kingdom of Heaven?

She so wants to be wrong, but the two men are still staring at each other. Hamid can see something deeply perverse behind those blue eyes and, for a moment, a shudder runs through him. The young woman is holding out her hand.

"Pleased to meet you. My name's Gabriela . . ."

He doesn't return her greeting. The other man's eyes are shining.

"There's a table over in the corner. Why don't we all go and sit down there," says Ewa.

A table in the corner? Is his wife going to leave her place of honor at the top table and sit at a table in a corner? Ewa has already linked arms with both men and is leading them toward the only free table, near the door through which the waiters come and go. The "actress" follows behind. Hamid detaches himself for a moment and goes back to his host to apologize.

"I've just met a childhood friend. He has to leave tomorrow, and I wouldn't want to miss this chance to talk a little. Please, don't wait for us, I can't say how long we'll be."

"No one will steal your places," says the host, smiling, knowing full well that the two chairs will remain empty.

"I thought he was your *wife*'s childhood friend," says the former Miss Europe waspishly.

Hamid, however, is already walking back to the worst table in the room, reserved for the celebrities' assistants, who, despite all precautions, often manage to slip in where they're not supposed to be.

"Hamid's a good man," thinks the host, as he watches the couturier walk away, head held high. "But the night hasn't got off to a very happy start for him."

THEY ALL SIT DOWN AT the corner table. Gabriela understands that this is her one chance, yet another of those many "one chances" that have happened today. She says how pleased she was to receive the invitation and that she'll do all she can not to disappoint.

"I trust you," she says. "I even signed the contract without reading it."

The other three people don't say a word; they just look at each other. Is something wrong? Can it be the effect of the champagne? Best to keep talking.

"I'm particularly happy because, contrary to what people usually say, the selection process was very fair. There were no special requests, no favors. I did the test this morning, and they didn't even let me finish reading the text they gave me. They just asked me to go to a yacht to talk to the director. That sets an excellent example, Mr. Hussein, I mean, treating people with dignity and honesty when it comes to choosing who you're going to be working with. People think that in the world of cinema the only thing that really counts is . . ."

She was about to say "sleeping with the producer," but the producer is sitting next to his wife.

". . . is what a person looks like."

The waiter brings the entrées and launches into his usual monologue:

"Tonight's entrées are artichoke hearts in a Dijon mustard sauce, drizzled with a little olive oil, flavored with *fines herbes* and served with slivers of Pyrenean goat's cheese . . ."

Only the young woman smiles and listens to what he's saying. He realizes that he isn't welcome and leaves.

"It looks delicious!" she says. Then she glances round at the others, none of whom has made a move to pick up knife or fork. Something is very wrong here.

"Look, you obviously need to talk. Perhaps I should sit somewhere else."

"Yes," says Hamid.

"No, stay here," says the woman.

What should she do now?

"Do you like your companion?" the woman asks.

"I've only just met Gunther."

Gunther. Hamid and Ewa look at the impassive Igor sitting beside her.

"And what does Gunther do?"

"Aren't you friends of his?"

"Yes, and we know what he does. But we don't know how much you know about his life."

Gabriela turns to Igor. Why doesn't he help her?

A waiter arrives to ask what wine they would like to drink.

"White or red?"

Saved by a stranger!

"Red for everyone," says Hamid.

"You still haven't told us what Gunther does?"

She hasn't been saved.

"He works with heavy machinery, I think. We hardly know each other really. The only thing we have in common is that we were both waiting for friends who never turned up."

A good answer, thinks Gabriela. Perhaps that woman is having a secret affair with her new "partner" or else an affair that her husband has just found out about—that would explain the tension in the air.

"His name is Igor," announces the woman. "He owns one of the biggest mobile phone companies in Russia. That's far more important than selling heavy machinery."

If this is true, why did he lie? She decides to say nothing.

"I was hoping to meet you here, Igor," the woman says, addressing Gunther now.

"I came looking for you, but I've changed my mind now," comes the blunt reply.

Gabriela suddenly gives her paper-stuffed handbag a squeeze and adopts a surprised expression.

"Oh, my phone's ringing. I think my friend must have arrived, so I'd better go and find him. I'm so sorry, but he's come a long way just to be with me, and since he doesn't know anyone else here, I feel kind of responsible for him."

She gets up. Etiquette dictates that one shouldn't shake hands with someone when he or she is eating, although the others haven't even touched the food. The wineglasses, however, are already empty. And the man who, up until two minutes ago, was called Gunther has just ordered a whole bottle.

"I HOPE YOU GOT MY messages," says Igor.

"I received three. Perhaps the telephone network here is worse than the one you developed."

"I'm not talking about telephones."

"Then I don't know what you *are* talking about," she says, but what she wants to say is: "I know you're not."

Just as Igor must know that, during the first year she was with Hamid, she waited for a phone call or a message, for some mutual friend to tell her how much Igor was missing her. She didn't want him near her, but she knew that hurting him would be the worst thing she could do; she needed to placate her own personal Fury and pretend that one day, they would be good friends. One afternoon, when she'd had a bit to drink and finally summoned up the nerve to call him, she found that he'd changed his mobile number. When she phoned him at the office, she was told he was in a meeting. When she rang on subsequent occasions—always with the help of a little Dutch courage—she was told that Igor was traveling or would phone her back at once, which, of course, he never did.

And she began to see ghosts everywhere, to feel that she was being watched, that soon she would suffer the same fate as the beggar and the others whose "promotions to a better life" Igor had hinted at. Meanwhile, Hamid never asked her about her past, alleging that everyone has a right to keep his or her life locked up and private in the subterranean tunnels of memory. He did all he could to make her happy and to help her feel safe and protected; he even told her that his life had only begun to make any sense since meeting her.

Then one day, Absolute Evil rang the doorbell of their apartment building in London. Hamid was at home and sent him away. Nothing else happened in the months that followed.

Gradually, she succeeded in deceiving herself. Yes, she had made the right choice; the moment we choose a path, all other paths disappear. It was childish of her to think that she could be married to one man and friends with her ex-husband, that was only possible between well-balanced people, and Igor was not well-balanced. It was best to believe that an invisible hand had saved her from Absolute Evil. She was enough of a woman to make the new man at her side feel dependent on her and to help him as much as she could, as lover, advisor, wife, and sister, and she channeled all her energy into doing just that.

During this period, she had only one real friend, who disappeared as suddenly as she had appeared. She was Russian too, but unlike her, had been abandoned by her husband and didn't really know what she was doing in England. They spoke almost every day.

"I left it all behind," Ewa told her once. "And I don't regret it one bit. I would have done the same even if Hamid—against my wishes—hadn't bought a beautiful estate in Spain and put it in my name. I would have made the same decision if Igor, my ex-husband, had offered me half his fortune, because I need to live without fear. And if one of the most desirable men in the world wants to be by my side, then I'm obviously a better person than I thought."

It was all lies. She wasn't trying to convince her only confidante, but herself. It was all a front. Inside the strong woman sitting at that table with two powerful and important men was a little girl afraid of being left alone and poor, never having experienced what it was to be a mother. Had she simply got used to all the luxury and the glamour? No. She was always preparing herself to lose everything from one day to the next, when her present companion finally found out that she wasn't what he thought and was incapable of meeting others' expectations.

Did she know how to manipulate men? Yes. They all thought she was strong and confident, mistress of her own destiny, that she was capable of leaving any man, however important or eligible. And the worst thing was that men believed it. Men like Igor and like Hamid. Because she knew how to pretend, because she never said exactly what she was thinking, because she was the best actress in the world and knew better than anyone how to hide her vulnerable side.

"What do you want?" he asks in Russian.

"More wine."

He sounded as if he didn't much care what answer she gave; he had already said what he wanted.

"Before you left, I said something to you, but I think you must have forgotten."

He had said so many things: "I promise that I'll change and start working less," "You're the only woman I love," "If you leave, it will destroy me," words familiar to everyone and which are utterly devoid of meaning.

"I said: If you leave me, I'll destroy a world."

She couldn't remember him saying this, but it was perfectly possible. Igor had always been a very bad loser.

"But what does that mean?" she asks in Russian.

"At least be polite enough to speak in English," says Hamid.

Igor turns to face him.

"I will speak English, not out of politeness, but because I want you to understand."

And turning back to Ewa, he says:

"I said I would destroy a whole world to get you back. I started doing that, but was saved by an angel. I realized that you didn't deserve it. You're a selfish, implacable woman, interested only in acquiring more fame and more money. You refused all the good things I offered you because a house deep in the Russian countryside didn't fit in with your dream world, a world, by the way, to which you don't belong and never will.

"I sacrificed myself and others for your sake, and that's not right. I need to go to the very end, so that I can return to the world of the living with a sense of duty done and mission completed. Now, as we speak, I'm in the world of the dead."

THIS MAN'S EYES ARE FILLED with a look of Absolute Evil, thinks Hamid, as he listens to this absurd conversation, full of long silences. Fine, he'll let things go to the very end, as Igor suggests, as long as that doesn't mean him losing the woman he loves. Even better for him, Ewa's ex-husband has not only turned up accompanied by some vulgar woman, he has insulted Ewa to her face. He'll allow him to go on a little longer and will know when to bring the conversation to a halt, when it's too late for Igor to apologize or to beg forgiveness.

Ewa must be seeing the same thing: a blind hatred for everything and everyone, simply because one person didn't do as he wished. He wonders what he would have done were he that man who is now apparently fighting for the woman he loves.

He would, he thinks, be capable of killing for her.

The waiter reappears and notices that the plates are all untouched.

"Is anything wrong with the food?" he asks.

No one answers. The waiter understands: the husband must have caught his wife in flagrante with her lover in Cannes, and this is the final confrontation. He's seen it all before, and it usually ends in a fight or a row.

"Another bottle of wine," says one of the men.

"You don't deserve anything," says the other man, his eyes fixed on the woman. "You used me just as you're using that idiot beside you. You were the biggest mistake of my life."

The waiter decides to check with the host before bringing them that other bottle of wine, but one of the men has just got to his feet, saying to the woman:

"That's enough. We're leaving."

"Yes, let's all leave, let's go outside," says the other man. "I want to see how far you would go to defend a person who doesn't know the meaning of the words 'honor' and 'dignity.'"

Two males fighting over a female. The woman asks them not to go outside, but to return to the table. The man with her, however, seems ready to respond to the insult. The waiter considers warning the security guards that a fight might ensue, but the head waiter is already complaining that the service is too slow, so what is he doing hanging around there? He has other tables to serve. He's right, of course. What happens outside isn't his problem. And if he admits to listening in on a conversation, he'll get told off. He's being paid to wait at tables, not to save the world.

THE THREE OF THEM CROSS the garden where the cocktails had been served and which is now undergoing a rapid transformation. When the guests come down from supper, they'll find a dance floor lit with special lights, a seating area furnished with armchairs, and several small bars all serving free drinks.

Igor walks ahead in silence. Ewa follows, and Hamid brings up the rear. There is a small metal gate at the top of the steps down to the beach. Igor opens it and asks them to go first. Ewa refuses, but he seems not to mind and goes down the many flights of steps that lead to the sea below. He knows that Hamid will not prove to be a coward. Until he met him at the party, he had considered him to be nothing but an unscrupulous couturier, a seducer of married women, and a manipulator of other people's vanity. Now, however, he secretly admires him. He's a real man, capable of fighting to the end for someone he believes to be important, even though Igor knows that Ewa hasn't one iota of the talent of the young actress he met tonight. She can't disguise her feelings at all; he can sense her fear, he knows that she's sweating, wondering whom to call, how to ask for help.

WHEN THEY REACH THE SAND, Igor walks right to the end of the beach and sits down close to some rocks. He asks the others to do the same. He knows that despite her terror, Ewa is also thinking: "I'm going to spoil my dress. I'm going to get my shoes dirty." But she sits down beside him. The other man asks her to move over a little, so that he can sit there, but she won't budge.

He doesn't insist. There they are, the three of them, as if they were old acquaintances in search of a moment's peace in which to contemplate the rising of the full moon before they go back up the steps to listen to the infernal racket of the discotheque.

HAMID PROMISES HIMSELF THAT HE will give Igor ten minutes, time enough for him to say everything that's on his mind, to vent his rage and then go back where he came from. If he turns violent, he'll be the loser because Hamid is physically stronger and, as a Bedouin, trained to respond swiftly and precisely to any attack. He doesn't want to cause a scene at the party, but the Russian should be under no illusion: he is prepared for anything.

When they go back up, he'll apologize to their host and explain that the situation has been resolved. He knows he can speak openly to him. He'll tell him that his wife's ex-husband had turned up without warning and that he'd felt it best to remove him before he caused any trouble. If the man doesn't leave as soon as they return to the party, he'll summon one of his own bodyguards to expel him. Igor may well be rich and own one of the largest mobile phone companies in Russia, but he's being a nuisance.

"You betrayed me, not just during the two years you've spent with this man, but during all the years we spent together."

Ewa says nothing.

"What would you be capable of doing in order to keep her?" he asks Hamid.

Hamid wonders whether he should answer or not. Ewa isn't a piece of merchandise to be haggled over.

"Can you rephrase the question?"

"OK. Would you give your life for the woman beside you?"

There is pure evil in the man's eyes. Even if Igor had managed to steal a knife from the restaurant (Hamid hadn't noticed him doing so, but he must consider all possibilities), he will have no problem disarming him. No, he wouldn't give his life for anyone, except God and the chief of his tribe, but he must say something.

"I would fight for her and, if it came to it, I think I would be capable of killing for her."

Ewa can stand the pressure no longer; she would like to say everything she knows about the man on her right. She is sure that he murdered the actor and destroyed her new companion's long-cherished dream of becoming a film producer.

"Let's go back up."

What she really wants to say is: "Please, let's get out of here now. You're talking to a psychopath."

Igor appears not to hear what she said.

"You'd be capable of killing for her, so that means you'd be capable of dying for her too."

"If I fought and lost, yes, I think I would. But let's not start a fight here on the beach."

"I want to go back up to the party," says Ewa again.

Hamid, however, feels his male pride is in question. He can't leave there like a coward. The ancient dance performed by males—humans and animals—in order to impress the female is just beginning.

"When you left, I somehow couldn't be myself," says Igor, as if he were alone on the beach. "My business was prospering, and I could keep control of myself during the day, but at night, I would plunge into black depression. I had lost a part of myself I could never recover. I thought I might be able to do that by coming here to Cannes, but when I arrived, I realized that the part of me that had died couldn't and shouldn't be resuscitated. I'll never take you back, not even if you came to me on bended knee, begging forgiveness and threatening suicide."

Ewa breathed easier; at least there wouldn't be a fight.

"You didn't understand my messages. I said I would be capable of destroying whole worlds, and you didn't get it. Or if you did, you couldn't believe it. What does it mean to destroy a world?"

He puts his hand in his trouser pocket and takes out a small gun. He doesn't point it at anyone, though; his eyes remain fixed on the sea and the moon. The blood starts to flow faster in Hamid's veins. Igor either wants to frighten and humiliate them or this really is a fight to the death. But will he kill them there, at the party, knowing that he'll be arrested as soon as he goes back up the steps? He can't be that mad; if he were, he could never have achieved all he has achieved in life.

Enough distractions. He is a warrior trained to defend himself and to attack. He must stay absolutely still because, although the other man isn't looking directly at him, he knows that his senses will be alert to any gesture.

The only part of his body he can safely move is his eyes, and he can see that there is no one else on the beach. Up above, the band is just beginning to tune their instruments, preparing for the most enjoyable segment of the party. Hamid isn't thinking, his instincts are now focused on acting without the interference of his brain.

Ewa is sitting between him and Igor, and she seems hypnotized by the sight of the gun. If he tries anything, Igor will turn and shoot and she might get hit.

Yes, perhaps his first hypothesis was correct. Igor just wants to frighten them, to force Hamid to show himself to be a coward and lose his honor. If he really wanted to shoot them, he wouldn't be holding the gun in that casual manner. It would be best to talk and try to get him to relax a little, while he thinks of some way out.

"What *does* destroying a world mean?" he asks.

"Destroying a life. A whole universe gone. Everything that person saw and experienced; all the good and the bad that came his way; all his dreams, hopes, defeats, and victories ceasing to exist. As children, we learned by heart a passage which I only later found out came from a Protestant priest. He said something like: 'When the sea bears away into its depths a single grain of sand, the whole of Europe grows smaller.' We don't notice, of course. After all, it's just a grain of sand, but at that very moment the continent is diminished."

Igor pauses. He's starting to feel irritated with the noise from up above; the sound of the waves was so calming, allowing him to treat this moment with the respect it deserves. The angel with the dark eyebrows is watching and is happy with what she sees.

"It was supposed to teach us that we were responsible for creating the perfect society, namely Communism," he goes on. "We were all brothers and sisters, they said, but, in fact, we were spies trained to betray each other."

He becomes calm and thoughtful again.

"I can't quite hear you."

This will give him a reason to move.

"Of course you can. You know that I have a gun in my hand and you want to come closer to see if you can grab it off me. You're trying to engage me in conversation in order to distract me while you consider what to do. Please, don't move. The moment hasn't yet come."

"Igor, let's just drop the whole thing," Ewa says in Russian. "I love you. Let's go away together."

"Speak in English. Your companion here needs to understand what you're saying."

Yes, he would understand, and later on, he would thank her for it.

"I love you," she says again, in English this time. "I never received your messages. If I had, I would have come running back. I tried several times to phone you, but never got through. I left many messages with your secretary, but you never called me."

"That's true."

"Ever since I started getting your messages today, I've been longing to see you again. I didn't know where you were, but I knew that you would come and find me. I know you don't want to forgive me, but at least allow me to live by your side. I can be your servant, your cleaner, I'll look after you and your lover, should you ever decide to take one. All I want is to be with you."

She'll explain everything to Hamid later. She has to say something, anything, just to get them out of there and back up the steps to the real world, where there are policemen who can stop Absolute Evil from revealing its hatred.

"I'd like to believe that, or, rather, I'd like to believe that I love you too and want you back, but I don't. Besides, I think you're lying and that you always lied."

Hamid isn't listening to what either of them is saying; his mind is far away with his warrior ancestors, asking for inspiration to make the right move.

"You could have told me that our marriage wasn't working out as we both hoped. We had built so much together; couldn't we have found a solution? There's always a way of allowing happiness in, but for that to happen, both partners have to acknowledge there are problems. I would have listened to what you had to say. Our marriage would have regained all its initial excitement and joy. But you didn't want to do that, you chose the easy way out."

"I was always afraid of you, and now, seeing you with that gun in your hand, I'm even more afraid."

Hamid is brought abruptly back to earth by Ewa's last comment. His soul is no longer somewhere in space, asking advice from the warriors of the desert, trying to find out how he should act.

She can't have said that. She's handing over power to the enemy; now he'll know that he's capable of terrifying her.

"I would like to have invited you to supper one day and tell you that I felt so alone, despite all the banquets, jewels, journeys, and meetings with kings and presidents," Ewa says. "Do you know something else? You always brought me really expensive presents, but never the simplest gift of all—flowers."

This is turning into a marital argument.

"I'll leave you two to talk."

Igor says nothing. His eyes are still fixed on the sea, but he's still pointing the gun at him, indicating that he should stay where he is. The man is mad, and his apparent calm is more dangerous than if he were screaming threats at them.

"Anyway," he says, as if unperturbed either by her words or by Hamid's attempt to move, "you chose the easiest way out. You left me. You didn't give me a chance; you didn't understand that everything I was doing was for you and because of you.

"And yet, despite all the injustices and humiliations, I would have done anything to have you back—until today. Until I sent you those messages, and you pretended not to have received them. In other words, even the sacrifice of those other people didn't move you; you just couldn't get enough of power and luxury."

The Star who was poisoned and the director whose life still hangs by a thread: is Hamid imagining the unimaginable? Then he understands something even more serious: with that confession, the man beside him has just signed their death warrant. He must either commit suicide there and then or put an end to the lives of two people who now know far too much.

Perhaps, Hamid thinks, he himself is going mad or simply misunderstanding the situation, but he knows that time is running out.

He looks at the gun in the man's hand. It's a small caliber. If it doesn't hit certain critical points in the body, it won't do much harm. He can't be very experienced; if he were, he would have chosen something more powerful. He obviously doesn't know what he's doing; he must have bought the first thing he was offered, something that fired bullets and could kill.

The band has started playing up above. Don't they realize that the noise of the music will mask the sound of a shot? Then again, would they know the difference between a gunshot and one of the many other artificial noises that are currently infesting—yes, that's the word, infesting, polluting, plaguing—the atmosphere?

IGOR HAS GONE QUIET AGAIN, and that is far more dangerous than if he were to continue talking, emptying his heart of some of his bitterness and bile. Hamid again weighs up the possibilities; if he's going to act, he needs to do so in the next few seconds. He could throw himself across Ewa and grab the gun while it's lying casually in Igor's lap, even though Igor's finger is on the trigger. He could reach out to him with both arms, forcing Igor to draw back in fright, and then Ewa would be out of the line of fire. Igor would point the gun in his direction, but by then, he would be close enough to grab his wrist. It would all take only a second.

Now.

Maybe this silence is a positive sign; perhaps Igor's lost concentration. Or it might be the beginning of the end, meaning that he's said all he has to say.

Now.

In the first fraction of a second, the muscle in his left thigh tenses, propelling him furiously forward in the direction of Absolute Evil; the area of his body shrinks as he hurls himself over Ewa's lap, arms outstretched. The first second continues, and he sees the gun being pointed directly at his head; the man moves more quickly than he had expected.

His body is still flying toward the gun. They should have talked before. Ewa has never said much about her ex-husband, as if he belonged to a past she preferred not to think about—ever. Even though everything is happening in slow motion, the man draws back as nimbly as a cat. The gun in his hand is perfectly steady.

The first second is just reaching its end. He sees a finger move, but there is no sound, only the feeling of something crushing the bone in the middle of his forehead. His universe is extinguished and with it the memories of the young man who dreamed of being "someone," his arrival in Paris, his father's shop, the sheikh, his battle to gain a place in the sun, the fashion shows, the trips abroad, meeting the woman he loves, the days of wine and roses, the laughter and the tears, the last moon on the rise, the eyes of Absolute Evil, the look of terror in his wife's eyes, all disappear.

———

"DON'T CRY OUT. DON'T SAY a word. Keep calm."

Of course she isn't going to cry out, nor does she need to be told to keep calm. She's in a state of shock like the animal she is, despite her fine jewelry and her expensive dress. Her blood is no long circulating at its normal speed, her face grows pale, her voice vanishes, her blood pressure plummets. He knows exactly what she's feeling; he once experienced the same when he saw the rifle of an Afghan warrior pointing at his chest. Total immobility and a complete inability to react. He was only saved because a colleague fired first. He was still grateful to the man who had saved his life; everyone thought he was just his chauffeur, when, in fact, he owned many shares in the company, and he and Igor often talked; indeed, they had spoken that very afternoon when Igor had phoned to ask if Ewa had shown any sign of having received his messages.

Ewa, poor Ewa, sitting there with a man dying in her lap. Human beings are unpredictable; sometimes they react as that fool reacted, knowing that he had no chance of beating him. Weapons are unpredictable too. He expected the bullet to come out the other side of the man's head, blowing away the top part of the brain, but, given the angle of the shot, it must have pierced the brain, bounced off a bone, and entered the thorax because he's trembling uncontrollably, but with no sign of any blood.

It must be the trembling, not the shot, that has so shocked Ewa. With one foot, Igor pushes the body to the ground and puts a bullet through the back of the man's neck. The tremors cease. The man deserves a dignified death; he was, after all, valiant to the end.

———

THEY ARE ALONE NOW ON the beach. He kneels down in front of her and places the barrel of the gun against her breast. Ewa doesn't move.

He had imagined a very different ending to this story, with her understanding his messages and giving the two of them a new chance of happiness. He had thought of all the things he would say when they were finally alone again like this, looking out at the calm Mediterranean Sea, smiling and chatting.

He doesn't want to live with those words stuck in his throat, even if those words are useless now.

"I always thought that one day, we'd walk hand in hand through a park again or along the seashore, finally saying those long-postponed words of love. We would eat out once a week, travel together to places we'd never been to simply for the pleasure of discovering new things in each other's company.

"While you've been away, I've been copying poems out in a book so that I could whisper them to you as you fell asleep. I've written letters telling you how I felt, letters I would leave where you could find them and then you'd know that I never forgot you—not for a single day, not for a single moment. We would discuss plans for the house you wanted on the shores of Lake Baikal—just for us. I know you had a lot of ideas for that. I planned to have a private airport built there, and, of course, I'd leave the decoration of the house to your good taste, to you, the woman who justified my life and gave it meaning."

Ewa says nothing, but stares out at the sea before her.

"I came here because of you, only to realize that it was all pointless."

He squeezes the trigger.

There was almost no sound because the barrel of the gun was pressed against her body. The bullet entered at precisely the right place, and her heart immediately stopped beating. Despite all the pain she had caused him, he didn't want her to suffer.

If there was a life after death, both of them—the woman who betrayed him and the man who encouraged her—were now walking along, holding hands, in the moonlight fringing the shoreline. They would meet the angel with the dark eyebrows, who would explain everything that had happened and put an end to any feelings of rancor or hatred; at some point, everyone has to leave this planet known as Earth. And, besides, love justifies acts that mere human beings cannot understand, unless they happen to be experiencing what he has experienced.

Ewa's eyes remain open, but her body grows limp and falls to the sand. He leaves both bodies there, goes over to the rocks, carefully wipes any fingerprints from the gun, and throws it into the sea, as far as possible from the place where they had been sitting contemplating the moon. He goes back up the steps, finds a litter bin on the way, and drops the silencer in. He hadn't really needed it; the music had reached a crescendo at just the right moment.

10:55 P.M.

Gabriela goes over to the only person she knows.

The guests are now leaving the supper room; the band is playing music from the sixties, the party is beginning, and people are smiling and talking to each other, despite the deafening noise.

"I've been looking for you! Where are your friends?"

"Where's yours?"

"He's gone. He said there was some problem with the actor and the director, that's all, and then he left. The only other thing he said was that tonight's party on the yacht has been canceled."

Igor realizes what has happened. He hadn't had the slightest intention of killing someone he greatly admired and whose films he always tried to see whenever he had time. Nevertheless, it's fate that makes these choices—man is just the instrument.

"I'm leaving. If you like, I can drop you off at your hotel."

"But the party's just beginning."

"Enjoy it, then. I'm flying off early tomorrow morning."

Gabriela has to make a decision quickly. She can either stay here with that handbag stuffed with paper, in a place where she knows no one, hoping that some charitable soul will give her a lift as far as Croisette, where she will take off her shoes to climb the interminable hill up to the room she's sharing with four other friends. Or she can accept the offer of this kind man, who probably has some very useful contacts, and who's a friend of Hamid Hussein's wife. She had witnessed the start of what looked like an argument, but such things happen every day, and they would soon make it up.

She has a role in a film. She's exhausted from all the emotions of the day. She's afraid that she'll end up drinking too much and spoiling everything. Men will come up to her, asking if she's on her own and what she's doing afterward, and if she'd like to visit a jeweler's with them the following day. She'll have to spend the rest of the night politely avoiding people, trying not to hurt anyone's feelings, because you could never be quite sure who you were talking to. It was, after all, one of the most exclusive parties at the Festival.

"Let's go."

That's how a star behaves. She leaves when no one is expecting her to.

They go out to the hotel reception, Gunther (she can't remember his other name) asks the receptionist to call a taxi for them, and she tells them they're in luck; if they'd waited very much longer, they would have had to wait in an enormous queue.

On the way back, she asks him why he lied about what he does. He says he didn't lie. He used to own a mobile phone company, but had decided to sell it because he felt the future lay in heavy machinery.

And what about his name?

"Igor is an affectionate nickname, the Russian diminutive of Gunther."

Gabriela is expecting him, at any moment, to come out with the words: "Shall we have a nightcap at my hotel?," but he doesn't. He leaves her at the door of the house where she's staying, shakes her hand, and leaves.

How elegant!

Yes, this has been her first lucky day, the first of many. Tomorrow, when she gets her phone back, she'll make a collect call to a city near Chicago to tell everyone the big news and ask them to buy the gossip magazines because she'd been photographed going up the steps with the Star. She'll also tell them that she's had to adopt a new name. However, if they ask her what's going to happen next, she'll change the subject. She has a superstitious belief that one shouldn't discuss projects until they actually happen. They'll hear all about it as the news leaks out. Unknown actress chosen for major role. Lisa Winner was the guest of honor at a party in New York. Previously unknown Chicago girl is the new sensation in Gibson's latest movie. Agent negotiates million-dollar contract with one of the major Hollywood producers.

The sky's the limit.

11:11 P.M.

"You're back early?"

"I'd have been here sooner if it wasn't for the traffic."

Jasmine kicks off her shoes, drops her bag, and throws herself down on the bed, exhausted and fully clothed. She says:

"The most important words in any language are the short ones: 'yes,' for example, or 'love' or 'God.' They're all easy to say and they fill up the empty spaces of our universe. But there's one small word that I have great difficulty in saying, but I'm going to say it now." She looks at her companion. "No."

She pats the bed, inviting her companion to join her. Her companion does so and strokes her hair.

"The word 'no' has a reputation for being mean, selfish, unspiritual. When we say yes, we think we're being generous, understanding, polite. But I'm going to say no to you now. I won't do what you're asking me or making me do, even though you think it's in my best interests. You'll say that I'm only nineteen and don't yet fully understand life, but going to a party like the one tonight was quite enough for me to know what I do want and what I definitely don't want.

"I never planned to be a model, and I didn't even think I was capable of falling in love. I know that love can only survive when it's free, but whoever said I was anyone's slave? I'm a slave only to my heart, and in that case my burden is a very light one. I chose you before you chose me. I embarked on what seemed an impossible adventure and never complained about the consequences, whether it was society's preconceived ideas or resistance from my own family. I overcame all those things so that I could be with you here tonight, in Cannes, savoring the victory of an excellent fashion show, and knowing that there will be other opportunities in life—by your side."

Her companion lies down next to her, her head in Jasmine's lap.

"The person who made me realize this was a man, a foreigner, whom I met tonight while I was at the party, lost in the crowd, not knowing what to say. I asked him what he was doing there, and he said that he'd lost his love and come here to look for her, but wasn't sure anymore whether she really was what he wanted. He asked me to look around at the other guests. We were, he said, surrounded by people who were full of certainties, glories, and conquests, but they weren't enjoying themselves. They think they're at the peak of their careers and the inevitable descent frightens them. They've forgotten that there's still a whole world to conquer because . . ."

". . . because they've got used to life as it is."

"Exactly. They have lots of things but few aspirations. They're full of problems solved, projects approved, businesses that prosper without them having to do anything. Now all that's left is the fear of change, which is why they go from party to party, from meeting to meeting, so as not to have time to think, and to meet the same people over and over and be able to believe that everything's the same. Certainties have replaced passions."

"Take off your dress," says her companion, preferring to say nothing more.

Jasmine gets up, takes off her dress, and slips between the sheets.

"You take your clothes off too and put your arms around me. I really need to feel your arms around me because today I thought you were going to let me go."

She does as Jasmine asks and turns out the light. Jasmine falls asleep at once in her arms. She, however, lies awake for some time, staring up at the ceiling, thinking that sometimes a nineteen-year-old girl, in all her innocence, can be wiser than a forty-one-year-old woman. However fearful and insecure she may feel right now, she'll be forced to grow. She'll have a powerful enemy in HH, who will doubtless create as many obstacles as he can to prevent her taking part in the Fashion Week in October. First, he'll insist on buying her name, and when that proves impossible, he'll try to discredit her with the Fédération, saying that she failed to keep her word.

The next few months will be very difficult.

What HH doesn't know, indeed, what no one knows, is that she possesses an absolute power that will help her overcome all difficulties: the love of the young woman now lying in her arms. For her, she would do anything—anything, that is, except kill.

With her, she is capable of anything—even winning.

His company jet already has the engines running. Igor sits in his favorite seat—second row on the left—and waits for takeoff. As soon as the seat-belt sign is turned off, he goes to the bar, serves himself a generous measure of vodka, and drinks it down in one.

For a moment, he wonders if he really had succeeded in sending those messages to Ewa, while he was busy destroying worlds. Should he have been more explicit, adding a further note or a name or something like that? That would have been terribly risky—people might think he was a serial killer.

And he wasn't: he had an objective, which, fortunately, had changed in time.

The thought of Ewa doesn't weigh on him as much as it used to. He doesn't love her as he once did, and he doesn't hate her as he came to hate her. With time, she will disappear completely from his life, which is a shame because he's unlikely to find another woman like her, for all her defects.

He goes back to the bar, pours himself another vodka, and again drinks it down in one. Will they realize that a single person was responsible for extinguishing those worlds? It doesn't matter. His only regret is the moment he decided to give himself up to the police in the afternoon. Fate, however, was on his side and he managed to complete his mission.

Yes, he had won, but the winner doesn't stand alone. His nightmares are at an end. An angel with dark eyebrows is watching over him and will teach him which path to follow from now on.

ST. JOHN'S DAY,
19 MARCH 2008

ACKNOWLEDGMENTS

I could not possibly have written this book without the help of the many people who, whether openly or in confidence, gave me access to the information it contains. When I began my research, I never imagined that I would find so much of interest behind the façade of the world of glitz and glamour. Apart from the friends who have asked for their names not to be mentioned, I would like to thank Alexander Osterwald, Bernadette Imaculada Santos, Claudine and Elie Saab, David Rothkopf (the inventor of the term "Superclass"), Deborah Williamson, Fátima Lopes, Fawaz Gruosi, Franco Cologni, Hildegard Follon, James W. Wright, Jennifer Bollinger, Johan Reckman, Jörn Pfotenhauer, Juliette Rigal, Kevin Heienberg, Kevin Karroll, Luca Burei, Maria de Lourdes Débat, Mario Rosa, Monty Shadow, Steffi Czerny, Victoria Navaloska, Yasser Hamid, and Zeina Raphael, all of whom collaborated directly or indirectly in the writing of this book. I must confess that, for the most part, they collaborated indirectly, since I never usually discuss the subject of a book when I'm writing it.

About the author

About the book

Insights,
Interviews
& More . . .

Read on

Meet Paulo Coelho

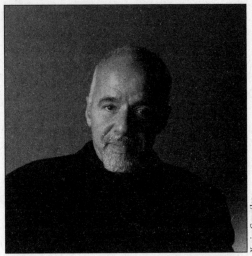

Xavier González

PAULO COELHO was born in Rio de Janeiro in August 1947, the son of Pedro Queima Coelho de Souza, an engineer, and his wife, Lygia, a homemaker. Early on, Coelho dreamed of an artistic career, something frowned upon in his middle-class household. In the austere surroundings of a strict Jesuit school, Coelho discovered his true vocation: to be a writer. Coelho's parents, however, had different plans for him. When their attempts to suppress his devotion to literature failed, they took it as a sign of mental illness. When Coelho was seventeen, his father twice had him committed to a mental institution, where he endured sessions of electroconvulsive "therapy." His parents brought him back to the institution once more, after he had become involved with a theater group and started to work as a journalist.

Coelho was always a nonconformist and a seeker of the new. When, in the excitement of 1968, the guerrilla and hippie movements took hold in a Brazil ruled by a repressive military regime, Coelho embraced progressive politics and joined the peace-and-love generation. He sought spiritual experiences traveling all over

66 The first edition [of *The Alchemist*] sold only nine hundred copies, and the publishing house decided not to reprint it. 99

2

Latin America in the footsteps of Carlos Castaneda. Coelho worked in the theater and dabbled in journalism, launching an alternative magazine called *2001*. He began to collaborate with music producer Raul Seixas as a lyricist, transforming the Brazilian rock scene. In 1973, Coelho and Seixas joined the Alternative Society, an organization that defended the individual's right to free expression, and began publishing a series of comic strips, calling for more freedom. Members of the organization were detained and imprisoned. Two days later, Coelho was kidnapped and tortured by a group of paramilitaries.

This experience affected him profoundly. At the age of twenty-six, Coelho decided that he had had enough of living on the edge and wanted to be "normal." He worked as an executive in the music industry. He tried his hand at writing but didn't start seriously until after he had had an encounter with a stranger. The man first came to him in a vision, and two months later Coelho met him at a café in Amsterdam. The stranger suggested that Coelho should return to Catholicism and study the benign side of magic. He also encouraged Coelho to walk the Road to Santiago, the medieval pilgrim's route.

In 1987, a year after completing that pilgrimage, Coelho wrote *The Pilgrimage*. The book describes his experiences and his discovery that the extraordinary occurs in the lives of ordinary people. A year later, he wrote a very different book, *The Alchemist*. The first edition sold only nine hundred copies, and the publishing house decided not to reprint it.

Coelho would not surrender his dream. He found another publishing house, a bigger one. He wrote *Brida*; the book received a lot of attention in the press, and both *The Alchemist* and *The Pilgrimage* appeared on bestseller lists.

Coelho has gone on to write many other bestselling books, including *The Valkyries, By the River Piedra I Sat Down and Wept, The Fifth Mountain, Warrior of the Light: A Manual, Eleven Minutes, Veronika Decides to Die, The Zahir, The Devil and Miss Prym*, and *The Witch of Portobello*.

Today, Paulo Coelho's books have sold more than one hundred million copies and appear at the top of bestseller lists worldwide. In 2002, the *Jornal de Letras de Portugal*, the foremost literary authority in the Portuguese language, bestowed upon *The Alchemist* (a *New York Times* bestseller) the title of most sold book in the history of the language. In 2003, Coelho's novel *Eleven Minutes* was the world's bestselling fiction title (*USA Today, Publishing Trends*). In 2007, he was named a United Nations Messenger of Peace.

In addition to his novels, Coelho writes a globally syndicated weekly newspaper column and occasionally publishes articles on current affairs. His newsletter, *Warrior of the Light Online*, has more than 223,600 subscribers. Likewise, his blog, www.paulocoelhoblog.com, has been visited by millions. His Web site at HarperCollins is www.harpercollins.com/paulocoelho.

Coelho and his wife, Christina Oiticica, are the founders of the Paulo Coelho Institute, which provides support and opportunities for underprivileged members of Brazilian society.

On *The Winner Stands Alone*
A Conversation with Paulo Coelho

With The Winner Stands Alone, *could it be said that you underwent a change of goals or objectives from what you had been writing before? Did you want to continue writing another book of values, sensations, and feelings?*

This new interest emerged when I went to the Cannes Film Festival in 2007, where I saw a lot of talent and courage being wasted in search of glamour, luxury, and fashion. I met very lucid people who were able to perfectly dissect that universe; however, that lucidity did not lead to any exit, to any alternative. From this view, captivated by appearances, I saw cynicism flourish, which for me is the beginning of the soul's death.

How could I avoid trying to penetrate the heart of that collective craziness? As a writer, I knew there was a whole world to be revealed. That's why I don't think I have distanced myself from the connecting thread of my books. I have always been interested in the fight for dreams. In *The Winner Stands Alone*, I am able to explore the pursuit for a dream that doesn't belong to us. It is something I felt I had to understand: How certain dreams can reach such tremendous scale, completely anonymously, and can drag so many people in to them?

But why talk about the world of celebrities, fashion, and glamour?

I've spent quite a lot of time in that world, and it always leaves me feeling uneasy. I'm more used to it now, but I'm still curious to know how things really work. The research I did was an attempt to explain those mechanisms. For my main characters, I chose people who are full of dreams and who are doing all they can to make them reality—but are going about it in an entirely wrong way. However materialistic their goals may seem, they are motivated by something that transcends the material world. I want readers to know that the people they imagine to be all-powerful superstars are, in fact, mere cogs in a machine manipulated by the few.

Do you consider yourself a winner? Do you stand alone?

People think a winner is someone who is loved by everyone. But as you climb the steps of fame, there's always another side to that. People might be fascinated by you, but on the other hand, those who haven't been as successful are bound to view you with a certain bitterness. That's where the loneliness comes in. I think I'm a winner of a different sort. I do go to lots of events and parties, and I'm sure that I'm viewed by people with fascination and envy. But I have other commitments beyond my life as a writer. I'm a United Nations Messenger of Peace; I travel all over the world, meeting with people of different nationalities and social classes. In fact, it provides the raw material for my work. I have my wife as well as many friends. However, I'm alone when I make decisions, but never physically or emotionally. A winner can be alone or not, depending on the kind of life one chooses.

Your central character, Igor, "destroys worlds" and is a social commentator without a conscience, how exactly did you perceive this character and the duality in it?

When I started to write the book, I had no clue where it would lead me. Somehow the characters take their destinies from the hands of the creator. With Igor, my main surprise is how he justifies his crimes in the name of love, a contradiction that gradually unfolds page after page. In a way, I was a spectator of my character: he had a will of his own and led me toward very dark places. But, I needed to follow him—in order to see how far we could go into our insanity.

The Alchemist *is about following your dreams.* **The Winner Stands Alone** *is about paying a terrible price for following your dreams. What* ▶

On *The Winner Stands Alone* (continued)

is the ultimate message you would like this book to deliver and is there a definite moral of the story?

I beg to differ: *The Winner Stands Alone* is not about paying a terrible price for your dreams. On the contrary, it is about the gigantic price we pay for allowing ourselves to chase illusions, instead of our true dreams.

I don't think it's a moralistic book—even though I describe it without concessions as a "dream factory"—but I do hope the reader will be able to see it as a warning rather than a manifesto.

You make a lot of pointed truths about the sham behind a lot of things modern life has foisted on us. Like the facade of superficiality, consumerism, etc. What triggered it?

I remember once being at a gala dinner and next to me was a beautiful woman that was inconsolable. She was at the prime of her life, yet she held this profound hatred toward the other women at the event. What was her sadness and hatred based upon? Fame—either she wasn't as famous as some other women or she wasn't as rich as other women.

How can I describe the feeling of looking into a beautiful flower and discovering that her scent was actually poisonous? It reminded me of "The Sick Rose" by William Blake—where he describes this beautiful rose that actually wishes to die in her own flower bed.

How can the ambition to forward oneself be channeled in the right direction so that one doesn't become self-destructive or meaningless?

It is a very personal process and experience is extremely important. But, as long as one is able to distinguish between being and having, I believe the force can be directed. It's always important to have in mind that the most precious things are invisible.

Have You Read?
More by Paulo Coelho

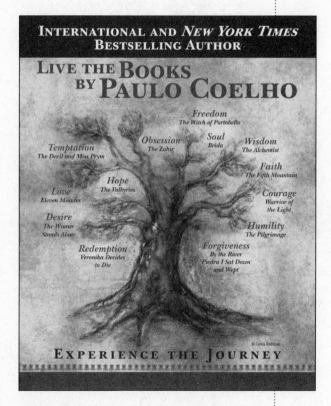

INTERNATIONAL AND *NEW YORK TIMES* BESTSELLING AUTHOR

LIVE THE BOOKS BY PAULO COELHO

Freedom
The Witch of Portobello

Obsession
The Zahir

Soul
Brida

Wisdom
The Alchemist

Temptation
The Devil and Miss Prym

Faith
The Fifth Mountain

Hope
The Valkyries

Love
Eleven Minutes

Courage
Warrior of the Light

Desire
The Winner Stands Alone

Humility
The Pilgrimage

Redemption
Veronika Decides to Die

Forgiveness
By the River Piedra I Sat Down and Wept

© Carlos Rodrigues

EXPERIENCE THE JOURNEY

With each of his beautifully crafted works Paulo Coelho has mapped out a literary pilgrimage. By encouraging *Freedom, Soul, Wisdom, Faith, Humility, Hope, Forgiveness, Redemption, Courage, Love, Obsession, Desire,* and *Temptation,* his writing transports us to the sacred place that the best books create between reader and text. It is a journey that proves that great literature has the power to influence lives.

BRIDA

Brida, a young Irish girl, has long been interested in various aspects of magic but is searching for something more. Her search leads her to people of great wisdom. She meets a wise man who dwells in a forest, who teaches her to trust in the goodness of the world, and a woman who teaches her how to dance to the music of the world. As Brida seeks her destiny, she struggles to find a balance between her relationships and her desire to become a witch.

This enthralling novel incorporates themes that fans of Paulo Coelho will recognize and treasure. It is a tale of love, passion, mystery, and spirituality from the master storyteller.

"Coelho's books have had a life-enhancing effect on millions of people."   —*The Times* (London)

BRIDA

Spanish-language edition available in trade paperback from Rayo.

THE WITCH OF PORTOBELLO

How do we find the courage to always be true to ourselves—even if we are unsure of who we are?

That is the central question of Paulo Coelho's profound novel *The Witch of Portobello*. It is the story of a mysterious woman named Athena, told by the many who knew her well—or hardly at all. Like *The Alchemist*, *The Witch of Portobello* will transform the way readers think about love, passion, joy, and sacrifice.

In 2008, Coelho launched the Experimental Witch Project in conjunction with *The Witch of Portobello*. To learn more about the project, please visit http://paulocoelhoblog.com/experimental -witch/.

"Narrated from multiple points of view, the portrait of Athena that emerges is as provocative and spiritually complex as one would expect from the author of *The Alchemist* (1993) and *The Devil and Miss Prym* (2006)."   —*Booklist*

LA BRUJA DE PORTOBELLO

Spanish-language edition available in trade paperback from Rayo.

THE DEVIL AND MISS PRYM

A stranger arrives at the remote village of Viscos, carrying with him a backpack containing a notebook and eleven gold bars. He comes searching for the answer to a question that torments him: Are human beings, in essence, good or evil? In welcoming the mysterious foreigner, the whole village becomes an accomplice to his sophisticated plot, which will forever mark their lives.

A novel of temptation by the internationally bestselling author Paulo Coelho, *The Devil and Miss Prym* is a thought-provoking parable of a community devoured by greed, cowardice, and fear—as it struggles with the choice between good and evil.

"Internationally acclaimed author and contemporary fabulist Coelho concludes his excellent And on the Seventh Day trilogy with another provocative morality tale." —*Booklist*

EL DEMONIO Y LA SEÑORITA PRYM

Spanish-language edition available in trade paperback from Rayo.

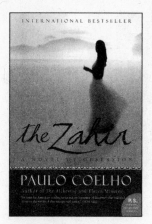

THE ZAHIR

The narrator of *The Zahir* is a bestselling novelist who lives in Paris and enjoys all the privileges that money and celebrity bring. When Esther, his wife of ten years, disappears with her friend Mikhail, who may or may not be her lover, the authorities question the narrator. Was Esther kidnapped or murdered, or did she simply abandon a marriage that left her unfulfilled? The narrator has plenty of questions of his own until Mikhail returns, promising to take him to his wife.

A haunting and redemptive story about the dark side of obsession, *The Zahir* explores its potential to both fulfill our dreams and to destroy them. It is also a thoughtful meditation on faith, celebrity, and marriage—and their relationships to freedom and creativity.

"Coelho is a novelist who writes in a universal language."   *—New York Times*

EL ZAHIR

Spanish-language edition available in trade paperback from Rayo.

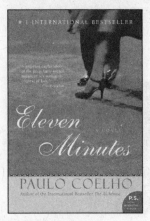

ELEVEN MINUTES

Maria, a young girl from a Brazilian village, endures a broken heart following her first innocent brushes with love. Convinced she will never find true love, she believes "Love is a terrible thing that will make you suffer." A chance meeting in Rio takes her to Geneva, where she dreams of finding fame and fortune, yet ends up working as a prostitute. Maria's despairing view of love is put to the test when she meets a handsome young painter. In this odyssey of self-discovery, she must choose between pursuing a path of dark sensual indulgence or risking everything to find her own "inner light" and the renewed possibility of love.

"Gratifyingly erotic. . . . The narrative embeds itself firmly in Maria's perceptions and experiences, her emotions, dreams, and struggles to understand life." —*Washington Post Book World*

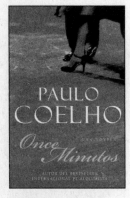

ONCE MINUTOS

Spanish-language edition available in trade paperback from Rayo.

VERONIKA DECIDES TO DIE

Twenty-four-year-old Veronika seems to have everything—youth and beauty, boyfriends and a loving family, a fulfilling job. But something is missing. So, one cold November morning she decides to die. She takes a handful of sleeping pills expecting never to wake up, but she does—at a mental hospital where she is told she has only days to live.

This poignant international bestseller takes readers on a quest to find meaning in a culture overshadowed by angst, soulless routine, and pervasive conformity. Based on events in Coelho's own life, *Veronika Decides to Die* questions the meaning of madness and celebrates individuality. Bold and illuminating, it is a dazzling portrait of a young woman at the crossroads of despair and liberation, and a poetic, exuberant appreciation of each day as a new opportunity.

Be on the lookout for the film adaptation of *Veronika Decides to Die,* starring Sarah Michelle Gellar. Coming soon to cinemas in 2010.

"Told with sincerity approaching urgency, Coelho's novel is surprisingly effective."
— *Boston Globe*

VERONIKA DECIDE MORIR

Spanish-language edition available in trade paperback from Rayo.

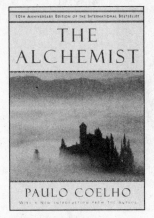

THE ALCHEMIST

The Alchemist, a *New York Times* bestseller, has inspired a devoted following around the world. The story, dazzling in its powerful simplicity and inspiring wisdom, is about an Andalusian shepherd boy named Santiago who travels from his homeland in Spain to the Egyptian desert in search of a treasure buried in the Pyramids. Along the way he meets a Gypsy woman, a man who calls himself king, and an alchemist, all of whom point Santiago in the direction of his quest. No one knows what the treasure is, or if Santiago will be able to surmount the obstacles along the way. But what starts out as a journey to find worldly goods turns into a discovery of the treasures found within.

"A magical little volume."

—*San Francisco Chronicle*

EL ALQUIMISTA

Spanish-language edition available in trade paperback from Rayo.

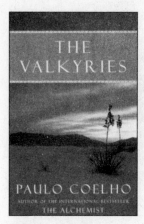

THE VALKYRIES

This true-life account—at once a modern-day adventure and a metaphysical odyssey—begins in Rio de Janeiro when Paulo Coelho gives his mysterious master, J., the only manuscript of his book *The Alchemist*. Haunted by a devastating curse, Coelho confesses to J., "I've seen my dreams fall apart just when I seemed about to achieve them." In response, J. gives Coelho a daunting task: He must find and speak with his guardian angel. Coelho and his wife set out on a forty-day quest into the starkly beautiful and sometimes dangerous Mojave Desert—where they encounter more than they bargained for.

"Reads like a suspense novel."

—*The Times* (London)

**A ORILLAS DEL RÍO
PIEDRA ME SENTÉ
Y LLORÉ**

....

*Spanish-language
edition available in
trade paperback
from Rayo.*

BY THE RIVER PIEDRA I SAT DOWN AND WEPT

What happens when, after eleven years, two
childhood lovers are reunited as adults? Pilar has
become an independent and strong woman while
her former boyfriend has become a handsome
spiritual leader. She has learned to bury her
feelings; he has turned to religion as a refuge
from his inner conflicts. Together they embark
on a journey fraught with difficulties, as long-
buried demons of blame and resentment resurface
after years of being hidden. But by the River
Piedra, in a small village in the French Pyrenees,
they discuss many of life's big questions and
reevaluate their own special relationship.

"Coelho's message . . . is invariably heartfelt and
challenging, emphasizing the feminine aspects of
the divine and the charismatic aspects of worship."
—*Publishers Weekly*

THE FIFTH MOUNTAIN

The Fifth Mountain is Paulo Coelho's inspiring story of the Biblical prophet Elijah. In the ninth century B.C., the Phoenician princess Jezebel orders the execution of all the prophets who refuse to seek safety in the land of Zarephath, where Elijah unexpectedly finds true love with a young widow. But this newfound rapture is to be cut short, and Elijah sees all of his hopes and dreams irrevocably erased as he is swept into a whirlwind of events that threatens his very existence. In what is truly a literary milestone, Coelho gives a quietly moving account of a man touched by the hand of God who must triumph over his frustrations in a soul-shattering trial of faith.

"A thought-provoking personal tale."   —*Time*

LA QUINTA MONTAÑA

Spanish-language edition available in trade paperback from Rayo.

Have You Read? *(continued)*

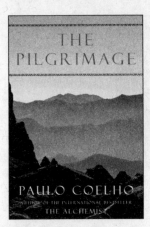

THE PILGRIMAGE

The Pilgrimage recounts the spectacular trials of Paulo Coelho as he journeys across Spain to discover personal power, wisdom, and a miraculous sword that seals his initiation into the secret society of the Tradition. With his enigmatic mentor, Petrus, he follows a legendary road traveled by pilgrims of Santiago since the Middle Ages, encountering a Chaucerian variety of mysterious guides and devilish opponents. Coelho's experiences and his mentor's teachings impart the spiritual wisdom that reveals itself as the true purpose of their exciting journey. Part adventure story, part guide to self-mastery, this compelling tale delivers a powerful brew of magic and insight.

"An exciting tale."   —*Library Journal*

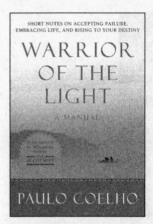

WARRIOR OF THE LIGHT: A MANUAL

Warrior of the Light: A Manual is an inspirational companion to *The Alchemist*, an international bestseller that has beguiled millions of readers around the world.

Every short passage invites us to live out our dreams, to embrace the uncertainty of life, and to rise to our own unique destiny. In his inimitable style, Paulo Coelho shows readers how to embark upon the way of the Warrior: the one who appreciates the miracle of being alive and whose quest leads him to become the person he wants to be.

Paulo Coelho is one of the most beloved storytellers of our time. In the long-awaited companion to his first novel, Coelho presents a collection of philosophical stories that will delight and guide seekers everywhere.

"Coelho is on a good thing, and he sticks to it."   —*The Courier Mail* (Australia)

MANUAL DEL GUERRERO DE LA LUZ

Spanish-language edition available in trade paperback from Rayo.

Have You Read? *(continued)*

EL VENCEDOR ESTÁ SOLO
....

Spanish-language edition available in hardcover from Rayo.

Don't miss the next book by your favorite author. Sign up now for AuthorTracker by visiting www.AuthorTracker.com.

BECOMING
NATURALLY
THERAPEUTIC

A Return to the True Essence of Helping

JACQUELYN SMALL

BANTAM BOOKS
NEW YORK • TORONTO • LONDON • SYDNEY • AUCKLAND

BECOMING NATURALLY THERAPEUTIC
(REVISED EDITION)
A Bantam Book / January 1990

PRINTING HISTORY

Library of Congress Cataloging-in-Publication Data

Small, Jacquelyn.
  Becoming naturally therapeutic / by Jacquelyn Small.—
Rev. ed.
     p.   cm.
  ISBN 0-553-34800-0
  1. Alcoholism counseling—Handbooks, manuals, etc.
  I. Title
HV5275.S6   1990
362.29'286—dc20   89-6925
                                                             CIP

Published simultaneously in the United States and Canada

PRINTED IN THE UNITED STATES OF AMERICA

0   9   8   7   6   5

To Mary and Jack who gave me
the parental blessing of unconditional love.

Acknowledgments

There are two people in my life without whose vision this book would never have come to be: Wayne Ewen, my supervisor at the Texas Commission on Alcoholism, who in 1974 recognized this material—originally a sixty-page memorandum to him—as one of significance and worthy of a larger audience; and Brenda Shea, of Eupsychia in Austin, who carried this book through several publications and kept it in print during its primary stages.

I would also like to acknowledge my editor at Bantam, Linda Loewenthal, who saw the vision and caringly midwifed this present edition through its transformational process of expansion—and whose dedication and insightful attitude made this coadventure one of great pleasure.

I thank you all!

Contents

ON THERAPEUTIC RELATING:

A Note to My Readers

If we are going to heal our addicted society, we must create a safe place for people to come and express their feelings of pain—feelings of anger or grief that may have driven them to drink, to take drugs, or to act out in other harmful ways at some point in their lives. This safe place is a cleared-out human heart. It is here that we can really listen to and share each other's intimate pain. And it is here that we can help heal each other's old hurts.

The true healer is within! And it needs only to be accessed to offer us its gifts. High-functioning psychotherapists have found their inner healers and have moved beyond their mechanical, outworn techniques by learning how just to be themselves and to speak the truth. Now it is time for all of us to learn how to access our healer within—for it is most often not in the therapist's office but in everyday life that we meet each other in our struggles and can help one another through difficult life transitions.

Fourteen years ago I was involved in doing the empirical research that revealed what makes a therapist effective in the life of another: This research showed what therapists actually *did* during those crucial hours behind closed doors and what about them really made the difference for their clients. Now we'd like to bring this knowledge to you, so that you too can see that you are a natural healer.

This is a book about therapeutic relating for ordinary people—human beings from all walks of life who can help when someone calls out in pain. It is also for the professional counselor who may be feeling lost in the sophisticated therapeutic jargon of today's multifarious psychological schools, wishing to return once again to the basics of creative counselor-client relationships. May all of you find your self all over these pages as you discover how the true art of therapy lives within us all. And remember, therapeutic relating heals not only the one seeking help, but the one being asked for help as well.

INTRODUCTION

You may never have thought of yourself as a therapist, having reserved that title for people who have professional counselor roles. Yet research has made clear that the most therapeutic responses to people in trouble often come from "ordinary people" who don't think of themselves as experts, teachers, judges, counselors, or ministers. They're *just people* who have experienced life and who have understanding, nonjudgmental hearts—a mother, an older brother, a friend at the office, a cab driver, a bartender. Or they may be professional therapists who have stayed in touch with their hearts without becoming lost in the dogma or formality of professional training. In any case they are people who do not hide behind roles and who can just be themselves.

Untrained people who listen with their hearts as opposed to their brains often have a much more healing effect on others than those who have trained themselves to be "helpful." Over the past fifteen years those of us who've worked in the area of counselor training have found that people with the highest college degrees, or with the most degrees, have often lost their inherent therapeutic abilities. It's as though these natural human responses were trained *right out of them.*

Distancing oneself from others' pain and trying to act like an expert are two ways professional psychotherapists frequently get into trouble—not only with their clients but with themselves. Sometimes this professional hazard is simply a result of the therapist's own ignorance about how real therapeutic healing happens. Professional counselors have been trained to remain professionally aloof, to stay neatly and appropriately clad in counselor "uniforms," sitting efficiently behind their desks. But even worse, sometimes we professionals fall into the category of "the codependent helper"; we may throw our own ego weaknesses and unfinished psychological business at our client or use the client's problems as a way to avoid looking at our own issues. Codependent counselor behaviors take many forms, such as the need for approval from the client, or the need to come across as having it all together. Some professionals consistently control situations with their clients or merge with clients and vicariously work on themselves at the client's expense. Therapists may have too much invested in being right—while thinking the whole time their conviction will help the client! All these examples illustrate how a therapist's own process can become activated and get in the way of the therapeutic relationship.

But lecturers, preachers, saviors, and judges come in all sorts of packages, not just in that of the professional psychotherapist. We are all in danger of hiding behind roles that block the essence of helping. And unfortunately some of us get attached to these roles as ways to make ourselves feel important or needed. We may even find a way to put seekers down or to punish them if they do not do what we say. (I will discuss how we let our lower-self needs get in the way of counseling in "Toxic Relating.")

When people in need are in the presence of this kind of "toxic helper," they begin to feel uncomfortable and confused; their hearts become constricted instead of free and easy. And they feel themselves shrinking instead of expanding into more self-love or confidence, or into forgiveness of others who've harmed them. At some point they will no longer feel safe discussing their problems with this person, as they have experienced nonacceptance and a lack of true understanding; they have not been heard.

4

All of us know intuitively when we are being subjected to someone laying his "trip" on us. It's the heart that knows. For the heart is a built-in "truth detector," although we sometimes ignore it and allow others to take advantage of us.

Counseling others can be a two-edged sword: It can enable us to hide from ourselves while ostensibly aiding another. Or if we are the one seeking help, it can keep us in a dependent (codependent) relationship, habitually giving our power and our heart away to someone we've decided to make into an expert on us. Claiming our own power and right to *be* is how we heal. Learning to believe in ourselves is how we grow. When we need help, we want to feel there is someone there who is *a real person*, someone we can bounce ideas off of who is open and receptive, someone we can risk telling our mistakes and perceived weaknesses to. We need to feel safe as we reveal our worst fears and expose our darkest secrets.

I believe that something within all of us is beginning to rise up in dissatisfaction with those who insist on calling us sick and crazy and who don't seem to remember how to come from the heart. As clients of professional therapists we are changing, reclaiming our right to be human and to expect a human response. And we are learning to expect the same from our relationships in general.

In my work with others in counselor training, I've discovered that the true healer and authority is *within the person* who is hurting and reaching out for help—not in the one who is listening! The very best "people-helpers" know this and see themselves as guides and fellow travelers, not as experts on another's situation. They are learning to struggle themselves and to accept life's disappointments and crises with grace. And they therefore have no emotional investment in making judgments or offering quick, easy advice. They are relaxed but caring and are not intensely involved in other people's problems—with no real ego investment in others' choices. These are the therapeutic helpers in the world. Sometimes they are professionals who have kept their hearts open—often in spite of their training—and who continue to work on themselves. But mostly these "helpers" are nonprofessionals; they are people who are busy loving and sharing in each other's difficult times, moments of bliss, and visions of the future.

Whether you are a professional or nonprofessional counselor, it is important to remember that people in crisis need to see if their way of expressing their problems and their reactions to these problems are making sense. They need to release the pent-up energies of rage and hurt that block clear thinking. And they need some reminders about who they really are beyond the current melodrama, grief, or fear they've gotten caught up in. They also need to be reminded of their strengths, as well as empathized with about the ways they've gotten hurt or off track. Sometimes you can offer a creative solution just by being there completely and sharing from your heart your own experiences—self-disclosures that make others feel a kind of kinship with you. Isn't this what *you* need when you are in trouble, feeling alone or lost?

Becoming Naturally Therapeutic describes the true therapeutic qualities that each of us has within our own hearts, our own essence, that serve as "therapeutic change agents" for people seeking help. This book can help you "straight-talk" beyond your own codependent ways of helping others; it will teach you to offer clear and loving guidance directly from the heart. And it will help you create a more natural response to life, getting you past the barriers of too much advice or too much therapeutic technique. It is for all of you who find yourselves in counseling roles, whether you wear an actual counselor's hat or not. It will teach you to have the courage to "come from the heart"—a phrase you will fully understand after reading this book—and will give you an understanding of certain basics that are good, true, and helpful, which many therapists may have learned from their professional training.

Being naturally therapeutic heals not only the one asking for help; it also allows helpers to become more integrated and comfortable with themselves, leading them to more creative roles in their own lives. This book points us toward relationships in which we can be our real selves, in which we can feel safe and can truly communicate.

In 1975 *Becoming Naturally Therapeutic* began circulating within the alcoholism treatment community as a guidebook for alcoholism counselors seeking ways to become more confident and professional in their work with alcoholic clients and their families. It achieved instant popularity, soon becoming a prerequisite for counselors at many governmental, agency, and academic programs that deal with counseling addicts or members of dysfunctional families who have trouble with issues of codependence. And the response from people throughout the country wanting help in their relationships was tremendous. I was rather amazed. To me the book was so simple and easy to write, I couldn't imagine why it was making such an impact.

Since it was first published, I've received feedback that has helped me discover the answer: *Becoming Naturally Therapeutic* is based on the universal law of love. And this Law is totally transforming; it is the driving force behind our essence. Love is truth. And when truth happens between two people, there is a noticeable exchange of energy. And conversely, when untruth prevails, no energy is exchanged—*nothing happens.*

In other words, the human self is an instrument designed specifically to concretize the law of love in the world. And this universal law can operate only within the context of relationship—otherwise it remains an abstract, formless concept, nonexistent. You will notice from your own experience that it is only through touching one another (not just physically) and observing what we reflect for each other that we are able to know ourselves. We remind each other of who we are. This is our purpose.

I've learned something that I wish to share with all of you—it is what motivated me to write this book. When therapeutic relating occurs, both parties have dissolved the boundary between the one needing help and the other offering it; they are simply two beings bouncing off each other *in truth*. Light enters when truth happens. Truth is not a concept; it is a *power*—the power to be real, or realized. It is the power to *be*.

Becoming Naturally Therapeutic is a study of the human qualities inherent within the personality structure that manifest practically and simply as the law of love. These qualities are our essence. They are broken down into distinct elements in this book, so that we can absorb each "flavor" of our self one at a time and thereby gain an understanding of how each one manifests itself through our ways of relating. As you go through the book, studying and practicing the traits of the self, you will see that they all bring about the absolute truth of a situation—pointing each person to himself, honestly and simply. Therapeutic relationship is no accident, nor is it a game: It is following the natural laws of human nature, bringing us closer and closer to the authenticity of our being. We all just need clear people to bounce off of so we can see our own light. Then we are capable of living from the heart, our true self.

Therapeutic relating can be recognized in operation, defined, taught, practiced, and mastered. It is no mystery! It is truth happening through a magnetic exchange of energy that makes dynamic contact with another person, heals, and then transforms. *We* don't do it; truth does! We are merely its instrument. This book shows what therapeutic relating looks like in the here and now, day-to-day life of a person placed in the role of helper to one in trouble—as we all are from time to time.

I have used the counselor-client relationship as an example throughout the book, both for the benefit of the professional counselor and as a metaphor for readers involved in relationships of all kinds. It will be beneficial for nonprofessional helpers to see the high-functioning therapist in action. There are also nonprofessional examples from everyday life (interactions between family members and friends) to remind us that therapeutic relating takes place not only in the counselor's office or in group therapy sessions. It happens in all aspects of life, whenever the heart is open and speaking its truth. This type of communication is our human heritage, for we all have hearts, and God knows, we've all had troubles.

The principles described throughout are universal in their application. This book is for all of you seeking knowledge and wisdom about the self and how it works to help others. I offer this to you from my experience, with love.

TOXIC RELATING

Before we begin our study of therapeutic relating, it might be useful for us to stop a minute and look at the negative patterns we all are in danger of falling into when someone asks us for help. Where did toxic communication come from in the first place? How could we ever allow ourselves to harm other people when they seek help or ask us to share in their stories and feelings of hopelessness or fear? You would think this type of call to relationship would only bring out the best in us. And sometimes it does. But other times we may find that we are feeling punitive, uninterested, or helpless and full of our own fear. Sometimes another's problems remind us too much of our own, and we become confused as to how to help the other person. At other times we may even discount what another calls a "problem"; we feel that this person should just "get over it." Or sometimes we feel ourselves becoming too preoccupied with someone else's difficulties, and we may even obsess about them or move into a "savior mode" and try too hard to be helpful. What is going on when these types of contaminated responses become the driving force behind our activities?

Well, I believe that when Jesus said, "Ye shall love thy brother as thyself," he meant it differently than many of us have been taught. He didn't mean for us to *try* to love our brother as we would want to be loved. He meant we just *will* love others as we love ourselves, for we are incapable of loving anyone else before we love ourselves. Similarly, if there are parts of ourselves we have not forgiven for certain types of behaviors, it is quite unlikely that we can forgive others, or even feel neutral toward them, if they remind us of these unredeemed parts of our beings. We will be inclined to punish the other person, or desire that person to suffer the consequences of his actions, just as we expect will happen to us. We may think we are being helpers when in fact we've only vented our own "stuff" around *our* issue. In counseling this is called overidentifying with the client and attempting to provide solutions that are really for us, not for him or her. We know we are overidentifying when we begin to react emotionally. This is our cue that we are not clear.

For example, let's say you come to me with a problem about your mother; you want me to listen as you tell me that she has the ability to make you feel guilty about almost anything. If I have individuated from my own mother— meaning that I can now see her as a human being, a woman, instead of as "mother" or an authority over me—I will have no trouble staying clear as you speak. On the other hand, if I am still tied up in knots every time my mother calls or comes to visit, or if I am still motivated by trying to please her or prove to her that I am an okay person in spite of what she may think of me, I will find myself projecting my feelings onto you as you speak of your difficulties. I will feel a knot in my stomach, and I will want you to change the subject or solve your problem very quickly. In such a case there is a contamination in my response to your issue, and I must either tell you outright about my reaction, or I should not try to discuss the issue at all; I am not the right person to help you. *Unconscious* contamination causes toxic responses.

In our lower selves, our ego nature, we all have "un-cooked seeds." There is hardly anyone alive on this planet who has completely cleared out all his or her old hurts, disappointments, and illusions. But if we react from this pain when someone else is asking for our help, our true self is not the listener: Our ego is—and we need to stop the interaction.

If the "wounded child" within us still has security needs, and someone else's problem is making us feel unsafe, we may seek security from the very person who is needing our help. "*I* need security! *I* need to feel safe! Yet there is someone right here asking *me* for help." If we are in touch with our need, we can "own" it by telling the person: "I know that I have a lot of needs concerning my own safety. Your situation is making me feel somewhat defensive and unsafe, so I may not be a good sounding board for you." This is honest and clear—and will prevent you from giving a nontherapeutic response. It also will give the other person assurance that he or she is not alone; others may have the same problem. This is therapeutic relating. Good therapists do not have all the answers! In fact, an attitude of "having the solution" makes the other person feel inadequate.

Toxic relating happens when a listener acts out of his or her own unmet needs and confuses them with those of the person seeking help. This lack of clarity will throw the "helper" into a role that can harm the very person seeking help. Those finding themselves in such a situation will usually resort to a role such as preacher, judge, teacher, or savior. "Preachers" take on a moralistic attitude, listening out of preconceived notions of what's good and what's bad. They say things like, "For shame! Didn't you know this would happen? Your actions were wrong, and you know it!" "Judges" are similar, although less moralistic and more logical. They sound as if they know the correct decision and that you will come to it yourself once you listen to their advice: "Write down your goals, and we'll get together tomorrow and I'll tell you what to do to straighten this all out. If we can't come to a conclusion, I will have some other suggestions to make at that time." "Teachers" will want to train you to think "correctly" so this will never happen again: "I've got two books on marriage I want you both to study before our session next week." "Saviors" need to fix everything—usually very quickly—and will try to take over your life for you, often frantically making sure they stay in the forefront of the rescue mission. Saviors need to be needed.

These are all roles of the "expert." Experts don't talk much about what they really know; they keep their own true experience a mystery for fear they might reveal deficiencies in their own knowledge.

All of the above are ways people-helpers hide from intimacy and the truth of their own process, which is too scary for them to face. They see themselves as the healthy ones, the ones who are supposed to be right, clear, and untroubled. After all, as helpers they must be complete, having "arrived." Right? Wrong! There is no place where we all arrive. The journey is our home! We must learn to accept this journey with grace, or else we will fight it and play ego games that will make us all sick and crazy, creating an unsafe world where we will be unable to truly explore our deepest human issues together.

The key question we must ask ourselves before setting out to help someone is, If this person is being natural and sincere, no matter how scared or screwed up, can he or she be safe with me while going into private pain and discovering much-needed lessons and personal truth? If your answer is "yes" and you *mean* it, then you can be a therapeutic listener. If you can stay in a cleared-out space while you listen to another person, you are being therapeutic. You are one who helps to heal others by your very way of being. And your ego can't do a thing about it. It is simply so.

COMING FROM THE HEART

The Heart is the place within each of us that we can count on to tell us what's really going on—bottom line! For only truth can reside in the Heart.

You've heard the expression "hitting below the belt." Well, counselors and people-helpers hit below the belt whenever they respond from the needs of the lower self—needs that come from the unintegrated parts of us that are still unclear, even to us. We react from below the belt when we act out of feelings of defensiveness, insecurity, anxiety, or fear. The urgencies and intensities of emotional overreactions are the ego's ways of taking care of itself when it feels threatened. We call these responses "coming from the lower self."

Above the belt resides the Heart, which has no "ax to grind." I am capitalizing this word *Heart* because the human Heart is a lot more than we've thought it was. Not only is it the anatomical heart that pumps our blood and gives us a heart attack if we become too constricted; it is also a metaphor for total and complete clarity, a place where we can experience our true essence—which is unconditional love.

When describing the Heart, we must use metaphor—the chamber, the chalice, the womb, the cave—for the Heart can never be truly known through logic or intellect. The Heart is pure consciousness and unlimited bliss. It is spontaneous, unbounded light that can appear in many forms. It is ultimate—both transcendent and immanent—simultaneously above the world and living in the midst of the world. When we say *essence,* we mean Heart. It is the essential nature of all created things. As Saint Exupéry said so beautifully in his book *The Little Prince,* "It is only with the heart that one can see rightly; what is essential is invisible to the eye."

The Heart is a *space.* It is the portal or gateway to a higher reality, a more expanded state of consciousness. When it is empty, it provides us with a feeling of bliss or serenity; this is the Heart's natural state. When we are empty, that is, clear of emotional hurts, fears, or excitements, even if only for a moment, our inner self and our outer life match completely. We feel as if we are space, or spacious. At moments like these there is no activity blocking our complete happiness and contentment. But usually the Heart is not empty; it collects all our hurts, our feelings of grief over people and things that we've lost. The impermanence of our material world is a sore spot for all human beings. We love and we leave—this is the human tragedy, the true human condition. And this truth—indeed our entire truth—resides in the Heart. Many believe the Heart is the seat of the human soul.

The Heart is where we really feel our feelings, the reminders of our humanness, our vulnerability. And after we've fully experienced these emotions, the Heart puts us in touch with the sacredness behind all our sorrows and hurts, showing us each lesson's meaning and purpose. It teaches us to live in surrender, eventually learning to accept fully every single part of the human condition in love, and in forgiveness.

> To behold with the eyes of the Heart; to listen with the ears of the Heart to the roar of the world; to peer into the future with the comprehension of the Heart; to remember the cumulations of the past through the Heart; thus must one impetuously

advance upon the path of ascent. [Our creativity]
is impregnated with the sacred fire of the Heart.

HEART
(New York: Agni Yoga Society, 1975)

When we are counseling others from the Heart, we are
living in our truth of the moment, with no hidden agendas
about what ought to be. In the Heart things just are as they
are. An example: A woman is trying to talk herself into
loving her husband when really her marriage has died. She
even asks you to validate the fact that she loves him. Yet
both of you are sitting there "just knowing" that the love
has gone, and no matter how smart, how patient, how
loving the wife may be, the fact remains that the love the
couple once knew no longer is. Now it is time for the
woman to act on this fact. No more pretending—the Heart
has spoken.

We all know this place. This is the place of clarity. And
there will be times that clarity will mean taking action or
making decisions that are painful and filled with difficult
change. This change may not only affect the one who is
discovering a truth, but others as well, and this makes
acting from the Heart even harder. This is life. This is the
way of love.

Counseling from the Heart happens when the listener
can really put aside all his or her own issues for a while and
just be there for someone else. It happens when the helper
is willing to offer his or her true reactions—physical, emotional, and mental—to those seeking help, who speak the
truth as best they can, given the confusion they are
experiencing.

When listening from the Heart, you can have absolutely
no intensity around or expectation about the outcome.
There is simply a willingness to tell the truth as you perceive it. From the Heart your perceptions will come not

only from the mind, but from the feeling nature. For example, I might be listening to you, and as you tell me, with great conviction, that you do not believe in divorce, I see your body constricting as you begin talking of going back home to that one you no longer love. I notice the constriction, and I feel it in my own body as well. And so I tell you my truth: "Mary, as you speak of going back home, I too am feeling a constriction around my own heart as I watch you close up." At this point Mary observes her own body and sees that she has folded up in a contracted position, a posture of deep, unsatisfied resignation.

As I listen to the parent telling me how he has kicked his son out of the house—"Good riddance!" he says. "The boy deserved it! He did not follow the family rules"—I feel myself beginning to tear. I look into the father's eyes, and I see his tears as well. And so I say, "My heart hurts as I see you making this decision. I feel that you have hemmed yourself in with your own rules." At this point the father breaks down and begins to cry, telling of his deep love for his son. This is therapeutic relating.

Counseling from the Heart resolves itself into truth. But this truth can come about only if we, as listeners, are willing to be ourselves completely, listening to our whole organism as we interact with the one seeking help.

As a therapist, I use the first few minutes of a session for my client and myself to sit in silence, holding hands and invoking our Higher Power, which we experience from within. I have learned that the soul does the work of transformation, and the ego merely cooperates with (or has the power to block) the soul, or Heart. If my client and I are both willing to remain in surrender to the real truth of the situation—not seeking impatient solutions or trying to be "right" or "good" or "dutiful"—truth will emerge and will eventually lead to loving action. Love is sometimes tough. Love sometimes even means withdrawing. But love is always real. And it emanates from a place beyond our ego's needs—from the temple of the Heart.

Now we are ready to proceed with the therapeutic qualities that manifest through the human Heart. These are the specific *aspects* of the workings of the Heart, ways we offer support to and challenge those who seek us out when they are in need. The chapters that follow teach us how to remind each other that the true healer is within; all people ever need is some help in accessing this reality. For no matter how damaged we think we are, no matter how dysfunctional our outer lives may appear to be, we are our own healers when we are in touch with our spiritual nature: This is how we are made, each and every one of us.

Therapeutic people know how to help us get back in touch with our inner healer. They help us in gently removing our masks—which may have literally grown onto our faces. It hurts to peel off our protective coverings. People who are natural therapists assist us in this process without even knowing they are doing it. They provide a safe, nonjudgmental space—like a temple—where we are led gently to the straight talk necessary for getting to the bottom line, our real truth.

> Something we were withholding made us weak
> Until we found it was ourselves.
>
> *ROBERT FROST*

We are all blessed with this sacred space of the Heart; it is built into our organism through nature's creative design. Without it we might never weave our way through the maze of illusion, doubt, and fear we have collected as we've traveled though life's events. The therapeutic variables described in this book do not depend on logic or on lofty degrees and titles. In fact, these very things sometimes get in the way—for we are the people of the Heart, not the mind! Therefore, we must resonate with the energies of the Heart in order to reach our full potential as relational beings. The true helper "comes from the Heart" and puts us back in touch with our own strengths, our own choices, our own dignity, and our own courage to pursue our lives.

The Heart is a temple, it is not an abode for idols!

HEART
(New York: Agni Yoga Society, 1975)

THE THERAPEUTIC
TRAITS

Regardless of your role in life—be it professional therapist, parent, supervisor, or friend—there are ten personal characteristics that accompany high effectiveness as a therapeutic person. These ten characteristics correlate with helping, as opposed to hindering, another person, regardless of your theoretical orientation if you have been trained as a professional therapist, and regardless of the extent of your love and caring for another if you are not a therapist.

From the work of Sigmund Freud to the growing transpersonal psychology movement that looks toward spiritual forms of healing; from the beginning of psychology all the way through its evolution into the newer forms of therapy; the characteristics of the self described in this book remain constant. In empirical counselor-effectiveness studies conducted during the 1960s and 1970s, professional counselors were rated on a scale of 1 to 5. An example of a high-functioning therapeutic individual would be someone who scores as high as a 3 on the variable scale. An example of a 5, the highest rating, would be a person who responds by helping the other person go deeper into self-exploration. A high response could also be a nonjudgmental comment that gives the troubled person a feeling of worthiness or *rightness* for experiencing what he or she is experiencing.

People who score 2 or below can actually be harmful agents in any type of interpersonal relationship. They cannot help others grow, and likely cause people in need to constrict rather than to expand, encouraging them to see themselves as bad, crazy, or sick. A toxic response would be one that causes a person to believe he or she is "bad" or too "tainted" to do the "right" thing.

The personal characteristics described in this book have been found to correlate with observable criteria of client improvement, including psychological tests, amount of time clients stay out of institutions, clients' self-reports, and therapist and supervisor ratings of clients. Even independently people list these characteristics in some form or another when reporting what qualities they seek in a helper. These ten variables hold constant, regardless of the diagnostic nature of a client's problem. They have been tested with alcoholics, schizophrenics, juvenile offenders, and college counselees, as well as many other kinds of groups.

It follows, then, that in relationships *other* than counselor-client relationships, the extent to which these characteristics are present determines the health or toxicity of interactions. For example, if these qualities are present in a family, a child will feel she can talk to her family members about anything, no matter how "loaded" the subject. However, if they are lacking, a child may lie to her parents out of fear of being misunderstood or punished for her self-disclosures during a crisis. The child with "toxic" parents (having too many unmet needs of their own) will likely seek someone outside the family to confide in, and the parents will learn of a child's difficulty only when it becomes apparent through "acting-out" behavior.

Emerging now from many years of extensive research in the field of counseling and psychotherapy, these counselor traits can be useful guides for any of us who wish to look at ourselves in terms of therapeutic relating. Those wishing to improve their counseling skills either formally or informally can benefit from a thorough understanding of these characteristics. By "thorough understanding," I do not mean merely "knowing about" these traits, but "knowing in your bones."

This involves understanding on your cognitive, emotional, and behavioral levels of being. This deeper wisdom comes from a higher *being* level: You as a helper need to align with your spiritual nature and not operate merely from your ego, that part of you that is concerned only with *your* needs, even sometimes at the expense of others.

From my own experiences as a counselor, parent, and friend, and from my observations of the many beautiful therapists I have encountered in my counselor-training experiences and people I have met on my path through life, I will attempt to describe these characteristics dynamically, in a way that I hope will bring them alive for the reader. For those of you who are already using your naturally therapeutic skills well, you will recognize yourselves in action— give or take a little, considering the unique style each of us possesses. Becoming aware that you have these characteristics, either budding or full-blown, can be an exciting experience and can build your potency as a helper, as well as expanding your effectiveness in every part of your life. You will also improve these skills through practice and validation from others, and you will see that you are indeed one who is helpful and transformative in other people's lives.

THE THERAPEUTIC TRAITS. The characteristics we will explore that correspond to effective therapeutic relating are empathy, genuineness, respect, self-disclosure, warmth, immediacy, concreteness, confrontation, potency, and self-actualization. These qualities are the essence of love in action; they reside at the core of our being. We all already have the potential to use these aspects of our love nature, provided we have removed any barriers to our just being real.

Most therapists who have been in practice for a while will tell you that therapy is not really a skill but an art— that being a good therapist is more like a way of being than a set of learned techniques. Anyone can memorize by rote a given set of rules, but the key to therapeutic relating lies in the power of the relationship itself. Somewhere within the helper and the person being helped a new phenomenon is created—not a summation of the parts but an integration of the whole. This process is the mysterious delight and pain of self-actualization. It is a two-way process: The helper changes and grows along with the seeker of help.

Many years ago a very wise supervisor told me always to remember: "Good counseling is made up of two very, very simple words that just happen to take a lifetime to fully comprehend—*support* and *challenge*." One without the other can be helpful but will seldom be sufficient to produce growth.

The therapeutic characteristics can indeed be broken down into three more or less distinct categories: support, challenge, and a total way of being. Empathy, genuineness, respect, self-disclosure, and warmth are basically supportive in their feeling tone, while immediacy, confrontation, and concreteness are ways of challenging people to be more real, truthful, and specific in their self-exploration. Potency and self-actualization measure a helper's overall manner and attitude that come from one's level of being rather than from one's training. In fact, research indicates that we cannot train to become more potent or self-actualizing; life itself teaches us these personality characteristics.

SUPPORT MUST PRECEDE CHALLENGE.
A warm, supportive, and genuine climate must exist before people who are troubled will feel enough trust in you to move into the real problem areas of their lives, and before they can read your challenging messages as helpful. This is especially true of alcoholics or people whose problems, for one reason or another, society labels as "immoral," who will automatically expect you to condemn them.

24

In the pages that follow we will concentrate first on the *supportive* traits, then move on to the deeper stages of good counseling, the attempt to *challenge* the individual seeking help. And finally we will attempt to capture the "flavor" of the therapist who is both potent and self-actualizing so that we may have a model of a high being level.

But can something as artistic, ethereal, and creative as therapeutic relating be taught as skill development? If good counseling is indeed dependent upon such ill-defined phrases as "a total way of being" or "just being naturally therapeutic," what on earth is this book attempting to teach? It sounds as if there is nothing to *do,* only someone to *be.*

My conviction is that we have entered into a paradox (a word that seems most aptly to describe life anyway). We must develop skills in order to discover and bring to fruition the creativity within us. Just as an acorn has the innate potential to become an oak tree, we, simply by being ourselves, have the inherent ability to be creative and therapeutic. If anything, we have trained out of ourselves our naturally therapeutic ways by becoming (often of necessity) frightened, defensive, closed up, and sometimes even rigid and unbending. Good counselor training may involve nothing more than merely letting go and being what we were intended to be in the first place—before we got so scared.

EMPATHY

Empathy is the quality that enables us to perceive another's experience and then to communicate that perception back to the individual. As listener I hear you as you speak to me, and although I do not experience your feelings, I begin to have a mind-picture of the essence of what you are describing. I share my perceptions with you in "I" language (statements about *my* perceptions rather than statements about *you* and what you ought to do).

EMPATHY IN THE COUNSELOR-CLIENT RELATIONSHIP

EMPATHY IN ACTION.

Client: (head down, arms crossed, squeezing her chest in a constricted fashion) I just can't . . . (sighing) . . . can't seem to take it. They all want me to . . . oh, I don't see how I can . . .

Counselor: I hear your pain Mary. It's as though your family is strangling you. . . . Some sort of struggle for breath is what I'm sensing. I see you looking sad and desperate, with your fists clenched . . . and your breath seems constricted as you talk about it. Am I hearing you correctly?

As the counselor talks, he has drawn closer to his client, animated and involved in what he is feeling and attempting to communicate. He even imitates the client's behavior at times during this interchange, in the way he has perceived it.

PROCESS. During this conversation the counselor has attempted to get "out of his head" (analyzing or interpreting) and just experience the essence of his client in the here and now. He has listened for the "process" instead of hearing only the "content" of the client's message: He has listened to the whole person within the context of her own unique existence, rather than listening only to her words. He looks at nonverbal behavior and the messages under the surface of what she says. As the counselor begins to gain a strong feeling of understanding, he becomes more active in the session and moves into sharing this with the client. He **reflects** and **mirrors** * for the client—meaning that he feeds back to her what he notices. We think we know ourselves so well, but usually we know our friends better than we know ourselves! Often we are not aware of our verbal or nonverbal behavior patterns and messages until someone points them out to us. Reflecting and mirroring are two techniques that are natural to the involved counselor.

In the above example of empathy in action, the counselor is also imparting **nonjudgmental feedback**—telling the client what he experiences in relation to her, using "I" statements. These are statements about himself rather than about the client: "I hear your pain . . . ," "I see you looking . . . ," and so on. Nonjudgmental feedback is an important concept in counseling, because the client is free to accept or reject what the counselor is perceiving. She does not take his statements as *facts* about her that she must defend against or accept. Instead they are statements about

*Words that have a technical meaning in the field of psychotherapy are in boldface and appear in the Glossary.

him in relation to her, which are by their very nature truthful statements. A counselor cannot know the facts about a client's experience, but he can tell her the facts and feelings about how *he* perceives her experience.

Empathy in action is often quite graphic and expresses itself in fantasy images. Notice the counselor's graphic depiction of "strangling" and "constriction." The counselor's mind-pictures match the client's nonverbal behavior, and when fed back to the client in such a dramatic manner, they can serve as a clarifier of unexamined feelings on the part of the client.

A counselor's perceptions may be wrong. One is never an expert on another's life. This point cannot be stressed enough. The client is the only true expert on herself. If the counselor is wrong in his perceptions, the client will communicate this: She will either tell the counselor directly that he is off, or she will simply not pick up on what he is saying. If he is on target, the client may gain a new understanding of her situation. He has created the possibility for a therapeutic moment through the use of empathy. However, the client may reject his perceptions even if he is right. She is free to do so. The healing element in operation here is not the accuracy of the counselor's perceptions, but his intense involvement with the client. The communication that is important is taking place on a subterranean, therapeutic level.

OPPOSITE OF EMPATHY IN ACTION.
Some examples of behavior directly opposed to the practice of this variable would include the following:

(1) A counselor who presents his own perceptions and **projections** as *facts* about the client. This confuses the client and takes her further away from her own reality.

(2) A counselor who analyzes a client's situation or dynamics as though he is (or could be) the expert on the client's inner experience.

(3) A counselor who is not "present" with the client in the here and now. He is not free to be with the client where *she* is because he is instead using his energy to handle his own needs.

Because it happens so often, I will elaborate briefly on this last example. The inability to be wholly with a client in the present happens most often when the counselor is preoccupied and reactive around **unfinished business** of his own during the session; when the counselor has a great need to be right and uses his energy to "lay his theories on" the client and attempt to prove them to her; or when the counselor spends a great deal of time talking about or listening to the client's past history—content "way out there somewhere"—which can be an avoidance mechanism to keep from painful here-and-now material.

IMPLICATIONS FOR THE ALCOHOLIC CLIENT.

The use of empathy in action enables the alcoholic to feel that you're present with her and that you are sincerely interested in trying to discover her specific reality. As I mentioned earlier, the perceptions that you share with your alcoholic client may be incorrect; they may be perceptions about *you* that you're projecting onto her, or you just may have heard her inaccurately. This is not important as long as you state perceptions as perceptions. As you begin to feel free to be with your client in the here and now, you will notice that you are most often amazingly close to her reality as you attempt to share with her your understanding of her world. The real healing that is occurring—the true therapeutic agent at work—is your atti-tude of committed interest and your attempt to understand your client. Her sensing that you care so intently and are not afraid to get involved with her emotionally is the real healing factor. This is the Heart in operation. This idea is so simple, yet so very difficult for most counselors to grasp.

So many of us get so entangled in trying to be right, we forget that the workings of the Heart, though invisible, are doing the real work of healing. Correct perceptions can sometimes be helpful, but your committed attitude of genuine empathy is more healing than any correct interpretation could ever be. And the need to be right on your part can be extremely unhelpful to the client. Experienced alcoholism counselors often report that understanding is the one thing the alcoholic talks of needing the most. You may be the first person in her entire drinking—and nondrinking—life to make a sincere attempt to understand her. The impact of empathy in action on her battered self-esteem will be profound and healing.

A PRACTICE EXERCISE FOR YOU.* Practice how you would use empathy in action in the following situation.

Client: After I've had my second or third drink, I begin talking to myself about not drinking any more. Can you imagine that? Talking to myself! I go back and forth, back and forth. I put the bottle down, walk outside, talk to myself, *cuss* at myself, on and on (sigh). Then I wind up saying I'll just have one more . . . and well . . . there I go . . . down into the deep pit again, sometimes not even waking up again for days (puts head down in his hands).

Counselor:

*When doing the practice exercises throughout the book, it would be helpful to make a mental note of your very first reaction to each hypothetical client before you begin to experiment with different ways you might choose to respond. Becoming aware of what it is we do *now* before we set out to change or improve our responses is the first step in discovering how therapeutic we are or which qualities we need to develop.

EMPATHY IN
EVERYDAY LIFE

And now let's take a situation between a parent and child to demonstrate how this same therapeutic process can unfold in everyday life. Empathy in action will lead to openness and warmth between a parent and his son, and this will enable the son to come to the parent the next time he experiences a crisis. When parents and children keep the lines of communication open, most children will grow up amidst the ambiguities of life without having to hide things from the parents; such hiding can lead to terrible family consequences.

EMPATHY IN ACTION.

Son: (entering the room with a cowed look on his face, frightened, yet obviously needing to talk) Dad . . . I think I might be in a little trouble at school. I think my coach is going to call you.

Dad: (gently) Well, son, come on over here and sit down with me. Let's talk about it.

Son: (comes over to sit down and begins to cry)

Dad: (sees the fear and embraces his son) Now, John, you know that I love you and always will, no matter what's happened.

Son: Oh, Dad. I've really let you down. I'm so ashamed, and I just want to get this off my chest (breaks down again).

Dad: (allows his son some time to feel his feelings, waiting quietly, with no sense of alarm) Well, whenever you're ready to talk, I'm listening.

Son: Dad, Coach caught a bunch of us smoking a joint behind the basketball court after practice yesterday. It's true, Dad. I did it (bursts into tears).

Dad: My God, John. You must feel awful! What a mess (takes son in his arms and embraces him). Go ahead, son. Let it out. You seem really terrified. (He waits while John cries more deeply. During this few moments of supporting John's need just to cry in his father's arms, the father has time also to collect his own feelings to avoid an *over*reaction to this news. It is natural for the father to have a reaction, but *over*reaction is not necessary.) Go ahead now. Tell me what all this is about. (There is concern in the voice, but not a trace of anger.)

Son: Well, Bill and Terry have been smoking dope pretty much, Dad. But I haven't. I promise. I haven't. I've known they were doing it, but I've just not been into it. Dad, this is the truth. I'm not a druggie. I just . . . I just . . . for some stupid reason decided to try it. We were all just cutting up. . . . Oh, it all just happened so fast. . . . I just . . . well, I just *did* it! It was so stupid.

Dad: (silent, while he absorbs this information) John, do you think *I* think you're into drugs?

Son: Well, I don't know, Dad. Coach says I've got to go to a drug abuse group now every week for six weeks! Dad, I'm not a drug abuser! I admit I've tried it before—but only one other time. Dad, it's everywhere. All the kids—well, nearly all the guys have at least tried it a few times. Please, Dad, will you believe me?

Dad: Of course I believe you. Why shouldn't I? Your mother and I see that you're making good grades. You're doing great in your sports. You don't seem to be a druggie to me. Now, come on. Let's talk about this. Just see if you can calm down (gives John another hug). This drug abuse group doesn't sound all that bad, now does it? Sounds like a lot of your friends will be there (a little humor here).

Son: Oh, Dad. I'm so relieved. I thought you'd kill me.

Dad: Well, Son, I'm certainly not pleased about this. But I must tell you that I got expelled for three days one time in high school for getting caught smoking a cigar! I guess in today's world joints are pretty common. I'm no idiot, you know. I do live in the real world. The main thing is that you learn something from all this.

PROCESS. The father is able to absorb his own feelings while his son is releasing his emotions. During this time the space between them becomes one of the Heart. Although the father is honest about being disturbed (obviously his son has been caught doing not only a drug, but an illegal one at that), he allows his feelings of love for his son and understanding about temptations we all encounter to come to the forefront. The father knows this is not the time for a lecture on morality, nor a threat of some punitive action. He sees that his son is already experiencing the natural consequences of his thoughtless act.

Natural consequences are often enough for a child to feel. Parents may forget this and try to lay other punishments on top of what life is already dishing out. These unnecessary reprimands can often turn a normal adolescent into a lying, fearful person, doubting whether or not his parents are safe people with whom to discuss "the real world."

OPPOSITE OF EMPATHY IN ACTION. A father who lacks empathy might respond to the same situation on the basis of his own philosophy or fears about the use of drugs that are completely out of touch with what life is like for teenagers today. Many parents live in denial of the fact that all kids experience plenty of opportunities to use drugs; and some parents try to take a strong stand that, to the young people of today, seems totally inappropriate. Parents may also not realize that every child who experiments with a drug is not an addict, nor is he likely to ruin his life. When parents take a hard-line approach, young people may resign themselves to the fact that they cannot safely discuss these matters with their parents. They look elsewhere for confidants and for the truth about drugs, and unfortunately this lack of communication between parents and children sometimes leads children to further abuse of drugs or other harmful activities.

Here's an example of the opposite of empathy in action.

Son: Dad, I think I'm in a little trouble at school (sighing and acting fearful and depressed). You're going to get a call from Coach.

Dad: Well, I better hear about it. What's happened? (He looks intently at his son.)

Son: (comes over and sits down and begins to cry)

Dad: (silent)

Son: Dad, I've got something to tell you. Oh, it's awful. I really didn't mean to . . . Well, Dad, I got caught smoking pot behind the basketball court after practice yesterday. I was with . . .

Dad: (interrupting) What? What did you say? Smoking pot? My God, that's illegal! Can you even imagine the trouble you're in? That's an illegal drug! My son? Oh, my God. What a mess. Well, I suppose by now everyone knows. Well, this is really awful. What's going to happen next?

Son: Dad, please . . . please listen. I'm not a druggie. . . . I just . . .

Dad: Not a druggie, huh? Then *why* are you using drugs? That certainly makes no sense. And besides, this is just so stupid. How am I going to deal with this? What in the world am I going to say to your coach? Surely you don't expect me to stick up for you! (The son leaves, goes to his room, and shuts the door.)

IMPLICATIONS FOR THE FAMILY. Because of American society's ambivalence surrounding the use of drugs, the above scenes occur frequently in normal as well as troubled families. The parents' attitude toward the issue of drug use is the key to whether or not there can be dialogue. In the first instance it is easy for us to see that this young person has the advantage of an open-minded, yet truthful and concerned father who is willing to face this issue head-on and deal not only with the content of the problem, but also with the son's feelings of failure and stupidity. This situation can lead to a family healing. At this point there is no need for the father to be concerned that his son is in grave trouble with drugs; however, the son's behavior has served as a warning. If John regards the consequences of his act as his "lesson"—assuming that he really is in no serious trouble with drugs—this will probably be the last of such behavior. The father is going to support John's attendance in the drug abuse group. Here, if there *is* a real problem, the teacher will undoubtedly pick up on it.

In the second example this son and his father are already in trouble. They cannot communicate about anything "loaded" because the father is *re*active, exerting more energy on venting his own dogma, and on *his* fear of being "found out," than on being concerned about his son. The father's contamination has led to toxic communication.

A PRACTICE EXERCISE FOR YOU. Practice how you would use empathy in action in the following family situation.

Daughter: Mom! I've got to talk to you! (She bursts into tears.)

Mom: Honey, what on earth has happened?

Daughter: Oh, Mom. I'm in terrible trouble, and I don't know what to do. The school principal's accused me of stealing something from the women's lounge, and Mother, I didn't do it. I'm so scared. He's trying to make me confess!

Mom:

GENUINENESS

Genuineness is the characteristic that allows us to be freely ourselves—it is nonphoniness, non–role playing, nondefensiveness. Our outer words and behavior match our inner feelings.

GENUINENESS IN THE COUNSELOR-CLIENT RELATIONSHIP

GENUINENESS IN ACTION.

Client: (fighting back tears) I'm just not going to think about it anymore . . . losing the kid and all. . . . It's just useless to think about it!

Counselor: (moves closer to client, touching him on the arm, obviously deeply moved) Johnny, I'm feeling very sad too about what happened to your son . . . and seeing your deep, deep hurt.

Client: (breaks down and weeps)

Counselor: (quietly shares this moment with client, responding nonverbally like a nurturing parent)

PROCESS. The counselor ignored the defensiveness of the client (the pretended toughness) and moved in as a human being. She responded with her real feelings of the moment in a way that kept the client in touch with *his* real feelings of grief and hurt. The result was therapeutic: a **catharsis** and another small step toward completing an unfinished grief process. Unexpressed grief or anger takes up a tremendous amount of psychic and physical energy. If we could see this energy in action, it would look as if a person were forcefully holding something in—arms crossed, fists clenched, pressing his stomach against his backbone. As long as energy is being used in this way, it is not free to flow toward the actual solving of problems in daily life.

Griefwork is a natural process that follows a fairly predictable pattern for most people: from shock and denial of the loss, into anger, then real mourning, and a letting go of the pain. In the next stages one gradually begins to accept the loss and turn toward new possibilities in life once again. This process cannot be hurried through. Nor can it be held onto for too long without creating negative effects on the psyche. The client must release the anger and hurt that come up. Then he can go on and say good-bye to the person he has lost and be free again to live a life devoid of the loved or needed one. Although the stages of grief are painful, they are normal and should be experienced openly among loved ones who can understand and therapists who are supportive. It is also human to try to avoid grief by hiding it from others or denying the feelings when they arise. If people in the client's life assist him in running from these natural feelings of mourning and anger, **morbid grief** can set in, which manifests itself through several types of unhealthy symptoms (see Glossary for further information).

OPPOSITE OF GENUINENESS IN ACTION. Many counselors believe they must stay in a "professional" role when working with a client. Unfortunately, psychoanalytic theory has supported this notion for years by training psychiatrists to use objectivity as a way to distance themselves, never touching a patient and keeping their own personality out of the way while the patient free-associates in a prone position with no eye contact. A counselor with this professional mind-set might have said to Johnny in the previous example: "I understand your feelings, Johnny. Now what was it you wanted to talk about today?" This response is toxic; it takes the focus off the emotional feelings and puts the client into his intellect, pushing him away from the real issue—his need to express his heartfelt sadness and pain at the loss of his son.

The genuine counselor is not afraid to involve herself with her client's human feelings. Whether the feeling is sadness, anger, or joy, the counselor expresses herself to her client in very much the same way she would with a friend outside the counseling relationship.

Honesty is necessary even when it may be very difficult for the therapist. For example, sometimes a therapist has a negative reaction to people with a certain personality type (such as depressed people who have very little motivation or energy, or people who have excess energy and pace nervously). Often the loving thing for the therapist to do is to level with the client and simply tell the truth—that a certain behavior is getting in the way and hindering the counselor's therapeutic ability. This affords an opportunity for the therapist and client to work through these feelings together. If they cannot, the therapist should make a referral, acknowledging these feelings as her own and making clear that they are not a reflection on the client.

However, there are some restraints inherent in a counseling relationship that are necessary to keep the client safe—and which make the professional relationship different from a friendship. There needs to be limited contact, a lack of social engagement, and a lack of opportunity for romance. These boundaries protect the relationship: They maintain the objectivity necessary for effective and ethical psychotherapy; they are not ways for therapists to hide from clients! A counselor who draws these kinds of boundaries around a therapeutic relationship is in no way failing to be *real* with her client.

If sexual or romantic feelings should arise between a counselor and client and can't be worked through without the possibility of acting-out behaviors, the relationship should not continue under the strains of a counselor-client situation. If it becomes clear that the relationship is to become a personal one, the issue should not even be further discussed until many months after the professional relationship has ended. Time and experience have taught those of us in professional helping roles that it is too easy for clients to confuse love or attraction with their need for a helper, parent, or healer, whom they may perceive as being above them or capable of rescuing them. Freud used the word *transference* to describe the client's feelings for the therapist and *countertransference* to describe the feelings the therapist develops for the client. These feelings can become a healthy part of therapy if the counselor maintains a professional stance and does not manipulate the client or give mixed messages.

Expressions of genuine feeling that a client is beautiful, desirable, or lovable can be very healing to a person who has never felt much acceptance or self-esteem. And they can be shared. However, the therapist must be careful that these feelings are under no circumstances interpreted as being any type of a "come-on." Genuineness can become toxic if the therapist ignores the necessary boundaries of the relationship.

Among friends who are seeking help from each other, this same boundary must apply. When someone is suffering, especially as a result of a primary relationship breakup, and comes to us for help, that person is vulnerable and in need of reassurance and attention. It is not the time for us to blurt out our own feelings of attraction or promises of a deeper, more personal relationship in the future. These types of communications can be misinterpreted and can create confusion; indeed, they sometimes result in fiascos of melodramatic proportions.

IMPLICATIONS FOR THE ALCOHOLIC CLIENT.

Genuineness is crucial in alcoholism counseling. An alcoholic client or family members will not remain in counseling with a phony, role-playing counselor. People from addictive homes are especially sensitive to dishonesty and phoniness. They have a history of experience with such behavior and have developed a "sixth sense" for it.

Moreover, alcoholics with long drinking histories and their families have been shunned by society in many ways; they have low opinions of themselves before they ever get to someone for help. They often project their self-doubt onto others and may see mirrored back a therapist who despises or misunderstands them. It is crucial that alcoholic clients learn very early on that you are someone who keeps your word and says what you mean. They need to know they can risk being real with you; and they will know this only if you are real with them. If ever during the therapy process you feel angry at or hurt by your clients, or dislike their treatment of you in any way, you must acknowledge these feelings to them openly with "I" statements. They have already picked up on how you feel anyway. Remember, they are masters at masking feelings, having learned the hard way all their drinking life. They will recognize this behavior when they see it. By being yourself you enable them to make contact with you. Genuine contact with another individual is the most beautiful gift you can give an alcoholic person or a member of a dysfunctional family who has seldom felt understood or intimate with anyone.

A PRACTICE EXERCISE FOR YOU. Practice how you would respond in a genuine way with the following alcoholic client.

Client: How've you been anyway? Thought I'd stop by. I stood you up for the last couple of times, but you know how it goes. . . . Sometimes it gets busy and . . .

Counselor:

GENUINENESS IN EVERYDAY LIFE

Now let's take this same trait, genuineness, and put it into a nonprofessional therapeutic situation, so that we can see how these same principles hold true in any relationship—no matter how intimate. Many professionals feel it is impossible to be objective and truly helpful toward someone we love and are close to in everyday life. I disagree. I believe that with the proper understanding and motivation to become a good listener, we can all learn to be therapeutic, discovering how genuineness (as well as the other traits described in this book) can aid us in helping one another. Let's look at the most important relationship in many of our lives—our primary love relationship—in order to see the therapeutic value of genuineness. For a lover to be an effective counselor, both parties may need to expand somewhat beyond their ordinary roles. And I can think of nothing more therapeutic for such a relationship! If even *one* member of a couple can get into his or her higher self for a while, this will automatically aid the other in seeing or hearing something more clearly.

GENUINENESS IN ACTION BETWEEN HUSBAND AND WIFE (OR LIFE PARTNERS).

Wife: I'm at my wit's end. I simply cannot get along with this guy they've said I have to supervise at work! It's driving me crazy. This is now the fourth week we've been at it, and I just don't see any improvement. I'm getting hopeless.

Husband: I'm sorry this is so hard on you, Jennie. Have you told him how you feel?

Wife: No. It would freak him out. He wouldn't understand.

Husband: Jennie. That's not like you. I know you well. You've never had trouble speaking your mind. What's really wrong?

Wife: Now don't *you* start telling me how bossy I am!

Husband: (not willing to buy into this accusation with an emotional reaction) Jennie, I didn't say you were bossy. I wasn't even thinking that. I just know your strengths, and keeping your feelings to yourself about such matters isn't like you. I've always experienced you as direct, but loving and to the point—a no-nonsense lady. Come on, now. I'm on your side. What's up?

Wife: Oh, Eddie, I'm scared. This guy is really bringing things up in me. He does everything just right. And yet . . . well, there's something I don't feel good about.

Husband: Can you tell me more about the feeling he brings up in you? Maybe I can help you sort this out.

Wife: He reminds me of some old . . . some very old feeling, or some person. I don't know.

Husband: What kind of animal or something does he remind you of? Maybe that will provide a clue.

Wife: (without a moment's hesitation) A piranha! Yes, that's it! A man-eating fish!

Husband: Wow! That's pretty devastating. Are you afraid of him, Jennie? Is he threatening to you in some way?

Wife: No! Absolutely not! I'm not a bit threatened by him. No matter how smart and well educated he is, I know I'm good at what I do. I've been around quite awhile now and have *much* more experience than he does.

Husband: (pulling her close to him and looking into her eyes with love) Jennie, you *are* good at what you do. In fact, you're a master at your profession. I've seen you work in the most unfavorable conditions, and you're a real trooper—always performing at your peak. Jennie, I love you as a husband, but I wouldn't lie to you about this. You're tops!

Wife: (falls into his arms and begins to weep) Oh, Eddie, thanks. You really do understand, don't you?

PROCESS. Because of their intimate and lengthy history, Eddie was able to tell Jennie the truth about her professionalism. And she believed him, because she knew that he really had seen her in operation. In addition Eddie picked up on her fear of this new employee's masterful qualities and the threat he posed to Jennie—perhaps about future advancements or assignments. Instead of confronting these fears head-on—which might have been humiliating to

Jennie—he let her know how good she is and helped her to recognize in the most loving way possible her own lack of confidence.

This type of validation is the most meaningful when received from people who know us very well. We are less afraid that we may have "pulled the wool over their eyes" through some form of short-term greatness. We know that a life partner will be able to see through any kind of cover-up on our part and that he or she will really see us as we are. Therefore, we can accept reassurance from this person, which will in turn allay our fears and help build our confidence.

OPPOSITE OF GENUINENESS IN ACTION.
When a therapeutic relationship involves life partners, the listener must be very careful not to use the other's vulnerability as a way to play out some of his *own* unmet needs or expectations within the relationship. Here is an example of how this might have occurred in the previous situation.

Wife: I'm fed up with this new guy at work. I'm supposed to supervise him, and even though he does everything right, there's tension between us. I don't know, maybe it's me. . . . It's just that . . .

Husband: Yeah, I bet he sees you as a bossy lady, right?

Wife: What do you mean "bossy"?

Husband: Well, *I* certainly have trouble being heard by you. Like last night. I said I wanted to make love, and it was really important to me. You weren't even nice about it. You're never even *around* lately. I bet *he* feels like you're never there for him, either. You're always the one in charge, right? Maybe you should try . . .

Wife: Forget it! (She walks out of the room to call a
          friend.)

Eddie used his wife's situation with her employee as an opportunity to unload his own pent-up anger about some of his unfulfilled expectations. His role thus became toxic rather than therapeutic. His strong feelings of resentment toward his wife should have been saved for a more appropriate moment. If he felt unable to put them aside, he should have ended the interaction and gently recommended that his wife go elsewhere for support on this issue (which she ended up doing anyway!). This way the relationship would have retained its integrity.

IMPLICATIONS FOR LIFE PARTNERS WHO COUNSEL EACH OTHER.

If one partner is always the counselor and the other the counselee, there is trouble in the relationship. There is probably an "over-under," one-upmanship dynamic, in which one person feels like a child, the other an adult. Usually this produces a real problem that may bring the couple into professional relationship counseling.

But when exchanged between each mate and used only during crises or dramatic life changes, the roles of therapist and client can be strengthening both to the individuals and to the relationship as a whole. If the partners become tangled up, or confuse each other, a third party can help provide neutral feedback—or they may just know they need to stop the process and seek help elsewhere. The listener must be able to suspend all other issues during a counseling situation and maintain a free space in the Heart, so as to be a genuine and clear sounding board.

A PRACTICE EXERCISE FOR YOU.

You are just leaving for work and your wife, Maria, comes running to the driveway and asks you to stop. She needs to talk to you.

You: What is it, Maria?

Maria: I can't believe this has happened. That old friend of mine I absolutely hated in college just called, and she's on her way over. She's the one who ran off with my boyfriend at the time. How can I see her when I have so much anger toward her I've never expressed? What can I do? I'm scared!

You:

RESPECT

Respect means communicating to others our sincere belief that they, like everyone, possess the inherent strength and capacity to make it in life; they have the right to choose their own alternatives and make their own decisions. Behind the quality of respect is the belief that all human beings are equal and all have the right to choose their own destiny.

RESPECT IN THE COUNSELOR-CLIENT RELATIONSHIP

RESPECT IN ACTION.

Client: I just want to divorce my wife and get busy forgetting about the whole mess! But I can't do it. I really need to stay in there and take care of her, but I can't seem to do that either. Whew, the whole thing's just got me trapped. What do you think I ought to do . . . divorce her?

Counselor: (concerned) Golly, Bill, I can tell you're torn in two on this. Sounds like there's one part of you that needs to stay, but another part of you that wants to get out for good.

Client: Yeah. That's sure it, all right.

Counselor: Could you go on and talk for a while about how part of you wants to get out? What does this part of you feel like?

Client: It feels like . . .

Counselor: Just a minute, Bill, say, "I feel like . . ." instead of "It." Start your sentences with "I." Go ahead now.

Client: Okay. I feel trapped! I want out.

Counselor: Go on, Bill, go on now. Put your *feelings* into what you're saying.

Client: (getting agitated) I feel trapped! *I feel trapped!* I want out! Really out! Away from the whole goddamn mess! (He puts his head down in his hands.)

Counselor: (quiet for a while, allowing the client to absorb his experience) Now, Bill . . . (softly) What about that other side of you, the side that needs to stay? Can you talk about that with me a minute?

PROCESS. The counselor has not responded to Bill's request to give him the answer to his dilemma, nor has he accepted Bill's perceived powerlessness. Instead the counselor has fed back to the client his observation that the client seems to have two feelings simultaneously. The counselor wants to help the client clarify for himself what each of these feelings really is. The client thinks he is powerless. Notice that he begins by saying "I can't" and "the whole thing's just got me trapped." Both of these statements say the power is "out there" and "I am victim. I am helpless." By asking the client to talk about each emotion separately using "I" statements instead of "it" statements, the counselor enables the client to stay closer to his real feelings and to take responsibility for them. When a client fully experiences both sides of a split in a safe counseling environment, he often discovers which side is a "want" and which side is an "ought to." This can be a clarifying insight that can lead to action. He may discover which side contains the most power, or which side is really him and which side is merely his *idea* of himself. Once he sees both feelings more clearly, he will be better able to accept them and make choices for himself that are closer to his own reality. When the energy that has been stored up inside him around these split feelings is released, he will experience an amazing feeling of integration or balance.

In the above example the counselor has put the responsibility of making choices back onto the client, where the power actually resides. The therapist has an attitude of respect for the individual, enabling the client to discover in a nonpunitive way both his own power and his own responsibility for his decisions.

OPPOSITE OF RESPECT IN ACTION. The most obvious example of the opposite of respect in action would be if the same counselor had attempted to give Bill *the* answer: "Oh, no, Bill, you don't want to divorce your wife"; or, "Well, I wouldn't divorce her if I were you, Bill"; or if the counselor had ignored Bill's split feelings and attempted to preach to him about what he "should" be feeling.

In any case the counselor would have come away "the expert" on Bill's experience, and Bill would have missed an opportunity to discover more about his own reality. He would be further confirmed in his fear that he is powerless and hopeless. ("I can never learn to manage my life like this smart counselor can!") As a guide, your role is to help lead another person to the core of *his* being, not yours.

Otherwise you may be in his way. Within him resides the true place of healing—his heart, where he knows his real feelings about everything.

IMPLICATIONS FOR THE ALCOHOLIC CLIENT.

Respect in action helps alcoholic clients take realistic responsibility for themselves. A person suffering from alcoholism often wavers between feelings of powerlessness and feelings of omnipotence. Neither extreme is realistic. Respect in action does not pamper, nor does it punish. It acknowledges your alcoholic clients as people who learn in their relationship with you what their actual strengths and weaknesses are. You enable them to discover these for themselves by offering a nonjudgmental, clarifying lens through which they can see themselves more clearly. Respect in action gives such clients hope—hope that they may actually be worthwhile individuals with the ability to make choices and govern their own lives! Chances are they have gotten out of touch with this possibility.

A PRACTICE EXERCISE FOR YOU.

Practice how you would use respect in action in the following situation.

Client: Boy, I've just got to level with my boss about this alcohol problem . . . but I'm too chicken to do it. I started to fifteen times this week, but something stopped me every time—how the hell can I get up the guts to do it?

Counselor:

RESPECT IN EVERYDAY LIFE

RESPECT IN ACTION.

Let's see how respect in action would look when someone is asked to help a friend who is troubled and needing to talk. Here the friend, Jody, is in a codependent relationship that is causing her to experience both emotional and physical symptoms. As is often the case, she is participating as a codependent without consciously realizing it. Jody has been abused both physically and emotionally since the beginning of her fourteen-year marriage. She has simply taken it as it comes, never dreaming of doing anything about it. But after a particularly abusive incident the night before, she decides to talk to her friend, Dan. She is in crisis.

Jody: I don't know why I've decided to talk about this. It's no different now than ever before. I love Bill. I know he doesn't mean it. But I hate him too. I can't stand living like this!

Dan: So you love him and you hate him at the same time? I think I can understand that. It's not such a cut-and-dried thing, is it?

Jody: (sighs in relief) You *know*, don't you? Have you ever been in love with someone who hurt you? And stayed anyway?

Dan: Oh, yes. I did that one time. I can put blinders on when I want to, especially when I really care about someone. Did something in particular happen that caused you to want to talk to me about it?

PROCESS. In just a few words Dan has already let Jody know that he understands why she may not want to leave her husband even though this man is obviously abusive, unaware, and does not show signs of changing. Yet Dan has let her know that he absolutely does not question her right to make her own choice. Now she is free to explore both sides of how she feels without feeling judged or looked down upon for who she has been. She feels safe unveiling a delicate part of her psyche to this caring friend. This is the beginning of a therapeutic experience for Jody— and for Dan as well.

Therapeutic relationships work both ways. In our hearts we live in brotherhood and sisterhood with each other. We are the happiest and most fulfilled when our experience of being therapeutic matches with someone feeling blessed by our presence. At this moment we've entered a very high spiritual relationship—one of complete integrity—that can happen only when deep truth is being shared. Our respect for one another validates each of our unique experiences; we truly honor each other as equal beings and understand that we are all here to share life together, no matter how each of us might choose to live it (so long as our choices do not impinge upon the freedom of others). We live in true comradeship. This sense of belongingness and mutual respect is how heaven begins on earth!

Of all the counselor traits respect holds the highest value—for without it one cannot begin to be a therapeutic person. It is the *basis* of healing. If we cannot respect another, the other traits that make up therapeutic relating become a sham.

OPPOSITE OF RESPECT IN ACTION. When we decide things for others, we are not respecting them. We are telling them they aren't smart enough or awake enough to handle their own lives. And soon they may start believing us! When we are low in respect we can become dogmatic or narrow-minded. This happens when we are afraid or uncertain. At times like this we need to believe that our way of thinking is the only way, which keeps us safe from having to explore new territory. We prefer the status quo. And the more frightened we are, the narrower our belief system will become. We need to realize that this can happen to any of us, no matter how loving we are, particularly when our own issues come up and we ourselves are not clear. Here would be an example of how we might become disrespectful, even with a very close friend:

Jody: I don't know why I've decided to talk about this with you, but I guess I just need to blow off some steam. . . . You know how much I love Bill, don't you? And I know he never means to harm me. It's just so sad. He hits me from time to time, and last night, for some reason, it was worse. I hate him when he acts like this . . . yet I've no doubt that he loves the kids and me. It's just that horrible temper of his! Oh, I'm so confused.

Dan: Well, I certainly wouldn't stay with someone who hits me. And to *think*—you've stayed with him all these years, knowing he's abusive! Frankly, I think you ought to leave.

Jody: We've got a lot going for us, you know. I don't see . . .

Dan: Well, most people wouldn't put up with this stuff. Can't you see that? You ought to just leave . . . or make *him* leave.

Jody: But what about the kids? He's a good father. And what about all that we've worked for all these years? Am I sick because I love my husband? I can't be that sure. . . .

Dan: (sighs in frustration) Jody, I don't want to discuss this anymore. After you leave him, or do something about this, come on back and we'll talk some more.

IMPLICATIONS FOR CLOSE FRIENDS.
Jody is being asked to deny her feelings of ambivalence—
simultaneous love and hate for her husband of many years.
On the surface this conversation may seem like a sound
one, leading Jody to make a needed decision. However,
upon deeper examination we can see that this kind of
advice giving is ill timed and based on insufficient information. Is the abuse the only part of the relationship? Is
everything about it dysfunctional? Is Bill drinking or drug-
ging and only abusive when intoxicated? It is all too premature for Dan to be making these kinds of suggestions—even
though the marriage may indeed end in divorce.

Both Jody and Bill need time and help from a professional in sorting out this dysfunctional situation before a
decision is made. This couple have had children and together have a long history behind them; they seem to love
each other. The marriage could be saved and could provide
a transformative experience for them both. It is too soon to
discount the whole fourteen years, even though the situation is grave and quite negative. Dan activated Jody's defenses when he all but called her stupid for staying with her
husband all these years. Instead of helping her clarify her own
feelings, he acted as if he had *the* right answer to her
dilemma. Dan is certainly clear that *he* would not have
stayed. But how do we ever really know what is right for
another?

A PRACTICE EXERCISE FOR YOU.
See how you might respond to a friend in need in the situation
presented below. Remember to notice your first reactions—
even though you may choose not to actually act on them.

Friend: Have you got a minute? I really need to bounce
something off you. Something just awful has happened.

You: Sure, go ahead.

Friend: Fred and I learned last night that Sarah may be pregnant. She's our daughter, and we didn't even know she and Tom were living together! And now we've had this dropped in our lap. Can you believe it? She's only twenty-one. After all we've done to try to make a *good* family! I went to our minister this morning and just cried and cried. I don't know what to do or even what to say to Sarah. I'm so ashamed even telling you about this.

You:

SELF-DISCLOSURE

Self-disclosure is the act of sharing our own feelings, attitudes, and experiences with someone in the effort to help that person. Self-disclosure must be meaningful and pertinent both in content and context in order to be therapeutic. It should be used with discretion, an accurate sense of timing and appropriateness, and with some idea of how the person in need will make use of the material we share. It should never be used to fulfill our own needs to confess or vent feelings. Therapeutic self-disclosure is an art, one that can be developed. It is the ability to use our self and our experiences as instruments of healing.

SELF-DISCLOSURE IN THE COUNSELOR-CLIENT RELATIONSHIP

SELF-DISCLOSURE IN ACTION.

Client: (crying) I just can't let my wife see me like this . . . She would think I'm such a stupid weakling!

Counselor: (moving closer to client, with tenderness) I know how you feel, Joe. I have a lot of trouble letting my wife see me when I'm hurting. When I do, I feel weak and stupid too. I've been told all my life that men are strong, and they don't cry . . . haven't you?

Client: (still crying, silently nods)

Counselor: I'm trying to learn to share this scared side of me with Susan. I've been able to do it a few times. And you know, it's amazing to me that when I do, she seems to really understand. In fact, we always seem to feel a lot closer to each other after I've been that open with her. I think it somehow must make me more human in her eyes . . . or more *with* her, or something.

Client: (looks up, with mild surprise in his voice) You mean *you* really feel like this sometimes too?

PROCESS. This self-disclosure on the counselor's part has helped the client feel acceptable as a human being. He discovers he is not so different from the counselor—that he too has problems and makes mistakes. Self-disclosure dissolves the "over-under" relationship of the judge and the judged. The client can begin seeing the therapist as another human being—which is the reality—rather than as his fantasy of the perfect one who has all the answers. Self-disclosure breeds trust and moves a counseling relationship to deeper levels more quickly. The client will now feel more free to disclose the parts of himself he may be ashamed of, or may be having trouble with. When we don't feel judged by another person—which means we see that person as being equal to us—we feel free to be ourselves, and that means exposing the parts of us we see as being weak or unacceptable.

OPPOSITE OF SELF-DISCLOSURE IN ACTION. Counselors who can never share anything from their own lives with their clients are people who have the need to maintain a role of expert, judge, or superior person. They will keep their relationships with their clients at a safe distance, creating a climate of caution and superficiality, which is nontherapeutic.

IMPLICATIONS FOR THE ALCOHOLIC
CLIENT. Self-disclosure on the part of the counselor allows the alcoholic to see what it is like to have an intimate relationship with someone; this is a form of **corrective emotional experience.** The alcoholic is terribly deficient in the area of intimate relationships—a deficiency that is both a cause and an effect of his drinking.

Sometimes it is easier to comprehend the alcoholic's felt reality if you can think of his drinking years as having been a time when his socialization process came to a grinding halt. During his years of alcoholic drinking, he literally buried himself in a bottle. His entire life became alcohol centered; the result has been a paucity in every other area of his life. He has been practicing and learning only two skills well: how to protect and maintain his supply, and how to rationalize his behavior to others in order to maintain the remnants of his self-respect. His job, his relationships, his talents, and his dreams—all have been tainted or have become nonexistent during his drinking years. If his alcoholic drinking has lasted ten years, he may have ten years of socialization skills to catch up on once a fairly steady sobriety has been achieved. A recovering alcoholic and a nonalcoholic may both appear at ease in a room full of strangers—but chances are the nonalcoholic knows what to do in this social situation, while the alcoholic may be feeling anxiety ridden and completely at sea.

I am generalizing at this point about "alcoholics" and "nonalcoholics," which makes me somewhat uncomfortable because in most instances generalizations are false. However, from my work in the addictions field over the past twenty years I have heard many recovering alcoholics say they never learned how to feel safe in social situations. I am contending that alcoholic behavior does produce some *direct* consequences that must not be overlooked in the counseling relationship. Your ability to disclose yourself

63

in a deeply personal manner will enable your clients to practice interpersonal sharing in a safe relationship. This will be extremely useful to them in their other relationships as they learn to relate without the comforting support of alcohol.

A PRACTICE EXERCISE FOR YOU. The situation described below affords a counselor the opportunity to help the client through self-disclosure. Practice how you would respond.

Client: I sure don't look forward to weekends at my house. . . . Oh, dear, that's a terrible thing to say. I didn't mean that I don't love my family. I really do love my kids very much. I know they're little, and bless their little hearts, *they* can't help it if they need me all the time. I just mean . . . well, never mind.

Counselor:

SELF-DISCLOSURE IN EVERYDAY LIFE

OPPOSITE OF SELF-DISCLOSURE IN ACTION. Self-disclosure is quite common in nonprofessional counseling situations. When friends or family members are sharing with each other, there is often much self-disclosure—but often it is not therapeutic. It can even get in the way of effective counseling and deny people in crisis their need to be listened to attentively.

Here is an incident between friends—let's call them Ann and Rachel—that I've seen happen a lot and that I consider nontherapeutic.

Ann: And I'll tell you, I'm leaving him! I can't stand how he's treating me. It makes me sick. But oh, how scary. . . . I really can't imagine how I'm going to make it financially. He's so mad, he probably won't help me at all! I'm so angry with myself for always thinking about *him* all these years and not getting the education *I* deserve. *Yes*, I'm determined to try! Oh, but I'm scared . . . like the bottom has fallen out and I'm just hanging . . . with no support.

Rachel: Scared? Forget it! I left Jeremy with absolutely no problem. Sure, it took me a while to find a good job, but I loved the feeling of freedom. I loved it. First I went back to the bank and got in with some of my old friends there. Then I went to . . . (She continues with a long history of her own employment after her divorce.)

PROCESS.   Instead of receiving help the friend in need was distracted away from her own self-exploration—her simultaneous feelings of fear and determination—and was dragged into Rachel's story line for a long period of time. Hence the emphasis shifted to the listener. In a case like this it becomes unclear who needs the attention.

   A good listener could have shared something with feeling very quickly: "I loved the freedom I felt when I left Jeremy, even though it took me a while to find a good job. I can hear the fear in your voice as you consider this big step. How scary is this for you?" This puts the emphasis back on the one asking for help, although the listener has also offered some disclosure that may be comforting. It is important to remember that self-disclosure can easily become the listener's way of processing her own "stuff." And that is okay too if the listener will claim this honestly with the friend asking for help: "This brings up some of my old feelings of how scary it all was to break loose from years of security. I may need to talk about them for a while. Let me know if I go on at too much length." This dialogue is remaining honest and from the heart. Bottom-line feelings are being disclosed.

IMPLICATIONS FOR THE FAMILY.   In most families there are specific dynamics that can get in the way of therapeutic relating. Fears of being misunderstood or condemned by closed-minded or troubled family members can keep conversations at the dinner table on the surface level so that deeper issues remain hidden. Yet we all know that these "hidden issues" are not really hidden at all; the mistrust and untruths being bandied about are out there confusing everyone and corroding the family's integrity.

"Family secrets" can become a stumbling block to honest, therapeutic relationships. Sometimes situations become so complicated and heated that a professional family counselor is needed to intervene and facilitate direct communication between family members. However, some families do not have access to good counselors or simply cannot afford them. In such cases self-disclosure, the willingness to risk revealing real feelings to each other, can serve as a catalyst for healing rifts, or for bringing the family into more meaningful therapeutic sharing. Disclosure of one's true *feelings* or *attitudes* can be as helpful as disclosing portions of one's personal history or *facts* about oneself. This is true not only when there is a family crisis, but in normal daily interactions as well.

Here is an example from a family where one of the older children, a nineteen-year-old daughter, has begun her first sexual relationship. This family belongs to a religion that disapproves of premarital sex under any conditions. No one in the family knows the truth of Jayne's situation except her confidant, her younger sister, Margo, who is seventeen.

66

One day the mother comes into Margo's room and says she needs to talk about Jayne.

Mother: (sounding very firm and determined) I want to talk to you a minute about your sister. I'm afraid something's wrong with her. She doesn't act the same anymore. I need your help. I don't know how to talk to her. What's going on; do you know?

Margo: Mom, please wait. . . . (She takes a moment to collect herself, breathes deeply.) This is making me uncomfortable. I wish you'd just talk to Jayne. I feel this is an issue between you and her, not me. I mean . . . well, gosh, Mom. I love you, and I see that you're scared (hugs her mom). But I just need you to know that I don't like being in the middle here.

Mother: (alarmed) What? Do you mean you know something I don't know? What's going on?

Margo: Nothing, Mom. I just mean . . . well . . . (again takes a deep breath) Mom, I wish you'd just ask Jayne. I think she'll talk to you. I can listen, Mom. But I can't be in the middle.

Mother: Well, it sounds like you're on *her* side. You can't really know how I feel.

Margo: No, Mom. That's not true. I love both of you a lot. I'll go get Jayne right now, so you two can talk. How's that? And maybe we can talk later. (She reaches out to her mother again, with warmth.) I *do* care, Mom. And it's not your imagination about Jayne: She *is* changing. She's growing up. We *both* are. (She pauses). I guess it's pretty scary for a mom when her daughters start becoming adults, huh?

Mother: (begins to cry softly) Yes, sweetheart, it's real scary. I'm afraid I'm losing her . . . and maybe you too. (They embrace.)

PROCESS. In this example Margo was able to express her real feelings, refusing to be used as a middle person between her mother and older sister. She was able to speak from the heart and thus serves as a model of effective self-disclosure for her mother. Margo let her mother know where she stands; now there are no hidden agendas, and the stage is set for Jayne and her mother to talk openly. Margo maintained her integrity and at the same time gave her mother support. She would have rated very high in a counselor-effectiveness study.

Triangulation is a real problem in families with alcoholism or other types of severe dysfunction. Two people having a serious problem will often draw a third, more neutral, person into the event to serve as a sounding board or ally. The third party may feel trapped in an "unclean" situation and be compelled to lie in order to get out of it unscathed. However, the third party, like Margo, can use self-disclosure from the very start, stating her exact feelings about the matter and drawing boundaries around what she is willing and not willing to do.

A cardinal rule in counseling is to get the two people in conflict to tell their feelings to each other face-to-face— even if you have to sit with them as a neutral third party, continually reminding them to talk to each other, not to you, about the problem. If they will speak honestly, their hearts will eventually open and the real feelings underneath the issue will surface: "I'm scared"; "I'm afraid I'm losing control"; "I'm afraid you don't love me anymore." Once this level of truth is reached, the two will dissolve their defenses and melt into each other with compassion. Or if the situation is unresolvable at this stage, you might suggest they take some time to cool off, or perhaps it will become clear that professional help is needed.

After some practice family members will learn to speak truthfully to each other, expressing their feelings, their boundaries, and their needs. At this point the family secrets and issues of mistrust will begin to dissipate, bringing more life and more integrity to the family as a whole. When healthy communication patterns can begin at home with the ones closest to us, they are sure to lead to greater intimacy and integration in every area of life.

A PRACTICE EXERCISE FOR YOU. Your son, Mark (age sixteen), runs into the kitchen.

Mark: Mom, oh, Mom! I've got to tell you something awful. I've wrecked Dad's truck. Oh, gosh, I'm so scared. Mom, please help me. I didn't wreck it much, just a little. But I think it needs a new fender. Dad will kill me, Mom! Please don't tell him! Please, Mom. Let's just get it fixed real quick. I'll help. I'll do *anything*. Please, just don't tell him (bursts into tears).

Mom:

WARMTH

We manifest warmth mainly through nonverbal communication with the person seeking help. Smiles, touching, and other natural responses to the humanness of the one in pain are evidence of warmth in action. When appropriate it is even therapeutic to shed tears along with someone who is hurting.

WARMTH IN THE COUNSELOR-CLIENT RELATIONSHIP

WARMTH IN ACTION.

Client: (crying and rocking back and forth, holding her hands tensely in her lap) Ever since John died, I've felt so lost and . . . and untouched. Sometimes it's just unbearable. I just die to be touched sometimes.

Counselor: (Leans forward and takes client's hands, and as she does so, the client falls into counselor's arms. Counselor holds client for a while, in silence, gently rocking client to and fro, stroking her hair.)

PROCESS.

This scene would be likely to receive highly negative responses from traditionally trained counselors or supervisors, who would view it as dangerous and a violation of the therapeutic process. Many of us have been trained, mostly on the basis of Freudian psychology, to believe the therapist should remain distant and unemotional at all times. However, research shows otherwise. Clients need touching. They need to feel the counselor's humanness. As therapists we are asking our clients to open up with us, to share their deepest feelings, hopes, and fears. Consequently we must model this ability to be open and responsive—thus allowing the client to feel what she feels without any awkwardness.

In the above example the client is attempting to nurture herself by rocking to and fro. Observing this behavior, the counselor chooses to become the nurturer herself and takes over the rocking as a mother might. The counselor remains silent to give the client space to *feel* without having to process comments from the counselor. It is therapeutic for the client to stay with her feelings of loneliness and need, to go through the feelings honestly. And the fact that the counselor has responded to the client's desire for nurturing teaches the client that others may also respond to her needs. This is a subtle, nonverbal message of hope.

I have found in my work that "it is not out, but through" that we heal our old hurts. We must be allowed to feel the feelings all the way through until they dissolve or balance. Sometimes this comes all at once as a complete **catharsis,** or total release. Sometimes it comes in waves, each wave of feeling becoming less and less intense. It is like a "bleeding out" of the pain until there is a quieting. This is how healing really happens. The human organism already knows this process instinctively. That's why we cry when we are hurt and yell when we are angry. Good therapists encourage this "wisdom of the organism" by asking people who are crying to cry *more*, and people who are angry to yell *louder*, creating a warm and neutral place for these expressions to occur.

Many of us have become so afraid of painful feelings that we've learned all kinds of ways to stop others from expressing their feelings so we won't have to feel our own. The medical model of helping often assists us in this denial of feelings by prescribing medicine such as antidepressants or mood alterers when people are feeling pain.

OPPOSITE OF WARMTH IN ACTION. A counselor low in warmth operates from an injunction against showing feelings too openly. This injunction may have come out of a childhood in which there was little touching: In some families children grow up learning to hold back their touching responses from others. It is also possible that the counselor's training may have mandated a "professional attitude" of emotional noninvolvement with clients. In either case the counselor would be uncomfortable responding to the client with nurture, as in the example above. Instead this counselor would either intellectualize, discount the client's pain, or freeze. Often a professional stance can be the opposite of warmth in action.

Intellectualizing

Counselor: It's natural that you'd miss John a great deal, Sarah. You've just begun the grief process. Can you tell me how long you've been feeling this terrible loneliness?

This response would put the client "in her head" to analyze her behavior and check out her recent history of dealing with the loss of her husband. It could produce some insight, but it will not aid her in moving through the grief process in a natural and healing way. Catharsis and learning to reach out for nurturing are much more therapeutic for this client.

Discounting

Counselor: Now, Sarah, you act as though you think no other man in the world will ever pay attention to you! Why, you're a beautiful lady. You'll have another meaningful relationship soon, I'm sure.

This type of response is premature and irrelevant at this stage of the grief process. This client is nowhere near ready to begin thinking of other relationships, and reassuring her of her desirability is extremely inappropriate at this time. Still stuck in the past, she is not ready to look ahead, and rightfully so, for there is still griefwork to be done.

Freezing

When a counselor freezes, it is apparent she has been confronted with a human situation in which she is not prepared emotionally to cope. Her behavior will appear awkward and irrelevant—not coming from the same emotional level as the client. Any type of freezing behavior shuts a client down for the moment, causing her to pull back, change the subject, or become silent.

Clients often mirror for us what we are allowing them to feel. They will most often follow our lead.

A NOTE TO COUNSELORS WHO FEEL THEY ARE NOT NATURALLY WARM. If your demeanor is reserved, and displaying feelings and touching are uncomfortable for you, please do not feel you must force yourself to develop the natural ability to express warmth. It is far better to be yourself and continue developing genuineness with your clients. If you are genuine and learn to self-disclose a little, you will find at an appropriate time that you can share with your clients your desire to display more affection with them, while telling them that it is not natural to you. This type of rapport will build a type of warmth that is a very special form of genuineness. It may require a little practice, but it might be good for you.

A SPECIAL NOTE ABOUT SEDUCTION.
Natural human warmth is not seductive, nor will it be interpreted as a mixed message by your client. It comes from "above the belt," from the Heart. We all know and trust the feelings of the Heart. Holding, touching, and intimate sharing are human qualities that surface during times of suffering and need. The *feeling tone* of warmth is different from the feeling tone of sexual or seductive advances or mixed messages. Warmth can easily be expressed between a counselor and client. It will, if anything, serve as a safety against seductiveness.

In our therapeutic work my associates and I take women into deep self-exploration and catharisis around issues such as incest and rape (the most horrifying kinds of sexual abuse). Many of our best trainers and therapists are men who have worked out their own sexual and seductive issues. The corrective emotional experiences are profound and moving when an injured woman can relive these issues with a male counselor who is safe.

IMPLICATIONS FOR THE ALCOHOLIC CLIENT.
A client's ability to deal with her feelings appropriately is a major step toward a stable sobriety. Fear of feelings is a significant part of what alcoholism is all about. People drink to hide or handle negative feelings such as anxiety, nervousness, uncertainty, anger, or fear. The more authentically and warmly you can respond when an alcoholic client begins to risk showing real feelings, the more therapeutic you are. Encourage feelings with an air of confidence!

A PRACTICE EXERCISE FOR YOU. This
client is a male, very rigid and afraid of contacting others.
He has been raised in a nontouching "chauvinistic" family
that views emotional sharing as a form of weakness. He is
losing his wife through divorce, and the feelings of sadness
are just underneath the surface.

Client: (looking scared and childlike) I've never known
whether or not it was okay to ask someone to
hold me. . . . I mean, sometimes I just would
like to be held like a little baby. But it's not
like me, I mean, I wouldn't know how, or what
to do. . . . I think I'm going to cry.

Counselor:

WARMTH IN
EVERYDAY LIFE

WARMTH IN ACTION.

Now let's take a situation between a man and his aging
father who is in the hospital and may be dying.

Dad: Well, Son, I'm scared. I admit it. I'm afraid that old
man in the sky is about to say, "It's your time." (He
holds back obvious tears, choking.) Son, I may be
leaving all of you. (He tries to look brave.)

Son: (moves over to the bed and embraces his father and
allows some time for them both just to feel) Dad, oh,
Dad. I'm also afraid you might be dying. I need you to
know that I love you so much. I feel I may have
been cruel to you sometimes, and I'm sorry about our
differences. But, Dad, I love you. I know you're scared.
We're all scared, Dad. But we're here to support you

no matter what. (He holds his father once more, tightly, and they cry together.)

PROCESS. Death, or fear of death, makes most families uptight and superficial with each other, just at the time when real communication is so very necessary. The infirm person needs to speak real feelings, and so do the family members, especially when they sense that death may come at any point. Truth spoken between family members at times such as this heals many emotional wounds and aids the person in the dying—or healing—process.

In the case of a person who is dying, he may really be wanting to let go—but something has gone unsaid. Some kind of unfinished business among his closest kin holds him here, as he hopes for some miracle that will enable him to speak his truth. When this truth can be offered by you first, it makes the feeble one more able to clear his consciousness of the things that are important to him. Being real, being warm, and being available are the best therapy for a dying person. And these interactions can transform an entire family when handled in an honest, from-the-Heart manner.

OPPOSITE OF WARMTH IN ACTION. We are making a grave error in interpersonal relating if we assume that a dying person needs to "gut up and be brave," or that family members need to act as if they are not hurting or scared. It is now known through research in the area of death and dying that open feelings and warmth among family members heal old issues, not only for the one who is dying but for the survivors as well. "Pretend" feelings are no longer acceptable in any kind of therapeutic relating. We are all coming back to our roots—the human Heart.

IMPLICATIONS FOR THE FAMILY. Unhealed wounds create barriers to warmth in action within the family. In a dysfunctional home, children may hold their feelings in, becoming rigid and withdrawn when feeling emotional pain—afraid to reach out for support and sometimes even afraid to feel their feelings at all! Consequently some of these children grow up not knowing what they feel, or with whom it is safe to let down their defenses. In severe cases a family may need to seek professional help. You can be the first one in your family to learn to reach out, either by seeking outside help when necessary, or by just being there emotionally for another—no matter how dreadful the secret in your family is, or how closed up you have all become. You may be the "pied piper" who brings all the others along. The following is an example of how a sensitive family member can provide a therapeutic response through warmth.

Roseann, who is fourteen, dashes into her room after returning from school and slams the door. Her older brother, David, who is seventeen, goes to her door and knocks gently.

David: Roseann, can I come in? What's the matter? Has something happened?

Roseann: (opens the door, pulling herself together with great effort) Hi, c'mon in. Have a seat. (She points to her desk chair.)

David: (sits down in the chair) Hey, Sis, you're obviously barely holding it together. (He speaks gently.) Can you talk to me?

Roseann: (now obviously fighting back her emotions) Oh, nothing. Nothing at all! I can handle it. (She sits down stiffly on the edge of her bed, uncertain, waiting for some response from David.)

David: (standing up) C'mon Rosie, let's have a hug. This is really hurting you. (He reaches down and pulls her up into his arms and just holds her lovingly while her tears pour out. He speaks after the sobs have subsided a little.) Sweetie, you don't have to say a word if you don't want to. You can just cry.

Roseann: Oh, David. I'm so humiliated. I could just die! I'm so scared. I could die! You know my friend Susan? The one who spent the night over here last weekend?

David: Sure.

Roseann: Well, *our father* has made a pass at her! He was drunk . . . remember? Well, he did it! And now Susan's told her parents. This is all so . . . so *yuk*, I could throw up. . . . I'm going to kill myself! I just want to die. (She bursts into uncontrollable tears.)

David: (holds Roseann—obviously shocked) Rosie, this *is* awful. We've got to get help. Rosie, I'll go with you. I know someone to call. It's time, Rosie. It's time we get help. You don't have to deal with this by yourself. We'll do it together.

PROCESS. David's warmth and insistence on being there for his sister made it possible for Roseann to pour out this delicate and excruciatingly painful occurrence—one that many young people in alcoholic families have to face. Her father has disgraced her with his drunken behavior. And she is not only filled with shame, but now there is threat of even more serious trouble. The secret is out. The way this situation is handled could have a dramatic influence on this family and its close circle of friends. These issues are not hopeless, or even unmanageable; they occur more often than we would like to think where family dysfunction runs high.

Warmth is not a mere gesture toward someone in trouble; it is a *power*. It is one of the most potent variables, for it helps others release feelings. Often a person in crisis is about to break from holding on so tightly to feelings that need to be expressed. David did two things that were highly intuitive. (He probably had no idea he was even doing them.) First, he lifted Rosie up to a standing position when hugging her, rather than sitting down on the bed with her. This is a family where incest or near-incest issues are evident, but unspoken, and Rosie could have felt defensive, closing up even more if her brother had sat down on the bed to comfort her. Wisely, he removed the threat. Second, while she was crying, before she began to tell the content of her problem, he gave her permission to just keep on crying. Paradoxically, when we give someone permission to hold on to something confidential, that person often feels okay about sharing it. David has moved both Rosie and himself— and perhaps the whole family—toward professional help, which is very appropriate for a situation this complex. The mother's feelings, for example, will need a lot of quality attention, not to mention the father's, as well as all the others involved. With the right kind of professional guidance, this family may be able to move into health, beyond denial and addiction; this seriously unhealthy situation may serve as a catalyst for deep healing.

A PRACTICE EXERCISE FOR YOU. You are a parent. You are sitting in the living room one afternoon around suppertime, and your teenage son bursts into the house from basketball practice, sees you, and instantly straightens up, acting as if there is nothing wrong. Yet you sense that he is pretending to be brave and together, when really he is obviously in trouble.

Parent: Bobby, you're acting very strangely. . . . I can tell something's wrong. Did something happen at practice that upset you?

Bobby: No! Just leave me alone. I don't want to talk about it! (He charges to his room and slams the door.)

Parent: (waits a few minutes . . . then hears things being knocked around in Bobby's room . . . goes to the door and knocks) Bobby, can I come in? Bobby, please (kindly). Let me in so we can talk. (Bobby opens the door and looks at you helplessly. He is on the brink of tears.)

Parent:

IMMEDIACY

Research has shown that the word *immediacy* is the best way to describe how high-functioning therapists keep their clients in the here and now. The relationship between the counselor and client *itself* becomes a therapeutic "tool." This quality, when artfully employed, takes the emphasis off the *contents* of the sharer's problems (that have happened outside the room) and places the emphasis on the *process* going on in the moment between the helper and the one seeking help.

IMMEDIACY IN THE COUNSELOR-CLIENT RELATIONSHIP

IMMEDIACY IN ACTION—WHEN THE FEELINGS OF THE MOMENT ARE NEGATIVE.

Counselor: I'm beginning to feel uncomfortable right now, Jerry, because I'm sensing that you're very angry with me and not wanting to talk with me about it. Are you mad at me?

Client: Well, not exactly. . . . but . . . well, I *do* feel like you're not listening to me today. It seems like your mind is on something else . . . or you're not interested in me . . . or something.

Counselor: (pauses to reality-check this feedback with himself) You know, you're absolutely right, Jerry. I can see why you're mad. I really *am* distracted. In fact . . . yeah, in *fact,* I'm annoyed with you for not showing up yesterday, and I'm really not wanting to listen to you today. I think this is my way of getting back at you. Yeah . . . I'm aware of it now. I'm mad as heck at *you!* I think we'd better deal with this first.

PROCESS. Counselors are not totally self-actualized people, either. Often a counselor is not herself altogether in touch with her feelings. In this example the counselor has projected her own anger onto the client, and until she asks for the client's feedback, she has not herself become aware of this. But she *was* aware that the session was getting nowhere, and the energy between her and her client had become blocked up (which happens when untruth is present). Because the counselor practiced immediacy, she and the client will now be able to confront the real feelings that were dwelling beneath the surface, cluttering up their ability to be truthful with each other. They have brought their honest feelings to the level of conscious awareness so they can be dealt with. The act of getting all this out in the open will cause the feelings to dissolve. The client and counselor will then be free to explore the client's real work. The therapist has modeled for the client how to **reality-test** and bring communication to a genuine level of involvement.

IMMEDIACY IN ACTION—WHEN THE FEELINGS OF THE MOMENT ARE POSITIVE.

Client: I've brought you a little present today. . . . It's not much . . . but it's something I wanted to give you.

Counselor: (deeply moved) Thank you, Nancy. I'm very touched by this. I'm feeling very strongly right now that you do care a lot about me. Is that what you're feeling?

Client: (blushes and smiles, self-consciously) Uh huh. . . .

Counselor: (grins broadly) Well, I do feel *good* hearing that! I care very deeply for you too Nancy. In fact, I think you're a neat lady, you know it? I really *like* you!!

Client: (embarrassed, but obviously very pleased) Well, golly . . . you're saying that . . . well, you're saying that . . . you *really mean* that? I don't know when I've . . . (She suddenly begins to weep.)

Counselor: (Allows client to assimilate this very intimate moment by quietly sitting with her as she goes on and feels moved. Speaks when Nancy begins to come out of the feeling.) You seem so moved by this, Nancy. I guess you're really lacking for good friends right now, huh?

Client: Yes. I think I am. I don't know *when* I've felt close to anyone . . . (weeps again) . . . and I really *want* to. (She puts her head down.)

Counselor: (very softly) Well, tell me something. What could you do about that? Does anything occur to you?

Client: You mean . . . in my day-to-day life?

Counselor: Yes, that's what I mean. What could you do about this feeling of being so starved out?

PROCESS. The counselor, by dealing with the immediate process (their sincere caring for each other), has kept the client close to her reality. By sharing honestly with the client he has enabled her to be herself in a direct manner. (The client's giving of the gift was an *indirect*, less satisfactory means of expressing a need to be loved.) The encounter with reality on the feeling level moved them to a very productive interchange that invited the client to experience genuine caring and a true intimacy of shared feelings in a safe environment. In addition this genuine human interaction invited her to look honestly at a crucial question in her life: What can she *do* to develop closer relationships with people—or how is she blocking herself from fulfilling this vital need? She has no doubt hidden her true feelings from others for so long, she no longer knows how to relate openly and clearly. Her therapy, if successful, will put her back in touch with who she really is—the greatest gift we can ever receive from life.

In both the above instances of immediacy in action, an honest exchange of genuine intimacy served as a laboratory experiment for the clients to learn how to give and receive honest anger or affection in a manner that leads to satisfaction. This is significant learning that can lead to growth. We are never the same after an interchange such as this, because real energy is felt by each of us. This is the power of love, and it is transforming.

High-functioning therapists and people who transform others by their very presence (people very high in potency) are masterful with the quality of immediacy. Getting lost in the details of a sharer's story lines is a way of missing the point in therapy sessions. The evidence of a client's difficulties in life situations will be right there in the therapy room expressing itself within the very relationship at hand. If we can tap into this here-and-now resource of information, we can go a long way toward helping others see their dysfunctional patterns of relating—and also our own.

OPPOSITE OF IMMEDIACY IN ACTION.

Immediacy is one of the most risk-taking techniques of therapeutic involvement for the counselor as well as for the client—it brings truth right up to the surface, leaving no language or content barriers to hide behind. The counselor will usually be the one to initiate immediacy and must be prepared to tolerate a certain amount of anxiety as a result. In the first example it would have been much safer for the counselor to ignore the hostility she was feeling from her client and within herself. The counselor would have kept a safe distance from her client and allowed him to continue discussing whatever subject was on the surface. Nothing very productive would have happened, but the counselor could have maintained safety in her role of "being on top of things," and the client would not have had to face possible rejection for verbalizing his feeling that the counselor was not listening. A defensive counselor would have denied that she was angry with her client, and consequently the truth between them would have been blocked. When an untruth is sitting between two people who are trying to relate, a feeling of deadness, of boredom, or of "nothing happening" will set in.

In the second example if the counselor had merely said thank you for the gift and moved the session into a discussion about something other than the process in the here and now, the client would not have experienced what it is like to share intimately in a direct way with another human being—nor would she have encountered so vividly her real feelings of paucity in relationships. Her indirect, apparently unsatisfactory, pattern of showing affection (gift giving) would have been reinforced, and no new learning would have occurred.

IMPLICATIONS FOR THE ALCOHOLIC CLIENT.

Most alcoholics live in a world of disassociation from their own feelings. By the overuse of **unconscious denial** and **projection** as protective devices, they try to recreate their reality in a way that will help them live more comfortably. But unfortunately this very maneuver usually produces more discomfort; their reconstructed reality is constantly out of tune with what is really going on in their lives. The use of immediacy can help the alcoholic client learn how to look at his own feelings and the feelings of his counselor within the safety of the counseling relationship.

The rewards of being accepted for one's real self are so great, and the relief of expressing what is actually going on inside so gratifying, that the alcoholic client will benefit from this practice immensely; as time goes by, he will begin to trust his experience more—and his fantasies less.

A PRACTICE EXERCISE FOR YOU.

In the following example there is something going on under the surface that is getting in the way of a productive counseling session. See how you would respond with immediacy in action.

Client: (laughing self-consciously) Well, I had this dream last night that you and I were in this boat (pauses). Yeah, it was you, all right . . . and we were in the water, and the waves were getting higher and higher, oh this is so silly . . . but . . . and I kept hanging on to you, and you got bigger and bigger . . . in fact you actually became a *balloon* . . . sort of a *life* raft or something. . . . (pause, looking helplessly and self-consciously at the counselor)

Counselor:

IMMEDIACY IN EVERYDAY LIFE

IMMEDIACY IN ACTION.

Immediacy is a very powerful tool for family members who want to become their true selves with each other. This trait will teach them to see their dynamics in operation and to discover new ways of relating in the here and now that are more satisfying for all concerned. What follows is a situation between a mother and a daughter; it illustrates a type of dynamic that occurs often in dysfunctional families in which one parent has had to take charge and feels overburdened due to the other parent's alcoholism or some other family situation that has imbalanced his or her load of responsibilities. Here the mother is needy for friendship, something that will give her some personal satisfaction, so she reaches out for an inordinate amount of emotional support from her oldest daughter, who is twenty-three and newly married. The mother is speaking about a situation surrounding her impending divorce from her second husband, her daughter's stepfather.

Mother: And so there I was *again*, humiliated half to death by the confessions of this woman who's having an affair with him. I just couldn't believe it . . . *again* I'm supposed to stand there and take it. Grrrr, it makes me so mad I can hardly stand it! I couldn't wait to get home and call Bruce and tell him to . . .

Daughter: (calm but firm) Mother. Stop. I'm sorry, but this is the fourth time you've told me this story. Honest, Mom, it's the fourth time. Now, I'll really listen again if you just have to say all this. Maybe you need to hear yourself or something, I don't know. I *will* listen, Mother. But frankly, I'm bored with this story.

PROCESS. This response would have been rated very high by judges scoring therapeutic responses. The daughter is loving and attentive, but firm—and to the point. She is providing her distraught mother with feedback that will give her actual data on her obsessive behavior. The daughter has also said she will listen again if it is really important. So now the mother has the ball in her court. She can decide whether or not to continue boring her daughter with this melodrama, or whether to seek a deeper way of expressing her obvious hurt and outrage. Perhaps she needs to cry. Or perhaps she needs to confront the soon-to-be ex-husband directly with these unfinished issues. Or she may need professional therapy to help her unleash the feelings beneath the melodrama.

OPPOSITE OF IMMEDIACY IN ACTION.
In the preceding example a lack of immediacy on the daughter's part would have encouraged the obsessive communication, likely cycling them into a morbid conversation that would have gone nowhere but further into melodrama. It would have produced a phony interaction where the daughter would have pretended she was interested in the story line, never admitting her own boredom. Nothing healing or creative would have occurred. This would have been a recycling of a family pattern that is neurotic—a mother overusing her daughter to vent her own perceived failures with men in her life (hardly a healthy pattern for a young lady just launching into her own adulthood, with issues of her own). This is not to say that a daughter cannot "be there" for her mother when she is undergoing a crisis. Not at all. But you will note, this daughter has had to listen to this same story four times. Something unhealthy is going

on when there is this much cycling around in dramatic content. The mother may be displacing a need for excitement onto the daughter (a form of emotional addiction), hoping to incite a reaction from her. This kind of obsession with conflict is common among people who live with constant upheaval in unhealthy families. Crisis may have become this mother's way of life.

IMPLICATIONS FOR THE FAMILY. "Telling it like it is" can also become a trap for families with a lot of pent-up hostilities toward one another. True immediacy comes "from the Heart," not from "below the belt." The daughter's response did not ring of hostility; it was firm, but loving—it was bare truth. One could, however, feel as if he or she has been bawled out and told just to "hush up and get over it"—depending on how the message of immediacy is given out. First, when offering uncomfortable feedback to a family member or close friend, it is important to use "I" statements when expressing feelings. Statements beginning with "You are . . . " often make us feel judged or labeled, creating a defensive response. By saying "*I* am uncomfortable with how you are," rather than "*You* are a boring person," or "*You* are driving me crazy," we can provide the other with an opportunity to look at his or her part without feeling "bad" or blamed. This is more neutral and invites the person to be self-evaluating rather than reactive: "You're right. I need help with this," or, "You're right. I'm just making myself sick."

Families who learn to drop their judgmentalness, to leave behind their "ought tos," and to tell the truth will grow in strength and transform through love.

A PRACTICE EXERCISE FOR YOU. Your married son and his wife are going through a hard time with the wife's mother, who has been visiting them for three months. You have become the sounding board for your son and daughter-in-law concerning the problems that keep arising. You have listened now for about a week, every evening almost, to the day-by-day, play-by-play issues that are going on in their household across town from you. It is nine P.M., and you've just finished a nice meal, about to settle down after a long, hard day. Your daughter-in-law, Judith, calls.

Judith: Hi, Mom. I'm so glad you're there. Boy! You'll never guess what happened today. I didn't even get out of *bed* this morning before she was in my—*our*—room telling me what *she* thought I should be doing with Marty and his school lessons. And *your* son . . .

You: Judith, . . .

CONCRETENESS

Concreteness is the act of keeping communications specific—getting to the whats, whens, wheres, and hows of present concerns. As concrete therapists we must not go off on tangents or get into generalizations or abstract discussions with the one seeking help. We must keep people in need talking about themselves and into their own feelings, rather than speculating or gossiping about other people in their lives. We are being concrete when we can detect others' unique ways of avoiding their own reality: We must also have the ability to point out these avoidance behaviors and gently draw a person back to relevant issues and feelings of the moment.

CONCRETENESS IN THE COUNSELOR-CLIENT RELATIONSHIP

CONCRETENESS IN ACTION—WHEN THE CLIENT IS GENERALIZING.

Client: Oh, well, about the fight with my husband . . . well, you know, all husbands and wives seem to have these problems.

Counselor: Martha, I'm not interested right now in all husbands and wives. I'm very much interested in what you started to say a while ago . . . something about you're feeling mad at yourself because of some kind of fight that happened with Mark. Can you go on with that?

CONCRETENESS IN ACTION—WHEN THE CLIENT IS GOSSIPING.

Client: Marge is always telling me what to do. She feels like she's got to be in the driver's seat all the blasted time! Just like last night. She felt hurt and mad at me because she seems to want some kind of expression of *something* from me. . . .

Counselor: George, I'm getting lost in Marge and trying to psyche her out. Where are *you* in all this? What are *you* feeling while Marge is trying to control you? You look very angry right now as you're telling me about last night. What are you feeling?

Client: Angry? No, not at Marge. She's really okay; she takes care of everything, like I've told you.

Counselor: Yes. You were really scowling as you were talking about Marge just now. You were also clenching your fist.

Client: (pauses, somewhat confused, but begins clenching fist again)

Counselor: George, what's this? (He mirrors the clenched-fist gesture.)

Client: (begins hitting the palm of his hand with his fist) I *hate* it! I can't *stand* her always telling me what to do! I want to tell her to . . . to go to hell! Yeah, go to hell, Marge! Get off my back! I'm as good as you *any* day. *Any* day, you hear? (As client's anger begins subsiding, he puts his head in his hands and begins breathing deeply.)

Counselor: What are you feeling now, George?

Client: Better (smiles). Yes. Much, *much* better.

PROCESS. In the first instance, where Martha is generalizing, she wants to avoid some unpleasant feeling about a situation between her husband and herself. She is escaping into generalities, which are much easier and safer to talk about than the scarier issue at hand—her negative feelings toward her husband. The counselor pulls her back to her experience of the moment by being concrete, and the intervention creates an opportunity for a productive session.

In the second example the client is using gossip about his wife's feelings, and inferences about her dynamics, to avoid getting in touch with a feeling of his own, which he imagines to be unacceptable—absolute fury at a "perfect wife and mother." The counselor again manages to draw the client into the much more relevant issue of his own feelings. The client cannot change Marge anyway; he doesn't have the power. But he *can* have power over what *he* chooses to do in relation to Marge—once he becomes clear on what he wants or needs to do.

This particular counseling session was especially fruitful for the client for three reasons: First, it helped to clarify for George what his real feelings were about Marge's domineering style. Second, by going into his feelings of fury (via the clenched fist), a lot of stored-up psychic energy became freed and could then be used in more productive ways. And third, George was given permission by his counselor to go ahead and feel fury at his wife and thus discover that his feelings were acceptable after all, and perhaps even natural.

Sometimes a client will continue to avoid a significant issue even when the counselor makes efforts at concreteness. If the client is not truly ready to face a certain painful area, this need for avoidance must be respected; the desire to avoid may be just as relevant at that particular time as the issue the counselor knows lurks beneath the behavior. It is always important that the counselor "be where the client is" in his process and not attempt to jump ahead of him.

But it is also crucial to constantly present the client with his here-and-now reality in order to give the client the choice, either to confront or avoid until the time is right. The counselor may tell the client that he feels **stuck.** Such an observation can itself be therapeutic; the beauty of working in the here and now is that everything the counselor observes can be used to help the client. When a counselor claims very honestly that he is stuck, this puts the responsibility on the client to move the session to some other area of the client's choosing, which often is the client's examination of his own avoidance behavior. In any event, if the feeling or pattern the counselor is trying to uncover through concreteness is important in the life of the client, it will recur with frequency, and the client will encounter it when his own inner timing is right.

OPPOSITE OF CONCRETENESS IN ACTION.
In the first example given, the counselor would have listened to Martha's statement about husbands and wives and would have contributed to it by additional generalities of his own: "Yes, it does seem to me that marriages are made up of . . ."

No one ever grows much by hearing about "people in general." For instance, when I am suffering in my relationship with my husband, all other wives and husbands in the world are totally irrelevant to my particular problem. At that moment in time I am unique. I hurt. I'm feeling bad about myself, and I need help with my very own special feelings. I may seek to avoid my hurt, and that is my choice—but my counselor is doing me no service by allowing me to avoid without helping me realize that I am doing so.

Counselors who have trouble being concrete usually discover that the client controls the session, going on and on about first one thing and then another. This situation can make a counselor feel impotent and exasperated, usually resulting in a desire to avoid this particular client! Counselors often blame the client for this, unknowingly. It might be illuminating to look carefully at your ability to be concrete in instances where you feel you are failing with a client.

IMPLICATIONS FOR THE ALCOHOLIC CLIENT.

Alcoholic clients usually assume that no one is interested in them anyway—or that no one really sees them as people of value. They may generalize and speak "around problems" to test the therapist's interest or just to make conversation. An astute counselor will watch for clues in the alcoholic's conversation that point to problem areas he or she would really like to discuss.

Many alcoholism counselors have noted the alcoholic client's amazing ability to intellectualize (another form of generalizing). It is almost as though such clients have an extreme need to keep their minds working overtime, processing ideas and information. Some recovering alcoholics have told me they are convinced that this is a way to keep themselves from living in the present. "It is easier for me to trust an *idea* about the world than it is to *really* experience it," one concerned client said.

Concreteness in your counseling sessions can be very useful both in helping the alcoholic get to very specific problems and in helping *you* communicate your specific interest in the client.

A PRACTICE EXERCISE FOR YOU. Practice using the skill of concreteness in the following situation.

Client: Hi, Mary. Golly, I had a hard time getting here today. I went to a party last night, and . . . oh, did I tell you my sister's here? We are really having a reunion! Wow! What a reunion! And Joey didn't come by all week, and oh, yes, I wanted to tell you what Dr. Smith said on Tuesday. Golly, this dress of mine is too tight. Whew. Well, anyway, at the party last night I met an old friend. I've told you about all I did when I was in boarding school, didn't I? Well, this friend is from way back in those days. Yeah, at that boarding school, we used to sleep in the . . .

Counselor:

CONCRETENESS IN EVERYDAY LIFE

CONCRETENESS IN ACTION. In a nonprofessional counseling relationship concreteness may be more difficult, especially if the two conversing are good friends. Friendship is a place where our guard is down, where we are free to gossip and play around in our conversations, trusting fully that we are accepted. We often just "shoot the breeze" or "let off steam" with no real point behind much of what we say. And we may resist taking a concrete role with a friend, even when that friend is in pain. We may prefer to talk about our own situation, or vent feelings about how tough life can be, or use the moment as an opportunity to gossip ourselves. However, we will probably sense our friend's disappointment and feel an emptiness within our own being after such an interaction: A friend was in need and left our presence feeling just as needy.

If you find this happening in your life, you may want to develop your innate ability to be concrete. The more friendly and outgoing our personality, the more trouble we will have learning to use concreteness as a therapeutic trait. Our verbosity and ability to keep center stage may get in the way of our being a good listener and sensing clearly what is needed by the other. Concreteness requires the ability to hear what is going on beneath the words, to discern the pattern that is creating the difficulty—and then to help that person identify the core issues. Attentiveness and concreteness go hand in hand. Practice is required by most of us. Here is a sample conversation between a husband and wife.

Husband: I've still got that problem on my mind about having to let Jerry go. I couldn't sleep again last night. I dreamed all night that I was abandoned by all my friends, and no one wanted me to be part of anything. It was awful. I think I feel guilty.

Wife: Harry, I'm willing to listen if you want to talk about it.

Husband: (sighing) Well, I feel guilty about firing Jerry, I think. I feel like I've done something really wrong. Maybe I didn't look at all the data correctly. Maybe I've formed the wrong picture, or I've not been open-minded enough. I don't know . . . I just don't feel good about it. Maybe John gave me some wrong information. . . . I know he never liked Jerry. I guess I . . .

Wife: Harry, can you be more specific for a minute? What exactly *are* you feeling guilty about? Tell me specifically what it is.

Husband: (thoughtful for a while) Well, Mary, Jerry was my best bud at work. I'm going to miss him. Maybe I've hurt a friend, Mary, when I could have just overlooked all the errors and let it ride.

Wife: In other words, you're saying you don't believe he really did anything all that serious?

Husband: Oh, no. That's not it. Of course he did. He lied to us. And he apparently misused a lot of the company's money and supplies—for his own personal use. He even tried to hide some of it from us. The evidence was clear. And he's cost us a lot of money. It was all so stupid . . . like a kid! I'm still having trouble . . .

Wife: Then he did something that was really untenable and had to be fired?

Husband: Well, when you put it that way—yes. Yes, he did. But I feel guilty.

Wife: Guilty? Is it really guilt that you're feeling, Harry?

Husband: (thoughtful again) No, not really. Not when I really think about it. I know I did the right thing. But I feel bad. . . . I'm really hurting. Gosh, Mary. I miss him! I've lost my friend. Mary, I'm sad. I can't believe I'm losing Jerry.

Wife: (gives him a warm hug and looks lovingly at him) Harry, it's really sad to lose a bud, isn't it? (Harry begins to weep, and she holds him.) It took a lot of courage to do what you did.

PROCESS. The wife kept Harry looking at the specifics of why he might be feeling guilty while he was rambling all around the issue. Once he became certain Jerry's behavior was indeed a legitimate reason to fire him,

Harry realized he was mislabeling his feeling. He was experiencing the most natural feeling in the world—the loss of a friend, someone he had had good times with. Harry received real listening from Mary; she provided him with an opportunity to become clear about his feelings. And Harry left the exchange feeling like an okay person. And rightly so!

What we learn from this example is simply that when you take an interest in what someone else is trying to communicate and even go to the trouble of questioning that person about the specifics, the person in need feels heard. This is therapeutic in itself—we all need to feel heard. If you can help someone clarify what he or she is really hurting about, you are serving a therapeutic function.

OPPOSITE OF CONCRETENESS IN ACTION.

If Mary had just listened halfheartedly to Harry, she might have decided herself that Harry was guilty and should not have fired a friend. She would have been no help at all—and might have even become part of the problem. He would have rambled on about his guilt, and her lack of interest in the specifics would have caused her to validate his mislabeled feeling. She would have placated him with cool inattention, and no real communication would have taken place.

Concreteness is innate within us all. But often we ourselves have issues with the person in need that get in the way of real communication. We may have pent-up anger at the person, especially if he or she is a life partner, a family member, or a close friend. These are the people we interact with and care about the most, and there have been plenty of opportunities for negative feelings to arise. In such cases where there is contamination between us and the one in need, we may become overidentified with the person who is the subject of the conversation (Jerry, in the above example). In this example Mary might have acted indifferently as a way to punish Harry unconsciously for harming *her*. In other words, Harry's problem with Jerry pushed *her* buttons.

Another way Mary might have been ineffective would have been if she became so preoccupied with the content and details of the story line that she lost touch with the process—Harry's hurt and unfinished feelings. Without concreteness we may use each other as sounding boards and simply cycle in our pain, never providing each other with a clue as to what is really going on. We must all be careful not to ramble on and on, bouncing from one subject to another, venting without ever reaching the bottom line of what is actually hurting us.

IMPLICATIONS FOR THE FAMILY.   Family members need to use concreteness with each other when accusations are flying, or when members are feeling depressed or irritable, and nobody is doing anything about it. Sometimes one family member can call a meeting, sit the family down, and say, "Okay, everybody, we're all glum and blaming each other for things. I want to get to the bottom of this. Can we all just take turns and say something truthful about how we are feeling right now? What is really going on? . . . I would be willing to begin."

Then when members begin to share, all must listen attentively, without interrupting, and without judgment— just listening. If there are accusations that begin with general statements like, "Mom, you always make me feel . . . ," or, "Dad, you never remember to . . . ," the person who called the meeting can say, "Can you be more specific about what Mom really did?" Then the real data will begin to surface. As communication becomes clearer and more relevant, there are surprises in store: Usually things are not as bad as they'd seemed. And people can apologize and be forgiven for specific events or thoughtless remarks.

A PRACTICE EXERCISE FOR YOU. In the following example Cathy is rambling on and on, and you are becoming confused as you try to listen to her attentively.

Cathy: I just want to leave this town. I want to get out of here. I feel awful all the time. My job is boring. I hate my boss. I can't stand myself in this town. *Everything* is wrong! I'm just miserable.

You: Cathy, can you be more specific? What's really bothering you?

Cathy: Well, I hate my life. I mean . . . I hate my job. Well, I hate what I do at work. It's Susan too. I hate working with her. She's a pill. And she's living with me too! Can you believe it?

You: Cathy, what's *really* bothering you?

Cathy: If Susan doesn't get out of my life, I'm going to die!

You:

Remember that the bottom line will always sound absolutely real. You will have no trouble recognizing it. It can sound like a non sequitur, blurted out in exasperation, but it will be a breakthrough into the light of conscious awareness—a surprise even for its host. Your continued questions in the above exercise keep bringing Cathy closer and closer to the truth—until she finally expresses it simply and completely. The feeling is always, "That's it." Now you may want to help her elaborate.

CONFRONTATION

Confrontation is used to bring people face-to-face with reality when we perceive an obvious denial or untruth on their part. Confrontation occurs when there is an observed discrepancy between (a) what clients are saying and your perception of what they are experiencing; (b) what they are saying and what you heard them say earlier; and (c) what they are saying to you this moment and their actions in everyday life.

Unfortunately, the word *confrontation* has become a loaded term, carrying negative connotations—when, actually, *helpful* confrontation brings the client into more direct contact with his or her own experience and creates a situation in which growth can occur. Nothing can benefit those of us on what Alcoholics Anonymous calls the "merry-go-round of denial" more than therapeutic confrontation. But because confrontation *is* such a potent, growth-facilitating tool—and because it is the skill most misused by people-helpers of all kinds—its use requires careful self-exploration. Let's take a look at how a trained therapist handles the delicate act of confrontation. Then I will provide some examples for nonprofessional helping relationships.

CONFRONTATION IN THE COUNSELOR-CLIENT RELATIONSHIP

The decision as to whether or not to confront a client is always within the control of the counselor, who confronts only when he or she believes it is appropriate. Confrontation can precipitate a crisis point in the client's life and usually results in some kind of breakthrough. A deeper level of trust grows between counselor and client as a result of the counselor having risked this kind of honesty.

Confrontation is difficult for most people because of its potential for harshness and negativity. Many of us have come from families where confrontation was feared and kept at bay, resulting in our shutting down whenever confrontational interchanges take place between people. Because of the complexity and sensitivity of the subject, I devote more space here to detailing this type of therapeutic encounter.

Confrontation is a crucial variable in alcoholism counseling because it is a way to approach a client's extreme use of **unconscious denial, rationalization,** and **projection,** or in the language of Alcoholics Anonymous, "stinking thinking."

CONFRONTATION IN ACTION. If we very carefully analyze the art of therapeutic confrontation that takes place during any of the three situations noted in the first paragraph of this chapter, we will discover that there are five different types.

Experiential Confrontation.

Experiential confrontation usually occurs when the counselor observes a discrepancy between what the client is saying and what she is apparently experiencing as she says it.

Client: (slightly intoxicated, whiskey on breath) I'm just feeling *awfully* good today! I'm not even *worried* anymore about controlling my drinking! In fact . . . I'm . . .

Counselor: Wait a minute, Sue. I'm feeling very uncomfortable with you right now. I'm thinking you had to drink today to boost yourself up just to see me!

106

Client: Oh, now, wait a minute. . . .

Counselor: No, Sue. Right now you remind me of a little girl scared half to death, feeling miserable, and worried to *death* about your drinking. I don't believe you're feeling good at all. Come on now, Sue. What's going on here with us—here, right now?

Strength Confrontation.

Strength confrontation occurs when the client is "pretending weakness" in the area where the counselor knows or suspects the client has strength.

Client: I just don't know how to go about getting another job (droops in chair). I guess I'm just . . .

Counselor: Now, Joe, I won't buy that. Just last week you outlined for me very clearly four or five ways you have successfully changed jobs in the past . . . and always toward a promotion! Now, come on, Joe. What's this? (He mirrors the client's slumped, "pitiful" posture and expression.) What are you doing here with me now?

Weakness Confrontation.

When the counselor observes a client "playing tough" to avoid an obvious difficulty he's having, weakness confrontation is useful.

Client: Well, let me tell you, she just can't get to *me* anymore with all that cryin' and yellin'. When she starts up, I just tell her to knock it off right then and there!

Counselor: (gently) Michael, I'm sorry, but I don't believe you. You look "gotten to" even now as you talk about it. Your eyes are sad; you're fidgeting in your chair. . . . (He leans forward.) I believe this problem with Carol is still upsetting you very much.

Action Confrontation.

Action confrontation boosts the client toward an agreed-upon goal or contract:

Client: Hi, Mr. Johnson. I'm sorry I'm late.

Counselor: James, I'm not going to keep my appointment with you today, and I believe you already know why.

Client: Well, I . . .

Counselor: You look doubtful. Well, Jane from Alcoholics Anonymous called me this morning wanting to know if I'd seen you, because she hasn't. You and I have a very clear agreement that I see you if you go to AA. I'm feeling very disappointed and annoyed, James, because I've felt we're really getting somewhere together. And I'm really liking working with you.

Client: Yeah, me too. Aw, come on. Give me another chance.

Counselor: Nope. Won't do either of us any good (rising). I'll see you next week, *if* you get to AA on Thursday. That's your part. I'll keep your appointment time open. It's up to you. (He terminates the session.)

Factual Confrontation.

This method of confronting occurs when the counselor imparts facts to correct the client's imaginings or some misinformation he or she is operating from.

Example of Correcting Imaginings.

Client: You know, when I walk into that classroom everybody in the whole room looks up at me with disgust.

Counselor: Everybody in the room?

Client: Yeah, every one of 'em.

Counselor: That's hard for me to believe, Pete. I've never known of a group of people anywhere who could all be having the same feeling at the same time, especially about me! I've never known of that many people even being that *interested* in me all at one time. Aren't these people almost total strangers to you?

Client: Yeah . . . but it sure seems that way to me.

Counselor: Pete, what could be going on in *you* that makes you feel so bad when you walk in there?

Example of Correcting Misinformation.

Client: I can't tell my husband I'm an alcoholic! And I also can't stop drinking completely right now, either. You see . . .

Counselor: Just a minute, Joan. You mean you *won't*. There are only three or four things you *can't* do: You can't go without food, and you can't go without water, things like that. . . . There are so few things you really *can't* change. Now, start over and say, "I *won't* tell my husband" and "I *won't* stop drinking." Tell me you choose not to. I want to see *you* take the responsibility for both those decisions. *You're* in control here—not someone "out there." Now (gently), go on. . . .

Client: Okay, dammit! I *won't* tell my husband, and I *won't* stop drinking right now! I won't, I won't! (She breaks into tears.)

Counselor: (silent while she assimilates this experience, then tenderly) How are you feeling now, Joan?

Client: Well, I feel stupid! It's like I do these things to myself . . . (sobs) over and over again.

Counselor: Joan! Did you feel the power in you when you were shouting, "I won't?" There was a lot of strength in that, coming from *you.* What do you want to do with all that power? What are you willing to do?

PROCESS. In all of these examples the counselors have enabled the clients to experience the ways they keep themselves from their own reality and from meeting their own vital needs. **Reality-testing** and learning to take responsibility for one's own behavior are two vital steps every client must take in order to lead a functional life.

In order to facilitate clients on the path of realization and discovery, counselors must always check out their own feelings as they respond to a client. These inner feelings become guidelines for a true response and help counselors avoid using confrontation as a way to vent their own anger or confusion. It is when counselors become aware that they are feeling disbelief or doubt about what a client is expressing that they have the option to confront the person with their perception of what is going on. If a relationship of trust has not been established with the client, the counselor may choose not to confront every discrepancy or to go easy until more rapport has been developed.

The therapist's manner and attitude are crucial. If one is uncaring or emotionally aloof with a client, confrontation can be useless or even harmful. Honest, helpful confrontation comes out of a deep trusting relationship—it comes directly from the heart. It also *creates* deep and trusting relationships.

A naturally therapeutic person intuits a choice of confrontation tactics, basing these choices on the whole situation—the uniqueness of the client's personality, weaknesses, strengths, and so on, and the uniqueness of the particular counselor-client relationship. There are no general rules to guide you—but the following conditions may help you determine whether confrontation will be helpful.

Counselor Conditions.

1. Am I sensitive to the amount of trust and kind of feeling tone that exists between my client and me?

2. Am I willing to become more involved with my client as a person?

3. Am I confronting behavior that my client can really do something about?

4. Am I making my confrontation positive and constructive, rather than negative and punitive?

5. Am I being direct and clear?

6. Am I representing facts as facts, feelings as feelings, and inferences as inferences?

7. Have I laid down my cards first? In other words, does my client know what is motivating me to confrontation?

Client Conditions.

1. Will my client accept my confrontation as an invitation to self-explore?

2. Is my client open to knowing how he or she is seen or experienced by others?

3. Can my client tolerate the discomfort and mental pain that may result from my confrontation?

4. Does my client believe that I care?

If the answer to all of the questions is yes, favorable conditions exist for therapeutic confrontation. But if the answer is no to any of the questions, we should not confront—at least not yet—even if we may see the need. Such choices not to confront are valid; we usually just need to wait for the proper time when all the above conditions are met.

However, sometimes we hold back from confrontation to protect *ourselves* from something. This is especially true when we are in a nonprofessional helping role, such as that of a life partner, friend, or co-worker, because we have an ongoing relationship with that person; but professional counselors also have a similar need, at times, to avoid confrontation, and they should be aware of this. If we feel at some point that we are avoiding confrontation that is clearly needed, we must explore ourselves first and see what it is that we fear. We may discover that our hesitation is simply due to our fear of losing the person, and we can share this out loud: "Gosh, Jim, this may ruin our friendship—or you may never want to see me again—but I feel I must tell you what is coming up for me. I'm wondering if you are able to see your part in this, because, quite frankly, I know you well, and this is a pattern, old friend. It may be something really holding you back in life." This approach is warm, truthful, and revealing.

On the other hand, our fears may be coming from deep within us; *we* may be the resistant ones. We may have a familiar feeling in our stomach from having undergone negative confrontations in childhood when there was fighting or disharmony. We may fear confrontation so much that we can hardly bring ourselves to confront another at all—

becoming overidentified with the feared reaction. We can also share these feelings with our client: "I feel a need to confront your drinking behavior right now, Jim. The feeling keeps coming up over and over. Yet I hesitate. And I know this is my own issue. I have always felt shaky around the need to confront someone else, and I know it comes from the kind of family I had. But I've decided to tell you anyway what's on my mind, which you, of course, are free to accept or reject." This kind of talk, even with our best friends or mates, is often useful confrontation.

The following list includes some of the most common fears we *all* will have from time to time when confrontation becomes an issue.

1. Fear of rejection. (I need his approval.)

2. Fear of being wrong. (Maybe I'll confront and then have to take it all back. Or, maybe I'll confront and mess up her life even more!)

3. Fear of unpleasantness—anxiety, tears, anger, hurt feelings. (I've never known how to act in the face of these emotions.)

4. Fear of intimacy. (Boy, this is going to bring us face-to-face with each other, with all the barriers down. Or, Gosh, I may have to deal with him now at close range for quite a while.)

If these kinds of fears are stopping us from confronting someone's messed-up picture of reality, they are invalid in the therapeutic relationship and must be worked through at the counselor's initiation. Counselors cannot be effective if they are not able to confront. It is important not to confuse being *able* to confront with being *comfortable* with confrontation. In counselor-skills training, people who are *too* comfortable with confrontation make me feel uneasy: Often I have discovered such counselors are using confrontation as a way to relieve much of their own pent-up anger (feeding off their clients' issues). Or else they are low in empathy and respect and actually get an adrenaline rush from the excitement of confrontation and conflict. This I call toxic confrontation; it is harmful instead of helpful for both parties.

OPPOSITE OF HELPFUL CONFRONTA-TION IN ACTION. Harmful confrontation results when counselors have ulterior motives, or "hidden agendas," of which they themselves may not even be aware. Another way of saying this is that counselors may have problems of their own that they unconsciously try to work out at their clients' expense. A counselor who harbors pent-up hostilities, for instance, might play what Eric Berne (one of the founders of the psychological school of Transactional Analysis) has referred to as the "NIGYSOB" game: "Now I've Got You, You Son-of-a-Bitch." Some recovering alcoholic counselors who have not yet forgiven themselves for their own drinking histories can play this game unwittingly. The confronter carefully watches for the client to make a mistake, then feels justified in venting anger with some kind of put-down, which is rationalized with the excuse, "I'm only trying to help you." Recovering alcoholic counselors, however, certainly do not have a monopoly on this well-known game!

Counselors can also confront in harmful ways when they have a need to show off their perception and knowledge; they will usually sound very clinical and aloof. They will pin diagnostic labels on the client in matter-of-fact ways, offer interpretations and inferences that are of little use to the client, and can in fact hurt the client if he or she happens to respect the counselor a great deal and accepts unquestioningly these absolute "facts." Often degreed professionals who are still insecure in their professional identity fall into this trap.

Sometimes a counselor will confront just to stir things up a bit—out of a sense of boredom or impotence. But it should also be noted that constantly avoiding confrontations is in itself potentially harmful. If I handle you at all times with "kid gloves," regardless of your negative behavior, what message am I really giving you? More than likely the message is that I think you are too weak or too pitiful to handle the truth about yourself. Hardly a therapeutic inference!

Please do not be put off by my elaboration here on the harmful aspects of confrontation. I am not implying that you should avoid it. Nothing could be further from my intention! Interpersonal confrontation is one of the most potent and therapeutic change agents a counselor can use— when practiced with care.

A PRACTICE EXERCISE FOR YOU. See what you would do with the technique of confrontation in action in the following case. You have seen Beth only one time. She has achieved only two weeks' sobriety and is leaning very heavily on you and AA to maintain sobriety. She comes in for her second meeting with you two days earlier than her scheduled appointment.

Counselor: Well, Beth, I'm glad to see you, but I wasn't really expecting you today. What's up?

Client: Oh, nothing. Nothing at all. I'm feeling *really* fine! No problems. Just wanted to come by for a little social-type visit. Is that okay?

Counselor:

CONFRONTATION IN EVERYDAY LIFE

Confrontation has a different meaning for the nonprofessional helper. First of all, in a professional setting client and counselor have a clear contract: One person is seeking help from another person who has been trained to perform this kind of service. Money and time are of the essence in this relationship; clients are spending their money for every session, hoping each one will be effective and will shorten the time necessary for the counseling relationship to unfold. Clients are more likely to *expect* to be confronted by their therapists. The stage is set for it. There is also a role boundary around the professional relationship—ethical standards that limit professional interactions in ways that do not apply to ordinary friendships and family ties.

Boundaries are less defined between family members, friends, and co-workers. Sometimes the ones seeking help have previously been *your* listeners when you were in trouble. Also we must remember that between family members or close associates there is an ongoing relationship. The person will be there again tomorrow, next week, next year, and there is always the risk that we may create tension we will have to live with, that we may be rejected and lose the relationship, or that we may create discomfort with other family members or friends who may not even be involved in the particular issue.

Professional counselors and clients can terminate their relationship if the confrontation becomes too toxic, or they can bring in a supervisor or another therapist to help them past the uncomfortable situation—all within the bounds of therapy and professional ethics. When a client and counselor terminate their relationship, their personal lives go on as usual. This is not so with a nonprofessional relationship:

It's there to stay! Consequently more caution and sometimes more softening are essential for these more intimate confrontations; they require more self-disclosure and warmth —and certainly more empathy. The skill needed here is clear communication and a certainty that one is not using the confrontation as an opportunity to meet an unstated need of one's own. We can sense these kinds of contaminations by our feeling state: If we are getting activated in our own emotions while the person is speaking to us, we may ourselves have an issue. In such a case we can share these fears, clear them with the person, and then go right on listening—as suggested many times previously in this book.

When I have times of trouble in my life, I must admit it is usually my close friends, co-workers, and family members who are my most effective and potent confronters. At first I feel anger and resentment. Then I act withdrawn and unwilling to relate. I begin to see their point. Then, reluctantly, I have to go to them and admit they are right-on.

One of my favorite stories (in retrospect—I *hated* it at the time!) came from a confrontation with a dear friend and mentor.

One day, after we had led a group together, he said he needed to speak to me privately. He told me quite frankly about an apparently unconscious behavior of mine in the group that he considered manipulative of certain group members. The more I listened to him, the angrier I got. I finally yelled at him quite defensively and continued to get more and more angry, telling him quite loudly all sorts of things about him that I thought he needed to look at! At one point he added a little comic relief (because I never once "hooked" him with my rage) by raising his fist up to the ceiling and saying, "Dear God, *why* have you put both my wife *and* this woman in my life to deal with?" To which I replied quite sarcastically, "Because *you* need us!"

Later, after venting more anger in a long letter to him, I gradually began to see what he was really trying to tell me. Then it dawned on me—he was absolutely right! I rushed to the phone to call and tell him he was going to get this epistle from me, but that I'd seen the light, that he was right.

In the meantime he had realized that some of my feedback to him had also been accurate. It ended with my having more respect for, more trust in him as a true friend than I'd had before. And to this day, I must admit, his remarks have enabled me to stay away from certain more dominating parts of my charismatic personality in group work—this has been beneficial for me and for others as well. This is a good example of what friends and co-workers sometimes go through in honest exchange and deep caring.

When you feel that a therapeutic confrontation is essential in a close relationship, you may have to risk a temporary alienation from the person—and perhaps, but rarely, long-term or permanent separation if the person just cannot hear it. This is the risk. But when it is successful, it is growthful and rewarding for both parties involved. We need to know that deep, caring relationships come from the Heart—and sometimes require tough love.

PROCESS. As we have seen, confrontation between friends or relatives can be risky, but it can also have great advantages: The very fact of the longevity of such a relationship offers one a deep experience of another person's patterned ways of relating and a real basis for confrontation. Clients can sometimes fool therapists about some of their issues or problematic behaviors because the professional therapist rarely sees these people in all aspects of their ordinary lives, as do good friends and relatives. Consequently the client being confronted by a therapist always has an "out": "Well, this was just a special case when she saw me at my worst. If she *really* knew me, she would know this isn't really true." When people do not know us very well, we can deceive them, as well as ourselves! It is human nature to want to hide. But it is harder to hide from someone who has known us over time.

When we confront someone, it comes out of deep caring; we want the ones we love to see the truth. The safest measure to use in intimate confrontations is our very established, loving relationship with the person: "Mother, I will listen, but I'm bored." Or the comic relief my mentor used with me—which indicated to me that he really did care about me, and that it mattered to him how I took in the painful information. The fact that he would not "let me off the hook" when I became defensive was even more proof to me that he cared and that he was not going to terminate our professional relationship just because he'd seen an error I was making in my work. There is potency and love at work in therapeutic confrontation. We just have to be careful how we do it, drawing upon our intuition as well as our skill and logic.

In order to strengthen your confrontation skills, you might ask for feedback whenever you do confront someone close to you—after it is all over. Ask the person what you did or did not do that was effective. Find out specifically what you need to learn more about, or where you are already highly developed. Honest feedback from people who care is growth producing for us all.

OPPOSITE OF THERAPEUTIC CONFRONTATION IN ACTION.
When we fail in this endeavor, it is likely due to our codependent relationships with one another.

Codependence is the way we give our power away to another in a relationship—because of a fear of rejection, or the need to be certain ways for that other person—ways to "not rock the boat." Often this means that we listen to each other, but we do not respond out loud with what we are feeling inside; we take the easy way out and remain silent, or we stretch the truth or literally deceive others about our true feelings. Or we may try to control the conversations so that we take over and don't have to deal with the feelings of vulnerability that would come from being really honest. There are also unhelpful ways that we all get caught up in each other's detailed story lines, as I described in the previous chapter.

Codependent behaviors usually come from our families of origin where we learned to play certain family roles. Maybe we were always the caretaker, the one who tried to keep the peace, or the controller who kept most events from becoming too outrageous, or the one who always caused the trouble and shifted the emphasis from the real issues—our parents' drinking or fighting. And now, later on in life, we find that we want to stay on the surface in relating and not risk intimate encounters. But we also grieve our lack of heart-to-heart intimacy in life.

Therapeutic confrontation is a way for us to grow past our fears of telling the truth. As codependents we must learn to confront by speaking from the heart. If we are truly coming from the heart the confrontation *can be heard.* Why? Because the heart can be trusted, first, to tell it like it is, and second, to have no ax to grind. Instead of something like this: "Sit down, Carol! You need to look at what you are doing," a heart response will sound more like this: "Carol, I have a feeling this may be a big one for you. I've known you for a long time, and I really am concerned. It seems this has been a long time coming. Here is how I see it." This kind of "straight talk" is telling it like it is, according to our perception. And it is always just *our perception;* we can never say it's the real truth. We must leave that decision to the one being confronted. And if we truly learn to come from the heart, and not from below the belt where our own ego issues reside, we will *act* creatively in the life of the other and not *re*act egoistically at the other's expense.

IMPLICATIONS FOR THE NONPROFESSIONAL RELATIONSHIP. Here are some important tips that will aid us in creating therapeutic confrontation situations. First, we should wait to confront until we are invited in as a listener or helper, although if a person's behavior is clearly getting in the way of our relationship, we may need to instigate a confrontation.

In any case we must remember to stay constantly in touch with our own feelings during a confrontation. When I feel the need to confront my family members and co-workers, I notice that it puts me immediately in touch with *my* issues. So I use my own experience as a way to self-disclose to the one I'm confronting, using "I" statements and telling them my reasons for needing this clearing with them. If I can stay in my heart, I will come from a real truth place, and I will feel expanded, open, and caring. If I drop below the heart, I will feel my own energy become defensive, and my solar plexus will wad up. When the latter occurs, it is my cue that I've become needy; something in the conversation is making me uncomfortable. I may even have to stop the conversation and allow myself to get in touch with what I am feeling and then have the courage to share these feelings with the person I'm confronting. Confrontations bring up our real selves. They can become two-way streets where both people are expressing their feelings, using immediacy, self-disclosure, warmth, and empathy. Therapeutic confrontation is loving but firm.

I want to emphasize that we often fail in confrontation or any human interaction simply because we do not listen to what the other has to say. We are either unwilling to trouble ourselves, or we are already busy thinking about our opinions and responses. We jump in and finish others' sentences or discount what they are saying, feeling our answers are much more important than their input. We may become so preoccupied with what *we* have to say that we find we have failed to hear anything the other person has said; we lack respect. We may think we are confronting, when really we are alienating.

The next time you have the opportunity to enter into this kind of relationship with someone close to you, bring your "observer self" along and watch yourself *as you are relating.* Notice everything about yourself—your feelings, your thoughts, and your behaviors—as you listen and relate to the other person. This is the two-way listening that high-functioning therapists are known for; they can remain in touch with themselves and with you all at once—without getting the two of you mixed up! This is true intimacy in action. And true intimacy is required if therapeutic confrontation is to become a part of your relationships. A deepening of the intimacy between you and the other person will be the result.

Be sure this closeness is what you want before you begin using therapeutic confrontation. It is one of the most potent aspects of our nature. And to develop this therapeutic variable as a skill requires courage, practice, and feedback in interactions with those you are close to.

A PRACTICE EXERCISE FOR YOU. You have fallen in love again! And you are so thrilled. Three years have passed since the breakup of your last primary relationship, which ended traumatically when your ex bottomed out with alcohol and refused treatment. You went to treatment for codependence without him. Not dreaming you could ever fall in love again, you meet Jonathon. In every way he is attractive to you. You notice he smoked a little pot when you two first met, but this behavior seemed to vanish. Now, however, you smell alcohol on his breath almost every day, and you are beginning to have fears. Tonight he comes by to take you to a party. When you arrive, you walk in and see that everyone is stoned on marijuana or cocaine or is drunk. And the room is filled with cigarette smoke. These are all the habits you've left behind! You ask Jonathon to step outside with you.

Jonathon: Hey, what's the deal? What's going on?

You: Jonathon, is this really how you want to spend this evening?

Jonathon: Oh, c'mon. This is just a little party with some old friends. Now don't tell me you're going to be a . . .

You: Jonathon, stop. . . . (Now continue.)

POTENCY

Potency is the quality that largely determines whether or not others come to us for help. It is a measure of our charisma or magnetic character. Potent people are in command of themselves and communicate a dynamic, expressive, and involved attitude to others. They embrace all of life's experiences, both positive and negative. Potent therapists are those who have relaxed into "just being themselves." People who are high in potency have *presence*. They are not incapacitated by adversity and are therefore models for effective living. Because they are in touch with their true being, they invite others to rise in stature and practice being themselves.

POTENCY IN THE COUNSELOR-CLIENT RELATIONSHIP

POTENCY IN ACTION.

Client: (pacing up and down the room, lost in thought) I just want to work harder on that job out there because I *know* things can get done better than they are. I believe I could change a few things for the better, if I could just . . . (He hesitates.)

Counselor: (gets up and starts walking around the room with the client) Golly, Bob, while you were saying that I got a feel for the power and the

> sensitivity you've got in you! (He speaks expressively.) I really *felt* it!

Client: You really did? You felt *my* power? Well, golly . . . (excitedly) . . . you know, I really mean it. I *could* do a lot more out there . . . I could . . .

Counselor: Go on. You could . . . ?

PROCESS. Because this counselor is truly involved with her client and doesn't hold back her expression of involvement, she has hooked into the client's potential power bank. This process enables the client to feel his own power and to believe in it. He feels accepted and encouraged to go on and use his potential, as he has just been validated by his counselor as a useful human being. His counselor is also serving as a model for her client—a model of someone who lives with hope and enthusiasm. As the client begins to act from his personal power bank, he will look to his counselor for rewards when he is successful, even in the smallest ways, and for encouragement and understanding when he falters or fails. It is very important that the counselor remember to praise each small step toward effective living that the client attempts or achieves, reminding the client on a regular basis that it is the *client's* own efforts—and not the therapist's—that create positive effects.

OPPOSITE OF POTENCY IN ACTION.
The counselor who scores low in potency is flat in affect—uninvolved and inexpressive. She is utilizing very little of her inner power and will consequently be unable to facilitate the discovery or releasing of power in her client. Clients often leave sessions with such counselors feeling uninspired or depressed. They may drop out of the counseling relationship, or if forced to see the counselor will merely go through the motions.

IMPLICATIONS FOR THE ALCOHOLIC CLIENT.

Because of his or her life history, the alcoholic client feels particularly demoralized and impotent. A counselor who rates high in potency can be a very effective model for the alcoholic client. Modeling after a potent counselor may sound as if it is too dependent to be healthy, but in fact it is a necessary stage for clients who have had few good role models in life. The dependency and "copying behavior" will evolve into a realistic balance of dependence-independence later.

A PRACTICE EXERCISE FOR YOU.

Practice a potent response to the following client situation.

Client: My wife's entire family was over last night. Boy, what a clan. I never felt so angry and confused in all my life. All of 'em talking at once . . . never once hearing what anybody else said. They never even noticed I was sober. I kept wanting to tell everybody off or to tell them what I thought they all sounded like. Sometimes I think maybe I've learned more about livin' than any of 'em. But then . . .

Counselor:

POTENCY IN EVERYDAY LIFE

People high in potency have an attitude of "knowing" rather than merely "believing in" goodness, truth, or justice. This attitude may sound egoistic, but it's not. It comes from people's own direct experiences with life; they have learned their lessons well and their attitude is actually more humble than arrogant. They are willing to involve with people, not in a codependent, needy way, but by offering others their views about things and then calmly letting them go, knowing they have to learn for themselves.

If you are one who just naturally exudes a high degree of magnetism or potency, you may have noticed that people ask for your help frequently and may even put you on a pedestal. Consequently you must remain conscious of your effect on others; even when you are not intending to have this effect, it simply cannot be avoided. You are blessed—and will remain so, as long as you do not misuse this natural gift.

POTENCY IN ACTION.

The following is an example of potency in action between a daughter and her mother.

The daughter is graduating from high school and has been awarded the scholastic honor of valedictorian, having made the highest grade-point average in her class. She is being invited to give a speech for the graduation ceremony. She is telling this news to her mother, who is a television talk-show host.

Shelley: Oh, Mom. I'm so excited! But gosh, I'm scared. You know, I've never really given a public speech to hundreds of people before. Oh God . . . this is awful. I'm beginning to panic at the thought. Mom, please oh please. Will you write the speech for me? Mom, you're so good. *Everybody* knows how good you are. Please, Mom. Will you do it? I *need* you (falls into her mother's arms).

Mom: Shelley, sweetheart (hugs her warmly), you know that I'm here for you. Of course I'll help. But . . . you don't *really* think I could say what's in your heart better than you can, do you? You have such a beautiful heart. And Shelley, you're so articulate yourself! Don't you remember how often I've relied on *you* to help *me* with *my* show? But I know you're scared right now. . . . You need a little more time just to absorb this news. I'm very proud of you.

Shelley: (begins to calm down . . . and settles into being more herself) Thanks, Mom. I guess I am getting a little carried away. But I really *am* nervous.

Mom: I never start one of my public programs without a few butterflies in my tummy. Even after all these years . . .

Shelley: Really, Mom? *Really?* Gosh, you always *look* so cool.

Mom: (hugs her again) Yes, you're right. (She laughs.) It's an acquired trait. You can develop it too! (And they both hug and laugh playfully with one another.)

PROCESS. You will note that the mother put the emphasis back on Shelley's own strengths when Shelley wanted to lean on her mother's advanced experience. The mother knows her daughter well—she has seen her daughter's own leadership skills emerge throughout her childhood and can now point those experiences out to the daughter, whose fear has made her lose touch for the moment with her own potency. Note the effective use of self-disclosure by the mother when the daughter referred to her nervousness. With her disclosure the mother did not discount Shelley's fear or nervousness, or try to talk her out of it. She provided Shelley with the opportunity to identify with one of her idols: "Even successful, experienced people like Mom get stage fright; so I am not so different." This provides Shelley with hope that she too can succeed.

OPPOSITE OF POTENCY IN ACTION.

There are two possible ways the above scenario could have failed: first, if the mother had just agreed to write the speech for her daughter, with an unspoken attitude that she probably *could* do it better. This response would not have acknowledged the daughter's own strengths, of which the mother is well aware; and such a response would have promoted hero worship at the expense of this growing daughter's own development as a leader. Second, if the mother had tried to discount her daughter's nervousness and fear. "Now, Shelley, you know better than to be scared. After all, it's only a speech to many people you already know love you very much." This would have made Shelley feel that her fears were simply dismissed and possibly even that she was stupid for having such fears—creating a harmful discrepancy between how she thinks she should be feeling and how she really *is* feeling.

POTENCY IN ACTION.

In the following example Michelle is recovering from an alcohol and cocaine addiction, with four years of sobriety. She is a member of Narcotics Anonymous and a codependent women's group and attends meetings regularly. For eight months now she has had her six-year-old son Tom with her after losing him temporarily to her sister while undergoing treatment and the first stages of recovery. She and Tom have been doing very well, except for the past week, young Tom's first week of school. During these past few troublesome days Tom has cried a lot and regressed to some old behaviors leftover from when his mother was using and sick. Michelle's family is very upset and is demanding that Tom go back to his aunt's home to live. Michelle is bereft and very frightened. She feels her family has the power to take her son away from her. Michelle has visited her best friend, Laura, to ask for help. She is feeling very threatened and upset.

Michelle: (sobbing) They're coming over tonight to talk to me, Laura, and I know they're ganging up. They're going to insist on taking him. And we're doing so well—really. It's just school, all this adjusting he's having to do. *All* children go through *some* kind of adjustment period when they start something new like school! But they're all making it sound like . . . oh, I guess it's me. I guess they think *I* can't handle it. They don't trust me, do they? Maybe they're right. . . . Maybe it's . . . (begins to cry softly).

Laura: Michelle, you sounded so strong and wise when you were saying you and Tom are doing well. 'Cause you *are!* We all see your relationship with your son just blossoming. He loves you so much. And you two are happy together. It *is* natural what he's going through. Your family's just scared and overreacting. Michelle, I really know you. I see how you and Tom are doing.

Michelle: (obviously sitting up taller, more like herself) Really? Oh, gosh. I was beginning to think no one had noticed (begins to sigh and weep, quietly).

Laura: You can look your mother and sister in the eye and tell them emphatically *and* lovingly that you're doing just fine! And they can ask your friends if they don't believe you! I can understand your panic, Michelle. There's some painful history here (hugs her). And my! Haven't you come a long way in four years? (And here Laura's body posture is important: She has pulled her shoulders back and her head upright in a cheerful, prideful position—which is mirroring Michelle's own taller, more centered position. This nonverbal gesture not only mirrors Michelle's, but it underlines the statement Laura has just made about coming a long way.)

PROCESS. When we are threatened by the loss of something precious, we often lose our potency. Even if things on the outside look great, if we are frightened inside, we may feel powerless—impotent. Others will tell us to "get over it," but we can't. We still feel threatened. This means some piece of psychological "unfinished business" has surfaced, prompted by some outside event. In the above example Michelle's low self-esteem left over from her years of being an active addict (and maybe even further back than that) came to the surface so that it could receive a little more light of understanding. This is how we heal; things will continue to resurface, like reminders, until we learn all the truth surrounding an issue then integrate it—meaning that our picture of who we are will balance into an acceptance of ourselves *just as we are*, and the symptoms of the low self-esteem (or whatever we are facing) will subside.

Laura, in her potency and willingness to commit herself to this friend in need, provided feedback that was real from her point of view and that validated Michelle's conviction that her relationship with Tom was okay. Michelle was thus encouraged to return to her own true self. Laura's entire approach in this example, especially her posturing, is a high-functioning form of potency in action. The use of potency provides a **context** for and **validation** of truthfulness that enables others to believe in themselves and to trust *their own direct experience*.

OPPOSITE OF POTENCY IN ACTION. A lack of personal interest in another's situation can be a sign of low potency. An example of the opposite of potency would have been if Laura had in fact observed that

Michelle was *not* a fit mother for Tom and had lied to her friend to make her feel good, bolstering her confidence artificially.

It is through the **recognition** of others' strengths and essential qualities that our Hearts unite in oneness. When our souls are aware, we see each other's essence. And when this happens, we sparkle with delight! When something important about us is validated by another through the recognition of the Heart, it becomes easier for us to expand into this acknowledged part of ourselves. Gradually we learn to live from that part with conviction. This is how potency is born, and this is how it is replenished throughout life.

A PRACTICE EXERCISE FOR YOU. You are a father, and your twelve-year-old son is working on a science experiment as part of a team for a school assignment. Your son is shy and tends to hold back in a group. You walk into his room and see that he is thoughtfully working something out on paper, concentrating deeply.

Dad: (waiting until his son lifts his head in acknowledgment of his father's presence) Hey, Gary, how's the project going? You look like you're really getting into it.

Son: Oh, it's nothing, Dad. I'm just working something out. . . . I can see that there's a place where we could really make this work better. It's really neat, Dad! Come here and look! (He shows his dad proudly the formula he's worked out.)

Dad: Well, Son, this looks really interesting. You know more about this than I do, but I can tell you that I think you're really on to something here. Are you going to tell your group?

Son: Oh, no . . . not really. No . . . I couldn't. They're all better students than me. And besides, I may not be right. . . . (He hesitates.) I'd probably feel really stupid. . . . (Hesitates again.)

Dad:

SELF-ACTUALIZATION

The extent to which people are self-actualizing determines how involved they are in the growth process. Self-actualizing counselors learn from their clients as their clients learn from them. Such people serve as models for creative living. They are able to express themselves freely because they don't see themselves as "having arrived." They don't fall back on roles or phoniness because they have no need to protect themselves from becoming known, or being "found out." Because they accept themselves as having both strengths and weaknesses—as being fully *human*—they do not have to judge or moralize to others who fall short of a goal or make a mistake in life. They have the capacity for spontaneous warmth and intimacy, and they have a sense of humor. Moreover, they are flexible: If a course of action does not fall into place, they can flow into another direction without getting all bent out of shape. They experience stress and tension, yet they are seldom immobilized by these feelings, or even knocked off center. They seek to know themselves more and more and will risk new behavior and new sets of circumstances in order to grow and discover new truths about themselves. Some self-actualizing people may have adventuresome spirits that lead them to seek out a lot of change, while others may be more meditative and lead quieter lives.

Self-actualizing people do not lean on dogma or preconceived ideas to determine their lives but flow with the "process of becoming," using *their own direct experiences* as the true test of authority. Since they do this for themselves, they also trust and respect others' experiences as being valid. They are not hung up on what is "right" and "wrong"; the only "wrong" for them is when people block getting their needs met so that they function through neediness when relating to others. And the only "right" is for people to learn to take care of themselves in ways that satisfy these needs, so that each one of us is free to be a giving person.

Self-actualization is really a technical word, the definition of which is based on scientific research. The chief theorist of self-actualization is the well-known psychologist Abraham Maslow. Studies of self-actualizing people indicate that humans must meet their "deficiency needs" in order to be healthy. These basic needs include the need for food, shelter, security, sex, belongingness, and self-worth. When these are taken care of, we just naturally begin to operate from a higher level of consciousness, at the level of needs Dr. Maslow calls "being needs." Being needs are gratified through love and enhancing one's creative potentials. Self-actualizing people have "settled down" into their identities as acceptable people, able to flow with life's ups and downs. People who rate high on self-actualization scales are more concerned with what is good for the whole. They naturally tend toward service or projects that have meaning and purpose for society at large—or they may withdraw from the melodramas of life, becoming meditative and keeping to themselves in ways that harm no one. Maslow concluded from this finding that human nature is basically *good*, or at least neutral—and that any form of uncovering therapy (learning to explore, understand, and accept oneself) releases the basic good that is already in us, rather than unleashing evil "animalistic" instincts. He asserts that the selfishness, greed, and evil we see in human beings result from a lack of self-support or environmental support, which causes the individual to react from deficiency needs that have gone unmet.

Self-actualization is not merely a trait or characteristic—it is a description of the whole person in process, encompassing all the other nine personal characteristics described in this book. What does a person actually *do* when he "self-actualizes"? As Maslow humorously asks at one point in his book, *The Farther Reaches of Human Nature,* "Does he grit his teeth and squeeze?" It might be helpful at this point to describe in behavioral terms some of the things that happen when we are in the process of self-actualization.

1. A person will begin experiencing in the moment more fully and vividly, with full concentration and without self-consciousness. Remember when you were an adolescent and had the feeling you were always being watched as though you were on stage, that whatever you were doing, public or private, was being judged? In the self-actualization process this feeling disappears, and we begin doing for ourselves rather than doing for an audience. This process is tied very closely to the process of creativity—being able to unite completely with the "other" in the moment. The other might be a piece of stone if you are a sculptor, or another person if you are a counselor.

In fact, becoming creatively preoccupied with anything in the moment causes time to vanish; we've all experienced this at some time or another. We just fall into a timeless state where we feel complete. This is the absorption of the mystic and the artist—and many now believe this state is the healer of codependence. We are codependent when we lose ourselves in things *outside* of us, events or people we cannot control. When we return to a creative stance in life, rediscovering the things in life that really turn *us* on, we are beginning to become self-actualizing, in touch with our own inner authority and rightful expression.

2. Self-actualizing people remain in the moment and have a "growth" response instead of lying or "weaseling out" when confronted with a painful or prideful situation.

They take responsibility for their decisions and actions and experience a sense of freedom in doing so. This freedom, however, can sometimes be lonely or painful at first, until one can shift the feelings of loneliness to an awareness of *aloneness,* which can be quite rewarding, especially for people who've spent most of their lives giving their time and energy away to others.

3. People involved in self-actualizing behavior will begin "checking themselves out" to see if attitudes or decisions are really *their* feelings, or if they are unexamined belief systems that come from significant people in their past. A self-actualizing person might begin asking herself questions like, "Do I really want to spend all my Sunday afternoons visiting relatives, or is this something I am doing because my parents always did it?" She may even discover that no one in the family is enjoying this ritual. She begins listening more to her own "impulse voices" and less to the noises of the world.

4. Self-actualizing people will often experience periods of renewed interest in their own unfolding. They may throw themselves into a chosen task or a newly discovered skill or interest. There is a shift away from losing oneself in others to a vital interest in one's own development, even when certain sacrifices are required. Such people might change careers midstream or go back to school to finish a degree. Values change; life-styles become obsolete; some relationships, even major ones, die while others bloom or begin to take on a different significance. Sometimes a person considered to be emotionally stable and the rock of his community will enter psychotherapy or behave in ways that seem unpredictable to his closest associates. Often periods of disorganization and chaos seem to crop up "out of the blue" at the very time in one's life when the pattern has become established and easy—as though some deep, intrinsic part of ourselves takes over and says, "It's time to change."

5. "Peak experiences" (moments of ecstasy or mystical, religious experiences) may begin happening to a person in the process of self-actualization. These inner experiences are difficult to describe unless one has had them. They are those moments in life when even the mundane can become sacred. They can occur under a wide variety of circumstances—while making love, giving birth to a child, listening to music, walking through a busy parking lot in the rain, or looking at a sunrise. Or sometimes they are set off by more dramatic conditions, such as having a near-death experience, accompanying someone through the process of physical death, or experiencing times of extreme emotional crisis. Besides being inherently profound and meaningful, these moments can open up new horizons for us—giving us a new purpose in life, curing a neurosis, offering new insight into ourselves, or increasing our regard for people or for the world in general. In short, these experiences assist us in releasing our fullest potential as human beings and remind us of our spiritual significance.

The self-actualizing counselor is not concerned with teaching in the ordinary sense of the word, but only with helping other people realize their own way, their own unique style of being in the world. It is the Taoistic attitude—the "noninterfering" way of helping another to unfold, to break through one's defenses against oneself, and recover or discover oneself.

People who come for help are always in conflict. They are experiencing discordant feelings that usually center on the valuing process—"I ought to" versus "I want to," or "I ought to, but I can't." When we begin examining "ought systems," we discover quickly that there are two kinds of "oughts." There are oughts that are external to us, and there are oughts that are intrinsically locked into our own self system, which when violated produce horrible chaos and confusion internally. Good counseling consists of helping a client discover which oughts are external (really introjects) and which oughts are actual needs of the client, which must be listened to and satisfied. If there were indeed such a thing as *complete* self-actualization, *what is* (facts) and *what ought to be* (values) would fuse—our authentic self would match our values, and there would be no more conflict.

Self-actualizing counselors are nonjudgmental and concerned with values in a nonmoralistic manner: They aid clients in discovering their own internal and external values (or oughts) and help them realize the difference between the two.

SELF-ACTUALIZATION IN THE COUNSELOR-CLIENT RELATIONSHIP

SELF-ACTUALIZING COUNSELOR IN ACTION.

Client: I'm seeing Betty on the side, you know. Janet doesn't know it. She'd die! She's telling everybody we're just about to get married. And you know how much our folks are counting on us marrying. But I'll tell you—Betty's making me feel real good about some things. I feel like I *need* her company. . . . At least, I just seem to keep going over there a lot . . . sort of like a return of the old manhood or something. I don't know. Yeah, that's what it is. She just makes me feel like some kind of man! (He sounds determined.) I *won't* be forced into giving her up just yet! I just won't!

Counselor: Sounds like you're choosing a course of action that feels right for you just now. But Bill, I'm noticing too that this choice doesn't seem all that easy for you to make—like maybe there's a lot of pain in it for you, considering the possible reaction Janet and both your folks might have if they knew about Betty.

Client: It's really just awful. I shouldn't be doing this. . . . Boy, am I confused.

Counselor: I think I know how that dilemma feels, Bill. I have to work on myself a lot about what consequences I'm willing to pay if I choose to do something that I know has a lot of pain in it for someone else. That's sure a tough one, all right!

Client: Yeah. Well, I *do* know I could lose Janet either way I go. . . . I mean, if I don't tell her about Betty and she finds out from someone else, or if I do tell her.

Counselor: What do you get for yourself from your relationship with Janet, Bill? Are you pretty clear on that?

PROCESS. Because the counselor is a searching, growing person himself, he knows life contains ambiguities that are not always resolved with a correct answer. Note that the counselor is not choosing to lecture his client on the issue of promises and commitments to a fiancée, or on how he should live up to his parents' wishes. Instead he is accepting the client as a human being who has choices and must face consequences unique to his own situation. The counselor is also illustrating the fact that both he and the client are part of the same human race, with certain needs and dilemmas that are similar. He is helping his client to reality-test his decision (to continue seeing Betty) against another very real human being (the counselor). This can lead to a clarification of actions and consequences for the client that can, in turn, lead him to face his decision more honestly and directly, based on his *real* internal "oughts" rather than on appearances or needs that are external.

IMPLICATIONS FOR THE ALCOHOLIC CLIENT.
Alcoholic clients will blossom in a relationship with a self-actualizing person and will themselves begin to self-actualize, learning to return to their own creative expression in life. These clients will feel encouraged and accepted by a self-actualizing counselor in spite of problems with drinking, which have likely been labeled by relatives and associates as weak behavior. Such clients will begin feeling that they have a right to *be*. They will learn ways to get "deficiency needs" met so that they can keep their lives alcohol-free and fulfilling. Being in touch with one's creative uniqueness heals addiction. Clients will have no need to lose themselves in bottles or other people's lives if they are in love with their own lives and their own unfolding!

Dogma, moralizing, and preaching will drive the alcoholic further toward drinking and away from the true self that lies beneath the years of alcoholic behavior. You will see the alcoholic shrink rather than expand, more hopeless and discouraged after every moralizing encounter.

Yet morals are important too. Recovering alcoholic clients need to be supported very carefully in a moral system they are comfortable with. Even the smallest amount of guilt may drive them back to the bottle. When clients share with you some moral dilemma they are having, it is crucial that you help them examine their actions very carefully in a completely nonjudgmental way. They may need you to help them clarify their needs and behavior *realistically* within the context of a caring relationship and a climate of human equality.

A PRACTICE EXERCISE FOR BOTH PRO-FESSIONAL AND NONPROFESSIONAL COUNSELORS.

See what response comes naturally for you in a relationship with the person described below and watch how your behavior compares with what has just been described as "self-actualizing" behavior.

Client: Yep. It's true. I'm flunking out of school, and I've really just blown the whole semester—tuition, room and board—all of it! I've really done it this time—blown every chance I ever had for getting into med school. My dad is going to . . . oh, God, I don't know if I can even *think* about going home (puts head in hands—long pause). You know, I've never really wanted to be a doctor anyway. . . . Well, yes I have. I mean, my dad and granddad are both doctors. . . . Oh, brother. . . .

Counselor:

SELF-ACTUALIZATION IN EVERYDAY LIFE

In nonprofessional helping roles the best way to utilize the power of self-actualization for the sake of another is to model this actualization in truth and in exuberance. Show the other person your own discoveries of how life can be a real adventure! You might share how you are unfolding—how you are working on yourself and learning to express yourself in life according to your own values and your own truth.

The one in trouble may ask you admiringly how it is that you seem so happy, or what it is you are spending your time doing these days. Take these opportunities to share from your heart some of your own discoveries about life, about love, and especially about yourself. This not only enables someone to learn from your example, but it also reinforces your own discoveries and enhances your ability to be a creative, loving person.

Sometimes when I try to visualize what self-actualization looks like, I see an image of all of us together making up a long chain of beings moving upward toward a very high place. The person just ahead holds out his hand to you, while you hold out your hand to the one just beneath you. This is not an "over-under" situation, but one of true companionship. As you are being lifted by the one in front of you, you are also lifting the one behind. Giving and receiving are in perfect balance. In this way we all feel of equal value; each person serves a vital role in our collective wholeness—every one of us becomes a link in the chain of being.

I know of no better way to begin self-actualizing than for each of us to make a commitment *right this minute* (if we've not already done so) to do whatever is necessary in our lives to begin discovering more deeply who we are. Do so in the good company of other people like ourselves, people who are beginning to think and act for themselves—not self-ishly, but self-actually. First, we must *have* a self before we can begin to give this self away to others in selflessness. We cannot transcend an ego we've never developed! And when we are being truly self-actualizing, we are by definition being naturally therapeutic.

A FINAL NOTE
ON COUNSELING
AN ALCOHOLIC

Alcoholism scares us all sometimes, even the most coura-
geous therapists, or those who are considered "experts" in
the area of family dysfunction. Many people believe that
alcoholism counseling is something unique or mysterious,
requiring a special kind of training and expertise. Many also
believe that you cannot effectively help an alcoholic unless
you have experienced alcoholism yourself. Neither belief is
true. However, a family member should not try to serve as a
regular counselor to another family member who is in trouble with alcohol or drugs. In this instance professional help
will work more effectively. Today we know that alcoholism
is a family systems problem in which each member becomes
involved. A family member's own issues can cloud the
counseling picture for the person in crisis.

But when we have the opportunity to be involved in
helping someone who is not a family member—someone we
feel we can remain clear and objective with—we will find
that we can be effective by utilizing our *self* as an instrument, as described throughout these pages. Remember that
alcoholics have trained themselves to be masters at keeping
others away from their deepest secrets; this is usually due to
their own self-disgust. But inside they crave relationships,
ones that are intimate and meaningful. For in their hearts
alcoholics are very deep people; they have the qualities of
the mystic, the artist, and the sage. In order to release this

creative potential, the alcoholic must find another way. He or she must learn to stay away from alcohol and drugs and learn to live with fascination and with hope.

I would like to leave you with a very simple thought. Alcoholic clients or friends need from you only two things:

1. Someone to help them withstand the temptation to drink—because they simply cannot handle alcohol, not one thimbleful. In order to withstand this temptation—because it is so great—they must find something else in life that turns them on as much as they hoped the alcohol would. For they are transcenders—"flyers"—seeking a way back to wholeness, to a life with spiritual meaning. The urge for transcendence is behind their urge to drink or to otherwise alter their moods artificially.

2. And someone to help them discover their unique creative expressions and needs—their internal oughts and how to gratify them realistically—because they cannot survive with the frustration of too many unmet desires. Alcoholics and addicts are some of the world's most sensitive people; they are seeking ways to belong and to make a difference in the world.

Alcoholism is a problem that affects *the whole person*. And for you to be significant in the life of an alcoholic and his or her family, all you need is your *own* wholeness—your eyes, your ears, your brain, your heart, and your sensitivity —in other words, your ability to be fully human and naturally therapeutic.

ANOTHER FINAL THOUGHT FOR US ALL!

One day a centipede was walking down the street, minding her own business. A passerby was struck by the awesome grace and beauty of the one hundred legs in concert, loco-moting the centipede through the traffic in perfect symme-try. "Wait!" said the stranger in an excited voice. "How are you doing this wondrous orchestration with all those legs of yours? I really must know." The centipede graciously stopped and began to analyze and explain her structure and condi-tion. And before she knew what had happened, she was so tangled up in her hundred legs that she collapsed in a heap at the mercy of the oncoming traffic, unable to regain her original dignity.

This could become *our* story if we try too hard to analyze ourselves and our therapeutic parts. Once you study these ten traits of high-functioning therapists, finding your weaknesses and your strengths, it is best to forget all this and return to this book only when you feel that one or more of these qualities is missing in your interactions with people. When an important relationship is in trouble, it is often because we have temporarily lost touch with a thera-peutic trait.

Learn to trust your natural style of listening. Coming from the heart is a simple matter as long as we don't focus too much on our process or attempt to separate our parts. When our therapeutic self is operating, we function as a whole. When our analytical self is in the driver's seat, we may be off the mark, just in our heads. Becoming a therapeutic person happens while we are looking the other way, when we can just relax and be ourselves; it is our naturalness and our highest expression.

I hope this book has given you the courage to be your *self* and to realize that you already have within you everything you need to help another person.

I hope you can remember how beautiful you are the next time you are asked to serve another or feel the need for a helper yourself! Recognizing the good in one another and learning how to share in this goodness is love made visible.

GLOSSARY

Catharsis. This is a Freudian term with a highly complex meaning. It is the act of releasing pent-up feelings and emotions that have been held in by inhibition and blocked awareness—maybe for years. Freud felt catharsis is therapeutic because it is a purification or release from tensions, eliminating serious psychological complexes (which are systems of repressed or suppressed desires and memories that exert a dominating influence upon the personality and can produce exaggerated reactions to certain subjects, people, or situations). Catharsis brings these complexes or pieces of "psychological unfinished business" to consciousness and affords them expression.

Context. The counselor provides a context for the client when using a mental picture or metaphorical explanation to clarify the client's symptoms or troubled feelings. This creates a framework or mind-set in which clients can better understand their plights and emotions, seeing them not only more positively, but more meaningfully as well. Much of our fear comes from what we believe is the unknown. By providing a context the counselor shows the client that his or her feelings are okay. This provides an opportunity for deeper exploration and resolution.

Example:

Client: And I've never felt so terrible. I'm falling apart, maybe even going crazy. Maybe I'm dying. . . . I've just never been so depressed, never felt more lost or hopeless.

Counselor: I can really sense your fear, Paul, and your desperation. Perhaps you're at that place the mystics speak of—the "dark night of the soul." They say it happens right before the dawn of something new . . . a crucial and profound stage in our process.

Corrective emotional experience.

Quite often a client unconsciously reenacts with a counselor feelings, wishes, and experiences involving the client's parents or some other significant figure from his or her past. In a sense the client confuses the counselor's identity with the identity of these past figures, usually parents. These held-over feelings from past relationships can be used therapeutically in the present.

For example, if I have a young female client who "transfers" to me feelings she had in relationship with her mother, and her mother made her feel ashamed of her sexuality, I have the opportunity to correct my client's emotional experience by making her feel *good* about her sexuality. Since I have become the "mother figure" for the time being, I can replace, or correct, some of this past injustice and help my client perceive herself differently. This is called a corrective emotional experience in psychotherapy.

Mirroring.

A nonverbal technique of copying exactly what the client is doing behaviorally—hunching shoulders, scowling, fidgeting, smiling, and so on. This action on the part of a counselor enables clients to see themselves in ways they may be unaware of. Since it is very hard to teach our bodies to lie, our nonverbal behavior is usually closer to the truth about our reality than our words.

I was telling a therapist friend of mine one day that I had decided to take a job I had really talked myself into taking. As I was telling her how glad I was about my decision, she mirrored my nonverbal behavior—frowning, fidgeting, head down, expressionless eyes. I was amazed at how beautifully I had fooled myself into thinking I was glad about my decision. Her mirroring my behavior was more helpful to me than anything she could have said on a rational level. I've never regretted turning down that job!

Morbid grief. *Morbid* grief is the technical term for griefwork occurring in unhealthy or indirect ways because of a person's resistance to feeling and expressing *normal* grief at the loss of a loved one. *Normal* griefwork follows a certain predictable course through various stages—anger, guilt, mourning, acceptance of the loss, and reintegration into a world devoid of the lost person. The amount of time griefwork takes varies with individuals, but usually the process will take somewhere between three months to one year. *Morbid,* or pathological, grief has several predictable outcomes too, all of which interfere quite seriously with a person's ability to function and maintain normal relationships with others. Some of the signs of morbid grief are depersonalization (lack of feeling), agitated depression, flight of ideas, extreme irritability, and some behaviors resembling schizophrenia, such as identifying with the lost person (taking on his or her characteristics). When you observe clients with any of these

symptoms, it is useful to ask them if someone significant in their life has died or rejected or left them. If
so, helping them get into the avoided feelings will be
therapeutic.

Nonjudgmental feedback. My basic assumption
as a counselor is that clients deal adequately with
their own life problems—*if* they know what they are
and can bring all their abilities into action to solve
them. Clients know better than I do what decisions
are right for them. The art of feeding back to a client
what you are experiencing in relation to that client's
personhood, words, or actions in a nonjudgmental
manner is the mark of a good facilitator of personal
growth. Nonjudgmental feedback is made up of statements that are objective, or "I" statements; they do
not contain a "right" or a "wrong" in tone or content.

Example:

Client: I really told her how *I* felt about it! I told her
off! Was that the right thing to do?

Counselor: What I'm hearing is that you seem happy with
yourself for what you did. Right or wrong, who
knows? The key is how *you* feel about what you
did. Can you trust that? Can you trust your
own experience?

      Nonjudgmental feedback takes practice, but it's
worth every improvement you can possibly make because it keeps you out of the deadly role of "judge."

Projection. The art of attributing disowned aspects of
yourself to others—or, put in another way, the phenomenon of directly experiencing a feeling as though
it were someone else's. If I experience someone else as

angry in order to block my awareness of my *own* anger at that person, I am less in touch with the whole transaction and am likely to act or react inappropriately. Projection and denial go hand in hand: I cannot project a feeling onto you unless I am denying it in myself. The task of the counselor in the face of this phenomenon is to help clients perceive or experience the feeling as their own.

Rationalization. To attribute one's actions, feelings, or ideas to rational and creditable motives without adequate analysis or understanding of the *real* and perhaps unconscious motives underlying the choice. A person will even lie sometimes, inventing plausible reasons for doing something to cover up guilt or shame.

Reality-testing. The act of comparing an idea, fantasy, or feeling with a real experience.

Example:

Client: My sister told me to quit flirting with John so much or he'd get sick of me, so I watch myself around him and try not to come on so strong.

Counselor: How does John act when you flirt with him?

Client: Well, gosh, he seems to love it. He always warms up to me, is more talkative, hugs me a lot, acts really at ease about it.

Counselor: What might be going on in your sister to make her think such a thing about John, I wonder? Sounds more like *her* thing.

Client: You mean my sis may be wrong?

Counselor: Well, which are you going to trust more—*your experience* with John, or your sister's notion of it?

Client: Well, I never . . . you know, I never thought of
it like that before. (She laughs.) Old sis . . .
wonder what her problem is?

Recognition. The innate intuitive capacity of human
consciousness to grasp its own nature. It is an honor-
ing *from the heart* of a truth at the level of essence.
Sometimes we recognize a soul mate or fellow traveler
with a similar life purpose; or we "see" or "hear" the
bottom line, a true sense of what is really going on.
The ego "cognizes" (intellectualizes, or creates stories); the soul *recognizes. Recognition* connotes a re-
membrance, a *reminder.* We feel uplifted when a
recognition is taking place. "Ah, she sees." Or "*Aha!*
the truth!"

Reflecting. A verbal technique of repeating to the client
the essence of what he or she said. "You say you are
happy at home but you don't particularly like weekends?" Often something will clarify for clients when
they hear their very own words coming back to them.
Many times the things we say are contradictory or
have several meanings on several levels, and we have
just never taken the time to discover what it all means
to us. This is a very common way we all keep ourselves confused. The art of reflecting can slow people
down and cause them to examine more closely the
assumptions that underlie their thoughts and actions.

Stuck. This is a Gestalt therapy term, coined by the
originator of Gestalt therapy, Fritz Perls. It means the
following: If you are working with a client along a
certain line of blocked awareness and the client resists
or balks—either trying to put the responsibility on you
to do his or her "work," or telling you that you are

really not in tune with where he or she is—you may get lost and become blocked yourself, truly not knowing where to go next, or not willing to go in the direction the client is trying to lead *you*. At a time like this, you are stuck and the most productive thing you can do is to claim this openly: "I am stuck right now and cannot think of a way to go with you." This declaration always produces some action on the part of the client. Often it will add to his or her reasons for resisting you. Whatever it produces will be material to work with and will move the session out of a bottleneck. This honest action on your part demonstrates that you are human. It also puts the responsibility on the client to work. Trying to fake it when you are honestly stuck *never* works. You will either increase the client's resistance, or you will waste time for both of you in inauthentic activity.

Unconscious denial. This is a psychological defense, a maneuver of the psyche that serves the purpose of keeping unacceptable material on an unconscious (unaware) level so that it is not available to the personality for reality-testing. By "unacceptable material" I mean anything about yourself or your world that does not fit in with the psychological system you are unconsciously using for survival, or anything that would make you feel too guilty or ashamed to handle without excess fear or anxiety.

Unfinished business. Perhaps the major consequence of blocked awareness is the phenomenon of unfinished business. Need cycles cannot become completed; tension is aroused but not reduced; and affect mounts but is unexpressed. Little new can happen in the ensuing constriction and frustration when a person is experiencing an overwhelming amount of unfinished business. These unresolved emotional needs carry over into our present relationships, distorting and distracting our ability to listen and involve fully with each other. Unfinished business can go a long way back into our past; it may pertain to our relationships with authority figures due to unresolved conflicts with parents—or it can be a very recent piece of unfinished business left unresolved from just a few minutes ago.

When you are aware that some of your unfinished business really cannot be resolved quickly, just being aware of it helps. Here is an example of a counselor's way of handling his own need to be authentic when he is aware of an area of unfinished business within him that dates a long way back: "John, as you begin talking about your problems with your dad, I am aware that I've still got some pretty bad feelings about my own father I haven't worked out yet. I want to be sure I don't get my needs mixed up with yours. I'll need to check us both out very carefully as we go into this. You stop me if I get too far off in trying to hear your problem. My own feelings about this could get in your way. Okay?"

Validation. The act of acknowledging something out loud for clients that will help them see something about themselves that will reinforce their sense of self-worth. It must be truthful, clear, and to the point. "I note as you speak that you are sounding more and more forceful in your presentation" (said to a shy woman just learning to express herself). Or, "Jamie, I want to honor you for the way you handled your father in that conversation" (said to a young man just learning to stand up to his overbearing father). Or,

"Meg, lots of people have inner mystical experiences such as these. I myself have had this type of experience. You are not crazy at all; these things are quite common throughout human history" (a self-disclosure that validates a woman's unusual religious or "peak" experience that goes against the teachings of her religion, and for this reason has made her doubt her sanity). Often *context* and *validation* go hand in hand.

REFERENCES

Credit goes to Sidney Wolf, Ph.D., for synthesizing the research findings on counselor effectiveness listed below. The following is a list of all the chief investigators responsible for the counselor-variable studies reported in *Becoming Naturally Therapeutic*:

Berenson, B.G.; Mitchell, J.M.; and Laney, R.C. "Level of Therapist Functioning, Types of Confrontation and Type of Patient." *Journal of Clinical Psychology* 25 (1969): 111–13.

Bergen, A.E. "Some Implications of Psychotherapy Research for Therapeutic Practice." *Journal of Abnormal Psychology* (1966): 235–46.

Cannon, J.R., and Carkhuff, R.R. "Effects of Rater Level of Functioning and Experience Upon the Discrimination of Facilitative Conditions." *Journal of Consulting and Clinical Psychology* 32 (1969): 189–94.

———. "Helping and Human Relations: A Primer for Lay and Professional Helpers." *Selection and Training*. Vol. 1. New York: Holt, Rinehart and Winston, 1969.

Carkhuff, R.R., and Berenson, B.G. *Beyond Counseling and Therapy*. New York: Holt, Rinehart and Winston, 1967.

Collingwood, T.R., and Renz, L. "The Effects of Client Confrontations upon Levels of Immediacy Offered by High and Low Functioning Counselors." *Journal of Clinical Psychology* 25 (1969): 224–26.

Foulds, M.L. "Self Actualization and the Communication of Facilitative Conditions during Counseling." *Journal of Counseling Psychology* 16 (1969): 132–36.

Small, J., and Wolf, S. "Beyond Abstinence." *Alcohol Health and Research World* 2 (1978): 32–36.

Truax, C.B., and Carkhuff, R.R. *Toward Effective Counseling and Psychotherapy: Training and Practice*. Chicago: Aldine, 1967.

Wolf, S. "Counseling: For Better or Worse." *Alcohol and Drug Problems of America, Selected Papers*, 23rd Annual Meeting. Washington, D.C.: ADPA, 1972.

Wolf, S. "An Investigation of Counsellor Type, Client Type, Level of Facilitative Conditions and Client Outcome." Ph.D diss., Catholic University of America, 1970. *Dissertation Abstracts International* 31, 70–22,093.

Wolf, S.; Wolf, C.M; Spielberg, G. *The Wolf Counseling Skills Evaluation Handbook*, Omaha, NE: National Publication, 1980.

These findings expand on and refine the work of Carl Rogers and Abraham Maslow on the therapeutic encounter and self-actualizing behavior. In the currently emerging field of transpersonal psychology, these therapeutic traits are again surfacing in explorations of the "guide" or "new paradigm therapist." Suggested readings follow.

Boorstein, S. "Transpersonal Context, Interpretation and Psychotherapeutic Technique." *Journal of Transpersonal Psychology* 18 (1986): 123–30.

Bradshaw, J. *Healing the Shame that Binds You*. Deerfield Beach, Florida: Health Communications, 1988.

Brown, M. *The Unfolding Self*. Los Angeles, Calif.: Psychosynthesis Press, 1983.

Carlson, R., and Shield, B., eds. *Healers on Healing*. Los Angeles: J.P. Tarcher, 1989.

Dass, R. and Gorman, P. *How Can I Help?* New York: Knopf, 1985.

Duce, M.I.O., and Mackie, J. *Gurus and Psychotherapists: Spiritual Versus Psychological Learning*. Layfayette, Calif.: Searchlight Seminars, 1981.

Ferguson, M. *The Aquarian Conspiracy*. Los Angeles: J.P. Tarcher, 1981.

Ferrucci, P. *What We May Be*. Los Angeles: J.P. Tarcher, 1982.

Grof, C., and Grof, S. *The Stormy Search for the Self: Understanding Spiritual Emergencies*. Los Angeles: J.P. Tarcher, 1990.

Grof, S., and Grof, C., eds. *Spiritual Emergency: When Personal Transformation Becomes a Crisis*. Los Angeles: J.P. Tarcher, 1990.

Hidas, A.M. "Psychotherapy and Surrender." *Journal of Transpersonal Psychology* 13 (1981) 27–32.

Khan, P.V.I. *Introducing Spirituality into Counseling and Therapy*. Lebanon Springs, N.Y.: Omega Press, 1982.

Scotten, O.W. "Observations on the Teaching and Supervision of Transpersonal Psychotherapy." *Journal of Transpersonal Psychology* 17 (1985): 57–75.

"The Health of the Healing Profession: An Interview with Bernard Siegal." *ReVision: A Journal of Consciousness and Change* 7 (1984): 87–93.

Small, J. "Spiritual Emergence and Addiction: A Transpersonal Approach to Alcoholism and Drug Abuse Counseling." *ReVision: Journal of Consciousness and Change* 10 (1987): 23–36.

Small, J. *Transformers, the Therapists of the Future*. Marina del Rey, Calif.: DeVorss, 1982. (To be republished by Bantam in 1990.)

Vaughan, F. *Beyond Ego*. Los Angeles: J.P. Tarcher, 1980.

Vaughan, F. *The Inward Arc*. Boston: Shambala, 1986.

Walsh, R. "Reflections on Psychotherapy." *Journal of Transpersonal Psychology* 8 (1976): 100–11.

Whitfield, C.L. *Healing the Child Within*. Deerfield Beach, Florida: Health Communications, Inc., 1987.

Wilber, K. *No Boundary*. Boulder and London: Shambala, 1981.

For those readers who would like more information about Jacquelyn Small's workshops, which she conducts throughout the United States and Canada, please send your name and address to:

Eupsychia, Inc.
P.O. Box 3090
Austin, Texas 78764

or call (512) 327-2795.

BESTSELLING RECOVERY BOOKS
FROM BANTAM

A NEW DAY
365 Meditations for Personal and Spiritual Growth
Anonymous
Offers spiritual and psychological guidance on overcoming
the struggles we face each day, by the author of the bestselling *A
Day at a Time*.
34591-5   *Paperback* $6.95/$8.95 in Canada

TOXIC PARENTS
Overcoming their Hurtful Legacy and Reclaiming Your Life
Dr. Susan Forward with Craig Buck
The challenging, compassionate and controversial new guide to
recognizing and recovering from the lasting damage caused by
physical or emotional abuse in childhood, by the bestselling
author of *Men Who Hate Women & the Women Who Love Them*.
05700-6   *Hardcover* $18.95/$23.95 in Canada

800-COCAINE
Mark S. Gold, M.D.
From the leading expert on cocaine abuse and treatment, an
informative, prescriptive manual with hard facts on America's
fastest-growing drug problem.
34388-2   *Large Format Paperback* $3.50/$3.95 in Canada

HOW TO BREAK YOUR ADDICTION TO A PERSON
Howard M. Halpern, Ph.D.
An insightful, step-by-step guide to breaking painful addictive
relationships—and surviving separation.
26005-7   *Paperback* $4.50/$4.95 in Canada

**THE ADULT CHILDREN
OF ALCOHOLICS SYNDROME**
Wayne Kritsberg
Real help and hope for adult children in a complete self-help
program that shows how to recognize and remedy the effects of
the dysfunctional family.
27279-9   *Paperback* $3.95/$4.95 in Canada

UNDER THE INFLUENCE
A Guide to the Myths and Realities of Alcoholism
James R. Milam, Ph.D. and Katherine Ketcham
This groundbreaking classic emphasizes treating alcoholism as a physiological disease and offers information on how to tell if someone is an alcoholic, treatment, and recovery.

27487-2	*Paperback*	$4.95/$5.95 in Canada

RECLAIMING OUR LIVES
Hope for Adult Survivors of Incest
Carol Poston and Karen Lison
A comprehensive, inspiring, and supportive guide with a concrete 14-step program for healing written by an incest survivor and a therapist.

28497-5	*Paperback*	$4.95/$5.95 in Canada

FAMILY FEELINGS
Daily Meditations for Healthy Relationships
Martha Vanceburg and Sylvia Silverman
Valuable insights on changing destructive family patterns with one's spouse, children, elderly parents, and grandparents. By the coauthor of *The Promise of a New Day* and her mother.

34705-5	*Paperback*	$6.95/$8.95 in Canada

BECOMING YOUR OWN PARENT
The Solution for Adult Children of Alcoholic and Other Dysfunctional Families
Dennis Wholey
Television host Dennis Wholey, author of THE COURAGE TO CHANGE and himself an "adult child," takes us inside a series of meetings where fourteen men and women learn to find within themselves the validation and nurturance they were denied as children. Also offers the wisdom of a dozen nationally recognized experts on recovery.

34788-8	*Large Format Paperback*	$8.95/$11.95 in Canada

POTATO CHIPS FOR BREAKFAST
The True Story of Growing Up in an Alcoholic Family
Cynthia Scales
The shocking true story of a young girl who grew up with every material comfort—and two alcoholic parents.

28166-6	*Paperback*	$3.50/$4.50 in Canada

Prices subject to change.